SAROPHIA

First Published April 2004
By: Stu Dunn
        Paraparaumu
        Beach Wellington
        New Zealand
Email: Stu@MicroExpressions.co.nz
Facebook/Sarophia

ISBN: 0-476-00669-4

SAROPHIA

BOOK ONE OF THE
XYCERMON SERIES

BY STU DUNN

"With Sarophia, Stu Dunn has created a magical world of adventure and fantasy. Nightmare creatures from the darkest parts of the subconscious mingle with characters as recognisable and human as the people in your street...the ability to blend the real and impossible, the mysterious and plain that makes fantasy writing so rewarding - and this is no exception.

Stu's heroes face a world in the grip of an unspeakable evil. What begins as a flight for life by a group of frightened youths develops into a quest for understanding and vengeance. Nothing is certain, allies are scarce and time is running out...

Sarophia will keep you on the edge of your seat; as each crisis is conquered, only to reveal a greater danger beyond, the pages seem to turn themselves toward the next chapter."

Peter Baillie

Check out www.facebook.com/Sarophia

DEDICATION

This book is dedicated to my son Callan
who is so much like an Elf –

Perfect in every way.

ACKNOWLEDGEMENTS

There's no way I can truly name and thank everyone who has helped me complete this book, but I will sincerely try.

I would like to thank my brother Matt, for lending me City of Thieves - Fighting Fantasy Book #5 – that began my passion for fantasy. This led on to reading such great writers as R. A Salvatore, David and Leigh Eddings, Raymond E Feist, J R R Tolkien, Gary Gygax, and so many more. You have all become my mentors, for this I thank you.

Huge thanks to Hamish Wilson, Adam Wade, Kerry Ewan, Peter Baillie, and Matthew Culver for your constant and unquestionable support, feedback, friendship and love. I know with you all I have brothers. Special thanks to Pete and Hamish for your ongoing chapter-by-chapter feedback.

I also wish to thank Chris Upton, Greg Doone, Tim Lewis, Steven Gibson, Nelson Shum, Hamish Wilson, Allie Emo, Julie Sinclair, Rebecca Charlesworth, Tanya Marriott and Rachael Allwood for your magical assistance in whatever way in helping me bring the characters alive.

Thanks to the fantastic cover art by Dean, as well as the great maps that help bring the world alive.

And a final word to my friend Cliver Conner. Your life was too short, however in the time we knew each other we shared many dreams – some of them have come to fruition within these pages. I know you'll be dreaming on wherever you are.

CONTENTS

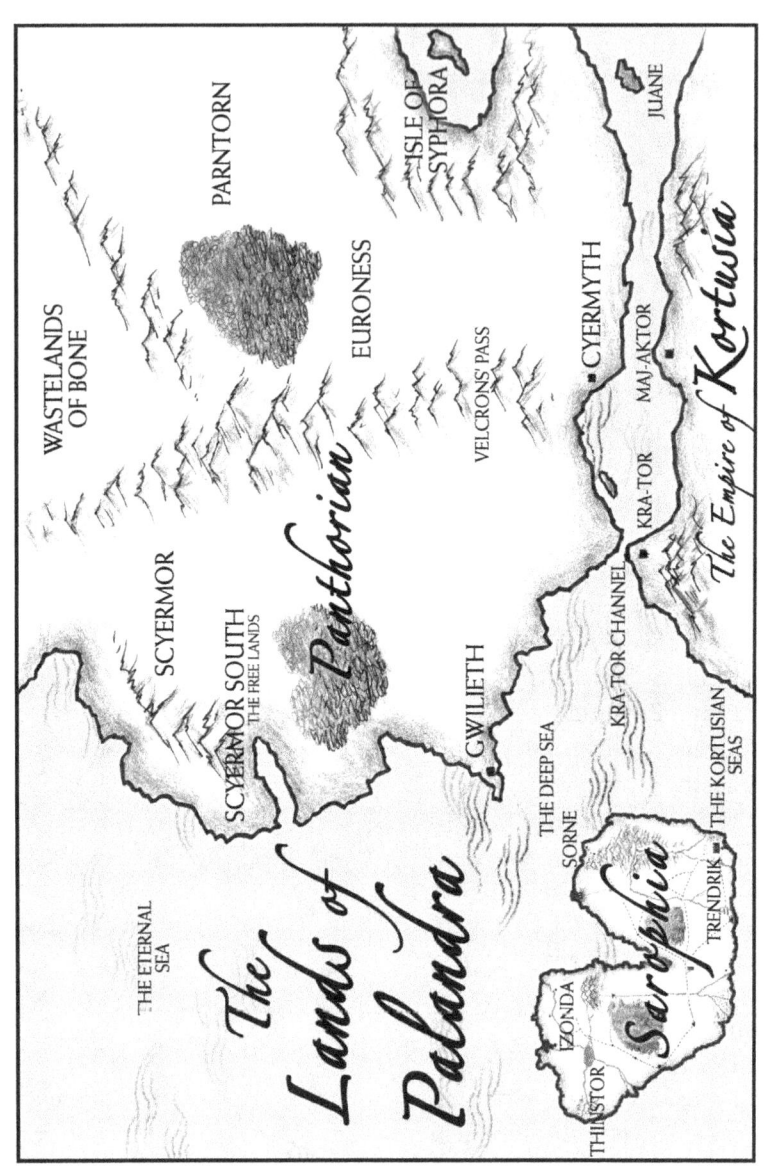

THE ETERNAL SEA

The *Lands of Palandra*

WASTELANDS OF BONE

SCYERMOR

SCYERMOR SOUTH
THE FREE LANDS

Panthorian

PARNTORN

EURONESS

ISLE OF SYPHORA

VELCRONS' PASS

CYERMYTH

MAJ-AKTOR

KRA-TOR

JUANE

The Empire of Kortusia

GWILIETH

THE DEEP SEA

SORNE

KRA-TOR CHANNEL

THE KORTUSIAN SEAS

IZONDA

THINSTOR

Sarophia

TRENDRIK

8

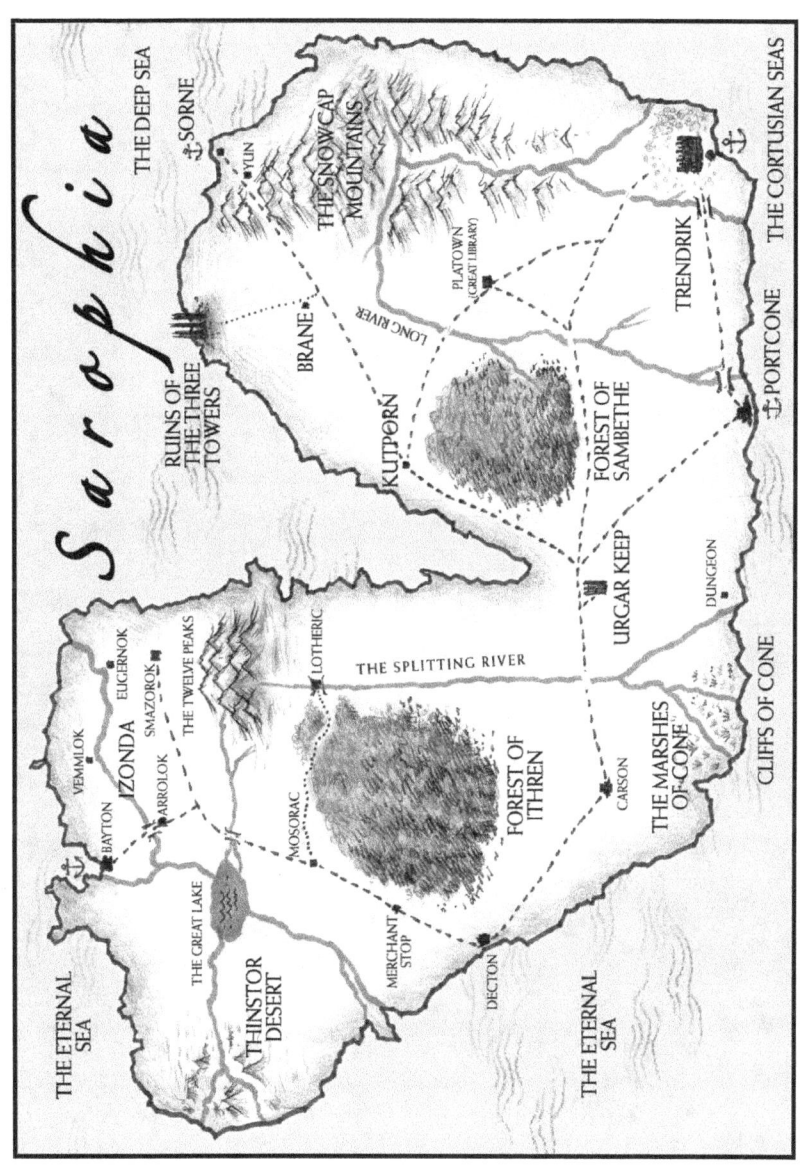

Sarophia

THE DEEP SEA

THE CORTUSIAN SEAS

⚓SORNE

YUN

THE SNOWCAP MOUNTAINS

PLATOWN
(GREAT LIBRARY)

TRENDRIK

LONG RIVER

RUINS OF THE THREE TOWERS

BRANE

KUTPORN

FOREST OF SAMBETHE

⚓PORTCONE

THE CORTUSIAN SEAS

URGAR KEEP

DUNGEON

LOTHERIC

THE SPLITTING RIVER

EUGERNOK

THE TWELVE PEAKS

SMAZOROK

IZONDA

ARROLOK

VEMMLOK

BAYTON

MOSORAC

FOREST OF ITHREN

CARSON

THE MARSHES OF CONE

CLIFFS OF CONE

⚓

THE ETERNAL SEA

THE GREAT LAKE

THINSTOR DESERT

MERCHANT STOP

DECTON

THE ETERNAL SEA

9

SAROPHIA: BOOK ONE OF THE XYCERMON SAGA

PROLOGUE

Under the evening stars she studied the encampment.

Neither *Lithloren* or *Tolorel* had risen so the evening was darker and lonelier than usual; the violet and pale white glows were absent through the branches of surrounding Elms. She needed to sleep, but the air was so bracing it kept her awake.

The dying embers of the campsite fire sizzled angrily as one of the five men below tipped water over it. She had been following them for two days now. She scrutinized each of them once more, committing them to memory.

The first two were big enough to pass for warriors; however that's where their similarities ended. One warrior with dark skin and short black hair rose and moved to the edge of the clearing. Overhearing his name as Kielmark, his clothing and black skin identified him as a horseman from the horse-breeder village of Arrolok. He turned back to face the group."Sudenora and I are going to find some food."

The man he called Sudenora rose to follow. He wore shoulder length brown hair, was unshaven, and was dressed a simple green woollen tunic and grey hose.

The others said nothing.

The watcher's attention turned back to the remaining warrior. Over the past two days she'd heard him called Anthron. He was a giant of a

11

man - his broad shoulders and muscular arms made him look formidable; yet he had an amiable face and blonde hair. Anthron's hand rested on the hilt of his sword.

Jelik sat nearest the smouldering embers of the fire, dressed in ragged black leathers.

The last person in the group joined Jelik by the fire. He was the least imposing sight in the group, overweight, with mousy coloured hair and a goatee. His name was Karlos. He seemed to be the least respected of the group, often being told to do the more menial tasks around the camp.

The watcher slid quietly down the tree and slunk off into the distance. She would visit these men again tomorrow - right now she would get some sleep.

* * * * * * * * * *

The sun rose over the treetops of the forest, banishing the darkness and waking Karlos. He could tell that it was going to be another crisp spring day. The others were awake already, discussing which way to go.

"If we continue north we should end up in Izonda by next week." Anthron calculated, his eyes scanning the surrounding forest as he spoke.

"But as soon as we arrive in Izonda we'll get arrested for escaping Selection," Jelik observed. "I suggest we head towards Sorne and sail our way out of trouble."

"Izonda is a big place, Jelik - we'll be fine. All of us have family back in Izonda, except you..."

"More likely you want to go back to your woman, who only cost three coppers an hour I hear," Jelik retorted maliciously, folding his arms across his chest.

Chaos erupted as Anthron swung his huge fist with a roar. Jelik rolled backwards and came to his feet, then dived to his left as Kielmark and Karlos restrained Anthron. The blonde warrior struggled briefly, then his shoulders slumped in resignation.

"Ah, look," Sudenora cleared his throat."We've got company."

Anthron shook off Kielmark and Karlos as he looked around quickly.

He relaxed slightly as he saw a female warrior standing twenty paces away. Although her features were Elvish, Anthron noted that she was the height of an average human woman. Her long blonde hair was plaited back into a ponytail which revealed the delicacy of her face. He estimated her to be about twenty-five years old, wearing snug soft leather armour and a green cloak which showed her slim figure to perfection. She was stunning, Anthron thought, and well armed as he spied her sword and daggers strapped to her body.

"My name is Anthea Fleké," she began, her voice soft, almost musical."I am here to offer you all an invitation."

"An invitation?" Jelik asked cautiously, eyes narrowing.

"To a village just to the north. It is a haven for people in your situation."

"Just what sort of 'situation' do you think we're in?" Jelik asked.

"You escaped Selection," Anthea stated."You are now considered outlaws throughout Sarophia. I've been tracking you for the last two days just to make sure you weren't being followed. The locals don't want uninvited guests."

"We aren't following you, lady. We can handle this ourselves." Kielmark interupted defiantly.

"You'd die within a week if you continued alone," Anthea replied as she gave Kielmark a penetrating glare."If you did actually make it back to Izonda, you'd be executed or re-captured as soon as anyone found out where you've been. Trust me, there *are* people looking for you."

"So we just live the rest of our lives out hiding in this forest?" Sudenora fumed. She didn't understand – he *had* to get home again.

Anthea shook her head."No. Within the village we can provide you with training and equipment. You can leave anytime you like, but with a better chance of survival. It's a good offer; however it's up to you."

"Well?" Anthron turned to the group,"What do you think?"

Kielmark turned and began to collect his things from the camp.

"I admit, our options are limited, so it sounds like a good plan." Jelik nodded to Anthron.

Anthron turned to Karlos."And you?"

Karlos was frowning,"I think she's right, Anthron. I think our old way of life is over. Trying to go back would be the death of us."

Sudenora looked pained and almost made as if to say something, however held his tongue.

"Okay then," Jelik motioned to the woman as he gathered his things."Lead the way."

As Anthron followed Anthea and the group through the forest, he thought about how comfortable his life had been until so recently. His father was a blacksmith, his mother a dressmaker. They'd all heard rumours in Vemmlok that people were disappearing from every town, city, and village in their vicinity. Anthron thought that this was just a coincidence - until someone he knew escaped. Lothor was an incredibly intelligent young man who had just celebrated his twentieth birthday - and he'd gone missing ten days before. He'd claimed that every month something called the Selection happened. Healthy young people with strong physical or mental abilities were taken - he didn't know where.

Within three hours of his re-appearance, Lothor was escorted away by black armoured knights accompanied by a man in a long black cloak.

Nobody tried to help him.

Anthron thought back to that fateful night when he had been taken. Drugged and tied in his bed, he had not chance of escape. He had woken to find himself in an enormous wheeled cage, being pulled by a tem of horses. Fourteen of the cages were linked together, each with thick metal bars they were treated like prisoners. Fed only scraps, the guards threw water at them through the cages each day to wash away the filth. It was under these conditions that he me his fellow cell mates; Sudenora, Kielmark, Karlos, and Jelik. Anthron had lost count how many days since his capture before Jelik managed to pick the lock of their cage one night using a bent fork he'd hidden, and they finally escaped into the darkness of the forest with several stolen weapons - intending on returning to their homes.

That was - until this encounter with Anthea. Now they were on their way to some village out in the middle of the Ithren Forest, blindly trusting someone they'd just met.

What was worse - they could never go back to their old lives.

"Terrific." Anthron thought to himself as he continued along the trail.

CHAPTER ONE

Anthron stirred from his thoughts.

The sun was just starting to peek above the treetops of another cloudless day near the end of summer. Anthron sat on his favourite grassy spot atop a small rise near the edge of the village. He had come to love this place.

The village itself was self contained, nestled safely under the tall trees of the Ithren Forest. It was made up of a series of thatched huts, which reminded Anthron of the farm hovels outside Vemmlok. They were sparse but comfortable and dry, but he'd often thought he wouldn't wish to spend a winter living in one. These huts housed the residents of this village, which Anthron thought numbered about sixty. There were also five larger buildings of better design. These were used for training purposes; what would pass as a Fighter's Guild and gym, a Temple of *Termolen*, the Library - where an Elementalist could also practice their skills, a place which was referred to as 'The Maze' - where stealth and sleight of hand were taught, and the town hall. Well, Anthron thought, not really a town hall - more of a place which the town leader Karter used as his base, and where he called meetings.

Anthron loved the people here as well. They weren't the bunch of rogues he'd expected. He cast his mind back to when he and his friends first arrived with Anthea. He and Kielmark had enrolled with the Fighter's Guild.

Sudenora picked up the theories of the Elementalists quickly, as his father had been a *Tolorel* illusionist. Instead of following his father's footsteps however, Sudenora chose to study the God of Air - *Servas*.

Karlos immediately began learning about *Termolen*, the God of Earth Healing. Karlos learnt how to enhance natural healing within a body and focus it in a positive way via channelling and prayer. Karlos was much more confident now. He had a look in his eyes as if he knew some great secret.

Jelik became a student of Furnar, the tutor of thieves. Furnar had shown Jelik all sorts of ways to conceal oneself, sleight of hand, how locks work, and many other things.

Anthron stood up and stretched to his full height, hearing a few bones creaking. He walked down from the grassy rise, eagerly anticipating being on the road, especially with Anthea.

Anthron halted at the Fighter's Guild, knocking politely on the hardwood door as he entered. The Fighter's Guild was the second largest hall in the village. The walls inside were decorated with several items of ancient armour and weapons, which, it was said, were used in The Great War nearly two and a half thousand years ago. Anthron didn't know much about the war - he didn't care for history.

The guild floor was polished wood that Anthron walked across noisily, leading into sand at the far end. Bowing as he reached the sparring area, Anthron sought out his teacher.

"You're as loud as an ox," the deep voice of Lepus boomed.

Anthron jumped. This man could still unnerve him. Each time Anthron began to think that he was getting the better of Lepus while they were sparring, he would suddenly realise that his instructor was just toying with him. Anthron was glad that they'd started out fencing with padded sticks!

Lepus came out from the back room. He was a short thin man, with black hair. As usual, he wore his rusty chainmail vest and shortsword.

"You're off today." Lepus, hands on hips, bellowed. Anthron still couldn't understand how such a little man could make so much noise.

Anthron nodded,"I've just come to say farewell."

"Well, bye then." Lepus then turned on his heels and disappeared back the way he had come.

Lepus wasn't one for social etiquette.

Anthron left, bowed again, and made for Adjur's hut. Adjur was the sage of the village. Their group was to meet outside his hut before they left for the Sambethe Forest. A man named Wilse had escaped from the Selection, finding sanctuary in the place to which they headed. He claimed to have found out the process and reasons for the Selection.

They were to make for Sambethe, question Wilse, and prepare for the Ithren village to join them.

Everyone but Sudenora was ready. He was reluctantly collecting their supplies.

Anthea sighed in boredom as she waited restlessly for Sudenora with the others. She'd been invited to go along with the group as a guide, and she'd accepted. It had been a while since she'd journeyed east, and her stomach was knotted with anxiety. Anthea turned her attention to Jelik. He was caught up in his thoughts, unconsciously toying with one of his daggers. She and Jelik had become quite close over the last six months and she wondered how they'd get along on the road.

Shrugging, she watched the others.

Kielmark sat in the grass dressed in a mis-matched set of leather, chain and plate armour. He polished his traditional Arrolokian sabre with a cloth.

Karlos sat cross-legged lost in thought, a morning star cradling across his lap.

At last Sudenora arrived with the town leader, Karter. Sudenora wore blue robes, brown leather leggings and boots and carried their rations under his arm.

"At last," Kielmark breathed impatiently, sheathing his sabre and standing.

Anthron hefted his backpack on to his shoulders.

The tall burly Karter shook all their hands bidding them goodbye."'Member to keep yaselves whole now, and we'll see y'all in a few weeks in Sambethe to find out what ya have. You'll have to see if these dungeons an' orcs are related to the Selection too," Karter said as he absent-mindedly brushed a stray curl of his bushy brown hair from his face."Good luck."

The party set off via the makeshift stables to collect their horses, and led them off into the forest.

The morning was quiet and passed uneventfully, the tall trees protecting them from the morning sun. Anthron noticed once again how beautiful this forest was. He listened to the birds, their mingled songs relaxed him, as he watched the animals scuttle out of their way.

He also wondered if there were any elves hidden in the forest watching as they made their way.

Little was said throughout the morning; everyone seeming to be pre-occupied.

About noon they decided to rest in a small clearing. They quietly ate a small meal as their horses grazed, then continued on, Anthea leading the way.

It was late afternoon when Anthron was roused from his thoughts as they came to an old country road which headed north west and south east. The road was about twenty feet across, bearing no wagon wheel marks or hoof prints although the dirt was very fine.

Anthea mounted her white mare as she looked south east."If we follow the road it'll take us east through Lotheric. If we keep to it we shouldn't run into any trouble."

"Trouble?" Kielmark inquired from his saddle."What kind of trouble?"

Anthea paused."I don't expect there to be any."

Karlos wiped the perspiration from his forehead and beard as he hoisted himself into his saddle."Still - it's better to be safe."

"Yes." Anthea agreed.

Anthron led the way as the rest of the party fell in behind him. That night they camped close to the road, not setting up their tents owing to the warm and clear weather. Jelik and Karlos collected firewood, Anthron dug a small pit, while Anthea and Sudenora prepared a dinner of bacon and fried potatoes. Kielmark cleaned up afterwards.

"That meal was just like home." Anthron acknowledged, licking his fingers.

Sudenora sighed."Pity it wasn't though."

Jelik and Anthea retired early, further from the fire than the others.

They soon all retired, with the exception of Anthron, who was on the first watch.

The next day dawned cloudless; promising another hot day as the group got up. They packed up their gear, and covered over the ashes of last night's fire. Then they continued their ride along the wide dusty road.

Everyone became more irritable as they rode through the hottest part of the day. Anthea had been forced to conciliate more than a few arguments, and had borne the brunt of one or two of Jelik's more nasty comments. Now the road began to turn directly east.

The forest had long since receded from the road, which now had tall dense bush running alongside it.

Karlos rode at the back of the group. He felt like he was being watched. He concluded that it was no more than his paranoia until he heard grunting sounds to his left. He stopped to listen. Probably a boar or something, he thought. He spurred his horse forward to catch up with the group who hadn't even noticed he'd stopped.

"Anthea." Karlos called. Anthea stopped and turned around.

"Do you hear anything. I mean in the bushes there?" he asked timidly, pointing at the dense bush to their left.

The rest of the group stopped. All eyes were on her as she listened attentively. They knew that if anyone could hear something, it would be an Elf.

"No, I can't," Anthea frowned,"What's wrong?"

"Nothing," Karlos stammered,"Don't worry."

The party started to move on.

Suddenly several armed figures sprang out of the leaves and branches. The whistling sound of arrows filled the air, mingling with snorted commands.

Anthron ducked under an arrow just in time to see Jelik's horse being killed. The young thief rolled away from his dead mount before he saw their ambushers. There were eight stooping creatures with brownish green coloured skin. Below their snouts protruded lower canines resembling boar tusks. Their reddish eyes were visible under rusty bronze helmets which covered most of their bristly black hair. They wore rusted scale armour and tattered yellow cloaks. They were orcs!

Anthron unsheathed his long sword and spurred his horse towards their foes, eager to take them on.

Kielmark drew his sabre as he urged his mount to rear.

Anthea closed her eyes as she made several symbols in the air, silently invoking the God of Fire to assist her. She remembered the first time she'd communicated with *Pharson*. She compared requesting a God's attention with Kortusian martial artists. The experienced martial artist concentrated before breaking boards or bricks with their hands, summoning their inner strength and releasing their energy with a kiai - a focus. Each God has a different focus. *Pharson* requires symbolic gestures whereas the moons require amulets before an Elementalist is able to borrow any power.

Slowly opening her eyes, she cupped one hand. Her palm sparked as a fire grew, until it slithered and wound its way around her whole arm like a flaming snake. Anthea pitched her arm back and threw the flame at the nearest orc, striking it dead.

Karlos dismounted, unfastened his morning star from his belt, and planted his feet firmly.

Jelik held his shortsword in one hand, a dagger in the other as he backed away from his arrow-riddled horse and the orcs.

Sudenora began murmuring under his breath as he raised his silver dagger in the air. Sparks began crackling around the dagger as Sudenora flung it into the ground. The blade sunk to the hilt in the soft dry dirt, setting off two sparks, snaking like fuse wire towards two orcs. They were struck dead on impact.

This all happened in a matter of seconds. Five still lived, Anthron observed. They dropped their bows looking at each other uncertainly, before there was a grunt from the biggest orc. Immediately they drew their wicked swords and ran towards the group calling battle cries.

The first to fight was Anthron. He rode past Karlos and kicked an orc in the face as he swung his sword in an arc over his head. The sharp blade bit deep into the orc's head, splitting it almost in half. The orc's body slumped to the dirt road in a series of grotesque twitches which seemed to unnerve Anthron's horse. Anthron felt the colour drain from his face at the sight of what he had done. He looked at the blood on his sword, caught a glimpse of Jelik's approval, then Anthron quickly sought to help his companions.

An orc ran at Karlos, its curved blade raised. Karlos swung his morning star in a figure-eight, keeping it at bay while Jelik ran behind it. The young thief slashed the orc across its back before running on to help Anthea. That was all Karlos needed. As the orc turned back, its face was rent asunder by a flying morning star.

Kielmark parried a thrust aimed at his horse's side, and counter-attacked with a head strike. His flashing sabre slashed the orc across its forehead just as it attacked again. The orc spun to the ground in a spray of its own blood as Kielmark felt the impact of the orc's blade connecting with his calf-plate. Kielmark resisted the urge to cry out just as Anthron ran the wounded orc through.

Anthea had her shortsword drawn and was trying to get behind the Orc Leader for a quick kill. Unfortunately the large orc noticed her, bared its yellow fanged teeth, and charged.

This orc was bigger than most - almost a foot taller than Anthea - wielding a battleaxe and a curved sword. The Leader had a golden ring through its nose, which added to its repulsiveness. It spoke in its guttural native tongue;"Nort...harish...carj!"

Without hesitation the orc sliced its battle axe towards Anthea's throat. She just managed to parry it, but the blow knocked her back. The orc continued to attack furiously, and Anthea was forced to roll backwards trying to escape the continuous attacks. She sprang to her feet and parried the sword, and ducked awkwardly under the axe. Anthea stumbled, then was kicked hard by the orc. She hit the ground heavily. As the orc lifted its axe to take advantage of the half Elf, its back stiffened and its eyes began to glass over. Blood trickled from its nose as Jelik's shortsword burst from the Leader's chest in a red spray. Jelik pushed the orc off his blade with his foot.

"Are you okay?" Jelik looked concerned.

She smiled and rubbed her bruised ribs."I'll live. Nothing a hot bath and a massage won't fix." She took Jelik's outstretched arm and got up."Thank you Jelik."

Jelik nodded as he leaned over the body of the dead Orc Leader. He retrieved its small golden ring, slipped it into his belt pouch, then began searching inquisitively for something to clean his blade.

Anthron chased the last orc up the road on horseback. When Anthron returned, the fight was over.

Karlos cleared his throat and walked over to Kielmark as he removed his calf plate."I'll look at your leg." The cut was only small, but it was very swollen. Karlos rubbed his hands together then placed them lightly on the wound. Kielmark twitched in pain as the tubby man massaged around the wound while murmuring a prayer to *Termolen*. When he finished his prayer, Kielmark could feel the pain ease noticeably.

"How do you actually do that?" Kielmark asked.

"Well," Karlos beamed,"I'm accelerating the natural healing processes which..."

"That's lovely," Jelik interupted,"But maybe you can tell us a little later, no? There's still the matter of my dead horse."

Kielmark was frowning as he climbed into his saddle."Was a good horse."

"You can ride with me." Anthea offered as she discarded an arrow from her saddlebag and mounted.

Jelik nodded and climbed behind Anthea."I guess this'll have to do then."

Anthron's eyes narrowed angrily at Jelik. The blonde warrior blinked several times and rubbed his eyes - he swore for a moment he could see a faint purple colour around the thief. Shrugging, Anthron led the way on his chestnut horse."We'd best be moving, there may be more orcs where these came from."

Sudenora pointed back at the smoking form of the orc Anthea had cremated."I'm sure that'll attract some attention as well. Should we hide the bodies?"

"I wouldn't worry," Anthea shook her head."You know, I think these orcs were actually waiting for us."

"What are you talking about?" Anthron queried."Can you understand them?"

"I know a little goblin - orcish is quite similar. The Leader said 'Nort, harish, carj.' Nort means dark or doomed. Harish is those picked, and carj is the word for soldier." Anthea replied.

Jelik toyed with a dagger from behind Anthea."So you're saying that these orcs are part of the Selection in some way? That they were sent to find us or kill us or something?"

"They might have wandered here by themselves, but I'm not so sure." Anthea shrugged.

Karlos spurred his horse on."How far to Lotheric?"

"From here...we'll make Lotheric about nightfall. We can stay there, find out what we can before moving onto Sambethe."

"Sounds like a good idea," Sudenora nodded.

SAROPHIA BY STU DUNN

CHAPTER TWO

The sun set.

The party dismounted and entered Lotheric through a narrow iron gate leading into the small town as the last light of the day dispersed, replaced by *Tolorel's* pale glow. Lotheric was a small farming village that was built on either side of The Splitting River, creating what was known as Western Lotheric and Eastern Lotheric. Vegetable gardens were located north of the little town, and to the south grazed several cattle.

Anthron thought it strange that even though the sun had just gone down, the streets of Lotheric were already deserted. Here and there the blonde warrior caught a glimpse of light seeping through a curtain.

"Times must have been hard," Anthea commented."Last time I was here there was a lot more activity."

"Possibly lost a few people to the orcs." Sudenora suggested.

"Possibly." Anthea muttered.

There was only one stable in Lotheric, which Anthron found unusual for a farming town. The stable was attached to a small inn, which was a modest two-storey building with a chimney puffing out smoke. The sign over the door depicted a sleeping lion in a cave mouth, naming it *The Lions' Den*.

They fed and watered the horses themselves - as there was no stable lackey to greet them - then pushed open the door to the inn.

The inn was simple but cosy. The smell of roast pork wafted from the kitchen. It had a dozen large round tables and a fireplace recessed into the northern wall that made the flickering shadows dance wildly as they entered. There was a healthy slab of pork roasting over the fire. On the east wall a flight of stairs led to the second storey, over what was obviously the kitchen. Only two of the tables were taken, so Anthron motioned the rest to follow. As they made their way to a table, the customers stared. Once they were seated, a plump middle-aged man emerged from the kitchen and noticed them immediately. He had greying brown hair and an honest looking face. He rubbed his greasy fingers on his apron as he approached."Good evening," he said with a smile."I'm Osile, the keeper of this inn. You'll have to excuse the locals - we don't get many new faces here any more."

"Not to worry," Anthron said."We're after some rooms..." Anthron turned to Anthea for an indication about numbers.

"Three rooms," Anthea replied."How much for a meal, three rooms, a hot bath, and breakfast tomorrow?"

"Let me see," Osile counted to himself on his fingers."That'll be sixteen coppers," he replied.

"I'll give you one silver," Anthea said flatly.

The plump innkeeper looked shocked, but recovered quickly."No disrespect, Lady, but a silver wouldn't cover my costs..."
Anthea interjected;"You look like you could do with our business. Take it or leave it."

Osile struggled for a moment before accepting."Alright. If you don't mind waiting a few minutes, I'll get your meals."

Anthea gave him a silver coin, then he returned to the kitchen. As he neared the kitchen a man in his forties wearing a brown woollen tunic called out,"Osile, how about three ales for a copper."

Osile put his hands on his hips stubbornly."You know the prices, Carlo."

His drinking friends supported Carlo's comment. A man in a green tunic added,"Take it or leave it!" This created a spate of drunken laughter. Osile looked around helplessly before retreating into the kitchen.

"A quiet town." Karlos noted.

"Agreed," Anthea said casually."I can't put my finger on it, but something's wrong."

"Like?" Kielmark inquired.

Anthea just shrugged.

"I feel like a drink," Jelik mused as he rubbed his chin."I wonder how much the ale actually is here." He stood and walked across the room, disappearing into the kitchen. He returned moments later with a triumphant look on his face, carrying a flagon of ale and four mugs.

Jelik sat, uncorked the flagon and sniffed."This must be a Bayton brew."

Karlos grinned."Pass me a mug my friend."

"The innkeeper said our meals won't be long." Jelik filled the four mugs, and began drinking. Karlos, Anthea and Sudenora each grabbed a mug.

Several minutes later, Osile appeared with their meals from the kitchen."Here you are, I hope you enjoy - roast pork, potatoes and gravy," He noted the ale with surprise."Good night." He shot a suspicious glare at the group, then attended another table.

"You did pay for that, didn't you Jelik?" Anthron whispered harshly.

Jelik looked concerned."Of course. You don't think I'd steal do you?"

"Jelik, I don't want you to get us into any trouble, okay?" Anthron warned.

"Not a problem."

They began to eat. Sudenora found the meal delicious, and he cleaned his plate thoroughly. So did the others.

As Kielmark leaned backwards in his chair and patted his stomach, the kitchen door opened again. A plump red-faced woman emerged wearing a grey woollen dress, a dirty apron, and a large smile. She approached the table unsteadily.

"I'm Hernsa." she giggled, and Jelik noticed the scent of whisky on her breath."If you'll follow me, I'll show you to your rooms." She took them slowly up the set of stairs, and pointed to three doors at the end of the corridor."The room at the end has the bath..." Hernsa paused to hiccup,"As soon as the water boils." She then curtsied and went down the stairs to clear their plates, swaying dangerously at the bottom.

Jelik and Anthea entered the room at the end of the corridor.

Anthron felt his stomach knot with envy as he swung open the door to the left room. Sudenora followed Anthron, and closed the door.

Anthron unbuckled his chain mail vest and sword, and was considering a bath too."I may just see when the water's arriving."

Sudenora sighed as he flopped down on his uncomfortably solid bed."Forget about it Anthron, just get some sleep."

Anthron climbed into his bed and lay there for a while, thinking. He heard the water being brought up, and later heard two people getting into the bath. He clenched his fists and put his pillow over his head, eventually falling into a dreamless sleep.

* * * * * * * * * *

Anthron woke late, and met the others in the quiet taproom. He sat silently, and was served cold pork and a mug of water that had a yellow tint to it.

"Care for any coffee with your breaking of fast?" asked Osile.

Anthron shook his head, and began eating.

Anthea looked at Anthron."We were just saying that the Sambethian Village is about seven days ride away."

Anthron nodded.

Sudenora absently scratched at his beard."I wonder just how much that guy Wilse at the village in Sambethe knows about the Selection?" he mused.

"If he did escape Selection," Kielmark replied."He probably won't know much more than us. Another thought too - if we know he's in Sambethe, how many others will know as well?"

Karlos squinted at the cobwebs on the low beamed ceiling."Good point. That also raises the question - how many knew we were in Ithren?"

Jelik stood to leave."The guy's probably a fake - who would be stupid enough to walk around the Sambethian Forest telling everyone he meets that he's escaped Selection. I'm going to get my gear."

Everyone except Anthea followed the young thief. She stared at Anthron."What's troubling you?"

He looked at her and sighed."I didn't sleep well, that's all." He went back to playing with his food.

"If it's lack of sleep bothering you, take some lavender to bed with you tonight. If it's something else...let me know when you're ready to talk. Now, we're looking at leaving in ten minutes." With that Anthea got up and went to her room.

Anthron's stomach knotted, and he knew he'd never finish his breakfast. He pushed his plate away and downed the contents of his mug. Wincing at the after-taste, he made as if to go upstairs. Suddenly the door to the taproom burst open revealing a middle-aged red headed woman dressed in a blue tunic and hose. Her red faced exposed her terror.

"The river, quickly!" she shouted hysterically.

"Muriel?" Osile called from the kitchen."I'll be there in a minute."

Anthron stared at her curiously. The woman locked eyes with him."Young Scotus!" she screamed."I've found 'im! 'E's dead, and 'e looks so terribly 'orrid!"

* * * * * * * * * *

Anthron looked at the sky. It was the first overcast day in what seemed like months. Winter was closer. Ominous grey clouds rolled quickly across the sky. Anthron pulled his green woollen cloak tightly around him as Osile and the shaky Muriel led them down to the Splitting River.

"Did she say what was so bad about the body?" Karlos asked the blonde warrior, nodding towards Muriel anxiously.

"No." Anthron replied solemnly.

"Osile." Anthea called. The portly innkeeper chattered while waiting for the half Elf.

"Yes?" Osile asked as the two of them walked together.

"Who was Scotus?" Anthea asked.

Osile stammered slightly."He was Jaress's boy, went missing at the beginning of last winter."

"Have many others gone missing?" Anthea inquired.

The innkeeper glared at her."Look around you, Lady," Osile gestured to the people that had gathered in the streets."Our children have gone!"

Anthea continued, unfazed."Could the orcs be connected with the disappearances?"

Osile frowned."I've never seen an orc in all my life, Lady. It would be easier to blame them though..."

"But you don't think so." Anthea continued.

Osile shook his head.

Anthea studied the people of Lotheric. No children ran or played. No laughter filled the streets. There was no distant sound of a baby crying. It looked like Lotheric had been decimated by the Selection. Perhaps Scotus had been another prisoner who had attempted to escape?

A sudden gust of wind whipped a purple coloured hat off a distraught man. He made a futile attempt to grab it, then chased it down the street. The howling wind took the hat up, and soon it was just a purple speck in the bleak sky. Jelik chuckled.

The tall thief had been keeping an eye out for any sign of a shop - but hadn't seen any. What kind of place was this? The party had only been walking for five minutes, and in that time it seemed to Jelik that everyone in the small town had come out to watch them as if they were some kind of procession. They stood in silence, clinging to what remained of their families. Jelik wondered if rumours had spread that hope had come to their town at last.

Kielmark shivered, wearing a dull gray woollen cloak that he decided wasn't warm enough. He winced at the sky, silently praying that it didn't rain.

They stopped at the river in front of a spiked iron fence that ran along the bank, ten metres upstream from the wooden bridge that crossed the Splitting River. Mist rose from the swift current as it sped south; its murky waters barely visible through the foam. The bridge looked derelict, parts of it rotten or missing altogether.

"The river isn't usually this swift, is it?" Anthea asked.

"It has been like this for a while now," Osile said."We think that this is how our children died." He waved to the iron fence."Obviously this didn't work."

Kielmark placed his hand gently on Muriel's shoulder."Where is the body, madam?"

"He," she hesitated."It is caught on a beam there under the bridge," Muriel indicated to a point near the bottom of the bridge."I saw it when

I was paying my respects to Brenot." She pointed out a bunch of dried gerbera tied to the iron fence. The flowers had not fared well in the wind.

Anthron stepped up to the flowers and peered through the fence."I can't see anything." he commented. The blonde warrior requested Kielmark's help, who stepped forward and knelt down. Anthron stepped on his back as he grasped the fence in both hands, then vaulted over, clearing the spikes.

A roll of thunder echoed across the sky as Anthron landed on the muddy bank with a squelch."I still can't see anything." he squinted.

Muriel clung to the fence, her knuckles white."It's down there," she insisted.

Anthron looked doubtfully at the muddy bank, then to the angry waters of the Splitting River.

"Maybe I should look instead." Jelik muttered quietly.

Anthron tentatively stepped away from the iron fence, peering as far as he could under the bridge.

"Stay there Anthron," Karlos warned."We'll get some rope for you."

Anthron nodded. He began to wonder if he should have volunteered so quickly. No sooner had the thought crossed his mind, his feet came out from under him. He grasped futilely at the fence as he began sliding slowly towards the fierce river.

"Quickly!" Anthea shouted, urging Karlos to throw the rope he carried to Anthron.

Anthron clawed at the bank but still he slid, the rope landing in front of him as he plunged deep into the freezing brown waters.

The rope nearly wrenched out of Karlos's grip until Kielmark rushed to help."He's managed to grab onto it!" Karlos puffed.

Jelik sprinted down to the bridge, tying a thin cord around his waist. He slowed as he came to the old bridge, carefully venturing a quarter of the way across. Squinting through the mist, Jelik stabbed a dagger deep into a support beam and searched for a suitable piece of wood.

Anthron surfaced, scratching at the bank, pulling fistfuls of mud while holding tightly onto the rope. Anthron knew that with his armour, he could not stay above the surface for long. He submerged again, his lungs filling with water. Things seemed to slow down while he was under the water, but it was deafening. He saw something ahead - a large pole! He could see the bridge supports. Losing grip of the rope he was swept up in the current of the river, smashing painfully into the pole. He surfaced once more, coughing water, winded, and his vision went black for a moment. As it returned he saw it.

He saw Scotus. Or at least what could have once been Scotus. Trapped between a beam and a pole were the remains of a grossly disfigured body. His eyes had rolled right back into his skull, and his skin was gray. Most of his hair had rotted out and he had no teeth. His tongue was swollen and purple, and his jaw was severely broken.

Then the stench got to him.

Anthron gagged and turned away, looking for a way to escape the putrefaction.

"He's under you!" Anthea screamed to Jelik.

Jelik barely heard her. Swearing loudly, he tied the other end of the cord to a piece of broken bridge railing. He then threw the railing over the side of the bridge downstream. Jelik had two concerns. The first was that Anthron might not see or be able to grab the wood. The second was that Jelik might very well get pulled in with him. The young thief braced himself, tightly holding the dagger he'd planted, and waited.

Anthron looked frantically around for an escape when something about Scotus caught his eye. His grey eyelids seemed to flicker, and he heard something come from his mouth. Granted strength by sheer panic, Anthron kicked out and hauled himself out of the water onto the beam which instantly began giving way. Anthron's foot collided with the body, and a jolt of pain ran up his leg. Ignoring it, Anthron's only thought was escape. That's when he saw a piece of wood about ten feet downstream. At least that would help him stay afloat. He jumped as the beam snapped. The icy waters swallowed him once more, but he felt the wood hit his palms. He held onto it, tucking it under his arms, and waited to surface again.

For some reason, Anthron was jerked backwards and up. The water's surface rushed up, kissing him with air, granting him an opportunity to breathe again.

"Climb!"

Anthron didn't know whose voice it was, but he was in no position to climb anything.

"Now!"

Anthron looked back and saw Jelik struggling from the bridge behind him. That's when he noticed that he wasn't being carried off downstream. He grasped the cord, feeling it cut into his hands, but he didn't let go. He climbed.

Jelik's arms hurt. His stomach ached. He felt like he was being squeezed in two from Anthron's weight on the cord around his waist. The young thief held on to the embedded dagger with his right hand, his left trying to ease the pressure around his waist. He could hear Anthron panting now, muttering something over and over. Just a little longer, Jelik thought. Anthron's hand appeared over the side of the bridge, and Jelik lunged to grab it.

"Give me your hand!" Jelik yelled over the noise of the river to the wild-eyed Anthron. The drenched warrior threw up his other hand without hesitation, and soon Jelik had pulled him safely onto the bridge.

"It wasn't dead!" Anthron cried.

Thunder boomed overhead once more, followed by rain. He suddenly felt the searing pain in his leg again, and he noticed the blood on his raw hands intermingling with the rain.

Then everything went black.

SAROPHIA BY STU DUNN

CHAPTER THREE

He heard the rain.

It sounded like a waterfall crashing down on smooth rocks, a constant, continual din. He must be indoors, because he wasn't getting wet. He tried to open his eyes, but gave up. He was so comfortable, not feeling anything, just lying there in the darkness with the noise of the rain like a waterfall. He remembered something...something had happened. Something else to do with water...maybe a river...yes...a fast flowing river.

He could hear distant voices, and he knew he should open his eyes and sit up, and say something like,"Don't worry about me, I'm fine." Fine? What had made him think that?

Water.

The voices seemed more insistent now; they were reaching out to him, trying to pull him back into consciousness. He resisted them.

River.

I'll stay just a little longer, then I'll open my eyes and get up, he thought.

Body.

Anthron remembered the body, the stench, the broken jaw, the teeth, and the flickering eyes! It wasn't dead!

Anthron sat bolt upright, startling his companions, blurting out his last recollection.

"It wasn't dead!"

Anthea pressed lightly on his chest, and slowly he lay back down.

A sharp pain ran up Anthron's leg, but it wasn't nearly as bad as it had been. Probably Karlos's doing.

"I'm all right." he whispered, noticing his dry throat. He sat up more slowly this time, and looked around. They were in a tiny cottage living room. Anthron was propped up on a squat ugly red couch that was badly fading. He was facing a small fire that kept the place warm, with two doors to his left which he suspected led to different bedrooms. The front door was behind him. Above the front door was a framed cross-stitch that read: 'Denkle and Muriel Genar - Together Forever'. There was a small desk in the corner of the room covered with papers, next to a rickety wooden chair. His companions were standing around him.

Suddenly the front door was opened, and they were all assaulted by the raging weather. Sparks flew from the fire in all directions, and papers from the small desk cartwheeled around the room.

Osile quickly closed the door, leaning hard against it. Somehow the small fire kept going.

"Ur...sorry." He looked around the room, then spotted Anthron, bleary eyed and pale."Ah, so you're up now I see." Osile vigorously rubbed his hands together to warm them, then shook his drenched coat in a futile attempt to dry it.

"He only woke a few moments ago." Anthea said."Any luck?" She asked, her eyes narrowing slightly.

Osile shook his head as he hung up his coat."No my lady. The body has disappeared. I don't understand it, Muriel said that the body was definitely there." He looked back to Anthron."Did you get a look at it lad?"

Jelik interjected."I'd say so. But tell us, Anthron. What makes you think that a body which has travelled all the way from The Twelve Peaks is still alive?" Jelik's usual sarcasm had returned.

"What made you say that?" Anthea snapped.

"Say what?" Jelik looked surprised, wondering if she was defending Anthron.

"You said 'a body which has travelled all the way from The Twelve Peaks'. What made you say that?"

"Well..." Jelik paused a moment in thought."Because The Splitting River comes from the mountains. Maybe Scotus was attempting to climb the seventh peak and fell into the river," Jelik glanced at Anthron."*Died*...and said one last farewell to his home town as he floated past."

"Scotus disappeared last year...like you five did a little over six months ago." Anthea paused, then gazed into the blank and confused faces of her audience. "Think about it! Perhaps the people who are taken for Selection are being taken to The Twelve Peaks."

Anthea stopped for a moment and watched a glimmer of understanding dawn in their faces.

Sudenora stepped forward with a puzzled expression on his face. "I was taken from Eugernok. Anthron was from Vemmlok." "I was abducted with Jelik from Smazorok," Karlos added.

"And I came from Arrolok," Kielmark concluded.

"We are all from Izonda. We travelled south around Mosorac in those wagon cages and came out with more prisoners." Sudenora took a moment to remember. "We headed south still, and stopped outside Decton, departing later with prisoners. We escaped about halfway to Carson and went directly north, into the forest. That's where we met Anthea." He looked at her, his confused face softening, and he smiled. "The rest we all know."

"Jelik and I thought we might be proceeding as far as Urgar Keep. That's where they take most prisoners if they don't execute them first," Karlos argued. "There are no roads to The Twelve Peaks, but if we were going there, they could have saved a long trip by going cross-country alongside the northern part of The Splitting River."

"But what's the use in going straight to the mountains with half a dozen prisoners," Anthea reasoned. "When they could cover whole countryside first, getting twenty times that number."

The party slowly nodded in agreement.

"Why can't we lie in ambush for another cage-train?" Jelik smiled wickedly.

Anthea shook her head. "We'd already thought of that back at the village. The problem is we don't know the difference between the police and the 'Selectors'. And the prisoners all look the same. If we attack the wrong group, we'll have Trendrik's men burning forests and draining lakes in retaliation."

"Fair enough," Jelik replied.

Osile had his mouth open, with water still dripping from the tip of his nose. Could these six people possibly find a clue which would answer the question: where have the youth of Lotheric gone?

"The town will pay you to go to The Twelve Peaks and find out if our children are there." Osile blurted.

Jelik's eyes brightened immediately. "How much are we talking about?" he asked.

"We can't take these poor people's money." Karlos started.

"I'm sure we could pay - let's say - thirty coppers if you go there, and another thirty if you find them."

"Make that thirty silver pieces and you've got yourself a deal." Jelik bargained.

"Jelik!" Karlos exclaimed. "I'm sorry about him sir, but we don't want..."

"Twenty pieces of silver." Osile pressed, ignoring Karlos. He wasn't sure if he could get the money from the Council, but he figured that he'd work it out later. Denkle would be the hardest one to convince. But first, they had to accept.

"Deal!" Jelik let out a triumphant laugh.

Osile sighed in relief as he looked at the group in front of him. Anthron had seen the body of poor young Scotus - one of the first to disappear - and it had spooked him. Anthron was pale looking, and had said nothing throughout the whole conversation. He was quietly thinking to himself.

Kielmark looked annoyed, as if his usually straightforward world had just become a lot more complex.

Anthea thought for a long while, and soon all eyes were on her. She sighed, knowing she had got herself into this. She looked at Jelik and nodded. This was officially part of their original mission - to find out what they could about The Selection. Wilse and The Sambethe Forest could wait a few days longer.

"Okay Osile," Anthea agreed, "We'll go to The Twelve Peaks. We'll see where things lead from there. We will need supplies. We'll head off tomorrow morning. Is that all right with everyone?" she asked.

The rest agreed.

Osile cleared his throat."Could you look out for a little girl? She's very pretty," the innkeeper stopped to think,"Nine years old. Yes, she'd be nine. She has brown hair and a bracelet with her name around her ankle. 'Harna'. Could you..?"

Anthea felt tears welling up in her eyes."We'll do our best." she replied, patting Osile's shoulder.

* * * * * * * * * *

Lotheric Hall was in the northwestern part of the town. It had a high ceiling of polished wood that matched the floor, the walls decorated with images of The Great War of 628. The six Council members sat in a semi circle around Osile.

"What's your problem?" Osile fumed."Don't you want to see if our children are still alive?"

The Major of Lotheric, Denkle Genar, squinted as he looked around the other five council members. Denkle was a pale balding man in his late fifties. He brushed his thin wisps of grey hair forward over his shiny scalp. He was tall and thin, dressed in a long red tunic, which matched his dark lips.

"Look fat man," Denkle's nostrils flared,"there's no point in creating false hopes around here. My wife caused a scene with the river - and we put up a fence. By *Bormal*, she did it again today! Now you want to pay vagabonds to go to The Twelve Peaks to look for our children? Have you gone completely mad?"

The other Council members shifted nervously.

Osile couldn't understand why Denkle was against the idea. He hadn't been himself since his son Brenot had died. Perhaps grief was still clouding his mind?

Several hours later, the five Council members out-voted Denkle. Osile was given the money, and the meeting adjourned.

Osile went home to The Lions Den, knocked on Anthea's door, and gave her the money. Then he went to his wife, Hernsa. He told her that their daughter might be up at The Twelve Peaks. She was very excited when she'd heard the news, and she had told him that she missed Harna so much. He said he did too. He told her that a group of newcomers were travelling up to the mountains, and she hugged him and asked if he thought Harna might really be up there. He said he hoped so. They lay in each other's arms all through the night, but Osile slept fitfully. Besides the smell of whisky on his wife's breath, he dreamt of bodies that seemed to have been dead for months, and somehow he saw them rise up and walk. They seemed to be looking for something. They were hacking at rocks with picks, clawing at dirt with their once warm-blooded fingers...

Osile lay awake, casting his mind back to when Hernsa's eyes had last been filled with such hope. Had he done the right thing in telling his wife about the mountains? Osile shifted slightly, one arm completely numb beneath her. He managed to retrieve his arm, and slowly flexed it, the numbness gradually changing into painful pins and needles. He placed his arm on top of his chest, and stared at the ceiling once again. It had all started about fourteen months ago. A young couple named Brenot and Silvra were planning to get married. Denkle and Muriel were proud of their son Brenot, but Silvra's parents weren't quite so happy. They apparently thought Brenot was a bad influence on their daughter. Lotheric was an old fashioned town, and the couple was caught committing immoral sins in the eastern fields by Silvra's father. He had told Brenot that he wasn't ever to see Silvra again, and sent him home. No one knew what Silvra's father did to her. He dragged her home crying, with bruises and ripped clothes. A week later Brenot and Silvra ran away. Three weeks after that they'd run away, Silvra stumbled back into town, near death from claw marks in her back and a bite on her wrist. Osile remembered thinking that she was very pale. Silvra fell into a fever, and deliriously described a fight she had witnessed between her love and a hooded figure. She retold how clouds surrounded them and it grew dark. She described Brenot at first greeting the figure, then threatening it. He swung his sword at it but the figure caught his sword arm and twisted Brenot's arm until bones popped out. Brenot fell and lay still.

Silvra then described how she'd felt a burning pain across her back. She turned to see a dead body standing before her. She took a step back, screamed, then passed out. She woke not far from Lotheric, and had managed to make it back into town.

After several days Silvra felt suddenly better. She wouldn't let anyone see her wounds, insisting that she was fine. When her father questioned her about what had happened, she accused him of being responsible for Brenot's death. She then broke her father's neck in the busy streets. An elderly Healer of *Termolen* accused her of being possessed, so she killed him too. She had then growled as a mist surrounded her. A silver wolf leapt from the cloud, and it bounded away. Three days later, Silvra's body was found in the eastern fields. She had died by impaling herself on a broken tree stump. People said that it took three men to pull her off that tree stump. Mysteriously, there was no trace of blood.

Since Silvra's death, one or two children went missing from Lotheric every month. Scotus was the first to go. At first it was teenagers, but very soon the younger ones were disappearing as well. Six months ago, Osile's own daughter was taken from her bed. He missed her. Tears welled up in his eyes, and he let them roll freely down his face. Something had to be done, and Harna had to be found - or avenged.

Osile wiped his eyes, and slowly drifted off into a troubled sleep. Hernsa didn't stir once.

CHAPTER FOUR

It was overcast.

The party rose early, the wind biting at them mercilessly as they moved through the sleepy town.

"What a wonderfully brisk day," Jelik noted sardonically as he gathered his grey cloak closer to his shoulders.

"Tell me again - why aren't we taking our horses?" Karlos complained as they came to the old bridge.

"How were you planning on getting them across that bridge?" Jelik shouted above the sound of the rushing water. He was in a particularly foul mood this morning.

Anthea started across the bridge.

Karlos continued grumbling."We could've gone around the town."

"The rocky terrain doesn't suit horses," Kielmark replied.

"Oh." Karlos held on to the loose railing of the bridge for support as he crossed.

"Watch out," Anthea shouted as she completed crossing the bridge."It's rotten here. Try the other side."

Jelik glared at the half-Elf."I can see that, thank you."

Anthea shot back a fiery look as she rubbed her temples.

"You okay?" Karlos asked as he arrived safely across the bridge.

Anthea just nodded but continued to massage her head.

The party crossed the damaged bridge safely.

Eastern Lotheric was completely deserted. The houses lining the roads had broken windows, missing roof tiles, and a permeating stench. Rubbish circled the alleyways in a turbulent frenzy as a chime clattered from an old weathered porch.

"Nice," Sudenora noted sarcastically as he covered his nose and mouth with a cloth.

Jelik breathed deeply."This place reminds me of home."

Anthea turned up her nose superciliously."Let's just get out of here as fast as we can."

Soon they'd passed through eastern Lotheric and reached the grasslands - but more poignantly - they'd come to a place where the air was fresh.

They followed a track north, alongside the Splitting River and fields.

Sudenora quaffed the air in happy gulps and studied the clouds."The weather should improve over the next few hours." He smiled as if that would lighten everyone's mood.

Anthron squinted at the Twelve Peaks that lay in the distance before them. They were colossal. Riddled with red volcanic dust, the twelve taller mountains stood out significantly further than the rest of the mountain landscape. Anthron imagined they resembled bloody fingers clawing at the clouds.

The hike in the wind was onerous. About noon they stopped and rested.

Sudenora took off his pack and searched its contents, taking out some cold pork.

Jelik rolled his eyes.

"You can go without then." Anthea snapped.

Sudenora then dug into his pack and retrieved a large wineskin."Osile gave us some wine," he grinned."Just in case it got too cold." With that he shared the pork, and drank from his wineskin. He wiped his sleeve across his mouth, then passed the wineskin to Jelik.

"Only a little each, we still have a job to do," Anthea said as Jelik handed her the skin."Only a mouthful," she smiled as she took a few gulps. She passed it around.

"Just remember, what she says goes." Jelik grated.

Anthea passed the wine on."Look, what's with you today?" she pointedly asked Jelik.

Jelik shrugged and looked away.

"This tastes awful." Anthron grimaced as he passed on the wineskin. Kielmark raised his hand while shaking his head."Arrolokians aren't allowed to drink."

Jelik scoffed."How come I've never heard that? If you don't want any you don't have to lie..."

"Leave him alone, Jelik," Anthea flashed, rubbing her temples slowly.

"Thanks," Kielmark said uncomfortably."I don't want any."

"No problem." Jelik replied.

They packed their belongings and set off again along the trail towards the red mountains.

As Sudenora had predicted, the wind dissipated as the sky gave way to snatches of sunshine after a few hours.

The mountains loomed above them - the twelve peaks now lost from view beyond the scattered cloud. After several hours of tramping they climbed up the last incline that led to the massive mountain valley, and stood rapt in awe. Inside the red valley rested The Twelve Peaks. The dusty trail they had been following wound off into the distance, disappearing between the red mountains. The sound of the Splitting River could be heard flowing somewhere below them.

"An impressive sight, no?" Jelik commented.

"I wonder what the view would be like from up there," Anthron asked rhetorically.

"You'd probably get a bird's eye view of the clouds," Jelik replied.

"There," Anthea pointed up at one of the peaks,"That looks like another track."

They picked their way carefully over the loose rocks into the red valley, their feet scuffing at the volcanic dust.

"I hope this stuff comes out," Sudenora said as he patted himself."It looks like it stains cloth."

"You know that having a track can't be good," Jelik kicked at a rock absent-mindedly."A track means life."

"Not necessarily." Anthea replied as she began to follow Karlos.

"Oh, so rocks make tracks in and out themselves do they?" Jelik taunted.

Anthea sighed irritably."Spare me."

"Would you two leave it?" Karlos huffed.

"Sure thing." Jelik said, then muttered something under his breath.

"What did you say?" Anthea shrieked as she spun to face the thief.

Jelik shrugged."Nothing important."

Anthea's eyes went steely as she drew several symbols in the air. Seconds later she was holding an angry ball of fire.

"Stop this!" Kielmark shouted, standing between the two adversaries. Anthron almost smiled.

"Couldn't agree more, Kiel." Jelik looked alarmed.

Anthea dispersed her fireball with a wave and began up the track, nursing her stomach.

"Are you okay Anthea?" Karlos asked. Anthea didn't reply, continuing to climb.

After a tense climb they came to a flat surface about twenty feet wide and fifteen feet long. There were human bones scattered about. At the far end was the cave that Anthea had spotted. Giant footprints were visible in the red dust, but none of them were anywhere near the cave entrance itself.

The view was quite impressive, Anthron thought, being able to see the town of Lotheric to the south in the late afternoon sun."Here we are." he said as the rest of the group climbed on to the dusty flat platform.

The party peered into the dark passage as Kielmark rummaged through his pack, finding two torches.

Anthron asked,"Think we need a scout?"

"I'll go," Anthea proposed."I don't need a torch." Anthea's eyes narrowed as she stepped past Jelik, disappearing into the cave.

Anthron shifted uneasily."What's up with you two?" he asked Jelik.

Jelik stared at the blonde warrior, making him edgy."We're not suited to spending all this time together. We can't get space while traveling."

Anthron nodded."So, what's going to happen...?"

Jelik waved his hand signifying the end of the conversation.

They waited in silence a few minutes before Sudenora spoke."We've given her enough time I'd say."

"I'll get a light." Anthron offered. He pulled out a worn flint, and began rubbing his dagger over it. Within moments the two torches were sparking and hissing with black smoke.

"I'll go next," Jelik stated. He took one of the torches, spun round and entered the cave, holding the light aloft as the others followed.

The passageway was about ten feet wide; the edges made up of loose sharp rocks that made it difficult to get in close. The ceiling was about seven feet high, dotted with hundreds of small red stalactites, but the floor seemed out of place. It was shiny and smoothly worn down the middle, looking like something had been dragged over it for several hundred years to create the effect.

"I really hate being underground," Karlos said nervously.

"Don't worry about it Karlos," Sudenora replied."If you don't make too much noise the roof should hold. Loud noises sometimes..." his voice trailed off.

Karlos then made a concerted effort to walk quietly.

After about twenty minutes the passage started sloping down, as well as leaning left. Kielmark spoke quietly."It seems we are descending in a spiral around the inside of the peak."

"I wonder if any of the other peaks are like this." Sudenora commented.

After walking on in silence for a while, Jelik motioned for the others to stop."I can hear something." Tilting his head he listened intently. There it was again - the echo of metal hitting rock."Anyone hear that?"

"Sounds like someone mining." Anthron observed, unsheathing his sword.

"Damn," Jelik swore."Why didn't Anthea wait for us?" He flicked his wrist to retrieve a dagger from up his sleeve, then turned and jogged quietly down the passage.

The others continued on at a slower pace.

Jelik increased his speed again as the metal-on-rock sound got louder. After a brief jog he stopped abruptly. Anthea suddenly appeared in front of him. Her eyes glowing dimly red, indicated she was using her Elven night vision.

Anthea squinted at the torchlight."We've got trouble."

Jelik cracked his neck to one side."What kind of trouble? What's that sound?"

47

"Let's walk and talk," Anthea turned to head back down the passage."Please put the torch out," she said sharply."The sound you can hear is pick axes."

"So there's just miners down here?" Jelik scoffed as he relaxed.

"Yes," Anthea stopped and stared at the thief."Dead ones."

"Ahh," he exhaled. He dropped his torch, stifling the flame with his foot."Is there anything else there?"

"Not that I could see." she wavered.

"What?" Jelik snapped.

"Well, I thought I sensed another presence."

"Do you know what the dead were actually mining?"

Anthea stopped walking, Jelik blindly crashing into her."Jelik, they're dead. They didn't chat about the weather."

The thief's eyes narrowed.

She sighed in frustration as she traced symbols through the air, then gently touched the thief's arm. Suddenly Jelik could see clearly in the dark corridor, thanks to Anthea's enchantment.

Jelik nodded his thanks. *How far?* For the first time he 'spoke' to her in the silent hand signal language of thieves.

Anthea replied in the same fashion. *No far. Ten by three walks.* She winced. It had been some time since she'd used sign language.

Jelik frowned. *Thirty paces?*

Anthea nodded. Jelik placed a dagger in the middle of the passage floor next to the torch then they continued on. The thief answered Anthea's raised eyebrow. *They'll probably blunder their way down. Leaving those will at least make them wary - perhaps even quieter.*

They moved on.

Just now, Anthea's hands flashed.

You mean we're nearly there? Jelik queried, screwing his nose up as the stench hit him.

Anthea nodded while covering her nose and mouth. The passage gradually became easier to navigate as torchlight flickered up ahead, strange sparks flaring off the walls themselves. The sound of metal hitting rock was now easily identifiable as someone wielding a pick.

We should wait for the others, Jelik suggested.

Why? Not bold? Anthea replied, smiling wickedly.

Fine. Jelik's hands made the sign sharply. In sign language, that was the closest one could get to shouting.

The torchlight was garish to Jelik's enhanced vision, so when his eyes began to stream Anthea removed her enhancement as she reverted back to her own normal vision.

The torch was mounted on the left side of the passage at a T-junction. The corridor they had been following kept going down, becoming steeper, with another branching to their right. This new passage was the same size as the other, well lit with torches.

Anthea pointed at the new passage. *There goes diggers, no that goes down.*

Jelik shook his head in dismay. *You need practice. So you haven't gone down there then?*

No.

Anthea let out a short yelp of fright and Jelik whipped out two daggers as a deep voice spoke from behind them.

"There's no need to be secretive," The voice came from a large pale man dressed in a baggy brown robe."I've known you were here for some time now."

Out of sheer habit of living on the streets of Smazorok, knowing the philosophy of he who hesitates dies, Jelik threw his daggers at the man who had startled him. The thief's reactions were lightning fast, both daggers striking the man's chest.

"Forgive me," the man responded as he withdrew Jelik's blades matter-of-factly from his chest. The daggers were bloodless."I have not introduced myself. I am called Gwyerson Dernas, third to The Master himself," he smiled, revealing a row of serrated teeth. He looked to Jelik."You were chosen originally as food. It looks like now you have another purpose - you should be honoured."

"What?" Jelik stuttered as he withdrew two more daggers.

Anthea unsheathed her sword and began advancing on Gwyerson. He responded with a raised eyebrow."*Shoth met likas toloth.*" he spoke softly.

Anthea's eyes went icy as Gwyerson spoke, and she clutched at her stomach. Gwyerson pointed to Jelik, and Anthea turned with her sword poised, a single tear rolling down her cheek as she struck the bewildered thief.

CHAPTER FIVE

The man pushed the door wide.

He was instantly affronted by the stench of stale beer and vomit - a putrefying disjunction from the fresh night air. *The Hive* was an extremely busy tavern and he jostled his way through the rowdy drunken throng.

He made his way to the stairs and disappeared into the shadows of the booth he wanted. An attractive woman wearing a white satin dress sat opposite."Sasha Quevnon. Or should I call you Quabeth White? It's been a while."

She smiled at him."Smit-Myer Crysin, you can call me what you like. In fact it's been two months and twenty one days since we last met," Sasha shrugged nonchalantly."But who's counting?"

Smit-Myer waved his arms around the tavern disapprovingly."A particularly loathsome choice of venue, I must say."

She sighed."Why do you want to see me?"

"I'm looking for more people, five others that have escaped. These ones have been missing for almost seven months. I need the help of your contacts around the Izonda border."

Sasha leaned back and screwed up her nose as she toyed with a fingernail."Why do you still work for *them*."

"That's my business. Will you help me? There's a full purse in it for you - the usual fee."

Sasha shrugged."I'll do it for you, not them. Just give me the money and descriptions."

Crysin reached into his tunic and passed a pouch of money to Sasha. She took it with relish, and counted its contents.

"This'll do." she nodded.

"The first one is a large man with blonde hair and blue eyes named Anthron Mikolnic. His father is a blacksmith, his mother a seamstress. They live in Vemmlok."

He paused before continuing.

"The next one is Sudenora Kiltorn. He has brown hair and eyes. His father was a street performer illusionist in Eugernok, his mother runs *The Jug* - a bar in Eugernok.

"Now, here's one you'll surely know. Brekon House."

"They took one of the Brekon children?" Sasha asked, stupefied.

"They'll take anyone, they don't care. Anyway, Karlos Brekon. He was a disappointment to Dathor because he was too portly to make a decent warrior. That's why his father ignored him. He's got mousy hair, and hazel eyes.

"Kielmark of Arrolok, a horseman. His father is completely blind, his mother's dead. Large muscles, squat with dark skin, and a mean spirit. You know the usual Arrolokian. Black hair and brown eyes."

"I've never really spoken to an Arrolokian. Are they really that rude?" Sasha asked.

"Not really, their faults have been terribly exaggerated. It's just their way of life.

"Now, the last one here is a little out of the ordinary. Jelik Qualis is his name. I checked him out, and his family was hit by the Ruby Brotherhood some time ago. He lived on the streets of Smazorok for eight years before he and the Brekon kid hit it off."

Smit-Myer paused, allowing Sasha time to commit the facts to her retentive memory."He earned his reputation for being the most adept man with a dagger on the streets of Smazorok." Crysin looked at the ruby ring on his right hand, the symbol of the Ruby Brotherhood. Sasha leaned forward and placed her hand on his just before they were interupted by a short plump woman with a red face."Excuse me," she held a jug of ale in one hand, a cask of wine in the other."Would either of you be wantin' somethin'?"

Crysin shook his head, knowing that his favourite green drink wouldn't be served in a place like this. He looked at Sasha."Quabeth my dear, would you care for something?"

She waved the barmaid away.

Crysin caught her eye."Before you go." he produced a silver coin and flicked it into her jug of ale. She blushed slightly as she looked awkwardly at Sasha.

Smit-Myer raised his hand in front of him and slowly shook his head."Make sure you get some sleep tonight." With that, he waved her away. The barmaid smiled and left hurriedly, just in case this generous stranger quickly changed his mind.

Crysin saw Sasha looking at him inquisitively. He explained."Every time I've been here, she's disappeared off upstairs with someone. It's really sad that anyone has to make a living like that." Crysin looked agitated about the whole thing.

Sasha smiled as she studied her old friend. He was thirty-eight years old, the lines around his tired grey-blue eyes made him look older. His tanned face was long, thin, and slightly leathery from travel, with his white teeth protruding whenever he smiled. He had long straight black hair pulled back into a ponytail, and a neat Scyermor styled moustache and beard.

"Anything wrong, my Quabeth?" Crysin asked.

"No, of course not. I was merely considering a strategy to track your targets." Sasha returned.

"They aren't my targets," Crysin snapped."Remember that."

"I'm sorry," she nodded her head respectfully.

"Of course," he replied.

"I'll get Sonat working along the Izonda border with a few men," Sasha began."Leaving word about, that sort of thing. I think Korsorn can cover Mosorac and Decton. We can probably forget about Lotheric."

"You know my feelings about being thorough. Make sure Korsorn checks out Lotheric as well. I don't want to have to call in my people just yet; they've got better things to do. How about Drans? The last job he did was very thorough, he found three people hiding in the Bayton sewers. Get Drans to check out Carson and the surrounding plains."

"Actually, I was going to suggest Lorol for Car..."

"Lorol's a thug - and not suited for this sort of work," Crysin interupted."Drans will do nicely."

Sasha unconsciously gnawed her fingernails."Have you checked east?"

"Yes," he nodded."We found a little village hidden in the Sambethe forest, very sequestered I must say. We sent Wilse to investigate with a story that he'd escaped Selection. The first thing he discovered was that there's another village in the Ithren forest somewhere. I'll have to send my own people to check that out." Crysin slouched back in his chair."The Elves would take out anyone but the best."

"So your game may well have been hiding in the forest for the last seven months and you didn't think to check it?" Sasha laughed derisively,"That's not like you."

Crysin's eyes glazed angrily."I was instructed to search east." he replied coldly.

"Ah. I should have realised."

Crysin rose from his chair, stretched, then leaned over and kissed Sasha's hand and bowed. Sasha noted that he never took his eyes off her the whole time. Charming he may be, but he was always cautious.

"As always, my Quabeth, it's been a pleasure. Let's agree to meet again in three days. This time, however, I'd like to change the venue. How does *The Merchant's Dream* sound to you?"

"That's fine. Three days then, same time." She stood as he left and watched him merge into the crowd.

"Why do you put up with that?" a rasping voice said from behind the booth.

Sasha slowly turned away from the crowd to seat herself once again in her booth. A thin man emerged from behind her, his head shaking distastefully."Thug?" he muttered.

"What's this, Lorol? Jealousy? Really, you ought to know me better than that. Business is business."

Lorol sat across from Sasha. He looked wiry, with a dark Kortusian complexion. He had slanted eyes and short black hair, with a scar running down the left side of his face, curving around up under his throat.

"Jealous, maybe. Do you have to do business so..." Lorol croaked as he gesticulated for Sasha to complete his sentence.

"Tell me, who has put the most business my way over the last little while?" Sasha asked."Crysin has, and that will continue."

She clicked her fingers as the barmaid walked past."Would ye be wantin' anythin'?"

"Yes, I would. A brandy - in a large glass." Sasha replied.

"It won't be long." the barmaid replied, then she headed off into the throng again.

"I'm not so sure Crysin will manage that, my Quabeth." he continued.

Sasha raised an eyebrow."Oh?"

"I might just hunt him down tonight, Quabeth, so that I may insult his severed head on those cold wintry afternoons when it rains and I've got nothing better to do."

"No." Sasha replied harshly.

Lorol stood up, placing his right fist over his heart."You don't think I can do it?" His rasping voice had a hard time reaching its desired pitch of obnoxiousness, but Lorol's expression said it all.

"I don't doubt you."

"I'll show you, Quabeth. I'll show you that my skill is far superior to his," Lorol then turned to leave.

Sasha caught his arm."Look, this isn't something to die for..."

Lorol pulled his arm away and barged through the drunken patrons.

"Now what can I do?" Sasha sighed, flopping back into her seat. She brooded until the barmaid returned with her large glass of brandy, and threw her a few coppers.

"How much for the rest of the bottle, missy?" Sasha asked. She picked up the large glass and downed it in five huge gulps. She winced slightly, wiped her mouth and continued."Because my glass seems to be empty, and I have a feeling I'm going to get very thirsty."

The plump barmaid gathered up her coins and nodded."This will be fine." And she made her way back to the bar via the path Lorol had just cleared.

* * * * * * * * * *

Crysin slipped through the back streets of Mosorac inconspicuously. He headed for the other side of town where five of his men were waiting for him in a derelict warehouse. What Sasha didn't know couldn't hurt her.

Crysin sighed, and watched his breath become a wispy cloud. His breath turned in on itself before diffusing into the cold night air.

From the next intersection Crysin could hear voices. He slipped into a doorway and hid in the shadows - listening intently. He could now hear the footfalls on the cobbled street close by, Crysin's best guestimate was there were about four people approaching. As they got closer, he could hear the sound of leather creaking; the sound of sheathed weapons slapping against their legs.

Their talking became louder and more intelligible as they came into view.

"I still don't think we'll find someone stupid enough to think we're the guards, Rali," a man with a handlebar moustache said glumly.

Rali, a man with short curly red hair, laughed. "It's always worth a try, Broan. If they suspect anything, the four of us can just wipe them out and loot them."

Low laughter crackled among them.

Crysin remained hidden until they were out of earshot.

Then he re-emerged from the doorway, completely invisible. He smiled to himself, grateful for the magical properties of his multi-faceted cloak. He went through the intersection, and changed course from east to south. After a few minutes, the magic wore off, so he walked in the shadows once again. He crept stealthily through another intersection, changing his course back eastwards. Suddenly he felt the hairs on the back of his neck stand on end - he was being watched! He moved further into the shadows, closed his eyes, mentally re-grouping. Yes... A watcher was on a rooftop on the other side of the street. He opened his eyes again and scanned the rooftops. Nothing. He could see nothing out of the ordinary. Crysin listened for a moment. He couldn't hear anything untoward. He continued along the cobbled road, loosening his sheathed wakizashi.

Suddenly he heard a whirling sound, the sound of something very sharp coming his way. He dove forward, got to his feet, leapt on to his hands, and did several handsprings before stopping to look around. In the wall right where he had been were three large shuriken, razor sharp metal disks, embedded deeply in the stone wall. He scanned the rooftops again. He could make out a figure on a small house opposite where he now stood. The figure somersaulted off the roof, landing on the cobbled road with barely a whisper.

Crysin had his curved wakizashi out of its sheath before his adversary's feet touched the road. His opponent drew two similarly curved blades, and advanced on him slowly.

Crysin was usually imperturbable, but this was an exception. His adversary was about twenty feet away now, covered from head to toe in black cloth. Crysin recognised his Kortusian features. This would be one hell of a fight he thought.

"I've grown tried of your games, Crysin." the Kortusian growled. His voice rasped like rusty metal being sanded.

"Ah, Lorol the Blade." replied Crysin, recognising his distinctive voice.

"This will be your last play, so try to play well. Quabeth White sees you as a threat. She is also weary of you. She wants you out of the game." Lorol then lunged at Crysin, and so the fight began.

Crysin feinted and missed his first attack and parried his second. There was a series of clashes of sword against sword, then both stepped back and re-grouped.

"Better than you thought?" Crysin taunted.

"You shall die painfully," Lorol spat.

"Oh, get on with it. Do you have any idea how many times I have heard that?"

With that Lorol charged.

Lorol's first strike was aimed at his throat; his second went for his right knee. Crysin blocked both attacks in one movement much more deftly than Lorol thought possible. Lorol then had to bring both weapons back as Crysin sent his wakizashi darting straight for his exposed chest.

Lorol caught the blade with both of his, deflected it downwards, trapping it in the X of his blades. He then pushed one of his curved swords aside and attacked with his other, aiming for Crysin's neck. Adrenalin surged as he noticed Crysin couldn't get his sword free from his other blade in time. His sword was almost home when Crysin raised his arm up into the sword's path. There was a dull thud, sending Crysin backwards.

Lorol couldn't believe his eyes. He could see little iron rods sewn into Crysin's sleeves.

"Terribly sorry, Lorol, but I'm going to have to hurry things just a little. I have some important business - business that I'd rather you didn't overhear."

Lorol was surprised that Crysin knew where he'd been earlier that night.

Crysin spun his wakizashi several times."Are you ready for another round?"

Lorol clenched his fists around the handle of his curved blades, and felt a slight pain in his left arm. He looked down at a small nick across his forearm. He cursed as he raised his swords once again in battle posture.

Lorol came in again, his twin swords lost in a blur of speed. He attacked from every conceivable angle, always frustrated and parried by the flashing wakizashi. He started to attack higher and higher, trying to lift Crysin's guard. Lorol attacked his neck and shoulders now, but still the wakizashi kept both swords at bay. Crysin saw what Lorol was up to and played along, allowing his guard to rise. Then Lorol pulled both his swords back at once, and lunged forward, attempting a double stab to his chest. His ruse would have caught most warriors off-guard, however Crysin was ready. He raised his wakizashi up, and brought it around in an arc as he stepped out of harm's way. Both blades strayed harmlessly wide. Crysin sidestepped and spun on his heels until he was standing alongside his attempted assassin. He then locked his left arm around both of Lorol's, and with Lorol's arms trapped, smashed the hilt of his wakizashi into his face.

Lorol's vision became befuddled for a few seconds - until he regained his composure. He was standing about fifteen feet from Crysin, weaponless. Crysin was so cocky that he'd put his own weapon away. Lorol reached down into his boot, and pulled out a long thin dagger. Crysin didn't look in the least perplexed.

Crysin unbuckled his sword belt, and placed it on top of Lorol's twin blades. He flicked his wrist, revealing a dagger. He undid his cloak, and placed it over the weapons.

"It doesn't need to come to this, you know," Crysin mentioned straightforwardly.

"I'll rest when you're dead," Lorol hissed.

The two assassins started towards each other.

Crysin lashed out - Lorol swayed back, then retaliated with a high swing, and a sidekick. His kick caught Crysin completely unawares, connecting painfully with his ribs. Seizing the advantage, Lorol kicked Crysin's dagger from his hand, and made a slash for his throat.

Crysin rolled backwards, coming to his feet as Lorol advanced with a series of slashes that were thwarted by Crysin's iron rods. Lorol made a horizontal slash - Crysin ducked under it and spun around putting his leg out. Crysin's heel caught the back of Lorol's feet, tripping Lorol on the cobblestones.

Crysin was quick, and he was upon Lorol in a flash. Lorol's dagger was sent scuttling noisily across the cobblestone road, as Lorol got back to his feet.

Both unarmed, they prepared to fight again, both unaware that their fight now had an unwanted observer.

Lorol's fist darted toward Crysin's head, but Crysin was quicker. His right hand deflected Lorol's punch, quickly followed by Crysin's left hand grabbing hold of the arm. Crysin pulled his arm as he shot out his elbow, smashing Lorol's nose. Lorol reeled back as he swung his fists wildly, catching Crysin's mouth.

They both stepped back again, catching their breath. Crysin darted out with a combination jab front kick, followed by a spinning kick. Lorol didn't see the latter.

Lorol stumbled back, blood flowing from his nose, fumbling in his belt pouch as Crysin kicked the side of his head. Lorol spun right round before dropping to the ground motionless.

Crysin wiped the blood from his mouth as he retrieved his items. He buckled on his sword belt and clasped his cloak over his shoulders. He decided to leave Lorol's blades."Sorry, my friend," Crysin began approaching the now stirring Lorol."Dead enemies are safe enemies. I find that live ones are more likely to come back and haunt you."

Lorol was now propped up on one arm, his hand searching through his belt pouch again.

"Oh no you don't," Crysin said as he began running towards Lorol. With a triumphant look on his face, Lorol pulled a shiny round object from his pouch and held it up."I shall see you again," he croaked. With that, he threw the object to the ground. Upon impact an explosion of thick smoke erupted into the overcast night.

Crysin was hesitant to enter the smoke - instead he circled around. Once the smoke had settled somewhat, Crysin scanned the area.

"Damn!" he cursed.

Lorol was nowhere in sight.

* * * * * * * * *

A dark figure slunk away from the fight into the receptive feeding ground of shadows. He was particularly ravenous this evening, but thought it in the worst possible taste to drain one of his employees.

CHAPTER SIX

Karlos covered his face.

"What in *Termolen's* name is that smell?" exclaimed the Healer, wrapping his scarf tighter around his nose and mouth.

"Smells like your boots," Sudenora muttered."I can also hear flies."

Kielmark peered further down the corridor."Where are the others?"

"What's that?" Anthron pointed, then picked up Jelik's extinguished torch.

Kielmark scooped up the dagger."One of Jelik's."

"How do you know?" Anthron inquired.

Kielmark turned the pommel of the dagger around to show Anthron."You see here, this is his symbol. He marks all his daggers this way."

Anthron frowned."What does this mean then? Are they in trouble?"

"I think he wants us to be cautious." Karlos replied.

The four continued down the corridor.

"Torchlight ahead," Kielmark hissed."The walls themselves seem to be sparking."

"And," Anthron whispered,"That sound has stopped."

"I've got one of those feelings." Sudenora muttered.

"Just be ready." Anthron responded as Kielmark doused his torch.

"That smell's getting worse," Karlos whimpered."Smells like something rotten."

They arrived at the well-lit T-junction.

"There's blood here," Anthron whispered."And it's fresh."

"Which way then?" Kielmark asked.

"Well..." Anthron stopped as Karlos yelled. Whirling around, he watched the Healer slump to the ground, his forehead bleeding. Standing over Karlos was Gwyerson Dernas.

Kielmark attacked instantly. Gwyerson caught the sabre effortlessly, wrenched it from Kielmark's grip, tossing it behind him up the passage.

Sudenora began mumbling words to *Servas* - but before he could finish Gwyerson bashed him off his feet. Sudenora stayed down.

"No more Elementalists." Gwyerson laughed.

Anthron glanced at Kielmark who was looking petrified.

"Who are you?" Anthron demanded boldly, holding his silver-hilted long sword in front of him.

Gwyerson smiled warmly, Anthron seeing his blood stained teeth. He gestured at Sudenora and Karlos."I do apologise, this isn't the easiest way to begin a relationship."

"What do you want? Where are the others?" Anthron demanded.

"First of all," Gwyerson stated with a nonchalant wave of his hand."Get rid of your toy."

Anthron's sword flew from his hand, ending up the passage near Kielmark's sabre.

"That's better," Gwyerson smiled."Now we can be gentlemen." He pretended to muse over it for a moment."Now that I have Xycermon," he motioned to a bat shaped dagger tucked in his belt."Your existence is superficial. I don't care myself, however the Master doesn't want any mistakes." Gwyerson tipped his head in farewell, then vanished into a green mist as Anthron and Kielmark heard shuffling footsteps coming from the torch-lit corridor.

"Anthron?" Kielmark's voice was shaking as he looked up the passage."Dead men walking."

The smell hit Kielmark and Anthron almost simultaneously and Kielmark was sick. The putrefying flesh of the approaching bodies was grey and maggot infested. Out of the five that approached only two were whole. Two were missing an arm each while the last was headless. They moved jerkily with each squelching footfall with hundreds of flies buzzing around them.

The image of Scotus flashed in front of Anthron's eyes. It wasn't dead.

Kielmark retched again.

"Anthron." A weak voice came from behind the blonde warrior. He turned around, dagger in hand, to see Jelik limping way up the passage covered in blood.

"Where's Anthea?" Anthron snarled.

"That doesn't matter any more." Jelik replied coldly.

Kielmark dashed up the passage, retrieving their weapons."Anthron, I'm going to need help."

"Fire," Jelik breathed."Use fire."

Anthron's eyes darted about."Jelik's right, Kiel. Use torches - the bodies will burn easily." The blonde warrior detached one of the mounted torches, while Kielmark grabbed another.

The first walking dead was mercilessly mutilated. Anthron swung his flaming weapon with all his strength at its head as Kielmark held it at bay by holding his torch at its torso. The head came off with a sickening crunch, maggots squirming about madly as they began to burn.

Anthron had just enough time to wipe bile from his chin as another approached."Three to go," he panted as another dropped to the passage floor burning.

"Anthron," Jelik pointed to the defenceless Karlos and Sudenora with a torch he'd plucked from the wall."We need to keep them safe."

The blonde warrior nodded in response as he ducked under a slow attack. Thrusting forward, Anthron discarded his torch that had punctured through the rotten chest and kicked the burning body over.

Kielmark was showered in flaming sparks as he blocked; then Jelik's flashing sword was there. Jelik severed the head and he kicked out the legs, leaving Kielmark to eradicate the fetid corpse.

The remaining animated carcass fell, caught alight from its spent drudgers.

"We have to get out of here!" Jelik wrapped his cloak around his face to protect him from the fumes and fetor.

Anthron noted the red dust on the walls flaring irregularly."I don't know what that means," he pointed."But I agree. Jelik - get Sudenora. We'll grab Karlos."

Kielmark and Anthron hoisted Karlos as Jelik threw Sudenora over his shoulder, and they began to run back up the smoky passage.

Anthron felt like his lungs had given out as they burst into the fresh night several minutes later. Gasping for air with a painful stitch wasn't a pleasurable experience. As he rolled in the red dust he vowed to get fitter.

It wouldn't be the last time he'd think that.

Jelik stood straight with his hands on his head, wincing while trying to catch his breath."Are we whole?" he gasped.

Kielmark wiped perspiration from his face."That was..."

The dark man was cut off by an underground explosion which shook Jelik from his feet. From the cave entrance they were assaulted by a wave of putrescence followed by a thick cloud of red dust. Anthron covered Karlos and Sudenora as several small rocks bounced off his back and forearms. There was one more shudder, then all was still.

"What was that!" Jelik coughed, peering through the thick dust.

"This dust could be flammable." Kielmark spat, rubbing his eyes.

Jelik opened his mouth to reply, but stopped as Karlos regained consciousness.

"By *Termolen*! My head!" Karlos groaned loudly before coughing.

Anthron examined Sudenora."You might want *Termolen's* help before too long," he hacked."He looks bad."

Karlos squinted."He'll live. I'll collect myself and be with you shortly."

Ten minutes later the dust had settled and Sudenora was awake nursing a headache.

"So," Karlos began."What happened?"

Anthron shook his head."I'm not sure. All we know is there's something powerful down there which wiped the floor with us - and Anthea's gone." The blonde warrior glared at Jelik."Where is she?" he said threateningly.

Jelik's eyes narrowed to slits."Don't take that tone," he snapped."She's one of them. She turned on me," Jelik revealed two slashes across his arm and back."That robed guy back there recognised her and she attacked me."

"Well," Sudenora urged."Go on?"

Jelik stared at his feet."She'd hit me twice before I could react, I obviously wasn't expecting an attack from her," he hesitated before continuing."I threw the daggers in my hand in her direction as I fell, then some kind of force hit me. I came too further down the passage when Anthron and Kiel began fighting."

Anthron's eyes were slowly reddening."She wasn't around when we got there. So you don't know where she is?"

"Damn it Anthron!" Jelik exploded."I have no idea!" Jelik's voice echoed through the mountains.

"What a mess." Karlos sighed.

Anthron studied Jelik, particularly his outline. For the second time, Anthron could see a purple hue lightly pulsing around him. He watched as it dissipated with the thief's anger.

"Anthron." Sudenora hissed urgently. All turned to where he was looking. A swirling green mist spiralled from the sky, slowly circling the party.

"What is it?" Anthron asked, drawing his sword.

The green smoke hovered above them for several moments before descending like a feather. As it touched the red ground it began to grow, slowly solidifying and taking the shape of a man - Gwyerson Dernas.

Jelik leapt in, daggers slashing, finding his attacks useless, as Gwyerson was intangible.

"Top effort," Gwyerson taunted as the group backed away."I didn't think you'd survive the blast." He held out his hand as a misty sword appeared."I'll have to finish you myself."

Kielmark was watching the man's feet, waiting for an indication that he had become tangible. Slowly the dark man noted the footprints in the red dusk sinking. That was what the Arrolokian was waiting for."Now!" He leapt forwards, sabre leading. Gwyerson swung his sword in deflection, grasped Kielmark's arm with his spare hand then swung his attack harmlessly wide.

Kielmark's eyes widened in horror as he realised the sheer strength of this thing. It couldn't be human. The vice-like grip on his arm hurt so much he had to drop his sabre.

Karlos swung his morning star over his head, smashing the spiked ball heavily onto Gwyerson's head as Jelik stabbed two daggers into his back.

Gwyerson snarled, twisting Kielmark's arm, then flung the screaming man away. Spinning on Karlos, Gwyerson's sword glowed an angry green as it cut towards the Healer. Throwing himself backward Karlos tugged on his embedded weapon, narrowly missing the hissing sword. His morning star came free as he tumbled backwards, winding himself. Karlos just had time to cover his head as Gwyerson's sword bit deep into the Healer's left arm. The cut itself hurt badly, but it was the burning from the blade that made Karlos black out.

Sudenora released his second batch of sparks before the first lot had struck. He hoped the sparks didn't ignite the volatile red dust, but threw caution to the wind as Karlos went down. Gwyerson's eyes - now glowing red - rested upon Sudenora as the sparks flared and bit at his feet. Gwyerson waved his hand and produced a globe of darkness on Sudenora's head, completely blinding him. Sudenora dropped defensively to his stomach and crawled away from the fight, the dark globe following.

Anthron and Jelik looked at each other, then to Gwyerson. The wound in his head where Karlos had hit him had gone, and Jelik's daggers in his back didn't seem to bother him.

They were in trouble.

Jelik circled around so Gwyerson was in between him and Anthron, daggers in hand, muscles taunt. Anthron glanced to his silver hilted sword, wondering if it was going to be any use. It had to be.

Gwyerson advanced on the blonde warrior casually, not afraid in the least. That annoyed Anthron. Anthron grasped his sword in two hands and begun a fighting routine his teacher Lepus had taught him, swinging with all his strength high, using his own momentum to instantly strike low, and so on. Anthron's attacks were easily defeated, and as Jelik came in poised to attack, Gwyerson Dernas vanished.

"Where is he?" Anthron panted, wiping the stinging sweat from his eyes.

Jelik turned, surveying their surroundings. Then, standing above the wounded Kielmark, Gwyerson reappeared.

"I must be out of practice," Gwyerson glanced at his nails."I would normally have you all by now." He smiled wickedly and sheathed his sword."I will end this now for you."

Anthron's heart pounded as he realised there was nothing he could do. Gwyerson summoned a fireball in one hand, and picked Kielmark up by his injured arm. The Arrolokian screamed out, his other hand tight in a fist."I may as well burn you all together." Gwyerson said as he threw Kielmark at Anthron.

Just as Kielmark flew from Gwyerson's grip, the black man swung his good arm as if to punch out. Instead Kielmark released a handful of red dust upon Gwyerson. Kielmark landed painfully, rolled, then blacked out.

Gwyerson's eyes widened as his fireball flared. He reached out to extinguish it just as it exploded, blasting his right hand to pieces.

Anthron and Jelik dived for cover but there were no more explosions. Gwyerson had stifled the blast so that it didn't contact any more dust.

Gwyerson let out an unholy howl of pain. Anthron and Jelik lost no time in taking advantage of that. Anthron raced forwards sword held straight out, and skewered the man through the chest. Gwyerson reached into his tunic as his stumped arm smashed into Anthron's ribs. The blonde warrior fell back gasping, just as Jelik jumped from behind. The thief sunk two more daggers into the back of Gwyerson's head. Gwyerson retrieved the bat shaped dagger from his belt, then he attacked. Jelik ducked the attack and kicked out, knocking the dagger harmlessly away. Gwyerson - now unarmed - snarled and launched himself at Jelik.

Jelik didn't expect such a straightforward attack, and they both fell.

Anthron winced as he stood straight, one hand on his side, the other shakily holding his sword. He would not give up.

Gwyerson was over Jelik, pinning him to the ground while the thief furiously thrashed and kicked. Anthron held his sword in both hands and struck Gwyerson with all his strength across his lower back. Gwyerson looked back at Anthron, his chin covered in fresh blood, and threw Jelik aside. Anthron watched in horror as his fatal cut on Gwyerson healed.

"What are you?" Anthron gasped, staggering back.

Gwyerson's red eyes glowed strongly as he advanced."I'm your death," he grated.

Anthron believed him. The blonde warrior's knees buckled and crashed to the ground, waiting for death. He couldn't move. He couldn't scream. He couldn't even look towards Gwyerson. He could just stare straight up at what stars he could see. The magic Gwyerson had placed on him was for torture he believed.

Gwyerson looked down on Anthron, blocking his view of the stars, two daggers protruding from the back of his head. Anthron then heard something fly past his ear and, being able to move again, turned to Gwyerson.

Gwyerson Dernas was gone, a gaseous figure dispersing in his place; the bat-shaped dagger appearing back in Jelik's waiting hand.

CHAPTER SEVEN

They camped at the base of the Twelve Peaks.

They settled cautiously as Karlos saw to their wounds. He'd asked for *Termolen's* assistance with no response, so the Healer did things the old fashioned way.

Kielmark was in agony, the ulna and radius of his right arm being badly cracked. Karlos splinted the Arrolokian's forearm, dressed with comfrey leaves, and bandaged it. He finished off with a sling, and lay the dark man down with his feet up.

Anthron's ribs were also dressed with comfrey leaves. Sudenora summoned *Servas's* power to provide ice, which was applied to Anthron's side.

Jelik's cuts and bite were treated with cayenne then dressed.

Karlos then tended his own arm. The sword slash across his left arm wasn't deep; it was the blistering wound left from the blade's flame which hurt the most. The bleeding had stopped, so Karlos instructed Sudenora to apply cayenne and ice.

By the time the sun had risen, Karlos's pain relief bottle of leopard's bane was empty.

They slowly picked their way back to Lotheric, stopping frequently. Neither Kielmark or Anthron could carry their packs, so Jelik and Sudenora carried twice as much.

They were a sore sight indeed, Karlos thought as they carried on in silence.

They rested for lunch on the overcast day and ate a lunch of bread, cheese and water amongst the tall grass as Karlos begun his prayers of healing.

"Jelik," Anthron started as he looked at the daydreaming thief. "That dagger..." Anthron waited as Jelik retrieved the bat-shaped dagger from his belt.

It was the first time Jelik had examined it since acquiring it from

Gwyerson Dernas. The thin black double-edged tail-blade was just over a foot long with faint silver designs. The crosspiece of the dagger was the bat's barbed wings, spanning out half a foot each side. A set of rubies were in place of the eyes, and from the crosspiece, running a little way down the blade were fangs. The hilt of the dagger was moulded for perfect grip, with the pommel itself looking like something had been broken off.

Overall, it was the blood red rubies which caught Jelik's attention. Staring for a moment longer, he then passed the dagger to Anthron.

Karlos shrunk back from it."It looks horrid! Something *Bormal* himself would find ugly."

Anthron turned it over in his hand before Sudenora reached out for it.

Sudenora examined it curiously."I haven't heard of a bat-shaped dagger. It might be worth while having it identified."

Jelik nodded."That dagger did what none of us could," Jelik glanced over his shoulder at the Twelve Peaks."It killed Gwyerson."

Anthron finished chewing on a piece of cheese."And it flew instead of spinning like a normal dagger."

Kielmark finished his mug of water, then went back to nursing his arm."Flew?"

"I didn't actually see it - rather I heard it," Anthron started."It sounded like a real bat flying past my head, and Jelik said that it didn't spin. Then it materialised back in his hand once that guy was gone."

"Gone?" Karlos leaned forward. He'd spent the whole morning in silence wanting to know what had actually transpired the evening before.

"Like Anthea." Sudenora offered coolly.

"One thing at a time," Kielmark interjected.

Jelik cracked his neck before answering."I threw the dagger at Gwyerson. It looked like he..." Jelik rolled his hand as he tried to find the right word."Evaporated."

Sudenora stared at Jelik."And Anthea? What happened to her?"

All eyes fell on Jelik, patiently waiting for an answer. The thief cleared his throat."I found her coming back up the passage. She'd found the corpses, and had a suspicion that someone else was around."

"So why didn't you wait for us?" Anthron shot.

Jelik shrugged."She wouldn't. She seemed to think it was a game. Anyway," He poured himself another mug of fresh water."We went back down, found the torches. Gwyerson Dernas somehow crept up on us - me. He then said something about us originally chosen as food, but now we have another job. I attacked but couldn't hurt him. That's when Anthea swung her sword at me," Jelik paused to finish his water."Her eyes were so icy, her attacks aimed to kill. I did what I could but Gwyerson hit me with something and I blacked out." Jelik looked up from his empty mug."That's it."

Sudenora let out a sigh while Anthron stood in protest."She wouldn't have betrayed us!" the blonde warrior boomed."There has to be something you're leaving out."

Jelik's eyes narrowed."You weren't there."

Sudenora passed the dagger back to Jelik, who slipped it into his belt. The Elementalist scratched his thinly bristled chin as he thought."So," Sudenora changed the subject."Should we get it identified?"

"How much do you think it would cost?" Karlos asked.

"Cost?" Sudenora thought."Your guess is as good as mine. Couple of coppers, a silver..."

"And where?" Kielmark added.

Sudenora shrugged."Maybe Mosorac? Maybe Decton? Maybe even at Lotheric..."

Kielmark shook his head."I don't think we should let anyone know about it at Lotheric. We could endanger the people."

Karlos frowned in response."How?"

Kielmark shifted uncomfortably."Gwyerson Dernas said to us in the cave; 'Now that I have Xycermon, your existence is superficial'. I think he was talking about that dagger. Perhaps the Selection has been collecting people to search the old mine in The Twelve Peaks for it."

"Was that cave an old mine?" Anthron asked.

Kielmark shrugged."It had all the signs."

71

Jelik shook his head slowly."No Kiel, we were meant to be something's dinner. I think the Selection is to feed..."

"Don't be absurd." Anthron looked back at the mountains."The people have to have gone somewhere. Don't you think it's strange that no one has noticed wheeled cages full of people being pulled across the countryside? What if we give this dagger back - will the Selection stop?"

"I don't think it would somehow." Karlos murmured.

"And," Kielmark began."Criminals are collected in a similar fashion as we were. Who's to say the last lot of criminals we saw in cages weren't innocent people?"

Karlos stood and began to pace."We don't know if they were taken to The Twelve Peaks do we? We looked inside but didn't explore very far - and now we can't."

"We just have to take the chance that the miners were a separate part of the Selection," Sudenora said."We can't go back to check - and I most certainly don't *want* to go back."

"Perhaps we can intercept the next lot of cages?" Anthron mused.

"An idea if we see one," Kielmark started."But if we get spotted we're back to square one. Fighting guards, possibly running away, possibly someone else dying or disappearing..."

Anthron flinched. He felt that out of everyone he'd lost the most so far, starting with his childhood friend Harson being killed in their escape...

Jelik rubbed his chin in thought."There's a couple of things remaining," he counted on his fingers."First, the cages have to go somewhere. Secondly, what were we going to be fed to?"

"If we were to be fed to anything," Anthron shot.

"And," Sudenora finished."What does the dagger have to do with all this?"

* * * * * * * * *

They reached Lotheric just before dark. Anthron pushed open the door to *The Lion's Den*, and led the party into the inn. The small tap room's fire burnt in the northern wall with welcoming warmth.

"Ah," the plump Osile called from near the kitchen."Come in, come in." He motioned for the party to sit near the fire. "Come warm your blood." Osile was rubbing his hands together, obviously excited.

"Thank you." Anthron said quietly as he and the group sat.
Osile frowned suddenly."Why, you're all hurt and - where is the woman who was with you?"

Jelik answered quietly and unemotionally, motioning to Osile and himself."The trip wasn't as successful as either of us had anticipated."

Anthron cleared his throat noisily."We can discuss this in private."

"Of course, sirs. But first, a meal?" Osile asked.

Anthron nodded in response.

They ate quietly a meal of chicken soup and roast pork, no one looking forward to telling Osile the news.

Within an hour, Osile was informed of the sad journey - and following Kielmark's advice - they didn't say a word about the dagger.

"So there was," Osile struggled as he wept openly,"no sign of Harna or the others."

Anthron leaned forward and spoke softly."I'm sorry. As we said earlier we found where Scotus came from. There were others like him."

"All dead then." Osile sobbed.

Jelik stood back from everyone. He sympathised what Osile was going through. No one should have their family taken from them.

Kielmark rubbed his slung arm."We don't want to create false hope, but we didn't see any evidence of your child. We believe they've been taken somewhere else."

Anthron looked at the Arrolokian, but his expression didn't give anything away.

"We have a few ideas." Karlos added.

"Yes," Anthron nodded as he turned back to the broken innkeeper."We'll keep looking."

Osile stared around the group, his glassy eyes confirming what they'd thought. He still had a little hope."Remember, she has a silver ankle bracelet with her name on it - 'Harna'. If I haven't heard from you in six months I may as well accept it in my heart that my little girl is gone, and move on."

They went to bed after that, Jelik sleeping on the floor of Karlos and Kielmark's room.

No one slept well.

Anthron dreamed of Vemmlok, of his parents, of his old childhood friend Harson. He dreamed of how he and Harson used to lie in a large field and talk about what they wanted to do with their lives. Anthron looked at Harson, his face full of happiness, and watched the joyous face crumble and decay before his eyes, his long brown hair rot and fall out. He then watched a silver hilted longsword strike out at the gruesome sight - his own sword. He watched as he slashed and cut Harson limb from limb, until there was nothing left but a mangled mess lying in the long grass. He tried to scream out that he was sorry, but no sound escaped from his lips.

* * * * * * * * *

Sudenora was on the streets of Eugernok, walking down the cobbled main street. He pushed his way through the crowd, aiming for the other side of the marketplace. He heard the people behind the stalls calling out bargains, but he couldn't pick out any particular voice. Then he heard a baby cry. The crying grew louder and louder until that was all he could hear. Sudenora looked around. Suddenly the crowd, the stalls, everything was gone. He was standing in the middle of a wide dirt road. Sudenora strained his eyes against the sun. He saw several black armoured riders galloping towards him. He gathered his wits about him and concentrated, suddenly finding *Servas* had opened his mind! Sudenora had gained the knowledge of the masters in the space of a few moments! He knew he could conjure anything - an ice storm, chain lighting, internal static pulses to control the riders' actions. Sudenora decided on lightning and sent it into the midst of the riders. There was an electric crackling sound and a sharp blue flash shot through the middle of the riders. Sudenora could feel the energy, smell the burning flesh.

He could see the girl.

A girl, perhaps about three years old, fell from the back of one of the horses. Why hadn't he seen her? Was he too cocky? She staggered to her feet shakily, her long brown hair singed. She raised an accusing finger at him as she locked her blue eyes on him. She looked slightly familiar...

Then she burst into flames.

* * * * * * * * * *

Jelik crouched beside a door to a huge cathedral, examining a lock. He drew out a small black leather wallet revealing his lockpicks and waited for the clouds to cover the bright moon.

Darkness.

Jelik's agile fingers started working on the lock, applying tension at the top of the lock while raking the tumblers with a pick. The lock let out a 'click' inviting the thief to enter.

Simple, he thought to himself.

Jelik looked down the deserted road, then silently slipped into the doorway. He was particularly cautious tonight, so he locked the door behind him. For some reason Jelik found it harder to lock a door than to unlock. Once the door was safely locked again he inserted a small twig and broke it. Now the lock was useless. He wasn't going to be followed.

Jelik scanned the entrance, and caught a movement in the corner of his eye. It came from the stairs. He moved to the stairs as he drew out a dagger, and silently ascended to the first floor of the great cathedral. This had to be the one. This had to be the assassin who'd killed his parents.

There. He saw movement again, this time coming from the stairs leading to the second level. Again he climbed.

Jelik followed the movement on the stairs until he reached the top of the twelve storey cathedral. Looking around, scanning the floor, he still saw nothing.

Jelik listened intently. He could hear a slight banging sound, the sound of a window left open in the wind. He followed it, and soon he was standing underneath a trapdoor in the ceiling sixteen feet above his head. He easily scaled the wall, and emerged onto the cathedral's roof.

"Help!" came a familiar woman's voice. Jelik rushed towards the sound.

A pair of hands clung to the side of the cathedrals roof, the knuckles white. Jelik sheathed his dagger, and ran to the woman in distress.

"Help me, Jelik! Don't let me fall!" the woman cried.

Jelik reached out to grasp the woman's hands, when he saw the ring. On the middle finger of her right hand the woman wore a ruby ring, a ring that was burnt into his memory, and had been for almost twelve years.

The Ruby Brotherhood membership ring.

Jelik hesitated and looked over the edge of the roof.

It was Anthea.

"Help me Jelik!" she cried.

Jelik, stunned, was unable to move. Could Anthea be a member of the Ruby Brotherhood that assassinated his family? Could she have finally tracked him down? Jelik shook his head, and took a step back. Anthea's face sank as he moved away, and she yelled all manner of things to get his attention.

"Jelik," she whispered after a moment of silence, "I loved you."

Jelik lunged forward to grab Anthea's hands but he was too late. The thief wept as he was forced to watch Anthea plummet towards the solid cobbled street twelve storeys below.

* * * * * * * * * *

Kielmark slashed a soldier, his sabre spraying blood. Another quick turn of his blade severed another soldiers' arm. Looking around quickly,

Kielmark saw that there were only two left.

The soldiers were wearing black plate mail, their faces visored. They wielded heavy broadswords. One soldier did an over hand strike. Kielmark blocked it, for some reason finding his sabre somewhat heavier. He spun the sword around, using the momentum perfectly, and hit the soldier straight on the arm. The blow which should have severed another limb, merely dented the black armour.

Kielmark was running out of strength.

The soldier came on again, the other circling Kielmark. Kielmark was now sweating profusely under the weight of his armour and holding his sword up. He managed to block another attack, but winced in pain as the soldier behind him struck him solidly. He felt slightly dizzy, and he could hear the soldiers laughing. He tried to raise his blade in defence, but the effort was just too much.

His sabre fell from his hand.

Kielmark could feel the painful attacks that were showering down on him as he crashed to the ground.

He opened his eyes one last time to see a huge barbarian hefting a battle axe walk past the soldiers and stand over him.

The last thing Kielmark heard was the laughing.

* * * * * * * * * *

Karlos stared up at his father, Danthor Brekon, straight into his cold eyes. Danthor was a big man, muscular, with a broadsword belted at his hip. Karlos considered his father quite intimidating.

"You know that you are a complete disappointment, don't you?" Danthor spat.

Karlos staggered back at the blunt comment. His father had always hinted that he wasn't the perfect son, but he had never been so blunt and to the point before. Karlos straightened up, and motioned at *Termolen's* symbol that kept his brilliant red cloak clasped around his neck. "I've started a new trend, one that's long overdue."

Danthor Brekon had three sons, and one daughter, and never had

77

any spoken more defiantly to him before! His face went red, the veins on his temples suddenly stood out. In one motion, Danthor drew out his well-used broadsword, and was advanced on his youngest son.

"You have broken the tradition of Brekon House, and you are proud?" Danthor bellowed.

Karlos asked *Termolen* to step in, to stop his father in some way.

Danthor shrieked and dived at Karlos, but suddenly froze where he was as Termolen listened.

Karlos studied the silent frozen man in front of him. "I'm following my heart, father, something you used to believe in. So, I may enjoy my food, but I am who I am. I'm not ashamed. Why should I be?"

Karlos turned to leave, then turned back as he remembered something. "Oh, another thing Father. You do know that Grethic, your oldest son, isn't that fond of women, don't you?"

Danthor Brekon's face was beyond red, as Karlos turned and walked away from his father.

As an after thought, he looked over his shoulder one last time, and to his horror, saw his father lying dead with his own sword stabbed through his gut.

* * * * * * * *

While Lotheric slept, Denkle Genar watched *The Lion's Den* from across the street. He used to be a regular there, when it was busy. Lotheric used to be such a nice place - people from Mosorac and Carson used to come here to get away from it all. It was quiet. Now it was too quiet. Denkle used to like it here. He was respected. He had authority.

Not any more.

His son went missing. Brenot. He couldn't help think that if his son hadn't met that harlot Silvra - he'd still be alive. Denkle had spent every spare waking hour grooming Brenot to become his successor in the council. Brenot showed so much promise that he could have made it in the city. Not now.

Denkle's wife Muriel hadn't recovered since Brenot disappeared.

Slightly mad, he'd heard her being called. To hell with her. To hell with this town.

He would be respected again.

He would be powerful.

He would crush whoever stood in his way, because Denkle knew something. Denkle Genar, councilman of Lotheric, upholder of the laws of Sarophia, humble Denkle, knew where Xycermon was.

Denkle slipped away to meet Korsorn - a man from Mosorac who promised much. Korsorn's Master would be very pleased with this news.

SAROPHIA BY STU DUNN

CHAPTER EIGHT

They rode in silence.

The cold dawn rose from behind as the companions travelled under the cloudy sky. They stopped for lunch on the edge of the road, and ate plain travelling rations.

Karlos used lunch as an opportunity to heal everyone a little more. Five minutes later Kielmark was flexing his arm gingerly - finally discarding his sling. Anthron's ribs had mended but were still tender, Jelik's wounds were gone, and Karlos's arm left a small scar. Sudenora waited patiently until Karlos was finished."Why couldn't you heal anyone two nights ago," The Elementalist started."Or last night? Or even this morning?"

The others turned to look at Karlos.

"Well," Karlos started."I'll put this as simply as I can. With *Termolen*, there is a certain pecking order. Since I'm a fairly new follower I have to wait at the 'back of the line' so to speak. Another Healer who had followed *Termolen* for longer than myself, or was high rank, would have their request listened to first."

"So," Kielmark rubbed his arm."He ignored you?"

"Sort of," Karlos defended."There was most likely some kind of battle over the last few days - a battle that involved a great deal of Healers. *Termolen* was most likely watching them closely and answering their prayers as quickly as possible," Karlos shrugged."I'm in no position to complain. We're alive, and I'm grateful."

Sudenora studied the clouds and sniffed the air."It doesn't look like the weather is going to hold much longer."

"Wonderful." Jelik grated.

"I wonder where the battle was?" Anthron asked no one in particular as he hauled himself into his saddle.

They set off, continuing along the wide muddy road.

"How long do you think it'll be until we pass the dead orcs?"

Sudenora asked Anthron.

"Couple of hours?" the warrior shrugged.

Soon it began to rain heavily, and they were quickly drenched. They plodded on gloomily.

Anthron blew a drip of rain from the tip of his nose as they came upon the dead orcs scattered across the muddy road.

Squinting through the rain, Jelik could see a figure crouched over one of the bodies."Hello there." he called.

The figure looked up, then started towards them.

"Hello yourselves." the figure called. As the figure came closer, Jelik saw it was a short man wearing a blue hooded cloak.

Anthron rode forward slightly, and loosened his sword in its scabbard."Unfortunate weather to be out in..."

The short man pulled back his hood, revealing blonde hair and a friendly face."Well put," he then bowed extravagantly."My name's Jassnik Corline - travelling merchant, gambler, and bard. I'm on my way to Lotheric, in the hope to relieve the good people of their silver."

Anthron nodded."We can save you a long trip."

"Oh?" Jassnik replied as he pulled his hood up, sheltering his face from the rain.

"We've just come from Lotheric," Jelik intercepted."The town has been going through a 'rough period'."

"A rough period, eh? I also see you've been in a fight of sorts," Jassnik shrugged."Say no more. I appreciate the advice - you just saved me three days. Where are you all heading?"

"Mosorac," Anthron replied.

"May I join you?" Jassnik glanced at the dead orcs."It would be safer to travel in a bigger group."

"Sure," Anthron nodded."Do you have a horse?"

"Of course, just over there," Jassnik pointed with his thumb over his shoulder."Now I shall endeavour to find out your names."

* * * * * * * * * *

It was still raining when they made camp that evening off the road in the same clearing they had camped four nights earlier. Jelik and Jassnik went in search of dry firewood as Karlos and Anthron erected the tents.

"So, how long have you been a merchant?" Jelik asked.

"Oh," Jassnik thought for a moment."I've sort of been trading a while."

"Sort of?" Jelik asked.

Jassnik looked at the ground."I decided about three months ago to become a merchant...I really needed a career change...one that wasn't quite so dangerous."

Jelik stopped walking.

Jassnik squinted in the rain."Being a gambler doesn't necessarily pay the bills..."

"What do you sell?"

"Trinkets, necklaces, bracelets - that sort of thing. Depending on where I go I'll stock up on different things," Jassnik explained."For example, Thinstor always wants weapons since they don't make very good ones themselves."

Jelik found a suitable dry log and took up one end in his gloved hands. Jassnik took the other and they returned. The tents were up, and soon they had a small fire going.

"Gruel. Mmmm." Karlos sulked after their meal.

"Are you complaining, Karlos?" Sudenora asked.

"Oh no, how could I possibly complain about gruel?"

"Stop whining and make yourself useful." Sudenora pointed at the dishes.

Karlos grumbled and began cleaning.

The next day was overcast. Biting wind whipped at their cloaks as they continued. It wasn't until after lunch that the wind died down.

Jassnik helped to pass the time by telling stories of Panthorian."There's actually a few places in Panthorian with no government."

Sudenora shook his head, looking dubious."How would that work?

Wouldn't it be chaotic?"

"There's one place which is better for it. Scyermor South, also called The Free Lands. No government or taxes, just morality ruling. Religious sects don't sway the common people's opinions. It's a great place, where chivalry is alive and there are many fair maidens to dazzle."

Jelik smiled."You're right, it does sound great."

Sudenora frowned."It's hard to believe that such a place can exist for any period of time though."

"Not everyone needs rule," Jelik returned.

Jassnik chirped a short tune on his little flute before replying."True enough. Parntorn has a government, but they broke away from the rest of the country. That's what got them into so much trouble."

"What trouble?" Anthron asked as he nudged his horse closer.

"Since they hadn't ever attended the Meetings of State since they'd began nearly two thousand years ago people became suspicious," Jassnik played another quick tune on his flute."So when the world's kings started dying off - killed off I should say - Parntorn was the prime suspect. Several states gathered their forces and attacked Parntorn. History states that most of the army died in the Parntorn Marshes before the fighting even started. The king of Parntorn at the time, Velgo II, survived the siege, but chose not to retaliate."

"I'm waiting for the moral of the story." Jelik smirked.

"What about the Cat People of Euroness?" Sudenora asked."Are they real?"

Jassnik thought for a moment."Yes they are, I think. What I mean is, I haven't seen one before, but I've seen where they've been," Jassnik shrugged."I believe they're real - and have proof."

Sudenora then changed the subject."Don't you get homesick?"

Jassnik chuckled."No, not really," he looked casually at an emerald ring on his finger."That's why I chose to travel. My family is quite demanding, quite public."

Jassnik's eyes became distant briefly before focusing back on Sudenora."How about you?"

Sudenora swallowed slowly."Yes. I miss home."

The rest of the afternoon went by quickly, and soon the party could see Mosorac in the distance.

Mosorac was a small independent trading town, with all the major roads of Izonda meeting at this one place.

"Within the spiked walls," Jassnik begun,"live over twenty thousand people of all races."

"What, like goblins, orcs, ogres..." Jelik teased.

"No, like humans, Elves, dwarves, halflings and Issa," Jassnik continued as the party trotted closer."Civilised races."

"I've never seen an Issa before." Anthron said.

"You probably wouldn't know if you have or not. They choose to look like whatever race they like." Jassnik commented.

"Will you be joining us for a drink this evening?" Karlos asked the short blonde man.

Jassnik scratched his chin."I'd like that. Are you staying long? I can take you to a great place on Constel Street - *The Merchant's Dream.* Classy."

As they rode up the eastern gate, a sleepy unshaven guard dressed in stained leathers approached them from a shed, carrying a nasty looking pike. Another guard skulked inside the shed.

Jassnik motioned for the group to stop, then dismounted and approached the guard.

"Corline," the guard said lazily."Back so soon?"

Jassnik cleared his throat."Yes Gret."

The unshaven guard held out his hand. Instinctively, Jassnik placed several coppers in his open palm.

Gret nodded."I think the Underground is looking for you."

Gret waved them past.

Jassnik remounted, and led the party through the gate.

"What was that about?" Anthron asked, eyeing Jassnik suspiciously.

"I find my wellbeing quite important, and Gret helps out. He hangs out with unpleasant people - but they talk," Jassnik shrugged."Gret finds out if anyone's after me."

"What's the Underground?" Jelik queried.

"Ah, bad people. Don't worry, I'll tell you over a drink."

Jassnik led them into the heart of what he'd referred to as the tavern quarter, to Constel Street. Constel Street was so crowded they had to manoeuvre their mounts on foot. Stalls lined the alleys, merchants yelled over each other even as they were packing their wares for the day. There were several jugglers and acrobats doing tricks along the road, and they were slowed as they pushed past the viewers.

"We're all cut-purse bait here, so watch yourselves," Jassnik commented.

They reached *The Merchant's Dream* stables, fed and watered their horses, then entered the tavern itself.

An enormous man dressed in furs stopped them."We want no trouble here." The man spoke slowly, then waved them on.

"He's huge!" Sudenora hissed.

"A Thinstor barbarian as a doorman?" Jassnik muttered."Come on, follow me. There's normally seats on the second level."

As Kielmark passed the barbarian, their eyes locked. Kielmark stopped, eyes narrowing, as a sneer slowly crept across his face. The barbarian mirrored the expression.

"A warning, Arrolokian," the barbarian started as he raised himself to his full height - eight inches above Kielmark."You want trouble here, I'll kill you."

Kielmark slowly reached for his sabre just as Jassnik returned."Come on Kiel, we'll miss getting a seat!"

Kielmark relaxed, then followed Jassnik without looking back.

The Merchant's Dream was a crowded two-levelled taproom with a small fire pit in one wall. Anthron could smell beer permeating throughout the noisy room as they followed Jassnik to the set of stairs leading to the next storey. Upstairs they found a large vacant table, and made themselves comfortable.

"What was that about, Kiel?" Jassnik asked.

Kielmark's face was void of emotion."The Thinstor Barbarians are mindless brutes whose only known action is killing. My father was maimed during the Arrolok - Thinstor War twelve years ago. He's now blind because of their stupidity," Kielmark's temple veins begun to stand out as he continued."There's no excuse. They kill their own families! They're animals!" Kielmark breathed heavily as he relaxed and unclenched his fists.

"Who wants a drink?" Jelik changed the subject quickly."And I assume we're staying the night here as well?"

"And I'm hungry," Karlos finished.

"Well," Anthron answered."I guess you two are organising it."

"Sure," Jelik replied. The two of them started towards the bar.

"Hold on," Jassnik called after them."I won't be needing a room, I've a place to stay nearby."

"No problem," Jelik nodded.

Karlos and Jelik returned several minutes later carrying a flagon of beer in each hand. A blonde maid dressed in a short blouse revealing her midriff carried empty mugs behind them.

"Thank you," Karlos eyed the maid as he placed the flagons on the table."What's your name?"

The young woman smiled."My name's Asidre." She curtsied, then returned to the bar, Karlos watching her all the way.

Jassnik filled the mugs, with the exception of Kielmark who politely declined, then Asidre brought their meals out."I hope you enjoy."

"I'm sure we will." Karlos replied.

Their meal consisted of chicken and corn soup, bread, and a variety of Trendrik cheeses.

"This is delicious!" Jassnik exclaimed as he cut more cheese from a block.

After several hours they finished all the food, their plates were taken, and they'd bought another four flagons of beer.

Anthron gingerly leaned back in his seat."I feel like I've rubbed my seat raw." he commented.

"You'll get used to it." the Arrolokian horseman said as he studied the room.

"Jassnik," Anthron squinted slightly as he looked at the little man. He was seeing the strange colours around everyone now, and he found it distracting."Would you know where we can find a sage that wouldn't cost us too much?" He finished his beer then poured himself another.

"That depends on what you want their services for," Jassnik replied.

"We want something identified."

"If you want an accurate guess I'd suggest 'Haloquad the Wise'. I've heard he's not too bad and doesn't charge that much," Jassnik drained his mug, then refilled it."If you want something identified, perhaps I can have a look?" He paused for another drink.

"Perhaps tomorrow, when there's less people about," Anthron rubbed his eyes and looked away.

"Are you okay Anthron?" Jassnik inquired.

"Yeah fine, just distracted."

"Now Jass," Jelik toyed with a copper coin, rolling it over his fingers."What's this about the Underground? Are they a Thieves' Guild?"

Jassnik shook his head."The Underground is more of an organisation that sells information. They're linked to most assassins and bounty hunters in Sarophia."

"So how did you get involved with them?" Jelik began spinning the coin with his other hand.

"I've had some dealings with their leader, Quabeth White. Very beautiful, but even more deadly. She and I had an arrangement, an arrangement of which I didn't necessarily honour completely..."

Jelik put the coin in his pouch and leaned forward."Care to explain?"

"Not really."

Anthron sipped at his beer."Aren't you afraid you'll run into her?"

Jassnik rubbed his chin."No, she doesn't come here. The Underground works from a place called *The Hive*. There's no reason for her to come here..." Jassnik sounded a little unsure.

"Hey, watch it!" Jelik called over his shoulder as a tall slender man with a moustache and beard bumped his seat.

"*Nga ka shalon*. Excuse me sirs." replied the man with a Kortusian accent. He bowed slightly, then moved away.

"It's been a while since I've seen a Kortusian in Sarophia." Jassnik watched the man walk to the bar.

"Since the new Emperor Chung took up in Kortusia, I've seen one or two in Smazorok." Jelik commented.

"Yes, he's a good politician," Jassnik mused."He's done a lot in three years to repair what his predecessors had done."

Anthron cleared his throat."I think something may be wrong with me."

Jelik laughed."We all know that!"

"I'm seeing coloured outlines around people." Anthron frowned at Jelik.

Jassnik suddenly looked interested."What do you mean? Auras? Intention? What sort of colours?"

"Well," Anthron stuttered."Around Jelik I've seen purple. Since we've been sitting here, I can see a colour around all of us. I'm green, Karlos is yellow..."

"Do you know what is represents though?" Jassnik persisted.

Anthron shook his head."No idea. Around that Kortusian I saw a grey/purple colour. Different colours could mean something, but I have no idea."

"Keep a note if you can," Jassnik suggested."Perhaps we can find a trend of some sort."

Anthron nodded.

"Jassnik Corline," the woman's voice made Jassnik freeze. A shapely brunette woman wearing a white satin dress approached their table."Jassnik Corline, I hope you were intending on seeing me tomorrow." Her voice was sharp, her eyes cold.

"Um...Of course Quabeth," Jassnik stuttered."How about midday tomorrow?" A bead of sweat rolled down his temple.

Quabeth's features softened."Very good, Corline. I'll look forward to it." She nodded at the group."Gentlemen." Then she left.

As soon as she was out of earshot, Jassnik began to swear."Of all the luck! Why was she here tonight of all nights?" He sighed before standing."Sorry to bring you into my personal affairs. I'll come by tomorrow and help you identify your item. An hour after dawn?"

Anthron nodded.

"Great. 'Til then." Jassnik bowed extravagantly, placed several silvers on the table, then left.

"Strange man." Karlos murmured.

"But quite likeable." Jelik returned.

"She was pretty." Sudenora muttered.

"It's late," Anthron stretched."I'm off to bed. Can I have my key?"

Jelik passed Anthron an iron key to one of the rooms they'd booked."They're on the third level."

"Thanks. Don't stay up too late." Anthron then headed for the stairs.

* * * * * * * * * *

Anthron awoke just after dawn, quite refreshed. He drew the curtains revealing a blue sky dotted with fluffy white clouds. Anthron wasn't used to buildings that were any higher than one storey, having lived in Vemmlok all his life. Already the stalls in the market were mulling with activity. He took several minutes to stretch, then washed using a towel and a small bowl of water. He pulled his rust-stained tunic over his head, followed by his chain mail vest. He jumped on the spot several times to get his vest in the most comfortable position on his shoulders, then he belted on his sword and dagger. Anthron crammed his cloak into his pack, then descended to the ground level taproom.

Jassnik and Kielmark were waiting downstairs, talking quietly.

"Ah, Anthron. Good morning." Jassnik chirped as he puffed briefly on his pipe to re-light it. Kielmark coughed briefly while waving the strong smoke away.

"Morning," Anthron returned as he sat himself down."Sleep well?"

Jassnik blew a smoke ring before replying."For most of the night. Then a racket woke me, a handful of knights clanking around outside my window." He blew another smoke ring as Jelik, Karlos and Sudenora joined them.

"Morning." Jelik yawned.

Jassnik nodded."Morning. As I was saying, these knights woke me. I tried going back to sleep, but then I heard voices. They were asking about, well, us."

"Us?" Sudenora burst.

"Yes. By name," Jassnik emptied his pipe and replaced it in a pouch."I feel I may have gotten you all into trouble. I'm very sorry."

Anthron stared at Jassnik in thought."I don't think it's you."

"Either way, Quabeth White will be quite put out that I stand her up this afternoon. I'm planning on leaving fairly quickly, and I recommend the same thing for you," Jassnik fidgeted nervously with his cloak hem."I can still examine your item, then you should pack. If you're going to Decton I'll come with you if you like..."

Anthron nodded to Jelik. The thief placed the bat shaped dagger on the table then slid it over to Jassnik. Jassnik's eyes widened as he saw it."This is a work of art."

"What can you tell us about it?" Anthron motioned for Kielmark to watch the entrance of the empty taproom.

Jassnik closed his eyes, turning the dagger around delicately. Jassnik's eyes flickered as the dagger began to pulse a faint blue colour."It fits the description of a set of daggers. From what I can recall, there are seven of these daggers in existence. The seven could be connected together at the pommel somehow, and were used in some kind of ceremony. A bad ceremony, but not Bormal," Jassnik screwed his nose in concentration before opening his eyes."That's all I can pick up. Tolorel referred me to The Great Library in Platown. There's a book there which has all the answers." He passed the dagger back to Jelik."What do you know about it?"

"It's been referred to as Xycermon and it can fly." Jelik answered.

"Ah." Jassnik was cut off as Kielmark spun towards them.

"The knights are coming!" the Arrolokian called."There's eight of them and they're armed to the teeth!"

SAROPHIA BY STU DUNN

CHAPTER NINE

The black knights approached.

"How far away are they?" Anthron bellowed as he drew his sword

"About a minute." Kielmark drew his sabre as he backed away from the door.

"Should we try and talk with them?" Karlos asked, wiping his forehead with the edge of his cloak.

"This is all my fault." Jassnik shoulders sagged as he unhooked a long thin metal shaft from his belt. He twisted one end and pulled the shaft in the middle. The shaft doubled in size. The metal shaft was now just over two feet long, one end having several small holes in it. Jassnik then held the end of the shaft with the holes, and twisted it, placing pressure on the other end. There was a clicking sound, and spikes appeared from the small holes.

"Should we run?" Sudenora asked in a shaky voice.

"No time to get the horses," Jelik hid the bat-shaped dagger away quickly. He unsheathed his sword and placed it on the table in front of him, then drew two daggers and waited.

The entrance to *The Merchant's Dream* smashed inwards, scattering splinters and shards of glass across the room. One knight stepped through the broken door to survey the room. The knight was dressed in intricately designed black plate mail. His visored helmet displayed the letter 'K' upon the forehead. He wore a sapphire-encrusted long sword on his belt and a double bladed battleaxe on his back. The knight looked around the room as the dust settled - eyeing the group one by one. He paused at Jassnik as Sudenora spoke."Can we help you?"

A smile crept across Jelik's face as his muscles remained taunt, waiting like a poised crossbow.

The knight motioned for the others to follow him inside. Eight? Anthron thought. I hope this doesn't come down to a fight.

Then the knight spoke with a deep voice, muffled by his

helmet."You're to come with us."

"Why?" Anthron asked."We've done nothing."

"Your presence is required."

"By whom?" Jassnik asked.

"I'm not at liberty to disclose that information," the knight waved his arm."Get them." The seven knights drew their broadswords and advanced.

Anthron made some room to fight, tipping over a table as Jelik threw his daggers at the closest knight.

Kielmark parried the first attack with his sabre using his left hand - his right still being too sore to use - and slashed back. His attack bounced harmlessly off the knight's armour. Kielmark managed to lash out again with his quick blade before retreating as two knights advanced upon him.

Jelik threw a dagger then picked up his sword, leapt onto the table and somersaulted over the two approaching knights. He landed and spun at the same time, his leg extended, managing to trip one knight. Jelik threw his sword up just in time to parry a heavy blow from the other knight, then rolled backwards to gain some room.

Sudenora held a fistful of electrical energy, waiting for the opportunity to help his companions. As Jassnik was pushed into a wall Sudenora let the energy fly. The crackling blue ball struck the knight attacking Jassnik on the side, the black armour conducting the energy enough to throw him to the ground. Stunned, the knight began to climb to his feet just as Jassnik sunk his spiked mace through the back of the knight's helmet.

Karlos swung his morning star in front of him, keeping his attacker at bay. The knight feigned a stab then spun backwards in a chopping motion. Karlos managed to duck under the attack, then stood while swinging his morning star up. The knight spun his broad sword about for another attack as Karlos's spiked morning star smashed into his groin. The knight dropped instantly.

Anthron ducked an attack and landed another hit on the knight he was fighting, again denting the solid armour. He could hear the knight panting from behind the visor. Anthron was wearing him down. The blonde warrior began an attacking routine, feigning low, striking high. Anthron risked a moment to see how the others were faring. There were two knights down. Three, he smiled as he put all his strength into a side cut aimed at the knight's neck. Anthron was shocked when the knight blocked the attack, then smashed his helmet into the blonde warrior's face.

Kielmark's arm hurt. He wasn't used to using his left arm in battle, and it didn't have the endurance of his right. He received another slash across his arm and staggered back, leaning against the tavern wall as the two knights closed in. Jassnik hit one of them with his shoulder, both falling to the floor. Kielmark pushed himself back from the wall and raised his sabre. He still had some fight left in him.

Jelik hit the ground and rolled as Karlos came to his aid. The thief was having trouble getting his hits through the armour. He dodged the attacks, hoping the others were doing better. As he came to his feet Jelik noticed the first knight still casually leaning against the smashed doorway. Jelik's eyes narrowed as he sprung into a forward somersault, sending the bat shaped dagger soaring towards the prone knight. As Jelik landed the dagger appeared back in his hand, and the fighting had stopped. All eyes were on Jelik as he looked around the room slowly.

Anthron was panting over a knight, his face and knuckles bleeding, his sword under a nearby table. Jassnik, his teeth gritted, was pinned to the floor through his thigh by a sword. Kielmark was covered in blood - his own - again facing two knights. Sudenora was holding another globe of energy and Karlos leant against a table puffing.

Only three out of eight knights were down, and the group already looked finished.

Finally Jelik looked to his original target, standing just as casual as he was earlier, the simmering globe of protection he'd erected now visible.

Jelik also looked at the dagger as the knight spoke."I will let you all live if you place Xycermon on the floor and kick it over."

Jassnik spoke before Jelik could respond."Jelik, think about this carefully. You hold our lives in your hands." Jassnik's subtle finger movements said something else however. *I've got to get myself free somehow. I've got a plan.*

Jelik thought for a moment."You're right," he faced the first knight again."As a sign of good will, won't you let my friends collect themselves?"

The knight nodded. The sword was pulled from Jassnik's leg with a cry of pain, and Kielmark helped him to his feet.

"The dagger." the knight insisted,

"Who do you work for?" Jelik replied rebelliously.

"The dagger!"

"Jelik." Anthron cautioned.

Jelik looked at the dagger. The ruby eyes glistened beautifully, almost suggestively. Jelik thought for a moment he could hear something - a chant perhaps - coming from it. He looked back to the knight.

"The dagger or you all die!" As the knight withdrew his sapphire-encrusted sword, Jelik heard a buzzing inside his head, and his eyes began to water.

Jelik focused on the ruby eyes and the irritation diminished. Looking up, he called,"Come get it." With that, the nimble thief back flipped over the hand rail and fled up the set of stairs.

"Thanks Jelik," Karlos huffed.

One knight chased up the stairs after Jelik.

"No more games," the first knight replied slowly."We've lost two of them."

It was only then that they realised Jassnik was nowhere to be seen either.

The knight continued."You'll have to be bait. *Bok morok gol tuelak!*"

First Anthron felt his legs buckle. Then he lost feeling in his arms. Painfully slowly, he sank to his knees. He managed to look to his right to see the others also falling. As he hit the floor Anthron passed out.

* * * * * * * * * *

"Okay Jelik," Jassnik winced as the Healer saw to his leg."Why do you have the Cyermyth Knights after you?"

Jelik stopped pacing the marble floor of the Temple of *Termolen.*"Cyermyth Knights?" He gaped.

"Never mind. Right now we need to get after the others," Jassnik shifted uncomfortably to face the Healer."How much longer before I can walk?"

"A few minutes," the priest replied."The healing is nearly ready, then we have these salves to..."

"Never mind the salves - just heal." Jassnik gritted his teeth.

Within twenty minutes Jelik and Jassnik were on horseback leaving through Mosorac's eastern gate.

"The knights went south? Thanks Gret," Jassnik threw a small pouch of coins to the unshaven guard.

They galloped south after Anthron, Kielmark, Karlos, Sudenora, and the five knights that held them captive.

By nightfall of the second day chasing the knights they reached a huge inn off the main road. It was the only building around, with a stable on one side. Both the inn and the stable were guarded.

"This is called the Merchant's Stop, designed for travellers in between Decton and Mosorac," Jassnik explained as they approached."It was built in 1918 when the road became too dangerous for the local merchants."

"Is that when the orcs and goblins and things came from the ground?" Jelik inquired.

"No, the dungeons were discovered nearly two hundred years before then. Urgar Keep was built on top of the biggest dungeon entrance at the same time as the Merchant Stop was built. The Kingdom believes that most creatures were sealed underground, but they still found their way back every now and then."

They dismounted and handed their reins to the guard at the stables.

"The boy'll look after 'em for ya," the guard promised."Ya can go right in."

"Have you seen any black armoured guys ride past here today -

maybe a couple of hours ago?" Jassnik asked the big man.

The guard shook his head."Nah sorry."

The hut was one big room, with a kitchen and bar at the northern end and baths at the southern. There was enough room to sleep fifty people in the hall, five lines of ten beds. There was no chance of privacy, Jelik noted.

"It costs about three coppers each the night here, which includes a complementary drink, a bed, and the use of the co-ed baths," Jassnik grinned."I met a nice woman there once."

"What about these knights?" Jelik changed the subject."You said they're from Cyermyth?"

"That's right," Jassnik replied."They had the letter 'K' on their helmets - Queen Kilandra."

"So they're coming from Cyermyth? Panthorian?" Jelik frowned."We need to find out what they have to do with the Selection."

"Maybe nothing," Jassnik mused as he studied his fingernails."But they're just the puppets. The real question is: what does Queen Kilandra have to do with the Selection?"

Jelik kicked his boots off and lay on his small bed."So, where do you think the knights are heading now?"

Jassnik shrugged."Maybe a port - heading back to Panthorian?" Jassnik leaned back on his bed, staring at the high ceiling."Maybe they're hoarding people close by."

"We need to find out what the Selection is about."

Jassnik nodded."I quite agree, and I think we'll find that out when we know what the dagger is for."

Jelik let out a deep sigh.

"What's that for?" Jassnik asked, still examining the ceiling.

"I feel that we should keep following the knight's tracks," Jelik explained."What if it rains and washes the hoof prints away? What if they don't rest and they get away from us?"

Jassnik turned his attention to Jelik."We first have to get a disguise. In the stable I saw some robes and cloaks drying. After a few hours sleep we can steal those, and pose as merchants or something. Secondly,

I have an idea as to where they're going."

"*What*?" Jelik exclaimed."Where? Why didn't you say anything?"

Jassnik let out a chuckle."It's just an idea, but they may be going to Urgar Keep - the prison. If they're not there we should try Sorne, stopping off at The Great Library on the way."

"What makes you think they're going to Urgar Keep?" Jelik asked sceptically.

"The keep was built over a dungeon. If people are disappearing without a trace, underground would be a good place to hide them," Jassnik explained."The dungeon is huge. It hasn't ever been fully explored. Anything could be down there."

"And we're going to explore it?" Jelik looked dubious.

"No, of course not. All we have to do is find a clue of some sort, something that tells us to go in or ignore it."

Jelik smirked."I've never broken *into* a prison before..."

"Neither have I." Jassnik returned.

* * * * * * * * * *

Jelik and Jassnik galloped away from The Merchant Stop, both moons high in the cloudy night's sky as their stolen clothes rustled in the wind. They stopped several times as Jassnik made sure they were still following the knight's tracks.

"Can you pass the water," Jelik asked, squinting at moons *Lithloren* and *Tolorel* as they trotted along.

"Sure," Jassnik threw his water skin."We're going to have to resupply soon."

Jelik drank several mouthfuls of water before responding."Yeah. I'm pretty hungry too. Sudenora carried all our supplies."

Jassnik stopped and dismounted quickly."The knights went cross-country here about twelve hours ago." He pointed east.

"To avoid Carson?" Jelik suggested.

Jassnik shrugged."Maybe. But maybe because it's a more direct line to Urgar Keep..."

"Does this mean we aren't getting supplies?" Jelik winced as he waited for the answer.

"Sorry Jel," Jassnik hauled himself back into the saddle. "We're going this way. Don't worry though, I've attended several courses in Panthorian. We won't starve."

"That's good to know."

CHAPTER TEN

Anthron awoke with a start.

The first thing Anthron noticed was the musky cold air. He could smell rotten straw and wet stone, and could hear dripping water from somewhere above him.

Anthron slowly opened his eyes, the first time since he'd fallen in *The Merchant's Dream*. He was alone in a small cell, three sides were rock, the last thick iron bars.

Anthron winced. His head pounded mercilessly and he had a foul gritty taste in his mouth. The blonde warrior recognised it - he remembered the taste from the wheeled cage he, Harson, Sudenora, Karlos, Kielmark and Jelik had woken in. So, they'd been drugged again, he thought. To travel where ever they were now, from Mosorac. Had they travelled in the cages again? How long had he been here? Was this where everyone from the Selection had been taken?

Anthron rose painfully from the puddle he'd been lying in on the stone floor, then noticed iron shackles around his ankles. Using the bars to help him to his feet Anthron squinted down the dark corridor. It ran off into the distance with similar prison cells stationed on each side, ending at a stairwell.

"Sudenora!" Anthron bellowed, closing his eyes and rubbing his temples as he did so. Swallowing hard to moisten his mouth, he tried again."Kielmark! Karlos!" His voice echoed down the corridor and through his head. Wincing again, he slid down the bars to sit back in the puddle.

"Anthron?"

The voice came from the other end of the corridor, close to the stairs.

"Karlos?" Anthron forced himself to stand up."Are you okay? Where are the others?"

There was a long pause."I don't feel too good," Karlos paused again."I think the others are here with us."

"In this passage?" Anthron called painfully.

Karlos's reply was cut off by the sound of heavy footfalls on the stairs.

"Wakin' up aye?" the descending guard called back upstairs with a throaty laugh."Call Sabriski."

Anthron watched the guard closely. He was a huge bald man bearing tattoos across his entire hairy torso, wearing bloodstained leather breeches - from his previous 'guests' no doubt.

"Who's up!" the guard bellowed as he began slowly up the passage, knocking a large hooked poker along the bars as he walked.

Anthron's head felt like it was going to burst. The noise in his head echoed around and around, and he felt suddenly dizzy and sick. After vomiting Anthron focused down the passage to see Sudenora being dragged from his cell by his foot, unconscious. Anthron watched painfully as Sudenora was hauled up the stone stairs, his head hitting each step heavily. Anthron tried to call out, to do anything, but vomited instead.

* * * * * * * *

Anthron woke at the sound of two guards returning Sudenora to his cell. The Elementalist was whimpering, his left eye swollen shut and fresh bruises around his face. Trailing behind Sudenora was the guard with the poker Anthron had seen earlier.

Once Sudenora had been returned, the guard with the poker cried out again;"Who's up!"

His eyes shifted quickly to another cell, and the three guards closed in. The cell was opened and Karlos was thrown out. He shot Anthron a plea for help before the hooked poker struck across his back. Letting out a quick yell, Karlos lay still on the passage floor.

The guards laughed as two of them grabbed a leg and dragged Karlos up the stairs in a similar fashion to Sudenora.

"Wait!" Anthron called. He had no idea what he was going to say or do.

The guards stopped, and the poker bearing tattooed guard approached Anthron's cell at the end of the passage."Wot?" the huge guard demanded."Wot you 'bout? Ya want a beatin' now?"

Anthron thought quickly."What are you wanting from us?" He climbed back to his feet as he spoke.

"We wantin' to hurt ya!" he replied to the delight of the two other guards.

"I can help you." Anthron began.

"How?" The guard stopped in front of Anthron's cell, waving his hooked poker about in between them.

"You want the dagger?" Anthron's mind was racing, his headache not so bad now.

Anthron wasn't quick enough to pull his fingers back from the swinging poker. He let go of the bars painfully, and restricted by his ankle shackles, fell heavily to the floor.

The tattooed guard motioned for them to replace Karlos in his cell and take Anthron instead.

Anthron tensed as his cell was opened, and allowed himself to be dragged feet-first up the passage after his shackles were removed. Eyes flicking left and right, he caught a glimpse of Kielmark through one of the cells. Just before he reached the end of the passage, Anthron spied a pale young woman staring at him, knuckles white, gripping the bars that held her captive.

"Back off Conear!" the tattooed guard yelled as he raised his poker, and she fled to the back of the cell.

Anthron waited until he was pulled up the first stair before he kicked out with all his strength. The guards pulling him lurched forward, and as they brought their weight back to compensate, Anthron flipped his legs backward over his head. The guards sailed over Anthron's head, crashing noisily further down the stairs. Anthron unsteadily scrambled to his feet just as the hooked poker smashed him across the back of the head.

* * * * * * * * * *

"This is it." Jassnik tied his horse in the thicket of trees where it could graze as Jelik stared at Urgar Keep's giant walls.

"They've got to be fifty feet high!" Jelik exclaimed as he pulled off the robe he'd used as a disguise."With a moat!"

They had been travelling solidly before they reached the keep at midday on the seventh day since leaving the Merchant Stop. Urgar Keep, built thirteen centuries ago, had been modified and expanded over the years. The massive walls had been extended, and a large moat had been dug to give the appearance of a Lords' castle. The keep was a giant prison, where the King's garrisons were also trained. It also rested atop the infamous Urgar Dungeon as it had been called - an unexplored underground mass of tunnels and caverns from which no adventurer had been known to return.

Having lived on the streets of Smazorok for years as a common thief, Jelik had heard most of the stories of Urgar Keep.

Jassnik nodded."We've a challenge ahead of us."

"So, what's your plan then?" Jelik grated.

"Well," Jassnik started."I was thinking that we could hide on one of the carriages that come and go so frequently..."

"And how are we going to get on one?" Jelik returned."Ask them to slow down so we can sneak on? Why don't we just become highwaymen for the afternoon and take an entire carriage?"

Jassnik scratched bristled chin."Not a bad idea, actually."

* * * * * * * * *

Anthron regained consciousness from a painful punch to his ribs. He opened his eyes to find himself strung up in shackles against a wall - his feet chained nearly a foot from the ground. The pain in his stretched arms was replaced as the iron knuckle-wielding guard struck him again - then again - all three striking the same spot. Anthron cried out as he felt his already tender ribs crack.

"E's awake." The guard backed away, removing his iron knuckles and flexing his fist as the tattooed guard approached.

The huge tattooed guard swung his poker at Anthron's exposed ribs. Anthron gritted his teeth, sweat stinging his eyes as he grunted in agony. His vision was covered in stars for a few moments before he regained consciousness.

"Dagger," Anthron panted, trying to get his mind together."I know who has it."

The huge tattooed guard seemed unimpressed. A punch to Anthron's jaw sent the warrior's head back into the wall.

The guard sneered."We knows who has it too, so hows you gonna help us?"

Anthron coughed and spat blood before responding."I can find him." Anthron bluffed. Truth was, he had no idea where Jelik and Jassnik were. For all he knew they were staying at an expensive tavern in Bayton, laughing at him...

"Why you betray yer mate?" The guard sneered again and pushed the hooked poker hard under Anthron's swollen jaw.

"He betrayed us," Anthron replied coldly.

The huge tattooed guard backed off, turning to a shadowy corner to Anthron's right. From the shadows stepped a man wearing a brown silk robe. He looked to be in his early thirties, his long brown hair hung around his tanned face, displaying his almost transparent blue eyes. He nodded in introduction to Anthron."My name is Zathorn Sabriski," he began in a clear Panthorian accent."I've been listening to your friend Sudenora Kilton display his loyalty, his character, on this rack. I've listened to you sell your friends out..."

"It's not..." Anthron begun, but Zathorn merely raised his hand in silence.

"Anthron Mikolnic, you will speak when spoken to," Zathorn continued in a calm voice."We already have the information we need. Since Xycermion has been unearthed, He knows where it is at all times. The Master knows your friend Jelik Qualis is carrying Xycermion here as we speak. What do you have to say?"

Anthron spat another mouthful of blood before responding."If you already know where the dagger is, why are you torturing us?" He demanded.

"Oh?" Zathorn looked amused, and the tattooed guard laughed."But we like it!"

Anthron struggled futilely with his chains in frustration."I'm going to kill you!" he swore.

"But how?" Zathorn asked in his quiet voice, not the least bit interested in the answer.

"When I'm free..." Anthron stopped as Zathorn and the guards began laughing.

"You want to be free?" Zathorn mused."Sure, we'll give you a fighting chance, plus an opportunity for revenge. How does that sound?" Zathorn motioned to the poker wielding guard, who then approached slapping his poker in one hand. Anthron could do nothing to defend himself from the poker slamming into his head again.

* * * * * * * * *

Jassnik and Jelik crouched on top of the south-eastern wall that ran the perimeter of Urgar Keep under the grey clouds of late noon. At each corner of the huge Keep, turrets rose about twenty feet above the outside wall. From their vantage point they could see most of the activity around the Keep, including a gathering of soldiers within the courtyard.

Jassnik pointed to the northeastern turret."That should be the way to the dungeon." Jelik frowned at the blue clad man before Jassnik responded."I was thrown in a while ago. Long story."

"So," Jelik thought for a moment."What's our plan now? We're inside..."

"One thing's for sure," Jassnik stated."I'm not going into the dungeon," He started patting at a muddy patch on his cloak."These stains will take forever to come out."

Jelik chuckled. They came up with the idea of stopping a carriage near Urgar Keep by someone lying in the middle of the road with a pouch full of money spilt around them. It happened to be Jassnik who ended up lying on the muddy road. The scheme worked well, with a rice merchant who supplied the keep being both interested and greedy enough to stop his large wagon and investigate. Jassnik knocked him out cold as Jelik knifed the one guard that accompanied the merchant. Dragging the bodies behind the tree line, Jassnik became the rice merchant, and Jelik was the hired blade. After entering the Keep, they ditched the wagon and climbed up to where they were currently hiding.

"I wonder what's going on down there?" Jassnik mused, studying the courtyard far below them. He turned back to Jelik."Okay, I'll go find out what's going on down there."

"While I find the dungeon," Jelik finished."Fine."

Jassnik and Jelik then ventured off in different directions, Jassnik whistling merrily.

* * * * * * * * * *

Anthron pushed back his matted bloody hair as he stood on a huge empty platform in the centre of Urgar Keep's courtyard, surrounded by several hundred jeering soldiers. He studied his surroundings. There was no escape. His head pounded and was bleeding, and he found breathing difficult as he nursed his side. Anthron shook his head. What did they have planned for him? He wasn't chained. There were no torture devices on the platform. He continued to look around - then he saw. Anthron understood what fate they had for him.

The soldiers quieted down and parted for a knight dressed in black plate mail. As the knight approached Anthron could see he had long raven-black hair and steely grey eyes that matched his thin pale face. At his side was a sheathed long sword that was adorned with sapphires. Under one arm he carried a black helmet with the capital letter K upon its forehead.

From what Anthron could tell, this was the knight from Mosorac who defeated their whole group with magic of some kind.

As the knight ascended the stairs the soldiers closed around and began chanting what Anthron assumed was his name:"Mort'l! Mort'l! Mort'l!"

As Mort'l approached, Anthron noticed just how big this man was. Shoulders wider than Kielmark, the knight stood over half a foot taller than Anthron.

Mort'l placed on his helmet and unsheathed his sapphire encrusted longsword. Instantly Anthron's eyes began to stream and he heard a buzzing sound come from the blade. Blinking profusely, Anthron concentrated on the dark blue colour he saw around the knight, and soon the noise died down and his eyes stopped running. He stood straight, unarmed and unarmoured, and locked eyes with his formidable opponent.

"His sword!" Mort'l ordered, and Anthron's silver hilted sword was thrown onto the platform. Not wanting to hesitate, Anthron painfully scooped up his sword, and the duel began.

Even though Mort'l was wearing heavy plate mail, he was still agile. Their swords struck, both ringing loudly.

The first few strokes Anthron threw were somewhat tentative as he assessed Mort'l's strengths and weaknesses. Within moments Anthron received a slash across his left shoulder and wheezed heavily. He nearly lowered his guard then and there, until he spied Jassnik. The little man's sky blue attire stood out in a sea of soldiers. He held his fists up - trying to tell Anthron to fight - to hold up for as long as possible. Jassnik then disappeared into the crowd.

Anthron gritted his teeth and threw his sword up in defence as he moved backward, knowing that one wrong move would end his life. He raised up his silver-hilted longsword and parried another heavy blow, which made his knees buckle and showered him in sparks. Anthron noticed then that his trusted silver hilted long sword had more than a few chips on the usually keen edged blade.

* * * * * * * * *

Jelik slunk through the darkness with ease. He descended the stairs of the turret until he eventually found an old barred gate. He examined the padlock with a sigh - it was completely rusted through. Jelik reached for one of his hidden daggers, and he smashed the pommel onto the lock. If he couldn't pick it, he'd break it. The lock smashed a little noisier than Jelik had anticipated, so he withdrew into the shadows for several minutes and waited. Not a sound. He winced slightly as he crept through the squeaky gate, hid the broken lock, then continued his descent.

* * * * * * * * *

Anthron's sword arm ached with weariness. He stepped back and lowered his sword slightly, traditionally indicating a mutual rest. Mort'l too stepped back and lowered his sword.

Anthron panted heavily, the pain in his side making him completely oblivious to the cheering soldiers.

"You do know that you're going to die, don't you?" Mort'l laughed over the crowd.

The fight resumed.

Anthron managed to score a solid hit on Mort'l's sword-arm, but the blow didn't change Mort'l's ferocity. Swing after swing Anthron blocked. Chip after chip was hacked from his sword, until finally it snapped completely in half.

SAROPHIA BY STU DUNN

CHAPTER ELEVEN

Anthron dropped his broken sword.

He backed away from the advancing knight. Mort'l relaxed and let out a laugh, and the soldiers roared in approval. Where was Jassnik? He stopped his retreat as several soldiers drew their swords and waved them threateningly as he backed towards them.

Mort'l grasped his black bladed long sword in both hands, and began spinning it in a routine of attacks as he slowly walked towards Anthron. The blonde warrior had one last idea. He stepped back just within range of a soldier. The soldier sneered, thinking Anthron was trying to jump off the platform, and swung a clumsy attack from the ground at Anthron's feet. Anthron easily dodged the attack, and stepped hard on the flat of the blade. In one painful motion, Anthron was away from the edge of the platform with a new sword.

Then Mort'l was upon him. Anthron's block was weak, his next even weaker. Mort'l was wearing him down. Anthron dared another search for Jassnik. Nothing. Mort'l's sword then rushed overhead at Anthron's head. The blonde warrior was running out of energy. His ribs were beyond description, and he knew they'd take a while to mend. He had to do something rash. Mustering all his remaining energy, Anthron blocked the overhead strike while moving forwards. As the weight hit his blade Anthron spun his wrist, creating a dangerous but incredibly quick attack. Anthron's blade came sideways at Mort'l's neck. For that moment, Anthron felt like everything had stopped. He could no longer hear the soldiers. Mort'l's own blade was too far away to block his own. Inch by inch Anthron's sword came closer to its target. His heart pounded noisily as suddenly everything sped up to normal. Mort'l threw an armoured arm in defence as his other arm smashed across Anthron's face.

Spinning to land heavily on the platform, Anthron lay still for a moment. Not one of the soldiers was looking at him. Did he kill the knight? Spitting blood, Anthron retrieved his stolen sword and pushed himself to his feet. Anthron's head spun as he staggered, until he saw Mort'l. The black knight was climbing back to his feet also, shaking his helmeted head. Mort'l's sapphire encrusted long sword was lying near Anthron, right next to the knight's severed forearm.

Anthron's heart raced as he found strength with the hope that surged through him. Anthron threw the soldier's sword down, scooping up Mortl's sapphire-encrusted sword as the knight climbed to his feet. There was blood everywhere, and Anthron was amazed that this knight could stand. Then the blood drained from his own face as he witnessed the spectacle. Slowly the severed limb within the gauntlet faded from view, as Mort'l's forearm replaced itself. No armour covering the new arm. Anthron felt hopeless. This guy could regenerate!

"Anthron!" Anthron looked up to his right to see Jassnik perched on a roof near the stables."Grab on!" Jassnik released a sack attached to a rope which swung down over the soldiers towards the platform. Jassnik cast a worried look towards the flagpole he'd attached to rope to. He hoped it'd hold.

* * * * * * * * *

Jelik withdrew his dagger from the back of the jailer's head, wiping it on the dead man's tunic. Glancing around quickly, Jelik noted that this was the only guard present in this cellblock. Spying down the corridor, he proceeded cautiously. Peering into the first dark cell, Jelik could make out a frightened young woman huddled against the cell's far wall. Upon seeing him, she scrambled towards the door. She brushed aside her matted brown hair, revealing dark rings around her eyes. Her skin was pale and dirty, covered by a tattered robe.

"You can get me out of here!" she wailed as she grasped the iron bars of her cell."I've been here too long! You're not like the others."

"Shut up!" Jelik hissed angrily, trying to silence the woman quickly. The woman scuttled back across her cell. Jelik calmed himself with several deep breaths.

"Jelik?"

The thief turned to see Karlos in the opposite cell.

"We're all here - except Anthron." Karlos said.

Jelik glanced back at the woman behind him before approaching Karlos's cell."Someone's made a mess of you," Jelik noted, as Karlos's bruised face was clearer to see.

"Jelik," Kielmark breathed from the cell next to the woman's."Thank the Gods you are here. Sudenora needs our help. The guards, they bashed him..."

Jelik frowned as he examined the lock to Karlos's cell. The lock mechanism on the barred door was fairly advanced, designed to keep thieves and buglars in.

"A disc tumbler lock," Jelik exclaimed under his breath as he made himself comfortable in front of the cell."May take a little time."

Jelik inserted his pick into the lock and proceeded to create a mental picture with what he felt. Jelik withdrew the pick and raised his eyebrows."Five tumblers?"

Jelik withdrew a second pick from inside his tunic, and placed it into the top of the lock. Applying a little pressure, the plug of the lock turned ever so slightly.

"Well?" Karlos asked, eyeing Jelik's expression.

Jelik shook his head in reply. The more the plug of a lock turns, the easier a lock is to pick. This lock didn't move much. Letting out a sigh, the thief proceeded to rake the tumblers with his first pick, the second keeping pressure on the plug.

It took Jelik ten minutes to open Karlos's cell, half that time for Sudenora's, and half that again for Kielmark's.

Karlos and Kielmark saw to the battered Sudenora immediately, Jelik stretched and twisted to relieve himself of his cramped muscles as he approached the woman's cell.

"Who are you?" Jelik asked quietly.

The woman looked up, covering herself as best she could with the dirty robe she wore. She stood slowly, but did not approach."My name is Gen'vieve Conear, last living descendent of the infamous Jea-ane

113

Conear."

Jelik interrupted, unimpressed."What are you doing here?"

Gen'vieve moved closer to Jelik as she spoke."What does it matter why I'm here? Are your friends not innocent of whatever crimes Urgar Keep has accused? This is not a just place."

"Fair enough," Jelik nodded as he sat himself in front of Gen'vieve Conear's cell.

Karlos approached."Sudenora was in quite a state, but thanks to *Termolen* he'll be fine."

Jelik nodded."Where's Anthron?"

* * * * * * * * * *

Anthron spun and ran towards the swinging rope, which had already started swinging back before he reached it. As the soldiers began climbing onto the platform Anthron reached the edge and leapt for all he was worth, grabbing hold of the sack Jassnik had used to weight the rope. Holding on with one hand, Anthron waved Mort'l's sapphire-encrusted sword underneath him in defense. He cleared the soldiers and got over three quarters of the way to Jassnik before the flagpole snapped. Anthron hit the cobblestone courtyard heavily, hauled himself to his feet, then continued towards Jassnik and the stables.

The courtyard soon bustled with swords as the soldiers drew their weapons and began chase. Jassnik appeared on top of the stables, swinging something above his head. Releasing a small missile into the middle of the crowd, it hit a soldier and spewed out thick gray smoke. Jassnik sent five more smoke bombs into the courtyard, smiling in satisfaction as he heard coughing and swearing.

"I love this," Jassnik jumped down onto a nearby straw covered roof, then landed lightly on the cobblestones below. Closing his eyes briefly, he summoned the ability to bend light as Anthron fast approached. Reaching out his hand to the blonde warrior, the soldiers surrounding them stopped short as Anthron and Jassnik completely vanished.

* * * * * * * * * *

"What's going on out there?" Jelik exclaimed as they raced back down the stairs.

"I have no idea." Karlos puffed.

Jelik had led them above ground just as the courtyard erupted into chaos. Unfortunately several soldiers had taken cover from the smoke inside the turret, and spotted the escaping group. There were now at least a dozen soldiers after them as they retreated back the way they'd come. They were heading back through the dungeon, without their weapons or armour.

After passing their own cells, they continued their descent until they came to a locked oaken door."Bash it!" Jelik urged Kielmark as he heard the jingling of armour from further up the stairs. Hearing the soldiers, the Arrolokian dropped his shoulder and threw himself at the solid door. His fourth charge smashed the old hinges off the door, and as they raced through, Jelik paused to drop several small tripod shaped spikes on the ground."That should slow them down a little."

Further down, they heard several soldiers cry out as Jelik's caltrop spikes pierced several soldiers' boots.

"Jelik," Kielmark drew the thief's attention ahead of them."We can't go any further. We've found the Urgar Dungeon entrance."

Kielmark, Jelik, Karlos, Sudenora and Gen'vieve stood in front of the stone dragon mouth entrance of the Urgar Dungeon. It looked as though there had been an attempt to seal the entrance, but there were tell tale signs of recent thoroughfare. This was their only exit, bar going back up the stairs through the soldiers.

Jelik threw the rest of his caltrops up the stairs before sighing."This is our only option."

"You're warriors, aren't you?" Gen'vieve pulled Karlos's cloak closer around her as she spoke."Why can't you just fight the guards or something?"

"I'm no use right now." Sudenora muttered.

"And we don't have our weapons." Kielmark stated.

Karlos screwed up his face. "The Urgar Dungeons are the biggest in Sarophia." he swallowed.

Jelik could see the soldier's shadows now. "I'm going in." Jelik pushed past Kielmark, kicked in one of the boards, and vanished through the stone dragon's mouth.

The rest followed quickly.

* * * * * * * *

Anthron and Jassnik walked carefully out of Urgar Keep. They made sure not to brush past any of the soldiers, as this would dispel Jassnik's light bending enchantment. Once they were safely hidden in the trees where Jelik and Jassnik had arranged to meet, Jassnik dismissed the enchantment.

Anthron lay back on the soft leaves as Jassnik saw to his wounds.

"I hope they're okay," Jassnik said.

"What can we do?" Anthron breathed painfully as Jassnik pressed some herbs against his swollen ribs.

Jassnik sighed as the sun went down over Urgar keep. "There's only one thing we can do to help, but with only two of us it'll be next to impossible. Jelik and I left our horses here. Can you ride?"

* * * * * * * *

Jelik passed his short sword to Kielmark, and handed Karlos, Sudenora and Gen'vieve a dagger each. "This is the best I can do," he stated.

They stood in a plain oval anti-chamber with two exits - one of which the soldiers guarded. They were relieved the soldiers hadn't dared follow them.

"Let's push on," Kielmark whispered, pointing with Jelik's sword at the other exit. Leading the way, Kielmark brushed the cobwebs away and entered the new chamber. It was pitch black in the new room.

"I don't like this," Karlos hissed."We need light."

"What was that?" Gen'vieve whispered urgently.

"What?" Sudenora asked.

A flash lit the room for a second. Kielmark and Jelik crouched cautiously. Another flash revealed a halfling striking two pieces of metal together. After another spark, a torch flared into life, displaying the little male halfling. He squinted, holding the torch at arm length."You take," he urged.

Kielmark took the torch. The halfling having rid himself of the torch, scuttled away from the light. They could now see they were in a plain, rectangular, stone room, with no visible exits other than the one they had entered. Pieces of broken furniture covered with thick spider webs littered the parameter of the room. The halfling hid behind one of the smashed tables.

"Who are you?" Karlos asked.

"I'm Tilsk. I can get you out, but you got to help me first," the halfling replied from the shadows.

Kielmark looked to the others before replying."Do you want us to help you escape?"

"No!" Tilsk snapped."Will you help?"

"What is it that you want us to do?" Karlos asked softly.

Tilsk let out a small growl."Will you help?" he asked more urgently.

"Yes, we will." Jelik replied.

Tilsk entered the torchlight and approached Jelik."You help me now, I help you next."

Jelik shrugged in reply. The halfling pointed at the dagger in Jelik's hand."You cut for me."

"What do you want me to cut?" Jelik asked.

"Me," Tilsk replied.

Karlos scoffed."This is ridiculous. He doesn't know how to get out of here. He's mad or something."

"Not mad!" Tilsk shouted."Will you help?"

"Yes," Jelik said quietly."Where do you want me to cut?"

Tilsk placed his right hand on the floor, fanned out his fingers, and pointed to his middle one. Jelik could make out tiny symbols around the halfling's digit."Cut."

Jelik frowned."You want me to cut your finger off?"

"Yes, yes," Tilsk nodded."Then I can help you."

Jelik leaned down as Karlos protested."Jel, don't."

Gen'vieve and Sudenora stood together uncomfortably as Kielmark held the flickering torch up.

"You help me!" Tilsk screamed, and before Karlos could say another word, Jelik sent his blade down, severing the halfling's middle finger.

Tilsk, without a sound, examined his missing digit as blood began spurting.

"Now," Jelik said coldly as he backed away."You help us get out of here."

Tilsk wrapped his bleeding hand in a rag, smiled, and pointed at his severed finger."That is how you get out."

Frowning, Jelik examined the finger on the floor.

"What's that?" Sudenora pointed as Jelik scooped up a small gold ring from the finger.

"There wasn't a ring on his finger before." Jelik mused as he examined it. It was a plain gold ring, with seven symbols running around the inside; a picture of a ghost, a cat's eye, a spider, a feather, a closed eye, a skull, and a fist. These were the symbols that Jelik now noticed had disappeared from the finger.

"You put it on and go through here," Tilsk pointed at a small crack in the wall."There's a lever to open door through there." With that, Tilsk dashed through the group towards the stone dragon mouth entrance.

"No! There are soldiers out there!" Karlos called as Kielmark made an attempt to grab the quick halfling. Tilsk quickly scrambled away through the debris, and out through the entrance. There was a painful squeal, followed by the soldiers laughing.

"So," Jelik began as he examined the ring, unfazed by the halfling's obvious death."This little ring will get us out. All we need to do is put it on and leave through that crack in the wall."

"We shouldn't trust that mad halfling," Kielmark retorted."That thing could be cursed."

Sudenora nodded."That would explain why he wanted you to cut of his finger."

"It may have affected his mind too," Karlos added.

Gen'vieve clutched at her cloak."It sounds like the soldiers are coming through now."

Sudenora swore.

"We are in no state to fight them openly," Kielmark began."Our best bet is to attack them as they come through the mouth."

Jelik crept closer to the entrance, turned to Kielmark and shook his head. He returned silently."There's at least two dozen out there!" He hissed urgently.

"Here comes the first one." Gen'vieve called.

Kielmark, brandishing Jelik's short sword, was upon the soldier in moments. Several powerful swings from the Arrolokian, and he'd hacked through the soldier's armour and pierced his heart.

Swearing, Jelik looked to Sudenora, then Gen'vieve, Karlos, and finally Kielmark who was hacking at another soldier. Without hesitation, Jelik placed the golden ring on the middle finger of his right hand.

* * * * * * * * *

Yarlyn Kontar sighed in relief as his last customer for the day walked out of his large office that overlooked the city of Trendrik. He opened a drawer in his desk and withdrew a small corked bottle. Yarlyn uncorked the bottle and smelt the aroma for a few moments before he poured himself a drink in a tiny glass. He looked at his glass for a second, then drank it down in one go.

"Ah... never misses the spot," he commented to himself.

Yarlyn Kontar was a young man in his mid thirties, with short curly brown hair and blue eyes. He stood about two inches below six feet, and he was quite thinly built, but any who knew who he was would not cause him any trouble. Yarlyn was King Trendrik's personal adviser, and Trendrik's Foreign Relations Minister.

Yarlyn placed his glass back on his desk, and hid his bottle back inside the drawer. He stood and attempted to mould the creases out of his expensive silk shirt and pants. He would have to change, of course, before he went out, or he'd be recognised. He was planning to go down to his favourite tavern, *The Drawn Bow*, and do some serious drinking and gambling.

This was something Yarlyn Kontar did quite often.

Ten minutes later Yarlyn was walking through the fast darkening streets of Trendrik wearing a plain tan coloured cloth vest, ripped breeches, and a crimson coloured cloak. Only two things stood out on Yarlyn; one was his shiny black knee high buckled boots, and the other was his clean shaven face that looked as untrustworthy as a thief. In truth Yarlyn did consider himself a thief, a shrewd businessman who could influence without notice. Oh well, he shrugged.

He entered *The Drawn Bow* through the front entrance and paused in the doorway to soak in the atmosphere.

The Drawn Bow was a tavern located a block away from the main western gate of what was referred to as The Walled, which made it popular with traders and merchants. A long bar ran along the northern wall, with a large amount of spirits displayed on the shelf behind. The entrance to the kitchen was positioned behind the bar, and the smells from within made Yarlyn's stomach grumble. Stairs ran above the unlit fireplace on the western wall.

Yarlyn smiled to himself as he walked towards the bar, noting how empty the tavern seemed at the moment. He ordered his usual drink from the shelf behind the bar, and sat at his usual table near the firepit.

Within half an hour the taproom had slowly filled up as the regulars came in and seated themselves. An ugly unshaven man with huge lips and dirty brown clothes sat down opposite Yarlyn at the table and nodded his greetings. He had short scraggly red hair, and alert green eyes.

"Well met, Kros." Yarlyn nodded as he winced away from the stench that Kros always brought with him.

"You're early today Hawke, wenching again?" Kros chuckled in a deeply lisped voice, his lips flapping.

Yarlyn sighed at Kros's obvious attempt at humour. He nodded just to keep Kros quiet.

"Good old Hawke, no? I'm going to win all your money tonight. I hope you don't mind." Kros chuckled again.

Yarlyn Kontar enjoyed working for the King, but his reputation would be ruined if the wrong people found he frequented a tavern such as *The Drawn Bow*. For this reason he went by the name Hawke between the middle and outer walls of the city. Another reason was that if half of the people here knew that Yarlyn was rich, they'd slit his throat when he was relieving himself and loot him for the chance of finding gold. He preferred himself whole.

Another man joined the table, sitting on Yarlyn's left. He was nearly six feet, in his early thirties. He wore a broadsword at his belt and a coat of shiny silver chain mail. He had shoulder length brown hair, deep blue eyes.

"Greetings all."

"Well met, Saralon. How was soldiering today?" Yarlyn asked with a hint of sarcasm.

"Not too bad, Hawke, not too bad at all. Something has come up in Urgar Keep though, so I won't be here for the next few weeks."

"So you won't be joining us next week then?" Kros asked slowly.

"That's right, Kros, I won't be." Saralon spoke slowly, purposely trying to irritate Kros. He then looked to Yarlyn, "Where's Jalesia tonight? You know I lose on purpose just so I can see her smile. I also like watching that beautiful pair of..."

"What happened at Urgar Keep?" Yarlyn interrupted Saralon, always wanting to keep updated on what is going on in Sarophia.

"Oh, some fairly powerful criminals escaped the Keep from right under their nose. One of them, their leader, fought the Great Carl Mort'l and lived." Saralon caught the attention of a passing barmaid and ordered a mug of ale.

Yarlyn whistled. He had heard about Carl Mort'l, head of the Panthorian Knights. Also an ex enemy of Cyermyth.

"And what of them?" Yarlyn asked. "Are you to hunt these criminals down?"

Saralon scratched his chin in thought."We have to help track them down and turn them over to the Panthorian Knights."

"What do the knights want with criminals?" Kros inquired to Saralon.

Saralon ignored Kros as a barmaid brought him a mug of ale. He placed a coin down the front of her dress and slapped her thigh as she left. Saralon took a gulp of ale."Ahh, that's better. Anyway, there's a reward for this group."

"How much?" Yarlyn asked quickly.

"Why Hawke? You turning bounty hunter?" Saralon grinned after another gulp of ale.

Yarlyn smiled weakly back, not particularly amused.

"The leader's worth one thousand silver, and each of his gang is half as much each. It's been said that even Smit-Myer Crysin is having difficulties finding them."

Kros's green eyes suddenly looked intelligent and alert.

Yarlyn pondered this information. There was no time to wait for the beautiful Jalesia to arrive for their card playing tonight, Yarlyn had too much on his mind. He had to find out more about this group, why the Panthorian Knights were after them. Yarlyn had a hunch that this group could be tied in with The Selection, but didn't dare say anything to his card playing companions.

Draining his glass, Yarlyn stood and excused himself. He had much work to do.

CHAPTER TWELVE

Jelik's screams echoed.

"What can we do to help him?" Kielmark bellowed as he charged back."The soldiers backed away as soon as Jelik began screaming," the Arrolokian explained to Karlos's unasked question.

Karlos stood over Jelik, trying to concentrate as he mumbled another prayer to *Termolen*.

Jelik gritted his teeth in agony. The ring was now smoking. He could smell his own flesh burning. He tried to pull the ring off, but it was almost like the ring wasn't there anymore. Just as Jelik's vision began to black out, the pain stopped.

"Well done, Karlos." Sudenora congratulated.

Karlos shook his head, leaning over Jelik."It stopped by itself. Jelik, are you okay?"

Jelik lay still on his back panting, nursing his injured hand, too scared to look at what horror the ring had done to his agile thieving fingers. He swallowed hard, then flexed his hand.

No pain? How could that be? He thought. Propping himself up on one elbow, Jelik examined his hand as the others leaned in closer. Kielmark, after hearing the soldiers stirring again, gripped Jelik's sword and went back to guarding the small entrance the soldiers had been climbing through in the previous chamber.

There was no sign of the ring at all, except for seven brown coloured symbols burnt into Jelik's flesh.

"Jelik?" Karlos asked again."Are you okay?"

The thief examined the burnt pictures closer, ignoring Karlos. The first was that of a wraith, the next was a cat's eye, third a feather, a closed eye, a spider, a skull, and the seventh picture was a fist.

Shaking his head, Jelik looked around his companions, then stood."Well," he casually held his scarred hand in the torchlight,"Maybe these pictures do something."

"Are you in pain?" Karlos asked, examining Jelik's hand.

"No." Jelik replied.

Sudenora examined the pictures after Karlos."What do these mean, I wonder?" Sudenora scratched at his stubble absentmindedly, and stood back."Press the wraith with your other hand," he urged Jelik.

Jelik's left hand trembled as he slowly brought it closer to his right. Pausing for a moment, he then pressed the picture.

Nothing happened.

Gen'vieve let out her breath."What do you think it is?" she asked the Elementalist."You obviously have some idea."

Sudenora wiped a trickle of sweat from his forehead."I though that these markings might have something to do with activating abilities. That halfling said something about putting the ring on and going through that crack over there - and from the pictures - only a ghost or wraith could have the ability to do that."

"Fair enough." Gen'vieve nodded.

Karlos jumped as he heard Kielmark bash at the soldiers as they began to tentatively enter the Urgar Keep Dungeon again."So, how do we activate it?" he asked urgently.

"Not sure," Sudenora thought."Jelik, do you feel any different? I mean, can you *hear* anything different?"

"I'm not sure what you mean." Jelik withdrew his hand from view.

"Some enchanted items, once worn, whispers to the wearer the fact that the wearer can do something new..." Sudenora explained.

Jelik shook his head."The ring is not talking to me," he replied sarcastically.

"The soldiers are coming back through," Kielmark called from behind them."We'd better do something soon."

Sudenora wiped another bead of sweat from his face as he tried a different angle."Jelik, try to close your eyes and focus on the picture. Visualise what it looks like in your mind."

Jelik closed his eyes, opening them quickly as he heard Kielmark cry out in pain.

"Damn it Jelik, concentrate!" Sudenora screamed in panic.

In that exact instant, Jelik disappeared, leaving behind the gaseous form of a wraith.

* * * * * * * * *

Jassnik slumped into the grass to catch his breath as Anthron grasped a pine tree to lower himself to the ground. Their progress had been very slow even on horseback, as Anthron's injuries were getting the better of him.

"How much further." Anthron wheezed as he lay on his back.

Jassnik dabbed the corner of his cloak to his forehead. "We are nearly there," Jassnik stared up at the cloudy evening sky, *Lithloren* high above. "But time is getting on. If we're going to be of any help to our friends, we must move quicker."

Anthron glared back. "Sorry to be a burden."

Jassnik held up his hand and shook his head. "I didn't mean to offend you. I was alluding to the fact that I have an Euroness vial. I was saving it for an emergency..."

"What is an Euroness vial?" Anthron coughed painfully as he held his side.

Jassnik began rummaging through his shoulder bag. "A Euroness vial is meant to be the saliva of a Cat Person. The Cat People of Euroness are meant to have healing properties within their saliva," Jassnik retrieved a small vial of thick clear liquid, wrapped in a purple velvet cloth. "Legend has it that they live for a long time because they clean themselves. Their saliva slows aging and heals wounds. Apparently, a fully grown Cat Person can regenerate for up to six hours after each 'bath'." Jassnik carefully uncorked the vial, and motioned for Anthron to lift his tunic and remove his bandages. "As you can probably guess, this stuff costs just less than selling one's soul."

Anthron tensed as Jassnik poured the small vial over his badly swollen ribs. The liquid slowly poured from the vial, and was warm on his skin. Instantly, Anthron could feel a tingling where the saliva touched. Watching with fascination, Anthron saw the saliva being absorbing through his skin. He could see his ribs begin to move of their own accord. With a painful crack, he felt a rib become repositioned.

Jassnik corked the empty vial and wrapped it back up in the thick purple velvet cloth."So?" Jassnik asked."How do you feel?"

Anthron was amazed."That stuff is great!" He exclaimed. He timidly touched his ribs, only to feel no pain. He felt a tingling around his mouth and head, then all his bruises were gone. Anthron jumped to his feet."I feel great, Jass!"

"Good, good," Jassnik waved."Be sure to buy me a couple of vials next time we're in Euroness."

"Where are we heading?" Anthron sat back down, his feet beginning to tingle.

Jassnik finished packing his shoulder bag then answered;"We're heading for one of the sealed entrances to the Urgar Dungeon. It obviously connects to Urgar Keep, where our fellow companions may be stuck." Jassnik then unwrapped some cold salted meat, offered some to Anthron, then began to gnaw on it.

Anthron ate the meat quietly, in deep thought."What abilities do you have, Jass?"

Jassnik looked up slowly."Why don't you have a guess?" he asked.

"Well," Anthron began,"You talked with *Tolorel* to identify the dagger, and you made the both of us invisible inside Urgar Keep..."

"We weren't invisible, we were bending light," Jassnik corrected. Letting out a sigh, he continued."I am a servant of the white moon, *Tolorel*, and her violet sister, *Lithloren*. *Tolorel* is the seeker of truths, the shedding of true light, if you will. *Lithloren* hides truths, shedding untrue light." Jassnik looked to Anthron."I have a very good relationship with them both. They have both gifted me with the ability to call upon them without the aid of an item." Jassnik beamed.

"What does that mean?" Anthron asked.

Jassnik frowned."It means I can talk to *Tolorel* and *Lithloren* personally. It means that I can call upon their help whenever I desire..." Jassnik looked up quickly."Well, to a point at least," he added quickly.

Anthron nodded."What can you tell me of this?" Anthron offered

Jassnik Mort'l's sapphire-encrusted long sword.

Jassnik took the sword carefully. He closed his eyes as the black bladed sword began to pulse the same faint blue colour the dagger had back in Mosorac."This is a powerful weapon," Jassnik began as his eyes flickered."Created by a blessed Cyermyth knight and an Elementalist in 2810, this weapon was designed to destroy chaos and evil. It has the chance to kill these things instantly, and to aggravate the senses of anyone who draws a weapon against the wielder," Jassnik's eyes popped open and the pulsing ceased."And you got this sword off one of the knights? Ha!"

"Yeah," Anthron took the sword back."The knights aren't exactly do-gooders now, are they?"

"No," Jassnik mused as he packed up the meat."But the Cyermyth Knights *were* do-gooders." He hefted himself to his feet and grasped the reins of his mount."It's time for us to move on."

* * * * * * * * * *

"By *Termolen*!" Karlos exclaimed as he looked at Jelik in the form of a wraith."Can you hear me, Jel?"

The smoky outline of Jelik's wraith form appeared to nod, then turned and slowly drifted smoothly towards the crack in the wall.

"It looks beautiful," Gen'vieve commented."Almost like transparent silk."

Karlos looked very uneasy."It doesn't actually look real."

"Whatever do you mean?" Gen'vieve laughed.

"Karlos!" Kielmark bellowed from behind them."Get in here!"

Karlos gave one final look as Jelik's wraith form slipped through the crack in the wall, then raced to help Kielmark.

The Arrolokian had dispatched eight soldiers, hacking away at their plate armour as they forced their way through the small opening into the dungeon. Two more were pushing their way through, and Kielmark was exhausted. He was gasping for air, blood flowing from several cuts on his arms. He threw the short sword to Karlos."I need to catch my breath." he panted.

Karlos awkwardly held the sword with both hands, and stepped in to begin chopping at the intruding soldier's armour.

Suddenly, there was a large shake, followed by a grinding sound, and the doorway leading to their companions began to close.

"Quickly!" Kielmark grabbed Karlos and swung him across the small room. Karlos landed heavily and skidded through the fast closing doorway.

"Kiel! Hurry!" Karlos called back. Kielmark staggered for a moment before finding the strength to launch himself towards the doorway. He collapsed several feet from the entrance, where Karlos and Sudenora quickly dragged him through. The last thing Karlos saw before the doorway was sealed was the pile of soldier bodies and blood completely vanishing, as if they'd never been there.

"What's happening?" Karlos turned to see a new door open, leading out into the dungeon.

Jelik, now back in his real form, approached through the new door, motioning over his shoulder with his thumb. "There was a lever to pull back there which opened this door. How was I to know it'd close off that one?"

Karlos shook his head. "Those soldiers back there," he glanced at Kielmark who had recovered somewhat, "I don't think they were real."

Kielmark scoffed. "What do you mean?" The Arrolokian displayed his cut arms. "You think I did this myself?"

Karlos shook his head, but it was Sudenora who spoke up. "Illusions will always do damage if you believe they are real..."

Karlos nodded. "I think we've been herded in here by illusions."

"So what are you saying?" Jelik crossed his arms. "You want me to find a way back through there again?"

Karlos shook his head. "I'm not sure what to do."

"Why did someone want us here?" Gen'vieve asked as she tended to Kielmark's wounds. She yelped in surprise when suddenly his wounds faded completely away.

"Okay," Kielmark admitted. "So they *were* illusions..."

"Giant game of cat and mouse," Jelik cursed."Well, let's not just sit here," he passed a torch to Kielmark, then lit another which Karlos took."Let's find a way out before what ever chased us arrives."

* * * * * * * * *

Anthron grasped the hilt of the sapphire-encrusted long sword as he and Jassnik ventured further into the darkness.

Jassnik had led them to a small group of pines growing on an unusual mound quite far from any road. After searching for some time, he found a buried piece of rotten rope, which he then pulled on to open a concealed trapdoor into the ground.

Jassnik now crept silently ahead of Anthron through the dark tunnel, while Anthron held a torch which flared whenever it came too close to the thick cobwebs.

"I don't care much for spiders." Anthron muttered as he examined the thick webs.

Jassnik looked back over his shoulder."I don't either," he replied."Just up ahead, there should be a T junction..."

"How do you know all this?" Anthron asked.

Jassnik turned to face the blonde warrior again."I once purchased an explorer's map of this place," he began."Vilgrane, ever heard of him?"

Anthron shook his head.

"Well, anyway, Vilgrane is a highly reputable explorer. We met in a tavern in Panthorian a while ago, and I mentioned that I was heading to Sarophia." Jassnik set off again down the corridor."He offered to sell me a map of the most famous dungeon in Sarophia. Of course it wasn't complete - no one has ever explored *all* of the Urgar Dungeon." They reached the T junction Jassnik had been expecting, then began off to the left."I bought the map off Vilgrane for twenty pieces of silver, and I examined it all night. Unfortunately, I got a little tipsy that night, and the map found its way too close to the firepit. In one moment," Jassnik paused and threw his arms out wide before continuing,"the map went up in smoke."

Anthron frowned."If you only had one night to remember it..."

Jassnik laughed."I've been gifted with a superb memory, my friend. I can close my eyes and still see the map, even now."

"So, where are we heading?" Anthron ducked under a particularly thick web.

"We are now on a westerly course, which should take us to Urgar Keep. If the others are still in the prison, we can sneak in from under them, free them, and flee back this way. If they've been moved though..."

Anthron thought for a moment."How much further have we got to go?"

"Not sure..." Jassnik then held his hand up for Anthron to stop.

"What is it?" Anthron asked.

"*Shhh!*" Jassnik cocked his head and listened intently."*Crap!*" he hissed."We're being stalked."

"Stalked?" Anthron asked quietly."By what?"

"I don't want to find out." Jassnik set off down the tunnel quickly.

There was a deep throaty roar from far behind them, followed by another not far in front of them."*Crap!*" Jassnik swore again."They are sensing our heat."

"We could cover ourselves with this mud," Anthron suggested, lifting up a muddy boot.

Jassnik snapped his fingers."That might help throw them off." Jassnik quickly collected a handful of mud, and with a look of dismay, covered his face and hands.

"The mud is definitely the smelliest part of the dungeon." Anthron gagged as he covered his arms and face.

There was another roar from up ahead of them, this time much closer.

"Do you know what they are?" Anthron asked, dousing his torch.

"No," Jassnik shook his head."They could be ogres, trolls, rock-fleshers...sounds too big to be goblins or orcs."

"Rock-fleshers?" Anthron asked as they fumbled onwards in the darkness.

"Nasty things," Jassnik replied quietly."As big as an ogre, strong as an ogre, but with a rock-like armour covering them from head to toe.

It's very hard to hurt them, so most people run away - they're quite slow."

Suddenly there was an awful bellowing roar from right in front of them. Anthron and Jassnik slunk to the side of the tunnel and froze. Anthron squinted through the dark. He could make out a large form squelching slowly through the mud. It took up most of the tunnel.

Anthron knew that he was going to have to fight his first rock-flesher. Slowly, he unsheathed his sword. Jassnik gave him an alarming look as he recognised what their opponent was, and how little room they had to sneak past. He placed a hand on Anthron's arm and shook his head in discouragement of what the blonde warrior was thinking.

As Anthron continued to squint at the dark shape approaching, he began to see a faint blue colour radiating around the rock-flesher. Blinking, he noticed the green outline of Jassnik. Anthron had seen these colours several times now, and they had always distracted him previously. However this time, he certainly found it very useful. He could now see the exact shape of the rock-flesher, the hulking torso, with its little head and neck. It was the thin weak neck which Anthron noticed.

As the rock-flesher stepped in front of Jassnik, the little man scurried past as best he could, to the safety behind. The rock-flesher didn't notice. Another step and it was in front of Anthron. Jassnik shook his head as he realised that Anthron couldn't get past.

Anthron launched himself at the head of the ten foot hulk, grasped the back of its neck, and climbed on its shoulder. The rock-flesher bellowed in frustration, then tried to smash Anthron apart with its massive rock like fists. Anthron ducked an attack as he held onto the head of the rock-flesher, then with all his strength, let out a primal yell as he wrenched the neck. There was a loud crack, and Anthron jumped clear of the falling rock-flesher's body. The body landed in a spray of mud, then all was quiet.

"What by OBPSULTTN did you do, Anthron?" Jassnik was awed.

Anthron picked himself up, his only injury a graze on his arm from the rock-flesher's tough skin."I could see that its neck was weak and unprotected, so I broke it."

Jassnik looked shocked."Well done!" he exclaimed."Now to find the others before its friend catches up."

CHAPTER THIRTEEN

Sudenora shivered.

The air was stale, ushered by a rotten stench. Sudenora stepped around another stalagmite that congested the tunnel floor. He gloomily thought the tunnel resembled a giant mouth.

Kielmark held his torch high. It flared furiously through the cobwebs above. Jelik crept silently ahead. Gen'vieve walked behind the Arrolokian next to Sudenora, her nose and mouth covered with Karlos's cloak as she walked on quietly. Karlos brought up the rear, eyeing the waning torch he carried.

"My torch is nearly spent," Karlos whispered.

Kielmark stopped and regarded the Healer. He passed his torch to Sudenora, as Jelik passed a small flask from his belt pouch. Kielmark then tore a length off his cloak, opened the flask and tipped it over the material carefully. Kielmark then repeated the exercise several more times, until he had six long pieces of treated material.

Kielmark passed three strips to Karlos."When it does go out, wrap that around your torch, and we'll re-light it."

Karlos took the smelly pieces of Kielmark's cloak."Thanks."

"Flammable liquid," Gen'vieve commented."So that's how they keep burning..."

Kielmark gave Gen'vieve a sidelong glance before discarding the remnants of his cloak. They moved on, finding Jelik waiting for them at a T-junction.

Shrugging, Jelik said,"My sense of direction's no good down here. Which way?"

Sudenora scratched his chin absently as he studied both possibilities closely.

"What is it?" Karlos asked the Elementalist.

"What do you mean?" Sudenora replied.

"You scratch your stubble when you have an idea," Karlos

observed."So, what's your idea?"

"I didn't realise I did that," Sudenora folded his arms."Well, I was thinking that I might be able to explore each direction of the corridor myself."

Jelik shifted uncomfortably."That might be a little dangerous for you..."

"Jel's right," Karlos agreed."He's the best man for exploring. He can blend into the shadows, move quietly..."

"Let Sudenora finish." Gen'vieve said.

"Thanks," Sudenora nodded."I was meaning that I could find something to look for us."

"What, like a friendly goblin?" Jelik chuckled.

"No, like this." Sudenora picked up a palm sized rock. He closed his eyes to concentrate, then began to mutter words to *Servas*. As Sudenora opened his eyes, so the rock opened an eye.

"What's this?" Kielmark jumped back, aghast.

"It's okay," Sudenora removed his hand, and the rock with it's new eye floated in front of him, blinking."It's sort of like a scout." Sudenora closed his eyes, then the rock turned and sped down the left tunnel. Sudenora's eyes flickered and twitched as he saw what his rock was seeing. After several minutes, the rock flew past Jelik, heading down the right tunnel.

"That thing can move!" Jelik exclaimed.

The others shifted in awkward silence before Sudenora's eyes opened."The enchantment has expired."

"So?" Gen'vieve asked."Which way?"

Sudenora pointed to the left."That way leads to some kind of encampment of rock-like people. They look nasty, and there's about a dozen of them. Past them the tunnel goes down quite sharply. That's as far as I went, since we're really wanting to go up."

"Fair comment. The other way?" Kielmark urged.

Sudenora smiled as he pointed to the right."The tunnel winds for a long while, opening into a charred cavern with gold and jewels everywhere."

"*What*?" Jelik exclaimed.

"Oh yes," Sudenora continued, wearing a smug look."Anthron and Jassnik are about to reach there too!"

* * * * * * * * *

"Is that what I think it is?" Anthron gasped as he and Jassnik peered cautiously into the gold littered cavern.

Jassnik's mouth was wide open."It sure looks like it."

The cavern was about one hundred feet in diameter, with rough charred and scratched walls. A forty foot hole in the top of which disappeared into the darkness. Anthron noticed the slight scent of saffron in the air. In the middle of the floor lay thousands of gold coins, escorted by brightly sparkling gemstones, and several ominous carcasses of various milieus. Jassnik held his torch up a little higher, but could not see any more of the cavern from their safe position.

"That's a lot of money," Anthron breathed, leaning against the blackened southern corridor."With that, we could buy all the information we need to expose The Selection." Anthron began counting on his fingers."We could hire enough people to clear out The Twelve Peaks, we could set up the villages..."

"We could get killed trying to remove it all..." Jassnik toned."What villages?" he asked offhandedly.

"We referred to them as outlaw villages. We were taken to one of them in the Ithren Forest after we'd escaped The Selection by Anthea..." Anthron choked back his emotions and looked away from the little blue clad troubadour as he fought to mask the painful thoughts of Anthea Fleké - the woman he loved.

"Anthea? I've heard you talk of her before..." Jassnik thought for an instant, then guided the conversation."How many of these outlaw villages are there? I'm fairly well travelled, but have never heard of them."

"There are two, one in Ithren as I'd said, the other in Sambethe," Anthron paused to let out a laugh."That's where our group was aiming for before we went to The Twelve Peaks. Things kind of got a little crazy after that, after finding that dagger..."

"So," Jassnik thought."These villages are where the people who have escaped Selection go?"

Anthron frowned."I'd never thought of that, I thought that we were the only...You know Jass, you might be right."

Jassnik said."Well, I hope for their sake they're well hidden from the Cyermyth Knights."

"I remember you calling our black armoured friends that before. Where are these Cyermyth Knights from?"

Jassnik sighed."Cyermyth," Anthron felt stupid at Jassnik's reply."They are Queen Kilandra's Palace Guard, her elite."

Anthron nearly choked."What? You know who's sending them against us?"

Jassnik stood back defensively."Hold on Anthron. Kilandra and her Cyermyth Knights *were* highly respected throughout all of Panthorian as being kind, reasonable and fair in all their ways just several years ago. Excuse me for having my doubts that the Queen of Cyermyth is sending her Palace Guard to Sarophia as a posse to abduct innocent people, responsible for cold blooded murder, dealing with creatures of the undead, and corrupting Sarophia's law enforcement - thus creating The Selection." Jassnik glared angrily at the blonde warrior.

Anthron rocked from the troubadour's sudden outburst."It does sound a little outrageous." he apologised.

"Now, back to things at hand," Jassnik changed the subject."We've got some gold to exchange ownership, and some friends to rescue." Jassnik cautiously crept into the cavern. He studied every inch of the cavern within the torchlight. After deciding there was no danger, he stood straight and began casually strolling towards the bed of gold in the centre of the cavern."I think it's safe, Anthron."

Anthron, sword drawn, started to follow the troubadour. After painfully slipping on the coins, he stood alongside Jassnik in the centre of the glorious lake of gold, the torchlight lending the cavern a magical sparkling glow.

"It's a beautiful sight my friend." Jassnik murmured, then crouched to gather a handful of coins. After placing several handfuls in his coin pouch, Anthron followed.

"We're now rich men, by anyone's standards," Jassnik beamed as he rejected a ruby over a larger emerald."Very rich indeed."

"What's over there?" Anthron motioned with a handful of coins."Looks like armour and weapons."

Jassnik's head shot up at the sound of more treasure, and they both eagerly approached the equipment."Maybe our imprisoned friends could do with some of these." he said.

Anthron spied a chain mail jacket. He lifted it and was impressed with how light it felt and that it made no sound as chain links normally would. Upon inspection, he noted a small design over the chest, in the shape of a drawn bow.

Noticing Anthron pausing, Jassnik inspected the symbol."Elven chain," he whistled."Very rare, and unfortunately made for someone of frame between us both - you're too big and I'm too small," he commented sourly."However, worth a lot of money. Look, some red bracers with the same pattern."

As Anthron decided to place the chain in his pack he heard what sounded like slow wing beats from the hole above them. He dropped the armour. He felt an overwhelming sense of guilt and the need to leave the cavern."We'd best be on our way," Anthron spoke quietly.

Jassnik nodded as he glanced upwards."Right you are." He took a quick look back at the pile of equipment. They began to slip their way across the cavern towards the northern exit. As they entered the northern corridor, a powerful force of wind smelling of saffron and incense hit them, as something landed in the cavern behind them. The gust pushed both Anthron and Jassnik into the side tunnel. They fell painfully to the ground. Pushing himself up, Anthron then helped Jassnik who had skewered his hand on a small stalagmite.

"What in the nine gods was that?" Anthron exclaimed, turning to examine the cavern. He froze as he saw a head the size of a small house level with his. It was covered with golden scales which Anthron noted were each the size of a kite shield. Its slender neck ran back to its massive body, with mighty wings folded across its back. Its long pointy snout revealed yellow teeth as long as a bastard sword.

It was a dragon.

Anthron felt the giant amber eyes resembling pools of molten gold fix on him. He felt an overwhelming fear which made his knees go weak, and his stomach churn. He tried to run, but couldn't command his body to take action. Chancing a quick look to Jassnik, he noted the troubadour was in a similar state.

"Humans," the dragon's voice thundered, like a boulder rolling down a mountain."I would assume thou dos speak the Common language of Palandra?"

Anthron felt ill, but stammered."Y-yes."

"What are you going to..." Jassnik let his sentence drift off, the dragonfear slowly fading.

The dragon laughed, a rumbling laughter which echoed loudly through the cavern and surrounding tunnels, shaking the ground, and loosing several stalactites. When the dragon finished laughing, it let out a large sigh along with a waft of stale smoke.

The dragon's amber eyes narrowed at Jassnik."Am I to kill thee? Maybe. Thou art already counted as thieves of my lair, my home."

Anthron cursed himself for his moment of greed. He'd known something wasn't right.

The dragon continued."Who art thou that ventures into Urgar Dungeon, and what is thy purpose - *thieves*?" The dragon spat out the last word.

Anthron took a deep breath."My name is Anthron Mikolnic, son of Arthor and Mari of Vemmlok, Izonda." Anthron tipped his head in a bowing gesture.

Jassnik pondered a moment before answering."And I am Jassnik Corline, son of Farim Corline, cousin to Queen Kilandra of Panthorian." Jassnik bowed extravagantly, his blonde ponytail brushing the floor as Anthron's mouth dropped in shock.

The dragon deliberated a moment."Human royalty. Be secure in knowing thou hast intrigued my curiosity, and shalt have time to explain thyselves."

Anthron felt in control of himself again, the sickening fear having past. He was obviously pleased the dragon hadn't turned them into vestiges - yet. Also from the neutral colour which ebbed from the dragon he sensed that it was not malevolent."We have come to Urgar Dungeon due to our companions having been captured and held in Urgar Keep." Seeing the dragon nod, Anthron continued."We are good people, not often picking from treasure not our own." With saying that, Anthron threw his money pouch back into the horde. Jassnik, seeing what Anthron was doing, followed suit."We are struggling against terrible foes, striving to unravel the mysteries of The Selection."

The dragon's eyes widened."The Selection you speak of, what is it?"

Jassnik stood quietly as the fighter explained."The Selection is a term the people of Sarophia have for the disappearances of their folk. For over a year and a half people have been going missing without a trace. Over six months ago my friends who are currently held captive within Urgar Keep and myself were taken from our beds as we slept and we were drugged. Once the effects wore off, we found ourselves being held in one of fourteen large wheeled cages pulled by horses - as are common when transporting criminals to Urgar Keep."

"So," the dragon urged."Are these people whom have been selected within this Keep?"

Jassnik answered."We believe they are not," Jassnik thought this a good time to find out if they had to thoroughly search the unexplored dungeon."Have there been large numbers of people brought underground over the last year and a half?"

"Thou already knows the answer, for there has been none save yourselves out of the ordinary," replied the dragon.

"We ventured up to the Twelve Peaks, since the body of someone who had gone missing had turned up in the Splitting River," Anthron shuddered as he remembered Scotus."We found a dozen undead drudges mining for a bat-shaped dagger. Also, we fought some kind of super human, whom we barely managed to beat."

"Go on." the dragon's amber eyes glinted with interest.

Anthron continued."Not long afterwards, these black armoured soldiers..."

"The Royal Palace Guard of Queen Kilandra," Jassnik corrected uncomfortably.

"The Royal Palace Guard," Anthron said."They began chasing us. We had escaped The Selection, and were a threat we expect. But we also had with us the bat shaped dagger they'd been mining for."

"Xycermon," the dragon stated."Continue."

"Well, we got caught - most of us anyway - and we're trying to free the others." Jassnik finished.

"Whatever her reason, Kilandra is sending her elite over The Deep Sea to aid the Selection process. We have two things left to do; learn about the dagger from Platown, and pay a visit to Queen Kilandra," Anthron finished.

The dragon was silent for a long while, as Anthron and Jassnik exchanged nervous glances. Finally, the dragon spoke."I am called Rhailk, offspring of Rhaal from the Snowcaps, father of none."

Jassnik noted the dragon's introduction with interest. He had read that dragon's pride themselves on their children's exploits, of which Rhailk had none. Jassnik decided not to say anything - he didn't want to be responsible for putting a dragon in a foul mood for centuries.

The dragon continued."I have heard of this Selection, known in my tongue as *Le Shoft Tear's Kra*. You have satisfied both my curiosity and my incantations. You are speaking the truth, therefore welcome Anthron Milkolnic of Vemmlok and Jassnik Corline of Cyermyth."

* * * * * * * * *

Anthron and Jassnik ventured a short way up the northern tunnel before meeting up with the tired group of Kielmark, Jelik, Karlos, Sudenora and Gen'vieve, after quick introductions were made to Gen'vieve and Karlos had healed Jassnik's bleeding hand, they returned to Rhailk's lair.

Anthron and Jassnik entered the cavern together, and explained to Rhailk they had found their companions. The newcomers were swept with dragonfear, which even made Karlos vomit. Afterwards, they were awestruck by the wealth. Rhailk growled smoke whenever anyone looked at taking a single coin. As soon as Gen'vieve had relaxed, the dragon narrowed his huge amber eyes and lowered his head so it was level with hers."Keep your mind to yourself, human." Rhailk warned. He sniffed, as if to remember Gen'vieve, then shifted his colossal body around the side of the cavern to observe Jelik closely, who didn't like the attention at all.

Jassnik moved closer to Gen'vieve, who looked shocked."What was that about?"

Gen'vieve attempted to brush out her knotted hair with her fingers nervously."I hear people's thoughts," she replied."Whether I want to or not." Her blue eyes studied everyone carefully, gauging their responses.

"You have nothing to fear from us," Jassnik reassured.

Gen'vieve closed her eyes briefly. Opening them again, she replied;"Thank you." Gen'vieve blushed slightly."I've been in the Urgar Keep dungeon for over a year now - for being a witch." She went back to trying to straighten out her hair.

"So much gold..." Jelik looked pained that he was unable to even run his hands through the treasure - any thief's dream.

"Where did all this come from?" Karlos asked.

"Mostly gifts from the orcs, goblins or rock-fleshers." Rhailk said.

"These creatures bring you gifts?" Sudenora asked.

"Yes," Rhailk said."I am not fond of their taste, and they fear me. They throw gems, weapons, or gold in here when one of my giants is guarding."

"You have giants as guards?" Gen'vieve exclaimed."What sort of giants?"

"Cloud. They own a portion of this horde for their services," the dragon replied.

"How did these creatures get hold of Elven chain?" Jassnik inquired,

141

nodding his head towards the pile of armour and weapons. Anthron felt glad that he at least hadn't stolen the Elven armour.

"Elven?" Jelik's head came up. Elven chain was always sought after by rogues, as the armour was as light as leather, but as tough as plate.

"He who wore that armour and bracers came here of his own free will." Rhailk said.

"An Elf came here?" Sudenora gasped.

Rhailk narrowed his amber eyes at the Elementalist."Long ago an Elven warrior came here from Sambethe. He stayed with me for many centuries and we enjoyed each other's company. He died here. Thou mayest take his armour and bracers, as long as they are the correct size."

Jelik rushed to where Anthron indicated, and found the chain mesh jacket. Unfastening his studded leather jerkin, he slipped the thin mesh Elven chain over his black tunic. The thief adjusted the straps then smiled.

"Fits perfectly," he commented.

The thief buckled his sword belt back on, then refastened his gray woollen cloak over his shoulders. As an afterthought, he strapped on the red leather bracers with the drawn bow design.

"One other item may leave here to help thy cause." Rhailk's deep voice rumbled. From the treasure Kielmark saw a faint blue glow, slowly becoming brighter. He noticed that no one else could see the light, so he made his way across the treasure towards the shining item. The blue glow winked out as Kielmark's hand touched it. When the light was gone, Kielmark noted that he held a plain silver helm. The others watched him closely.

"The helm, which belonged to Sir Rodol the Invincible of Cyermyth, hath chosen thee, Arrolokian." Rhailk announced.

Kielmark bowed low to the mighty dragon."My thanks." The dark skinned warrior then strapped the helm on.

"What do you know about the Selection - and the dagger?" Jassnik had been waiting for the right moment to ask."You seem to know so much."

Rhailk dipped his great head."Xycermon is known to all of my kind. There are seven such daggers, which are attached at the hilt and used as a mighty weapon of destruction." the great gold wyrm continued."Each dagger contains the soul of a thousand devils, which can act as a beckon to all who know how to look. They are hungry wicked knives." A burst of thick smoke erupted from Rhailk's throat."That they are once again being sought would indicate the beginning of the Second Great War," he finished.

"Is Xycermon the name of one dagger, or the weapon of destruction you'd mentioned?" Sudenora asked.

"Xycermon is sentient, thus it is both one dagger and all of them. Xycermon calls for the other daggers when they are apart. The longer you hold this one, the closer you will all come."

Karlos frowned."Closer to what? What are these knights wanting with this great weapon?"

Rhailk revealed his gigantic teeth in what could be likened to a smile."I will say this one thing - Xycermon, although a formidable weapon, is not being sought as a weapon of destruction. Xycermon is a summoning tool also."

Jassnik mused,"If these daggers are going to be used to summon something, then I highly doubt that the Cyermyth Knights are behind all this. Queen Kilandra doesn't think much of magic, so her knights are trained not to trust it..."

"What about that Mort'l guy then?" Anthron burst."First he knocks us all out with some enchantment - then he grows an arm back after I severed it!"

Jassnik held up his hands in peace."Calm down Anthron," Jassnik let out a sigh."Carl Mort'l. I'd heard of him before - one mean guy from Parntorn. He led a small army against Euroness's northern border about fifteen years ago, and fled into the Wastelands of Bone when Cyermyth soldiers turned up to help. He'd have to have made a deal with *Bormal* himself to have survived up there, and now he's leading squadrons of the Palace Guard?" Jassnik shook his head.

"Maybe he did make a deal with *Bormal*," Anthron said soberly.

Rhailk reared up and extended his wings, scrapping the tips on either side of the cavern at full stretch."It is time to rest. Do not touch anything." The great wyrm circled the cavern several times before curling up, his sharp golden tail resting over his snout. A faint amber glow come from his eyes, warning the group that Rhailk may have an eye on them still.

The group rested uncomfortably until Jassnik guessed that it was about two hours before midday.

"Do you know any short cuts out of here?" Jelik asked the lethargic dragon.

"If thou can fly," Rhailk lazily nodded his massive head towards the hole in the ceiling."The passage empties into the fields many miles east of the Keep."

All eyes shifted to Sudenora. He shrugged."I think I can do it."

They gathered in a circle on top of the pile of gold, and linked hands. Sudenora spoke several words, and they began to rise off the ground slowly. They had nearly cleared the lip of the hole when they shuddered suddenly and dropped several feet. Sweat appeared on the Elementalist's brow as he regained control. Rhailk merely looked on with interest. Sudenora forced them up the last few feet, then shifted them to rest upon the stone platform which signified the dragon's flight tunnel. Sudenora sat nursing a headache, breathing heavily, while Karlos saw to him.

The tunnel was massive, one hundred feet wide, forty feet high. The stones were smooth and charred, with the exception of the irregular markings that signified where the dragon's immense tail had scrapped the surface.

"I'm intrigued to know where this comes out, and how it remains hidden," Jassnik exclaimed.

Looking back over the lip, Anthron judged Sudenora had lifted them at least sixty feet.

The others gathered around the lip and stared down at the massive gold dragon.

"A beautiful creature." Gen'vieve murmured.

"We're not likely to ever see another dragon in this lifetime." Jelik mused.

Anthron waved down to Rhailk."Thank you." he called.

The great wyrm nodded, then rested his head once again and closed his amber eyes.

* * * * * * * * *

Smit-Myer Crysin watched the seven figures leave the valley through eyes which were temporarily enhanced for binocular vision. He closed his eyes and rubbed his Will storing ring once more, and whispered:"Closer." Again he opened his eyes and the group was closer. They had a new member with them now, a dirty but attractive brunette. He stroked his little moustache and beard as he considered his options.

First he could summon the butcher Carl Mort'l here with the Cyermyth militia. He could see the party was ill equipped, and could be easily taken.

Second. Yes, he thought, what is second? The assassin let out a long sigh. Tracking people who had escaped Selection was easy when he'd been in it for the money. But since the last time he had shared Quabeth White's bed, she had woken something in him which the assassin thought long dead.

Smit-Myer Crysin wanted to retire.

He shook his head with a laugh. Him with children? Maybe. He probably already had several children to whores around Sarophia. But he certainly couldn't just tell his current employer he was dissolving their contract. No, there had to be another way out.

Crysin followed the group at a respectable distance, until he reached the valley they had emerged from. Magic had told him to seek them around here, now he wanted to know how they had appeared here. Urgar Keep was still in utter chaos.

Massive charred rocks littered the valley floor. He dissolved his ring's ability as he descended through the grass to the small valley floor. He nimbly climbed a rock and looked. Nothing. It appeared as if the party had been transported here magically.

As he turned to continue after the group, his attuned sense of smell picked up something. He could smell saffron and incense.

CHAPTER FOURTEEN

It continued to rain.

They had spent a miserable night huddled together under a thicket of pines, exposed to the late autumn southerly. Only Jelik and Jassnik had their packs, and neither carried a tent.

Anthron flexed his cold limbs. His oil-treated cloak was soaked through, and he chattered as the wind bit through him.

"So," Karlos wiped rain from the tip of his nose."Where to?"

"To Cyermyth?" Kielmark asked Jassnik. Anthron had informed the group of Jassnik's royal ties and the source of the black armoured knights.

Jassnik shrugged."Perhaps. We could march up to Queen Kilandra and demand to know what she's doing sending the Palace Guard to Sarophia to aid the Selection."

"What is it we need to know," Anthron started."First, we need to know what the Cyermyth Knights have to do with the Selection - and what Queen Kilandra has to do with it. The dragon may be right in saying the Second Great War might be brewing.

"Secondly, we need to find out more about Xycermon. Rhailk said that it was not being sought as a weapon of destruction, but as some kind of summoning tool."

"Platown will have something on it I'm sure." Jassnik shivered. Platown, also known as The Great Library City, was where any seeker of knowledge went.

"So, what does it summon?" Sudenora echoed their thoughts."Does it require all the daggers together? And, are there any other components the summoning needs?"

"Good point," Karlos nodded."Sounds like *Bormal's* work, if you ask me. Spells of conjuration usually require a special candle too. If we can find out what else this spell needs, maybe we can destroy it..."

"Yes," Jassnik agreed."I think we can safely say we are heading to

Platown then."

"We should also find out what we can about this 'ring'." Jelik stated, holding up his gloved right hand.

"In Platown." Gen'vieve smiled, answering for Jassnik. Jassnik closed his mouth and nodded.

"We also have our original task." Kielmark said.

Karlos stepped next to the dark Arrolokian."We are still meant to be making for the other village in Sambethe, to question Wilse about his escaping Selection and prepare for the Ithren relocation." he chimed.

Kielmark continued."I have often thought of our original quest with guilt that we have forgotten it, and wish to complete it before burdening ourselves with new tasks."

Sudenora nodded."I agree, but still think going to Platown to be more important."

"Okay," Anthron said."Let's have a vote - who is for going straight to Sambethe from here?"

Kielmark, Karlos, and Jelik raised their hands. Hesitantly Anthron raised his own hand.

Gen'vieve, dressed in Jelik's spare tunic and trousers, shrugged."I don't mind where we go. I'm along for the ride, and even this rain is better than a year in the Urgar Keep dungeon."

Jassnik nodded."Obviously I wasn't part of your original goal, but I completely understand your need to tidy it up."

Sudenora folded his arms with a frown."Fine." he said.

Jassnik looked to Gen'vieve."I'm pleased that you've decided to join us, although it may not be very safe..." He looked doubtful.

Gen'vieve let out a laugh, her face lighting up, making her look quite attractive, Jassnik thought."I can take care of myself Jass. Give me a dagger and I'll be fine."

Jassnik looked to Jelik who nodded, flicked his wrist, and produced a long thin dirk. He pulled up his sleeve to unbuckle the sheath, then handed it to Gen'vieve.

"How many daggers do you carry, Jel?" Gen'vieve teased as she tucked the dirk into her belt.

Jelik grunted before shaking out his soaking cloak.

"Right, from Sambethe we can head to Platown then," Jassnik said.

"From there, we could continue on into the Kingdom Territories, to Trendrik," Karlos offered.

Jelik frowned at the Healer."Why?"

"We aren't outlaws, even though it seems like we are." Karlos explained.

Jelik nodded."So you think we might be able to muster an escort of sorts..."

"...and maybe visit Cyermyth..." Karlos continued.

"...and maybe start a war?" Gen'vieve added.

Jassnik shook his head."We would call it an escort to ensure an urgent message for Queen Kilandra does not fall astray. Now, let's be off to Sambethe. Perhaps if we're lucky, we may see an Elf, or even *Elvenméson!*"

* * * * * * * * * *

They met a travelling merchant on the evening of the second night out from Urgar, who had managed to lose his bearing. He was a young bald man dressed in brightly coloured silks, riding atop a covered horse drawn wagon.

"Greetings, my name is Flanc Du Mur." The bald merchant jumped from the platform of his wagon, and extravagantly bowed low in the rain.

"Pleased to make your acquaintance," Anthron nodded."I am Lothor, and these are my friends." Referring to the name he'd made up, he swept his arm in an arc behind him.

"Well met Lothor. I seem to have gotten a little lost," Flanc Du Mur said shyly."Do you know if I'm on track for Carson? My map was ruined in this rain."

Anthron looked to Jassnik, the most travelled person amongst them with the best sense of direction. Jassnik shook his head."You're currently heading north west. You should really head west until you hit the Kutporn road, then follow it south west until you reach the fork. Head directly west along the Carson-Urgar Keep road and you'd have to be blind to miss it."

The merchant bowed."Thank you, kind sirs. I would surely have ended up in Panthorian before reaching Carson without your aid. There are not many travellers out in this weather."

"What do you sell, merchant?" Jelik asked, quickly adding,"Our last job robbed us of much of our equipment."

Flanc Du Mur's eyes lit up."I have a wide range of equipment, which would be of much use to a group such as yours." He began unfastening the weatherproof cloth that covered his goods, and pulled it away. Underneath were all sorts of useless junk, as well as clothes and weapons.

"What do you mean 'a group such as ours'?" Karlos inquired.

"Oh," Flanc Du Mur exclaimed."I mean no offence! I merely considered yourselves veteran mercenaries..."

Karlos nodded.

"How much for that hat?" Jassnik asked Flanc as he dusted off a wide brimmed light blue hat with a single green feather attached.

Flanc scratched his chin for a moment before replying."Five coppers."

"Three," Jassnik retorted immediately.

"Four," Flanc said a little less sure of himself.

"Three or nothing," Jassnik replied.

"Let us see if any other items are to be purchased before I agree to such a demand."

Jelik put aside an advanced lock pick set in a rolled up leather case. Anthron found a sharpening stone and a long dagger. Sudenora picked out an oil-treated brown cloak and a silver dagger, and Gen'vieve selected a provocative pair of tight fitting black leather leggings that exposed an inch of flesh down the outside of each leg, a navy tunic and black woollen cloak. Gen'vieve was quite irritated that she couldn't find a pair of boots to fit her. Karlos found a large oil-treated piece of material, which could be used as a makeshift tent. Kielmark just stood waiting in the rain.

"For all this," Flanc Du Mur said,"I require two silvers and eight coppers. This is non-negotiable."

Jassnik smiled."Everything's negotiable."

Flanc Du Mur began packing the equipment back into his wagon.

Jassnik thought a moment."How about a trade? I've collected some items you may find of..." His voice trailed off as the merchant continued to pack.

Anthron put his hand on the merchant's arm."We agree."

Jassnik frowned as he paid the smiling merchant. Flanc Du Mur bowed low once more, before seizing the reins and mounting himself back up in his wagon."A pleasure, my friends, and thank you for the directions." He flicked the reins lightly, and the dark horse began to trot away to the west.

"He would have dropped his prices." Jassnik muttered.

"A merchant has to make a living," Anthron replied."However, we're nearly out of money now."

"Finding money isn't hard," Jassnik said."It's the spending of it which irritates me."

* * * * * * * * *

Large ancient branches covered with gray beards of lichen arched high overhead, shielding the party from most of the late morning rain. Hundreds of faintly perceived paths wound away from the track they followed.

It was the fourth morning since their escape from the Urgar Dungeon, and it continued to rain. They had reached the Sambethe Forest just before dusk, and had camped under the trees and waterproofed canvas. It was close to noon and they were already deep in the forest, but had not seen any sign of Men or Elf.

"Do we know where this village is?" Jassnik asked Anthron.

Anthron shook his head."Not exactly, no. From what Karter told us, we would be guided, and I think that guide was Anthea."

Jassnik scoffed."That's pretty vague." He was particularly tired and hungry.

"Are we going in circles?" Sudenora asked."I know it seems that we're walking in a straight line into the heart of the forest, but sometimes I feel disoriented - almost like we've been spun about several times without us noticing."

Karlos nodded."I've noticed that too. The leaves are green, then I see the odd gold-coloured leaf. My stomach twists and we're walking into the ordinary trees again."

"I can hear whispers all around us," Gen'vieve said."Non-threatening thoughts."

Jassnik stopped and looked around."I think I know what's going on." he mused.

"Elves?" Kielmark asked.

Before Jassnik could answer, a voice from within the trees spoke. It was a male voice with a musical tone, and it seemed to be coming from all around them."You are correct, travellers." From behind trees as close as ten feet away, ten figures revealed themselves. The speaker looked like a young man in his mid-twenties, with pale blonde hair from which protruded the lobeless pointy ears of an Elf. He was dressed in brown leathers and a gray cloak that seemed to shift colours and shades with the light. On his belt he wore a long sword, and over his shoulder was a bow and a quiver of arrows. His clear blue eyes studied each of the party in turn as he approached silently, his smooth tanned face concealing his expression. Anthron assessed that he was about the same height as him. The nine other Elves were dressed in similar attire, with several hanging back with an arrow notched to their bowstrings.

The blonde Elf quickly glanced at Jelik's Elven chain then bowed gracefully, never taking his eyes from the party."I am called Auréle," the Elf smiled warmly."You are perceptive to notice the deceptions of our home."

Anthron bowed awkwardly."I am Anthron Mikolnic." He gestured behind him, introducing each in order."These are my companions, Jassnik Corline, Gen'vieve Conear, Jelik Qualis, Sudenora Kiltorn, Karlos Brekon, and Kielmark of Arrolok." As they were introduced, each inclined their heads or bowed. Auréle nodded politely in turn to the companions, then said;"We have learnt much from you as you have walked backwards and forwards across our doorstep. We understand that you are here to visit with the village of Men within Sambethe, and that you have no mean intent. Many eyes are turned towards you, but are blind within our home. Here you are safe - or so we thought." Anthron noticed a tear rolling down the cheek of the Elf to Auréle's right. Auréle continued."We have lived here since *deastr' auÉ terrÉ-seisme* - The Earthquake of Change - and nothing has endangered us for nearly three thousand two hundred years. But now we are aware of *Le Shoft Tear's Kra* - what Men refer to as The Selection. This has forced us to communicate with Men again, and this has caused us harm. But come, we will guide you through the threshold you have been circling where you may rest, eat and meet with our King. King Armand will talk more of these things."

Guided by the Elves, the party travelled without any disorientation. Anthron learned from Auréle that the Elven City was protected by ancient magic, which would turn away any uninvited or those unaccompanied by an Elf. Those that searched for the city by themselves would circle in their footsteps for a day before becoming overcome with drowsiness and fall into an eternal sleep. Of course the Elves were not cruel Auréle assured, and there were always patrols of Elves which would either lead the travellers away or guide them into the city."Until recently, that is," Auréle said coldly."But again, I am ahead of myself."

Each of the party walked with an Elf, while the three other Elves shadowed them silently amongst the trees.

The Elf that accompanied Jassnik was called Antaeus. He was Auréle's nephew. They looked quite similar, even though there was a large age gap between them. Jassnik considered that they looked more like brothers.

They rested after several hours under a clearing of massive trees that reached up higher than any building Anthron had ever seen. Each branch of these trees was adorned with large full green leaves and every third leaf was a golden colour. Through the clearing swept a stream, the sound of which Anthron found soothing.

Auréle noted Anthron studying their surroundings."I forget strangers are in awe of our home. These trees are called *arbré Auréle*, which means golden trees. As you may have guessed, I was named after them. They shelter us from the rain, let in the sunlight, and when the sun sinks the golden leaves let out a faint light. We are planting more *arbré Auréle* as they are declining in number. This stream - which was once the *rivi're aué refraíce* - can refresh even the weariest of travellers."

After drinking and bathing their feet from the stream, the group set off again full of energy and at a much faster pace."We aim to reach *Elvenméson* before dark," said Auréle.

* * * * * * * * * *

 The sun began to sink behind the thick storm clouds as they moved steadily through the heavy forest, and the golden leaves of the *arbré Auréle* were beginning to let out a faint yellow glow.

Then they entered a massive clearing - *Elvenméson* - the Elven City.

Staring up, Anthron saw hanging paths spanning between the high branches of the *arbré Auréle*. They heard the soft sounds of an occupied community. The golden leaves illuminated the clearing, displaying hundreds of Elves moving quickly about. To their left Anthron saw several Elves attaching red feathers to what looked like another batch of long arrow shafts. To their right was a recently returned hunting party skinning their game. In the centre of the clearing was the largest tree any of them had ever seen before - an enormous *arbré Auréle* oak with a circling stairway carved into the trunk.

The sight overwhelmed them. Anthron stood breathless, feeling the magic of *Elvenméson* wash over him. Sudenora gasped, while Gen'vieve held Jassnik and wept. Karlos and Kielmark stood in silent wonder and Jelik nodded with approval.

"If you'll follow me," Auréle said as he once again took the lead, heading for the giant tree stairway.

The Elves that had guided them dispersed, with the exception of

Antaeus who smiled and brought up the rear of the group."I hope you don't mind heights." he smiled to Kielmark as they began their climb.

Karlos puffed and dabbed his forehead with a scarf after he had lost count how many little bridges he had passed. He let out a long sigh before continuing to climb the stairs."Just how high are we?"

Auréle said;"In your city terms, we would be roughly thirty stories up." They reached a rope bridge that was wider than the countless others they had passed on their journey up the outside of the giant *arbré Auréle*, able to fit three of them side by side."And we are here." Auréle motioned for the group to follow the hanging pathway so far above the forest floor.

Gen'vieve looked over the edge of the bridge and instantly went pale. She could see the tops of some of the shorter trees in the Elven City, a network of passages and ropes spanning between trees, and further down she saw the ground. Her knees went weak, and she began to sweat. Jassnik slipped an arm around her waist to support her.

"It's so far down..." she stammered."Just rope and wood holding us up..."

Sudenora frowned."You had no problem when I levitated us a few days ago."

Auréle and Antaeus exchanged smiles. It was normal for any non-Elf that had come to meet the King to be uncomfortable with the height.

Gen'vieve madly clutched at Jassnik as he tried to keep her in the middle of the rope bridge."Yes," Jassnik said."But she mustn't have looked down then."

Karlos moved up to Gen'vieve, and placed his hand upon her forehead as he spoke quietly. Within seconds of him removing his hand, Gen'vieve had been pacified. Jassnik wiped tears from her eyes and she smiled."I'm okay now," she said slowly."Thanks Karlos."

Auréle nodded his approval to Karlos at handling Gen'vieve's fear of heights."King Armand awaits us straight ahead." Auréle waved his hand towards the other end of the rope bridge where a large circular platform begun, which led to a small hall. Anthron assessed the platform to be about forty feet in diameter, the wooden structure taking up most of that space - leaving three feet of space around the entire building. At the large double doors stood two Elven guards, dressed in gray cloaks, mesh chain, and a mix of green and brown leathers. They wore brilliant long swords at their hips, and a long bow lay within arms reach of either of them, accompanied by a full quiver of long shafted arrows. Their boots were of soft brown leather, which folded over to finish just under their knees. Their faces were tanned and pleasant. They snapped to attention and bowed as Auréle stepped from the bridge to the platform.

Auréle bowed in response."Please tell King Armand that our guests and I have arrived."

The Elf with a ponytail nodded and quickly entered through the doorway, returning shortly afterwards."He will see you," the Elf returned to his post.

Auréle led the seven companions into the hall, with Antaeus closing the doors behind them.

The first thing Anthron noticed when he entered the hall was the warmth. To his left was an impressive range of bows, from a short bow right through to a great bow which was well over six feet long. Each bow was unstrung. In between each bow was a full quiver of red feathered arrows, and unsheathed blades of various sizes. Anthron thought it odd that several of the swords would require two hands, and couldn't picture a slender Elf wielding it with ease.

Along the right wall of the hall ran a long table, atop which were large polished silver candelabras, flasks of wine, mugs, and fruit. Above the table there was an amazingly detailed mural, depicting Elves in brown and green at war against other Elves and Men wearing dark armour. It clearly showed the Elves in woodland colours being massacred.

At the end of the hall sat an Elf wearing long red robes upon a simple throne. He looked older than the other Elves he'd seen, with wrinkles around his eyes, but was still unlikely to be considered old amongst Elves. Atop his blonde white hair sat a simple wreath and his alert green eyes studied the group as they were brought forward. Next to his was an empty throne.

Behind King Armand stood four Elves, dressed much as the sentries at the door, and Anthron noted there were four more at the back of the hall, hidden from view upon first entering.

King Armand pursed his lips and drummed his fingertips together in thought as he silently deliberated. Finally, he looked to Auréle. To Anthron's surprise, his voice was strong and clear."My son, explain why you have brought Men to my court."

Auréle shifted uncomfortably under his father's gaze."These Men..." Gen'vieve cleared her throat at the comment, but Auréle continued."...have been involved in *Le Shoft Tear's Kra.*" One of the Elven guards at the back of the hall took a sharp intake of breath, and each sentry visibly tensed. Armand waved for Auréle to continue."I have told them nothing of our clashes, nor of our knowledge on the subject. They refer to this as 'The Selection'. From what we understand, they escaped *Le Shoft Tear's Kra* about seven months ago, and have uncovered much. I see that we can benefit from aiding these Men." Auréle finished with a bow and waited for King Armand to acknowledge him with a nod, allowing Auréle to retreat to the side of the hall.

Armand muttered something, and Anthron felt the hairs on the back of his neck raise. As Armand swept his hand across the room, Anthron found that he was unable to move anything beside his head. Twisting in alarm, he managed to see Gen'vieve and Karlos similarly stuck in place.

King Armand began drumming his fingertips together again."I'm not sure what to make of you, or whether you are dangerous yet. I'll not apologize for my caution. You..." Armand pointed to Anthron."Please tell me your involvement with 'the Selection', and why your companion is wearing armour of our kin."

Anthron began to sweat under the piercing gaze of the King of Elves in *Elvenméson*. Anthron began;"As Auréle has pointed out, the five of us," Anthron attempted to nod behind him. Armand lazily waved his hand. Anthron felt the tingles of magic down his back, then he alone was free to move. Anthron pointed to Jelik, Kielmark, Sudenora and Karlos."We were taken from our homes just over seven months ago. We were drugged, and thrown in wheeled prison cages used to transport criminals. Between Decton and Carson we manage to escape, stole some weapons, and most of us managed to make it into the Ithren Forest," Anthron still felt a pang on sorrow for his childhood friend Harson. Armand seemed to understand Anthron's pause, and waited quietly."Once we'd killed or lost the guard that had chased us, we headed north through Ithren, and we found..." Anthron paused again."We found a village."

Armand leaned forward."Like the one that was here in Sambethe? Of Men?"

"Was?" Anthron blurted.

Armand nodded slowly."It was raided and destroyed two weeks ago, by orcs and Men. I sent three dozen archers to their aid. Only one made it back. His dying words were telling tales of necromancy - the walking dead. One of our kin that died was seen raising after life and attacking our own."

The image of Scotus flashed before Anthron. Armand raised his eyebrows at Anthron's response."But I see this is not new to you. Please continue."

Anthron swallowed hard. He looked at each of his companions, Karlos and Kielmark particularly looked defeated. Turning back to the King he then continued."We were trained at the village in Ithren, by some people who may well have escaped The Selection. We were given the mission to come to Sambethe and question a man named Wilse..."

There was a sudden discussion between the guards behind the King. From behind his throne stepped an elderly Elf with the assistance of an iron shod staff, wearing gray robes. His thin lined face looked tired, and his thin light brown hair hung loosely down his back. He shuffled close to Armand's ear and began speaking quickly in Elvish. After several minutes of hushed words, the elderly Elf which Anthron assumed was the King's adviser shuffled to the side and leaned heavily on his staff.

Armand looked back to Anthron."This Wilse you speak of was invited into their village. He was a spy, an assassin, sent to learn what he could about the village, then alert his superiors. He was the key to the downfall of the village."

Anthron stood still. He didn't know what to say. Were they to blame for the destruction of the village because they took too long? Would they have picked that Wilse was a fake? He shook his head as it began to ache.

King Armand smiled weakly and waved his hand, releasing the group from his enchantment."Please continue."

Anthron swallowed slowly as he looked around the group then continued their story."We left Ithren due east, following the road to Lotheric. Our intention was to cross the Splitting River there, and follow the coast south, then north east from there into Sambethe."

King Armand nodded; agreeing this was a fairly normal course.

"However, when we reached Lotheric we realized the town had been hit by the Selection particularly badly," Anthron decided to leave out the orc ambush."The towns' children had gone. We found a body under the bridge spanning the Splitting River - our introduction to the necromancy you referred to. We were then enrolled by the town to venture up to the Twelve Peaks to search for signs of their children - since it was a logical thought that the body we'd found may have come from there."

Again King Armand nodded quietly as his adviser quickly whispered in his ear.

"At the Twelve Peaks, we found a tunnel - it could have been a mine. There we were attacked by half a dozen dead men...rotting...maggots..."

Jelik decided not to make an issue of Anthea's betrayal - just yet.

Armand nodded again, his fingertips drumming together."Please continue." he said again.

"We set fire to them, which caused a reaction with the red dust found on the peaks. We managed to escape before the tunnel exploded."

The King's adviser pursed his lips impatiently and stepped closer to Anthron. King Armand motioned to the gray robed Elf."Let me introduce Majaré, oldest living Elf in Sarophia, wisest amongst us."

Majaré leaned heavily on his staff as he shuffled towards Anthron. Anthron thought that the old Elf would have been tall and proud in his youth. Majaré looked up at Anthron."Was the creature known as Gwyerson Dernas destroyed in the explosion?"

CHAPTER FIFTEEN

The hall was silent.

Anthron stared down at the King's adviser."Just how much do you know?"

Majaré's wrinkled face drew back in a half smile, but it was King Armand who answered."We have kept information from you until you proved you were no threat. We acknowledge that you have been speaking the truth, and mean us no harm." Armand paused, sizing up what he was going to say next as he tapped his fingertips together. After taking a deep breath he continued."You know the name Anthea Fleké?"

Anthron's jaw dropped. He nodded dumbly.

"She is here," Armand said."Four days ago her fever broke, and our healers could confirm she would live. She talked much of your group. She too wept when she heard of the destruction of the village."

"She's got a lot to answer for," Jelik shot through clenched teeth."She betrayed us!"

Anthron's eyes flashed with anger, going as far as putting his hand on his sword before he realised - Anthea was alive! She was here! She would sort out for good what happened in the Twelve Peaks, and Anthron was certain that it would be Jelik who'd be left behind...

King Armand held his hand up for silence."Enough. Clearly we must discuss matters further." Armand indicated toward the table furnished with fruit and wine."Please refresh yourselves. Moraglin shall show you to your quarters, where you may rest and discuss what you may between yourselves. We shall meet here again at sunrise tomorrow - Anthea will join us if she feels fit."

* * * * * * * * * *

"I can find out the real story." Gen'vieve said as she took another bite of an apple.

161

Moraglin, in the garb of a sentry with auburn hair, had led the group half way back down the enormous tree and across several rope bridges to a small hut. It was warm, with a dozen cots, a large table and chairs. Anthron noted that the Elf positioned himself just outside their door.

Jassnik nodded."Gen could read Anthea's thoughts during the meeting."

Anthron had to admit that it was a good idea."I don't have any other ideas."

Karlos nursed his head in his hands."If only we hadn't gone to the Twelve Peaks..."

Kielmark flexed his mended right arm, still tender from its recent break."We need to stop looking at what we should have done, and look at what we can do now."

"If we share everything we've learnt with the Elves, I think we can build a better picture of what's happening." Sudenora said.

Jelik stopped pacing and held up his gloved right hand."Do we tell them about this?" he whispered harshly.

Anthron shrugged."I don't see why not..."

Sudden sounds of activity outside made Anthron pause. Jelik, who was closest to the door, stepped outside. Moraglin regarded Jelik closely.

"What's happening?" Jelik asked, looking far below at what looked like the arrival of a hunting party in the golden glow.

The Elf studied the thief's Elven chain and bracers."One of our patrols discovered a band of orcs fairly close by. They are somehow moving through our forest's magic."

"Can we assist in some way?" Jelik offered while studying the motions of a community used to working together.

Moraglin raised his eyebrows. Peering into the hut he examined the group. Nodding, he said to Jelik;"You, the short one in blue, and him," he indicated to Anthron. The Elf left the hut, letting out a bird whistle. It was answered immediately from the ground."If you three want to head back that way." he pointed towards the enormous *arbré Auréle*."A guide is on their way to take you down. They will give you boots and cloaks so you will have a chance to move undetected through the forest."

Jassnik stopped in front of the Elf. Poking at his blue silk shirt, he said;"I think I will need a little more than a cloak and boots if we're snooping in the forest." The Elf let a smile escape.

The Elf pointed to the forest floor. Jassnik nodded, and the three set off across one of the many rope bridges leading to the great *arbré Auréle*.

Sudenora looked to Gen'vieve, Karlos and Kielmark."What about us?" He made towards the door.

Moraglin raised his hand."Please. Use this time to rest. I selected those three for their ability to keep up with an Elven scouting party."

Sudenora frowned."The orcs will hear Anthron from a mile away."

The Elf shook his head."Not when he's wearing a pair of Elven made boots."

* * * * * * * * * *

The forest floor was a hive of organised activity. Under the glow of the *arbré Auréle*, Anthron, Jelik and Jassnik were escorted to a weathered Elf of larger build. He stood tall, with a large chest and powerful arms. He was clothed how Jelik had seen human rangers attired: fitted brown leather pants with tall soft leather boots. His green tunic was covered with light brown leather armour and a gray cloak that seemed to reflect the colours of the forest around them. Upon his left hip he wore two swords, his right sporting a large hunting knife. Over his shoulder he carried a longbow and quiver. His tanned face had a strong jaw, and his gray eyes watched them approach. Something else stood out about this Elf, Jelik thought - not only was he bigger, but he was the first Elf he'd seen in *Elvenméson* with dark brown hair.

"I hear you're coming with us," the large Elf said, his voice strong and clear.

Jelik looked to his companions before replying."We are here to help however we can."

The dark haired Elf appraised the three."Name's Zéale, Hunt Master of *Elvenméson*. We have a band of orcs coming this way. Looks like they have one of us with them as their prisoner. That must be why they have not been turned around by the forest," he motioned to an Elf nearby who was dressed like Zéale."Bring boots and cloaks for these three." Zéale continued to study the group."Also bring some tunics and breeches, and some weapons."

Jassnik nodded his appreciation.

Zéale pointed at Jelik's chain mesh armour and bracers."Where did you get them?" he said pointedly.

"Ah," Jelik started. After deciding the truth wouldn't hurt, he said;"These items were gifted to me by a dragon named Rhailk."

The Hunt Master nodded, then looked disinterested as he waited.

The Elf returned shortly carrying a bundle."I have brought a selection," he eyed Anthron."I was unsure of size."

Another Elf followed soon after carrying several bows, quivers and swords.

"Please equip yourselves with what we have here," Zéale said, pointing to a small hut close by on the forest floor."You may change in there. We shall be ready to leave very soon." Zéale then nodded and went to supervise the equipping of his tracking party.

Several minutes later Anthron, Jelik and Jassnik emerged from the hut. They were dressed as Elves, wearing brown leather pants and green tunics. Anthron found that he was too big to fit any of the breeches comfortably - even the tunic he wore clung to him. Their cloaks were warm and light with large hoods. They were gray to look from sideview, but to look at straight on, their colours changed to blend with their surroundings. Their boots were made of soft tan coloured leather with a padded sole. They came up over the knee, then they were folded back just under the knee. Anthron wasn't used to such tall soft boots.

Anthron wore his sapphire-encrusted sword under his cloak, and had decided not to carry a bow. Jelik carried a slender Elven long sword as well as his short sword, with a bow and quiver over his shoulder. His Elven chain was hidden from view beneath his tunic. Jassnik also wore an Elven long sword, his shaft mace hidden from view.

"Ah," exclaimed Zéale as they approached."Here come the Elves." Antaeus and several other Elves standing around the Hunt Master let out a laugh."Follow me." The Hunt Master placed his bow in his left hand and set off at a fast jog, easily loping down a faint track. Antaeus and nine other Elves followed. Anthron, Jelik and Jassnik set off as another two Elves closed in behind.

Anthron noticed how tireless the Elves seemed. They ran silently, their attention alert. Anthron found himself panting within a short time, the Elves pace being expeditious. The blonde fighter was impressed at the silence of his footfalls whilst wearing Elven boots. After thirty minutes they stopped for a short rest. Anthron sat catching his breath as Jelik and Jassnik stood with their hands on their heads, sucking in the air.

"That was a workout," Jassnik puffed.

Zéale smiled."You have done well to keep up. We have always moved through the forest as such."

Anthron was amazed that none of the Elves even looked winded. The current rest was for their benefit alone. Looking around, Anthron noticed that, although it was evening, how green and fresh smelling the forest was. He was surprised at how alive the forest sounded. Taking a deep breath, he felt relaxed and peaceful. He nodded."Okay," He pushed himself to his feet."I'm ready when you are."

Jelik winced as he rubbed his side."Haven't had to run like that since the streets of Smazorok."

Jassnik let out a breath and wiped his face."Ready."

The Elven patrol paused again after another twenty minutes. Zéale motioned silently for two Elves to move off to the left, and another two to the right. The four Elves disappeared silently into the bush.

Zéale unsheathed his two swords, and crept closer to Anthron, Jelik and Jassnik."There is a party of two score orcs approaching, with an Elven hostage amongst them."

Anthron nodded, and withdrew his sword. Jassnik did likewise, as Jelik withdrew two daggers. Antaeus motioned that they should follow him off the path. They moved about twelve feet from the path, crouched and waited for the approaching company of orcs and their Elven prisoner.

* * * * * * * * * *

Sudenora stifled a yawn.

"Should get some rest," Karlos said, stretched out on one of the cots. He lazily picked at his teeth after eating an orange.

Kielmark shook his head."I can't rest either," He walked towards the door."I feel filled with anticipation."

"It's the thought of meeting Anthea again," Karlos said."I'm looking forward to it too."

Kielmark waved out to Moraglin. As the Elf approached, the Arrolokian said;"Are we able to re-equip ourselves with weapons?"

Moraglin noted that Kielmark, Sudenora, and Karlos carried no weapons. Gen'vieve only wore the long dirk Jelik had given her. Nodding, Moraglin said;"What are your weapons of choice?"

"A quick blade for myself," Kielmark made the motion of slicing quickly."A sabre, rapier, light long sword...Karlos?"

Karlos lay on his back, his hand making sluggish clubbing motions."Something to bash with..."

"A staff or sword." Sudenora continued his pacing.

Moraglin looked to Gen'vieve, who was quietly stretching on the floor."I'd really like some footwear."

Moraglin nodded once, then departed.

"What do you think happened between Jelik and Anthea in the Twelve Peaks?" asked Kielmark once Moraglin was gone. They had all been wondering the same thing for the last hour, but hadn't voiced it.

Karlos shrugged."Don't know. I believe Jelik, but..."

"But don't think Anthea would have attacked him?" Sudenora finished.

"Yeah," Karlos said, a little less sure of himself."They did start to fight a lot..." The Healer propped himself up on an elbow.

"I think we would have picked it up if Anthea was actually working against us..." Kielmark mused.

"What do we really know about Jelik?" Sudenora scratched absently at his dark whiskers.

"She was very sincere, she took us to the village. Without her, we may have made it back to Izonda...untrained..." Kielmark continued.

"But home." Sudenora snapped.

"All you've done for the last seven months is moan about going home," Karlos fumed."I've known Jelik for a few years, and can vouch for him!"

Gen'vieve let out a sigh."It normally takes a lot longer for cabin fever to kick in," she said quietly."As we'd discussed with the others earlier, I'll find out what happened back in the Twelve Peaks. When you ask her questions regarding it, I'll scan her surface thoughts. Until then..." The attractive brunette let her sentence fall.

Kielmark nodded, and stepped outside to wait for Moraglin's return. Karlos looked at Sudenora, who was studying the floor with great detail.

"Sorry." Karlos said to the Elementalist.

Sudenora looked up and smiled."Me too. I know we can trust Jelik...it's just..."

"It's not home?" Karlos finished.

Sudenora looked away as his eyes rimmed.

"What is it?" Karlos sat up."You don't have to say anything if you don't want to..."

Sudenora smiled weakly."This has been bothering me more as time has gone on, as my guilt continues to nag at me," A tear overflowed Sudenora's eyelid, rolling down his cheek, which he quickly wiped away."Before I was taken from Eugernok, I was with this girl, Carlae..."

"Oh, so it's about a girl." Karlos exclaimed with relief.

"Karlos!" Sudenora hissed quietly, his eyes flitting to see if Kielmark or Gen'vieve were listening."She was with child!"

The Healer looked stunned."Are you sure?" Karlos asked little above a whisper.

"Look, I'm positive Karlos. I just don't know what to do. This Selection thing messed everything up. I've tried to think of everything. If I go back, I would endanger Carlae - and our child. I don't even know if it's born yet, or if it's a boy or a girl."

"Do you want my advice?" Karlos asked.

Sudenora nodded as he wiped another tear away.

"Well, when we get to the next city, why don't you send a letter to Carlae and tell her you're fine, tell her you miss her, etc. The main thing is to tell her that you haven't abandoned her and you and your companions have vowed not to stop until you have made the world a safer place. Something like that."

Sudenora smiled and nodded."You're right, I..."

Sudenora stopped as Kielmark returned quickly, making Gen'vieve jump.

"Something's wrong," the dark man said."I can hear fighting below."

"Fighting? Here?" Gen'vieve exclaimed, climbing to her feet."Isn't anywhere sacred?"

Outside they could hear urgent whistles sounding though the trees. Suddenly Moraglin appeared in the doorway."Quickly," he passed a sheathed Elven blade to Kielmark, Karlos and Sudenora."We are under attack. Your assistance would be appreciated."

Gen'vieve looked hopefully for a pair of boots. Moraglin shook his head in apology."I'm sorry, but there was no time for your footwear." The Elf motioned for them to follow him. Gen'vieve kept her eyes locked straight ahead as she crossed a rope bridge.

"Who can attack you here? Other Elves?" Kielmark asked, wishing he was again wearing his armour. At least he had the silver helm from Rhailk's horde.

Moraglin stopped."Other Elves?" Kielmark could tell that his eyes were rimming under the soft golden glow of the *arbré Auréle*."Yes, our kin that were slain weeks ago have led orcs and renegade Men into our home."

* * * * * * * * * *

The forest was still. Antaeus notched an arrow, and adjusted his quiver for better access. Jelik lightly stabbed two red feathered arrows into the ground before him, and notched a third. Anthron crouched with his black bladed sword drawn, next to Jassnik.

They waited silently.

The orcs came into view, stooping as they jogged through the forest as quietly as they could. Their red eyes darted nervously, scanning the trees for possible ambush. To Anthron's surprise the orcs seemed to move through the trees with ease in the dark, their brownish green coloured skin helping them blend in. They wore no helmets, and their bristly black hair was either tied back or roughly cut off. They wore blood stained green tunics over their scale armour, carried small wooden shields, and each held a wicked looking curved sword. Their dark green cloaks trailed behind them as they ran. Anthron assessed that this group had been specially selected and dressed in camouflage for their ability to manoeuver through the forest.

As the first ten orcs past them, Anthron could see the Elf Zéale had referred to. The Elf was dressed as one of Zéale's company, running amongst the orcs with his hands tied. The hood of his cloak was pulled over his face, so Antaeus indicated that he didn't know who the Elf was. Anthron frowned as he saw that the Elf wore a sword as his hip, even though his hands were tied. Concentrating, the blonde warrior could make out a dull gray colour surrounding the Elf. Inhaling quickly, he felt his blood run cold. He had seen a gray aura only once before - around Gwyerson Dernas.

The first orcs were close to leaving the area, just as the last orcs became visible. Anthron heard a sharp whistle, and Antaeus nodded to Jelik. They released their taut bowstrings; the long shafts speeding through the forest. Antaeus's arrow instantly killed an orc as Jelik's missile struck an orc in the shoulder. Within seconds, another twelve orcs fell dead or injured. The seven remaining orcs moved immediately, one cutting the rope tying the Elf's hands.

With speed verging on supernatural, Antaeus fitted another arrow, killing another orc. Several more blurred arrows came from the forest and all the orcs were dead. The Elf stood silently amongst the carnage of orc bodies, his face still hidden from view. From within his deep hood, he surveyed the surrounding trees. Several Elves appeared from hiding places and began approaching, and still the lone Elf was silent.

Anthron motioned with his sword."It's a trap - I don't think that's an Elf."

Antaeus frowned."You noticed he's armed?"

Six Elves approached as the lone Elf stood vigil.

Antaeus grimaced."You may be right..." he stood and let out a sharp whistle while notching another arrow. The six Elves looked to Antaeus quickly, not sure what the warning was for.

Suddenly the lone Elf moved with an incredible display of speed. He sank to one knee as he withdrew his sword, then spun and stepped forwards with his blade out as he stood again. Four Elves fell with their throats cut. The remaining two drew their swords quickly as Antaeus released his arrow. The shaft struck the hooded Elf in the head, throwing him off his feet.

The Elf lay still.

Antaeus notched another arrow and motioned for Anthron, Jelik and Jassnik to follow him.

All was silent in the forest as Zéale, Antaeus, Anthron, Jelik, Jassnik and the remaining five Elves approached the carnage of bodies cautiously.

"How did you know it was an ambush?" Antaeus asked Anthron.

Anthron shrugged sheepishly."I saw a colour around it which I recognised."

Antaeus nodded."*Orlon* will be pleased."

"I'd stay back, if I were you," Jelik warned, depositing his bow in order to withdraw his new long sword.

There was a stir from the hooded Elf, and within seconds the body was riddled with arrows. The body began to move again, and again there was a volley of arrows fired at it.

Zéale held up his hand, signaling a cease-fire. Drawing both his swords, he said;"This may take more than arrows."

Almost instantly the body of the hooded Elf rolled, snapping most of the arrow shafts as it came to its feet. The scouting party created a large ring around the hooded Elf, all with swords drawn. It stood silently, regarding the Hunt Master.

"We must attack in pairs, for we do not want to get in the way of each other." Zéale commanded. Nodding to the Elf opposite him behind the hooded Elf, Zéale launched his first attacks. The lone Elf rushed forward to meet Zéale as the Hunt Master plunged a sword through its chest. Without flinching, the hooded Elf continued attacking, forcing Zéale to release his sword and fall back. Zéale's opposite struck across the Elf's back to no avail.

Antaeus motioned to his opposite, and they simultaneously struck the hooded Elf. Antaeus grasped at the tattered cloak, pulling while he thrust his sword point. He stumbled back as the cloak tore free to reveal decaying grey skin. The undead Elf's eyes were glazed and swollen, and from the open mouth trafficked disturbed flies. The once blonde hair was mattered with blood across the back of the Elf's hair - likely that was the killing blow when it was alive, Anthron thought.

The undead Elf lashed out at Antaeus as he retreated, then focused back to the Hunt Master. Zéale slashed viciously across its throat then received a cut across his shoulder.

Another pair of Elves attacked as Jelik positioned himself, ready to spring. As soon as the undead Elf's back was clear the thief darted forwards, avoiding Zéale's blade protruding from its back, with the bat shaped dagger in hand. The undead Elf stopped as Jelik sunk the dagger up to the hilt in the back of the creature's head, its mouth open in a silent scream. Jelik gagged and fell back as the fetid odour overwhelmed him. Zéale seized the opportunity, and with one powerful move decapitated the undead Elf.

Anthron heard what sounded like a deep sigh coming from the body as it slumped, as if invisible string holding it up were cut.

Collapsing back, the Hunt Master's face was grim."An abomination," he breathed in disgust."This Elf's life ended two weeks ago while assisting the village of Men."

"Could this have been a diversion?" an Elf to Anthron's right asked. Antaeus paled."*Elvenméson!*"

Zéale nodded."We must get back. Our home is under attack."

171

SAROPHIA BY STU DUNN

CHAPTER SIXTEEN

The barmaid approached with his drink.

Yarlyn Kontar slumped into a seat at *The Drawn Bow*. He felt exhausted. The last few days had been incredibly tiring. He drank down his first drink in one go, then waved the young barmaid off to fetch him another.

Saralon was still away and Yarlyn didn't know if Kros would show up tonight, so he was drinking alone unless Jalesia turned up. The pretty teenage barmaid quickly placed another drink in front of him, and he held up his hand to stop her. She turned to face him, her young attractive face shining through Yarlyn's bad mood. He downed his new drink, and placed a copper into the young girl's hand. She smiled and scooped up the empty glass, retreating back to the bar to refill the drink. The girl knew that Yarlyn - known as Hawke here - had large credit at *The Drawn Bow*, so that any money she was given was a tip. The girl brought another clear drink to Yarlyn, curtsied, and left to remedy the other patrons' thirsts.

Yarlyn sipped his drink this time, brooding over the last few days once more. It had all started when he had begun to investigate the group Saralon had been searching for, the group that had escaped from Urgar Keep. King Rogor Trendrik had assigned Yarlyn to find out what was causing the Selection and have it stopped. Yarlyn had informed his spy network to investigate why Queen Kilandra of Cyermyth had sent her personal knights to Sarophia - in particular to find out why she hadn't informed him or King Rogor about their presence in the Kingdom.

Yarlyn hated being uninformed.

The following day three of his informants were found dead. Yarlyn suspected the Ruby Brotherhood was involved somehow, which added to his assumption that the Brotherhood of Assassins was involved with the Selection.

Since then four more of Yarlyn's spy network had been found dead.

He could tell he was getting closer to piecing together the puzzle of the Selection.

Yarlyn sat back in his chair and again sipped at his clear drink. What did he know? It had started over a year and a half ago, mainly in the smaller towns and villages like Vemmlok and Lotheric. It was mainly the youth that was going missing, and there was no pattern that he could work out. There was an increased sighting of prison wagons, however they appeared to be bypassing Urgar Keep. He counted on his fingers - one, he must work out where the wheeled cages were going. The latest out-of-the-way sighting was near Kutporn. The City of Thieves, he thought. He had abundant contacts there.

What else had he discovered? Queen Kilandra. What part did she play in this? Cyermyth was a long way away - what interest did she have in this part of Palandra? And her knights taking over the offices of Urgar Keep...Yarlyn counted on his next finger - two, what are Queen Kilandra's Personal Guards doing here?

Yarlyn's thoughts were interrupted by a familiar voice."You look terrible Hawke." Yarlyn looked up to see the beautiful face of Jalesia, her long brown hair streaked with red, pulled back, her blue-green eyes studying Yarlyn with concern. She wore fitted brown leathers with the odd plate strapped on here and there, and had a pair of swords at her left hip.

"Have a seat, my dear." Yarlyn stood and pulled a seat out for Jalesia. She nodded in thanks and sat down, then attracted the attention of the young barmaid.

"Ale thanks," Jalesia said, paying for her drink. The girl raced off to fill the order."What's wrong, Hawke? I haven't seen you for a while, you'll have to fill me in." She had a sip of her drink when it was placed in front of her.

"Where have you been, Jalesia?" Yarlyn asked the beautiful woman as he continued to sip his clear drink.

"I've been working. Had to go on a road trip on short notice, so I couldn't tell you all that I was going. Speaking of which, where's Saralon and Kros?"

Yarlyn placed his empty glass down onto the table."Saralon's around Urgar Keep, searching for some *criminals* for Kilandra's elite."

Jalesia raised an eyebrow."Panthorian Knights in Sarophia?" She thought deeply as she drained her mug."Hawke, is Queen Kilandra here too?"

Yarlyn shook his head as he ordered them another drink each."No, but she's not responding to our inquiries either. She's somehow involved in The Selection."

Jalesia's eyes narrowed."So, where's Kros then?"

Yarlyn shrugged."Who knows and who cares where Kros is."

"There's a lot more to Kros than you'd think, Hawke. There's something about him..."

Yarlyn held up his hand, interrupting Jalesia."I'm not particularly in the mood to be kind to Kros, sorry. I know that he's a bright chap, he just smells like a sewer."

Jalesia giggled quietly, but recovered quickly."You should just be nicer to people."

Yarlyn laughed."And this is coming from a body guard. I bet you're really nice to people with those swords."

Jalesia made a face but said nothing more. She knew Hawke quite well, knew his moods, his way of dealing with people.

"I'm sorry for snapping," Yarlyn started,"I've just had a hell of a time keeping my business going..." After toying with his glass, he drank it down in one.

"Care to tell me about it?" Jalesia asked.

Yarlyn looked at Jalesia. He had known her for six years, since she was apprenticed to the Sword Master of Castle Trendrik at age fifteen. She had proven an apt student and had joined the Guild of Bodyguards just under a year ago. Yarlyn always felt safe around her. Jalesia had been playing in Yarlyn's regular card games at *The Drawn Bow* for six months now. He had tried becoming romantically involved with the beautiful woman, but she had let him down. He was now content to be good friends...

"Hawke?"

"Sorry, daydreaming," Yarlyn replied, remembering her last question. He decided to get straight to the point."I've been trying to investigate The Selection."

Jalesia's eyes twinkled, which made Yarlyn's heart beat a little faster. He considered that she would think more of him if he seemed somewhat noble, and trying to stop the Selection fitted that description."Finally the King is doing something?"

"Yes," Yarlyn absently examined his nails."I finally convinced him it was a plague that wasn't going away." Jalesia smiled warmly, making Yarlyn blush slightly. Quickly ordering another drink, he continued."I'm just not getting all the pieces of the puzzle yet."

"What have you found out?" Jalesia took a long pull from her fresh mug of ale.

"Well," Yarlyn made himself comfortable, sipping at another drink."It looks like..."

"No Hawke," she interrupted."What do *you* think is going on. You can drop the diplomacy."

Yarlyn chuckled nervously. She did know him well."Okay, here goes. I think that Queen Kilandra is behind the Selection. I think that her soldiers are somehow making off with the citizens of Sarophia, and she has hired the Ruby Brotherhood to cover her tracks."

"*Yarlyn*!" Jalesia hissed, forgetting to use the name he went by at the tavern."You're talking about war!"

"And we've always had great relations with Cyermyth too," Yarlyn mused."Unless it wasn't Kilandra who was organising it. That Carl Mort'l's one mean bastard."

"So, what are you going to do now?" Jalesia asked.

"Firstly, I'll try to stay alive," Yarlyn finished his drink and stood shakily."Then I'm going to find that group of 'criminals' Saralon has been commissioned to find. I think they escaped from the Selection and Kilandra's knights, the Ruby Brotherhood, and whoever else is working with them is trying to silence that group. And..." The thin man pressed his fists on the table as he looked seriously at Jalesia."I need your help on both counts. You can keep me alive long enough to locate this group, if I only knew where to start..."

* * * * * * * * * *

The Elf died.

Kielmark took a moment to survey the chaos, dark orc blood dripping from his blade. Screams erupted from all directions - both Elven and orcish. Small fires had been set in the ground level huts and the smoke begun to sting the Arrolokian's eyes. Kielmark wiped his streaming eyes and braced himself as an orc came at him. He stooped and thrust the tip of his sword through the orc's chest. The orc fell dead.

Kielmark quickly scanned to where he could assist, and found two Elven women brandishing their bows in defense, their quivers empty. They were fair skinned, wearing simple tunics, and wore their golden hair pulled back off their faces. Three orcs pressed them, thrusting curved swords as they grunted and squealed in excitement at having trapped the maidens. Around the three lay four dead orcs obviously slain by arrows, and an Elven lady whom had not been so lucky. Kielmark approached swiftly, hamstringing one orc as he shoved another forward into the path of a swinging bow. The bow snapped around the orc's head as it fell and lay still. The last orc turned on Kielmark and attacked quickly, forcing the dark man to duck and roll across his right shoulder. Kielmark enjoyed the freedom of not wearing armour, however he hardly felt prepared for a battle without anything but his silver helm. Rolling to his feet he blindly lashed out where the orc had been; satisfied to see that his blade had gutted the creature.

"*Mercu, fron amos,*" the Elven woman who had broken her bow nodded. "Thank you, my friend." she said in the common language. The ladies glanced at their dead companion, then turned their attention back to Kielmark.

Kielmark flushed as the beautiful ladies stared at him. He guessed that he might well be as strange to them as they were to him - they had probably never seen dark skin before. Nodding at the orcs he said, "Grab their weapons until you can refill your supplies." He made a motion over his shoulder as if to grab an arrow, and they nodded. Picking up an orcish sword each they turned and fled, leaving their companion amongst the seven orcan bodies.

"Kiel!" The voice was Sudenora's. Kielmark saw the Elementalist in between a billow of smoke, and ran towards where he had just seen him. Kielmark ran, as did his eyes, and he wiped them as he continued. Through his blurred vision he noticed something moving to his left. He slowed his pace, then felt an agonizing burn along his side left. He grasped his side in pain as he fell, crashing to the ground heavily and loosing grip of his sword as his vision darkened.

"Kiel!"

The smoke cleared, and Kielmark could see the wound he had received was from a human man dressed in black leathers, his sword dripping with Kielmark's blood. Shuffling backwards he looked at his wound, surprised at how little it bled compared to how it felt. Clenching his teeth Kielmark rolled backwards to his feet as the human mercenary slashed the dark man across the chest. Crying out, one of Kielmark's legs faltered, and he fell to one knee. His head was suddenly shot backwards as the mercenary brought his knee up into Kielmark's face.

Blood splattered from his nose as he fell back onto something hard. He was vaguely aware that he was lying across his own sword. Kielmark began to roll onto his side as the mercenary stabbed him. Kielmark coughed blood as he grasped at the blade with his bare hands, slicing them as he tried to pull the sword from his body.

The human mercenary seemed amused. Checking to ensure no one threatened him nearby, he withdrew his sword and watched the dying man. He rested his sword tip casually, kicking Kielmark's bloodied side. Then the colour drained from the mercenary's face.

Kielmark rolled and grasped his sword, and in one motion had thrust the point through the man's gut. Both men fell to the forest floor, the mercenary shaking his head with a frown.

Kielmark lay on his back, realizing that his breathing had become easier. I must be close to dying, he thought. He didn't feel any pain from his first wound, his nose only tingled, and his skewered side stung.

"Kiel! Where are you?"

Sudenora was still calling. Summoning what he thought was his last breath, Kielmark bellowed;"Over here, I'm down!"

Sudenora was there within seconds. Sudenora studied Kielmark quickly."For a moment I thought you meant you were hurt! Come on." The Elementalist offered his hand.

"What?" Kielmark spluttered. Was his friend blind?

"Looks like that guy did a great deal of bleeding on you." Sudenora commented.

Kielmark checked himself. He felt no pain at all. Looking through the blood soaked hole in his tunic he found no wound. Grasping Sudenora's hand he got to his feet. Frowning, he said;"I don't understand...I swear I was finished..." He tested his nose, finding it wasn't fractured. Pulling up his tunic he prodded his side."I was stabbed..."

Sudenora shrugged."We're needed over there." He pointed with his sword.

Kielmark nodded and wiped his sword on the dead mercenary's cloak, then followed Sudenora.

Three orcs rushed from Sudenora's side to intercept them. Sudenora whispered a phrase then swept his sword in an arc towards the attacking creatures. They fell away as Sudenora created a massive wave of wind, the orcs crashing into a burning hut. Smoke blew horizontally and sparks flew angrily. Then the air was still, the screeches of burning orcs fading against the sounds of battle nearby.

Kielmark inclined his head to Sudenora.

"This way." Sudenora indicated with his sword into the smoke.

Kielmark and Sudenora passed several dead orcs and a decapitated human mercenary as they closed in on the sounds of fighting. Kielmark wiped soot from his face as the smoke cleared ahead.

Numerous Elven bodies littered the forest floor, as well as on the rope bridges and platforms above. Kielmark could see that there were at least triple the amount of dead orcs. Looking up the great *arbré Auréle* he made out a duel between an Elf and what looked to be a

Cyermyth Knight. His heart pounded heavily as he and Sudenora approached the great tree. From the base of the *arbré Auréle* two Cyermyth Knights revealed themselves. Their black armour was covered with mud, their broad swords bloodied. Kielmark spied the 'K' on the forehead of their visored helmet, and whispered;"Kilandra."

Neither knight approached. They merely blocked passage up the *arbré Auréle*. Looking up through the smoke Kielmark could make out Auréle fighting the sole knight, bleeding and tired.

Sudenora spoke sharply in a language Kielmark didn't recognize, then released a long bolt of blue lightning in the direction of the two knights. The knights dived sideways. Kielmark sprang between them and leapt up the stairs that ran around the trunk of the great *arbré Auréle*. Sudenora's lightning bolt shot wide, hissing angrily into the ground near a knight. It was close enough to jolt the black armoured figure off his feet. The other knight advanced on Sudenora, who held his sword up in defense. He knew he was no match for a warrior using a sword, so he began retreating. Whispering an incantation, he released a charge onto his sword and held it. He trembled with concentration as the knight approached. The broad sword was raised, then swung quickly at Sudenora's Elven blade. Just before the steel connected Sudenora released the charge, blowing the sword arm right off the stunned knight. Sudenora's arm throbbed with pain, and dropped his sword as he staggered into the smoke.

* * * * * * * * * *

Kielmark reached the platform where Auréle fought the Cyermyth Knight, and paused to catch his breath. Auréle was bleeding from a deep wound through his left shoulder, and his movements were sluggish - almost as if he were drunk. The knight however seemed tireless. The knight noted Kielmark's presence, then cursed the sentries he had posted. The knight chanced a kick and knocked Auréle's sword arm wide, then followed up with a vicious horizontal slash that caught the tired Elf across his back. Auréle fell and lay still, his sword clattering over the edge of the platform.

The knight turned to regard Kielmark."Where's your blonde friend with my sword?" His deep voice grated as he advanced.

Kielmark knew instantly that this must be Carl Mort'l, leader of the Cyermyth Knights. Anthron had told him how the knight could regenerate, was a skilled fighter, and he was fully armoured. Kielmark swallowed and hoped that whatever magic had saved him from dying earlier was still with him.

Their blades met with a loud ring, then Mort'l's armoured fist lashed out at Kielmark's chin. The Arrolokian tilted his head, his silver helm deflected the blow as he stabbed straight out. The black armour turned Kielmark's blade, and they both stepped back to assess one another.

Kielmark raised his blade and stabbed forward, Mort'l spinning to his left as he swung a backhand attack at Kielmark's neck. Kielmark ducked, then received a kick to his side. Gritting his teeth, Kielmark retaliated quickly.

They fenced for minutes; Kielmark impressed that he hadn't become as fatigued as he thought he would have. Although his muscles burned, the dark man had energy in reserve. Ducking another attack for his head, Kielmark stabbed his blade at the plate armour beside Mort'l's left knee. Mort'l's leg gave out as he slashed Kielmark across chest, just an inch below his throat. Kielmark sat backwards in shock, his tattered tunic falling to the platform beside him. The agony in his chest made his sight begin to blacken as his own blood poured over him. Struggling to sit forward he lost grip of his sword and fell back with a cry. Kielmark lay still for several moments before his chest began to tingle, then itch. His vision cleared slowly, and his breathing became easier. He sat up easier as Mort'l approached. Kicking Kielmark's blade off the platform, the black man rolled frantically backwards.

Kielmark silently thanked whatever had enabled him to heal.

Kielmark was instantly forced to roll with a sideways cut by Mort'l's sword while the knight kicked at his knee. Kielmark nearly lost his balance, but instead of retreating he moved inside Mort'l's attack. Mort'l raised his sword over Kielmark's shoulder, then the Arrolokian heard a click and caught sight of a blade protruding from the sword pommel. Without thinking Kielmark picked Carl Mort'l up in his powerful arms, then strode four long steps and dived off the platform.

* * * * * * * * * *

Karlos held out his left palm, while his right thumb and forefinger created a circle in front of his palm. The circle within the hand symbol of *Termolen* began to glow, then a white light shot out and struck another undead Elf down.

Sweat dripped from the Healer's brow.

"Good work, *fron amos*," the Elven woman named Trasa commented. Trasa was an angelic Elf with large green eyes that stood out against her tanned face. Her long auburn hair was braided and fastened behind her head with a silver clasp. She wore a simple gray dress with a rope tying a pouch around her slender waist, and a pair of brown Elven boots.

"Thank *Termolen*." Karlos bent over, hands on knees.

Gen'vieve rubbed his back. "Your faith must be strong."

Karlos stood straight and wiped his forehead. Two dozen bodies lay scattered between Karlos, Gen'vieve and Trasa and the edge of the clearing signifying the edge of *Elvenméson*. Squinting upwards, Karlos could make out at least a score of Elves with bows ready to defend their home. Looking around, he was pleased that the nearby fires had been doused with soil.

"*Ennei*!" an Elven sentry called from above. Karlos saw the Elf point to the edge of the clearing, then notch an arrow. Within seconds of firing the red feathered cloth yard arrow, the Elf had fitted another and let loose.

An undead Elf advanced from the trees with sword drawn, quickly followed by four more. From behind the undead Elves approached a man who looked in his early thirties. He wore brown silk robes, his brown hair tied back, his tanned face was relaxed as he approached behind the Elves.

Karlos recognised the man instantly - Zathorn Sabriski, from Urgar Keep. Zathorn had been the interviewer throughout his torture during their short stay at the Keep.

Another score of arrows rained upon the five figures as they advanced.

"He's unafraid of the arrows, so must be protected somehow." Karlos growled as another missile arched harmlessly wide from some aversion Zathorn had erected. To Trasa he said;"We need to concentrate our efforts on him."

Trasa nodded. Closing her eyes the auburn Elf spoke quietly. Karlos noted that her voice was questioning. Karlos felt the hairs on his neck prickle and stand up as Trasa gathered her power and opened her eyes. Reaching into her belt pouch, she withdrew a large seed from a plant Karlos didn't recognize. As she threw it towards the six approaching figures, Zathorn stopped and went through several incantations of his own as the five undead Elves continued their advance.

The seed landed in front of the leading Elven carrion. Instantly the earth beneath the dead warrior shook, then erupted in a furious billow of soil and leaves that took the Elf to the ground. As the dust settled Karlos could see a hulking humanoid creature, standing about eight feet. Muscles rippled beneath the creature's thick bark-like skin as mud and slime slithered down its back and legs. The creature's head was large, covered in some kind of natural armour, and Karlos caught sight of its glowing green eyes - it was an earth elemental.

The earth elemental stepped forward in challenge. The undead Elf that had been knocked down gained its feet as the other four advanced with their swords drawn. The brown-robed mage left the elemental a respectful distance. The undead Elves attacked the earth elemental furiously, creating small chips of clay or bark with each attack. The elemental bellowed in anger before grabbing an Elf in each massive hand. The elemental easily crushed the undead Elves, then smashed its fists together, destroying another.

"Impressive," Gen'vieve said. Pointing with her long dirk at Zathorn;"He's up to something. I can't quite read him from here, but I get the impression that things are going his way."

Karlos frowned."Well, that's the last of the undead. I don't know what he's got planned..."

Zathorn Sabriski made several gestures, then pointed at the advancing earth elemental and shouted a command. The elemental stopped its thunderous approach abruptly, seemingly confused. As the elemental began to turn towards Karlos, Trasa, Gen'vieve and the Elven City, Trasa cursed and began chanting.

As the elemental approached, the Elves above divided their targets - now aiming for the brown robed mage and the giant elemental. The red feathered arrows seemed to bounce harmlessly off the elemental's thick wooden-like skin.

"Trasa!" Karlos said urgently, as the earth elemental pounded closer and closer.

Gen'vieve began backing away, realizing that her dirk would do nothing against the magical creature.

Karlos held his sword with both hands, ready to swing as hard as he could. If he could hurt its leg, they may have a chance.

Closer, closer. Karlos barely noticed that Zathorn had left the clearing unharmed.

Closer.

The enormous earth elemental raised its fist above Trasa as she finished her chanting. With a tremendous crash the earth elemental collapsed to its knees, allowing Karlos and Trasa enough time to clear away as the torso of the elemental toppled forwards with a boom.

As the dust cleared Trasa scanned the tree line, her face a mask of rage."Where is that mage!" she called out in Elven, to be answered from a nearby Elven archer."Damn." she whispered.

A whistle sounded from the centre of *Elvenméson* followed by several other whistles and cheering. Trasa frowned then relaxed."We have beaten them back, but they have succeeded. They have stolen Xycermon from our care."

CHAPTER SEVENTEEN

The Elven City smouldered.

Anthron stood in silence, staring at the damage inflicted upon *Elvenméson* while they had been drawn away. Perspiration trickled and stung his eyes as he stood motionless.

Anthron watched a group of Elves throwing orc bodies onto a bonfire, as another group marched into the forest with an Elven body between them. He noticed that not one Elf showed any form of emotion.

Anthron squinted as smoke caught his eyes, and the breeze brought the smell of burning orc flesh. His legs were still shaking from their urgent thirty-five minute run back to *Elvenméson*. He forced himself forward slowly, working his way to the group of Elves burning orcs.

"Can I help?" Anthron asked, his voice a little croaky.

An Elven woman with light brown hair dressed in green leathers looked to Anthron as he approached and smiled. Anthron didn't know if it was a smile at how absurd he looked dressed as an Elf, or one of thanks. Motioning behind her, Anthron saw several dozen orc bodies filled with arrows still to be burnt."I'd thank you for a rest." Her voice was soft, and Anthron could tell that it was emotional.

Anthron took her place, and with another male Elf began swinging the orcs onto the raging bonfire. Anthron was surprised at how tough the orcs' skin felt. He grasped another orc by its ankles as it was brought forward, and began the three count before launching it. Anthron gasped as the orc kicked out and began struggling, even though its right arm had been severed above the elbow. With a cold expression, the Elf holding the orcs' shoulders dropped it then slid a hunting knife across the orc's throat. The Elf waited for the orc to stop gurgling, then motioned for Anthron to pick up the ankles again.

Thirty minutes later Anthron shovelled dirt onto the last of the bonfire, and patted it down. Satisfied that the fire wouldn't ignite, he leaned the heavy shovel against an oak and washed his hands and face from a bowl provided to the bonfire group. Using soap to rid his hands of the stench of orc, he looked up at the gigantic *arbré Auréle.*

Anthron felt a hand on his arm. He turned to see the female Elf he'd relieved earlier."Thank you for your help." Anthron thought that her gentle musical voice could soothe him to sleep, so gentle and musical."My name is Béus." she smiled shyly.

"Thank you for finding Anthron, Béus."

Anthron turned at the familiar feminine voice. Standing at base of the steps of the great *arbré Auréle* was Anthea. Anthron's heart leapt as he dashed from Béus's side into Anthea's arms.

"Careful Anthron, I'm not quite myself yet," Anthea said, choking back tears.

He pushed the half Elf back gently so he could study her. She was thinner than when he'd last seen her at the Twelve Peaks, and her eyes were lined and gray as if she hadn't slept in weeks. She was dressed in green and brown as any Elf in *Elvenméson,* and wore the cloak and boots of the Sambethian Elves. She wore an Elven blade at her hip, and Anthron noticed an iron shod staff propped at the base of the stairs.

"I've missed you," Anthron's eyes brimmed as he stared into her silver-flecked green eyes.

"And I you, Anthron." Anthea smiled warmly, then pulled Anthron closer and kissed him gently.

A rush of emotions surged through Anthron. His legs felt like they would buckle. Ushering Anthea to sit on the steps, he sat heavily beside her.

Thoughts flashed through Anthron's mind; he pictured himself lying naked beside Anthea amongst the forest next to a clear lake, he visualised perspiration trickling between her firm breasts - her mouth open in ecstasy as they made love. Then he caught images of his friends frowning - of Karlos, Kielmark, Sudenora and...

"Jelik?"

Anthea tensed, then smiled uncomfortably."Jelik and I are not meant to be together. He knew that long before I did. Come on." She motioned for Anthron to help her to her feet."Let's catch up somewhere more private. We are expected in King Armand's hall at sunrise tomorrow."

Anthron offered his arm as Anthea used the staff with her other arm to slowly ascend the great *arbré Auréle*.

* * * * * * * * * *

King Armand sat upon his throne with an arm in a sling, the other clasping hands with Trasa who sat in a throne to his left. Karlos nearly choked when he had been announced upon entry then introduced to King Armand's wife, Queen Trasa. She still wore her simple dress. Around her neck she wore a golden necklace of intertwined leaves that were sprinkled with diamonds, giving the effect of morning dew reflecting the sunrise, Karlos thought. Trasa smiled wickedly at the Healer, obviously enjoying his surprise.

The hall was set up differently to when they had been there the previous day. The two thrones were still in place at the end of the hall, where the King and Queen of *Elvenméson* sat. Armand's adviser Majaré stood just behind him to his right. There were no sentries behind the thrones, but two stood at the entrance and back of the hall. The left side of the hall where the weapons had been displayed was now bare. In a semi circle around the thrones were twelve empty wooden chairs, with delicate arms and red velvet cushions. Karlos was pleased to see fresh fruit and wine on the table running along the other side of the hall.

"Please," Armand motioned with an incline of his head."Sit where you will."

Trasa rubbed her husband's hand gently as she watched Karlos sit closest to the refreshments table."How are you feeling Karlos?"

"Somehow I slept very well," Karlos replied. He stroked his goatee."Even though the attack was yesterday, I felt safe..." Suddenly feeling guilty that his friends weren't there, he said,"I'm not sure where everyone is, but most of our group will be up shortly."

Trasa nodded in reply.

Karlos blushed as his stomach rumbled loudly, even though he had broken his fast earlier. Trasa let out a giggle and Armand half smiled. The King said,"Help yourself to the fruit." Turning to his right he said,"Majaré, you may join the council."

The old Elf nodded and shuffled from behind the throne, easing himself into the chair closest to his King next to Karlos's.

One of the Elven guards entered the hall."Presenting Jelik, Sudenora, Jassnik, Kielmark and Gen'vieve." He waited as King Armand nodding his acceptance of the people named, then retreated back to the entrance as the group entered.

They looked refreshed, and none bore wounds from the previous day's battle. Jelik still wore his Elven attire, as did Jassnik. Sudenora's blue robe was torn and blackened, but still presentable. The Healer smiled as Gen'vieve proudly displayed the pair of Elven boots she wore. Karlos assumed that she had made quiet a fuss until she had got her way.

Kielmark wore a green tunic, which clung tightly to his powerful torso. Karlos saw that the Arrolokian's face was deep in thought. The Healer hadn't had the opportunity to catch up with either Kielmark or Anthron since yesterday.

Jelik sat next to Karlos with a nod of greeting."You left early. Why didn't you wait for the rest of us?" he whispered.

Karlos shrugged."I didn't want to be late I guess. I'm quite excited..." The thief nodded, knowing that Karlos was about to say he was excited at the thought of seeing Anthea and, wondered if she was well enough to come.

Sudenora sat next to Jelik, then Kielmark, Jassnik and Gen'vieve. Gen'vieve stretched her legs out in front of her and clapped her booted feet together like an excited young girl. Noticing Jassnik looking at her, she said,"What? I haven't worn footwear in over a year. It's a very novel experience." She smiled warmly at the troubadour, and rested her head on his shoulder affectionately.

"Presenting Prince Auréle, Prince Antaeus, Lady Anthea Fleké and Anthron.

Without knowing the appropriate etiquette in the Elven Court, they stood in respect of royalty. Only Majaré remained seated. All eyes turned to the entrance as the four entered. Antaeus assisted Auréle who looked pale and weak, leaning heavily upon a crutch. The King's son searched out Kielmark and smiled."I thank you again for saving my life."

"As we do also." Queen Trasa said.

Kielmark lowered his gaze and shifted uncomfortably under the attention.

Anthea stood in the entrance leaning on Anthron's arm, studying each of the old and new faces. Jelik broke eye contact as Auréle and Antaeus seated themselves next to Gen'vieve.

Anthron escorted the half Elf to a seat, and he sat between her and Antaeus.

No one spoke and no one smiled.

King Armand released his wife's hand and gestured to the last seat to his right that remained empty."Yesterday we bled in *Elvenméson* for the first time in our history." his strong voice echoed throughout the hall, bringing each from their private thoughts."Yesterday we won a great battle - however we lost a greater one.

"We can now see that yesterday's attack was planned well in advance. Our Seers have pieced things together as follows: it appears that the human agent named Wilse was placed within the village of Men in Sambethe. His role was to ascertain who had escaped *Le Shoft Tear's Kra* and where any other villages lay, and to notify his principal. We believe the attack on the village in Sambethe was to flush out an Elven guide to bring them to *Elvenméson*. We obliged by sending three dozen to aid the village. Out of those thirty-six, thirty-five returned yesterday as abominations, the walking dead, guiding both orcs and Men through our defenses into our city.

"And came into our city they did. We believe they had one purpose, and they succeeded in their objective." King Armand inclined his head towards the bare wall that had been covered the day before with various weapons."We have been safeguarding one of the daggers known as Xycermon. It has been in our care for over two and a half thousand years - since the end of the Great War.

"The Great War started in Parntorn by a small cult dedicated to worshipping the Lesser Gods and one of the Ruling Lords that had disappeared during the War of the Giants. They fuelled existing hatreds and organised an enormous army that overran both Euroness and Cyermyth. Their army was all the stronger for they possessed five of the seven daggers of Xycermon. An agent within their ranks stole three of the daggers, and used their power to escape to Sarophia with half the army following. The agent threw one dagger into The Deep Sea, hid one with us, and the other..." Armand looked to Jelik."The other you found at the Twelve Peaks. Due to the Parntorn army using their resources to destroy the ports in Gwilieth, Sarophia and Kortusia, Scyermor and Sarophia were able to defeat the remaining army. The two remaining daggers disappeared with the cult members from the host.

"We believe that *Le Shoft Tear* was one of the original cult members that started the Great War. It would seem logical that *Le Shoft Tear's Kra* - or the Selection as you call it - will cause another war. Caution has had them choose Sarophia for their needs. Although we have no idea what their *kra* is, we are sure it has to do with re-assembling Xycermon.

"This is all we know on the subject." King Armand finished.

The hall was silent again as the information sunk in.

Karlos leaned close to Jelik and whispered,"Rhailk said something about the Second Great War..."

The thief just nodded, glaring at Anthea. Finally, he said,"I have to know what your story is Anthea. Why shouldn't I run you through?"

Anthron tensed and began to rise before Anthea smiled weakly at Jelik and held the blonde fighter's elbow. Anthron eased himself back into his chair.

Antaeus patted Anthron's other arm in assurance."Just listen, *fron amos.*"

Anthea brushed her blonde hair back behind her human ears. Swallowing, she looked at Jelik, then the rest of the seated. Stopping at Jassnik and Gen'vieve she said,"You two are unfamiliar to me. I apologize for your having to endure this 'trial'."

Jassnik nodded respectfully. Gen'vieve smiled, revealing petite dimples, her eyes locked on the half Elf.

Anthea continued."About fifteen months ago I shadowed a prison trailer being led from Mosorac to Decton. By the end of the second day as the wheeled cages were rolling in towards the Merchant Stop I knew the prisoners were innocents. Even though the Selection was just beginning I took a chance and freed the prisoners," Anthea scanned every face staring at her before she continued."I secreted myself into their camp that night. I was aided by the fact that most of the guards decided to sleep in the Merchant Stop. I managed to open the locks of three of the cages before we were discovered."

Jelik closed his eyes and remembered using the bent fork to pick the lock of their cage as they escaped.

"I covered the eighteen escaping prisoners as they fled east towards Ithren. I fought several guards, set fire to several more..." Anthea absently curled her hands as if she was holding a fireball."One of the guards stuck his sword into a full cage, and killed a young girl. Soon each of the remaining seven cages had a guard with their sword poised, ready to kill another prisoner unless I threw down my weapons. I can still remember the children crying..." Anthea paused, her eyes downcast as Anthron rubbed her back.

A tear rolled down Gen'vieve's cheek as she let out a sob."Sorry," she muttered as Jassnik passed her a handkerchief.

Anthea looked to Gen'vieve and smiled. She continued,"I surrendered, and they...had their way," Anthea choked back her tears."They raped me, beat me, tortured me for pleasure in front of the prisoners. The guards didn't say anything - they were just having fun. Finally, near morning, a man appeared before me. The guards seemed afraid of him. He wore a brown robe, but looked quite plain. It was Gwyerson Dernas.

"He stood over me, untied my wrists, then spoke in a language of magic I didn't recognize. I woke near death, lying on the Highway outside the Merchant Stop. Thankfully a Healer of *Termolen* had stayed

191

the night at the Stop, and saved me from death. I think that if I had died...I may have become one of those...undead things."

Jelik no longer sat back with his arms folded. Anthea could see concern in his eyes.

"Within a week I had returned to the Forest of Ithren and found every one of the prisoners I had helped escape. We had begun to build the village which I brought you to," Anthea motioned to Karlos, Jelik, Sudenora, Kielmark, then to Anthron."Karter, Furnar, Lepus and Adjur were with those eighteen I had freed."

Karlos nodded, recognizing the names of the town leader and their teachers from the village in Ithren.

Queen Trasa indicated that one of the Elven sentries at the back of the hall should fetch Anthea a drink.

"Just water, thanks," Anthea said. She nodded in thanks as the guard handed her a goblet. She emptied it before passing it back to the Elf, then continued."Since that time, the village grew. Some were people who'd escaped Selection, some were dodging the authorities. It was about three months before I found you that a group headed here to Sambethe to set up, since we thought Ithren was soon to be discovered."

Jelik let out a sigh."Why did you betray us?"

Anger flashed across Anthea's features briefly before she calmed herself. She and Jelik weren't meant to be together, she reminded herself."The magic that Gwyerson Dernas placed upon me didn't reveal itself until we left Lotheric on our way to the Twelve Peaks. Something in the pit of my stomach began twisting, my mind became clouded and violent," she smiled at Jelik."You would have noticed that I'd become more irritable."

Jelik let out an uneasy chuckle.

"When you and I came across Dernas, he somehow forced the enchantment that he'd placed on me to another level. I understand now that it was a sort of *Geas* spell - one that makes the victim do as the caster instructs, or slowly and painfully die. I had already begun resisting the call - the call to kill you all - although I never knew I was hearing it. I remember losing control, attacking Jelik, and then being taken further into the tunnels where the dead miners worked. Dernas had found Xycermon then I think..." Anthea squinted as she struggled to remember the details."Dernas seemed pleased, then threw me down a pit near the end of the cavern. I recall falling, then hitting freezing water. I finally managed to climb out of the water in the darkness when there was an explosion...I fell, then woke in Lotheric," Anthea looked to Anthron."I think that pit must have been where Scotus had fallen, for I was found clinging to the same bridge in the Splitting River the same morning you left Lotheric. I thought that you'd be heading for Sambethe, so after I was healed, I bought a horse and followed the Splitting River south on the western bank.

"I gradually became sicker as I travelled. It took me twelve days to reach Sambethe..."

Auréle leaned forward to look at Anthea."Our hunting party found her seven days ago, unconscious, her horse dead nearby. We took her to the *rivi're aué refraíce* before she showed any signs of life. If she had not..."

"I lived through the peak of the spells fever, so it has expired, leaving me weak but alive five days ago." Anthea finished.

"Welcome back." Karlos said, dabbing his wet eyes with his scarf.

Jelik looked to Gen'vieve who gave a nod indicating that Anthea was telling the truth. Jelik let out a long breath before saying,"Yes Anthea. Welcome back."

Anthron visibly relaxed.

"Who is this *Le Shoft Tear*?" Sudenora asked, the rest of the group nodding."Is it Dernas?"

Armand leaned back in his throne, Trasa once again clasping his free hand."We do not think it is so. He is male, born in Parntorn sometime before the Great War. We do not believe he is of the long-lived."

Queen Trasa continued."We know he is powerful. He is master of necromancy, and disguise. He is likely in a position of some power within the Court of Men."

"Can you think of anyone, Jass?" Anthron asked, causing Trasa to frown. Anthron explained,"We believe that Queen Kilandra of Cyermyth is involved."

Majaré coughed loudly then cleared his throat."It would be the perfect hiding place..."

Jassnik thought."There are a few creepy people in the Cyermyth Court...is there anything else you can tell me about him?"

Armand rubbed his smooth chin in thought."Perhaps a feeling of being watched, or whenever you walk near and the hairs on your arms and neck rise?"

Without hesitation, Jassnik said,"Aracon. His name is Aracon, and he is Queen Kilandra's personal adviser."

King Armand stood."We shall break for one hour. Auréle, please ensure Zéale joins us then."

* * * * * * * *

"I don't know what to say," Jelik said. Jelik and Anthea leaned on a railing, overlooking *Elvenméson*. Squinting skyward, the thief noted storm clouds through the towering *arbré Auréle* and oaks."The rain doesn't seem to make it down here," he said absently.

Anthea glanced upwards."It never appears to rain, however the *arbré Auréle* soak up the water and nutrients and supply the forest from the ground." She surveyed the boundary of the clearing, indicating the perimeter of the city itself.

Jelik turned to look Anthea in the eyes."I'm sorry..."

"I think we both are." she interrupted.

They watched the activities of *Elvenméson* far below in silence.

Finally Jelik said,"Why didn't you tell me what had happened before we met?"

Anthea watched several Elves repairing hut roofs on the forest floor."You know me fairly well Jelik, I'm not one to be the victim," She turned to face the thief as she continued,"Besides, it's not a terribly pleasant thing to talk about."

Jelik nodded in response.

"It appears we are going to be travelling companions again," Anthea studied her nails, avoiding eye contact with the thief."You okay with that?"

Jelik half smiled."Not a problem." With that they embraced uncomfortably."Don't know about you," Jelik said as they lightly pushed each other away,"But I'm getting hungry again. I'm going to grab a bite to eat before the Court re-commences."

Anthea waved farewell then went back to watching the Elven community. Besides the huts being mended far below, her keen eyes couldn't pick any other evidence that there had been an assault in the city the day before. No Elven, orc or mercenary bodies were in sight, and the fresh sweet smell of the golden *arbré Auréle* leaves surrounding seemed to magically eradicate any traces of burnt flesh.

Anthea hadn't spent much time in *Elvenméson* during her fifty-five years of life, considered a child in the eyes of most Elves. Born on a farm east of Decton on the borders of the Forest of Ithren, her mother had been one of the few Elves that still lived within that forest. Her mother had died during the birth - as she had heard time and again from various Elves - Men and Elves should not mate. Their make up was so different that half-Elves were very rare, and for the human or Elven mother to survive was unique. Anthea had adopted the Elven way, never speak the name of one who had passed on to the next place.

Her human father had been a successful cat burglar who had retired from Carson some time before she had been born. He called himself Amlore the Tamperer - which she knew wasn't his real name - but he wouldn't embellish the truth at all. A handsome man in his youth, her father was an aged man now. Anthea quickly calculated her father would be seventy-six years old, seventy-seven at the end of winter if he had survived another. He still lived at the farm she had called home for eighteen years. I should visit with him before he...

She thought of Anthron. Anthea knew she would out live him tenfold - one hundredfold, and if they were to have children...would she survive? Would Anthron become the resentful father, crying into an ale mug each night, missing his wife...?

Shaking herself out of her thoughts she noticed Anthron approaching from the same rope bridge Jelik had left from.

"You okay?" Anthron asked as he leaned on the railing next to her.

Anthea looked at Anthron's tanned handsome face. Blonde stubble had begun to grow on his square jaw from the warrior missing several days of shaving. Anthron's shoulder length blonde hair had been tied back, his blue eyes looked concerned.

She was surprised at how much she felt for him."I'm fine now." She reached out and kissed him. They held each other high up on the platform in the Elven City of *Elvenméson*.

* * * * * * * * * *

"We have accounted for the thirty-five undead creatures," Zéale accounted to King Armand and Queen Trasa in the hall where the Elven Court was held. The Hunt Master had taken the remaining seat closest to the Queen."All have been destroyed. We tracked the last, destroying it earlier this morning by my own swords."

"*Tra brans*," King Armand nodded."This has ensured that we have no more uninvited guests." Looking around the twelve seated in the semi circle before the thrones, Armand aimed his question at Anthron,"What are you plans?" He aimed his question at Anthron.

Anthron stammered, having not anticipating a direct question."W-we are...were heading to Platown to find out more about Xycermon, and what spell it is part of... but you may be able to assist?"

Armand shook his head, then looked to Queen Trasa and Majaré who also indicated the negative."We do not know any more than you on the subject of the spell - other than Xycermon is used as a component in a summoning of sorts. It is suspected that since the cult is involved, they may be trying to summon or raise a Ruling Lord. We are unaware of any other components that are required." Armand motioned for Anthron to continue.

Anthron swallowed."So, we shall still visit the Great Library. We hadn't discussed it fully, but we were also thinking of going before King Rogor Trendrik to plead our case and ask for help. We thought he might..."

"...lend you an army?" Trasa asked, an eyebrow raised.

"Not an army, but an escort so we may next call upon Queen Kilandra," Anthron replied, sweat forming on his brow.

Armand brushed a long blonde strand of hair behind one of his lobeless pointy ears. Letting out a long sigh, he grasped his Queen's hand."Now we must decide how the Elves shall assist you," King Armand mused a moment then frowned, looking frustrated at his strapped arm."You may stay as long as you wish, to refresh and recover. When you leave, you shall be accompanied north by a patrol of Elves with full provisions." Armand thought in silence for a few moments before continuing. He looked to Antaeus."Antaeus, you shall accompany them to Trendrik. It has been too long since we have conversed with the Kingdom and perhaps you can assist in persuading the need for assistance under the threat of war."

Antaeus let the corner of his mouth curl in a half smile.

SAROPHIA BY STU DUNN

CHAPTER EIGHTEEN

Jassnik strummed the lute and sang.

It was their last night in the Elven City. The festivities had started early in the day with Elven children dressing as various forest animals, excitedly racing about terrorizing the adults. A range of fruits, breads, salads and salted cold meats initiated the breaking of fast. The midday meal set out on the forest floor consisted of roasted venison and wine, which continued late into the day. The companions lazed through the late afternoon rubbing fully bellies and sipping fine wine.

Instruments were fetched during the magical evening meal. Anthron couldn't believe how good everything tasted, how well the wine went down without clouding his mind, and how much he was enjoying himself. He looked to Anthea, who was laughing as she watched a nimble young Elf perform amazing acrobatics to Jassnik's song, while trying not to spill the contents of his wine goblet. She was beautiful, he thought. During the week they had stayed in *Elvenméson* Anthea had grown in strength, and was looking like herself again. She caught him staring at her and smiled warmly.

During their stay in the Elven City, each had found their own activities to keep them occupied. Anthron and Anthea had spent most of their time together, a pleasant mixture of talking and making love.

Sudenora learnt how to better use the sword, and spoke at length with Majaré of the Elven histories - at least that which the elderly Elf felt he was able to tell a non-Elf. Karlos made himself known to the Elven clerics. He was taken aback that the clerics didn't seem to possess the elemental restraints of himself and Sudenora. This had them discussing late into the evening at times.

Jelik took up Zéale's offer and learnt how to use two swords effectively together, instead of Jelik's usual sword and dagger. He had been astonished at the Hunt Master's speed and accuracy, and silently vowed to come back one day and give the large Elf a run for his money.

Jelik thought himself fast, yet he never came near to getting a strike throughout their entire training. Zéale had also taught him effective ways to move silently and unseen through the forest.

The Elven community considered Kielmark close to a hero, as he had saved the life of the King's son. The Arrolokian had questioned both Karlos and the Elven clerics about the miracle of his still being alive. Kielmark discovered that the plain silver helm he had picked up from Rhailk's horde could regenerate him quick enough, that given a moment's pause he could recover from nearly any physical wound. He spent most of his time in quiet contemplation or speaking with Karlos.

Jassnik and Gen'vieve drank. During their stay they had sampled every wine the Elves had to offer, and spent a great deal of time talking. Jassnik had taken up smoking an Elven pipe, which let out a sweet odour. He had found out that Gen'vieve's father had been a priest of *Nermion*, and that a year ago her mother had lived in the Duke of Carson's castle as a wet nurse for his baby son.

Jassnik finished singing the amusing story of the unsuccessful marriage between an ogre and a Kortusian woman and passed the lute to a waiting Elf. The acrobat finished with the splits and drank his wine down in one to the applause of the crowd nearby.

"That was great Jass," Gen'vieve's dimples grew deeper as her smile broadened."You'll have to write something for me someday."

The troubadour sat heavily beside Gen'vieve, who was playing with her long brown hair. She had begun wearing a silver Elven headband that kept her long hair away from her face. Her face was flushed from a long day of drinking wine.

They sat at one of many long tables on the forest floor, bathed in the golden light of the *arbré Auréle*. King Armand and Queen Trasa ate at a separate table along with Majaré, Auréle, Antaeus, Zéale and several Elves they didn't recognize, situated at the base of the great *arbré Auréle*.

The entertainment continued during the night, Jassnik playing several more songs before the evening was through. *Tolorel* was high in the sky by the time the jubilation ceased. Anthron led the half-Elf away to her quarters with a wave. Karlos and Sudenora leaned on each other, as they decided it not wise to climb the great tree and negotiate the rope bridges. They collapsed on the floor of one of the huts that had been rebuilt but was still unoccupied.

Jassnik extended his arm to Gen'vieve. She looked at him for a moment as they silently communicated then Gen'vieve blushed. Nodding, she allowed the shorter man to escort her away.

Jelik and Kielmark were left sitting alone at their table. Pouring the last of a bottle of red into his goblet, Jelik raised it to Kielmark."Sure you don't want one? This is probably your last chance."

Kielmark shook his head, and continued to think in silence.

Jelik studied the Arrolokian for some time before saying,"What was it like, I mean to nearly die?"

Kielmark continued to look away."It was so fast, but also very scary. If it wasn't for this helmet, I'd be dead twice over...It makes you think, Jelik."

"I bet it does," Jelik sipped at his wine."I remember back in Smazorok," he hitched his thumb over his shoulder, indicating to the northwest."The first time I had to really fight for my life. I got cornered by two pickpockets from the Thieves Guild." Jelik shook his head slowly."That was the most scared I'd been since..." Sudden emotion swept over Jelik as he remembered watching his parents assassinated by the Ruby Brotherhood as he hid under the floorboards of their small house. He remembered squirming out from under the house, and running to the other side of the city through the crowded streets. He remembered being alone, hungry...and the feeling of hatred so strong that he survived for eight years on the cutthroat streets.

Jelik turned away from Kielmark as he forced his emotions back under control and ignored the lump in his throat. When the thief turned to Kielmark, he saw the Arrolokian regarding him with interest.

"Perhaps we have more in common that either of us first thought." Kielmark said quietly.

Jelik shrugged."Maybe. I'm off to get some sleep, although I don't know where we'll be welcome tonight." The thief imitated Jassnik escorting the taller Gen'vieve away with a grin, which caused Kielmark to let out a laugh.

"It's going to be an early start," Kielmark agreed.

* * * * * * * * * *

"For whatever your reasons," Jelik read the rough signpost aloud."Whether business or pleasure, Kutporn will satisfy." Jelik rubbed his chin with a smirk.

The party had travelled four days north through the Sambethe Forest until their escort bid them farewell and good journey. The group was supplied with Elven cloaks and boots. Antaeus then embraced the eleven Elves in turn, speaking at length with each one. Anthron considered that they were acting as if the King's grandson was not going to be returning.

They stood up on the rise of one of the many muddy paths that led towards Kutporn - the City of Thieves, as it was known. The sun had just sunk behind the Ithren Forest far off in the west, robbing what little warmth the party had felt in the southerly winds.

"Interesting sign," Gen'vieve commented.

"It's an interesting place," Jassnik replied."I'd make sure you watch your money belt, as Kutporn has some of the best cut purses in Palandra."

Kutporn, housing fifteen thousand, was nestled in a shallow valley amongst the grasslands. Due to the winter weather, each road and path leading to the City of Thieves was ankle-deep in mud, carved by wagon wheels. During the warmer months it wasn't uncommon for a horse to stumble on the jagged dry mud and break a leg. The only royal presence in Kutporn was Baron Ihan, still unmarried, and considered a rogue by most of the nobles of Trendrik. The city watch kept enough order in the city that murderers were still hung and thieves were still flogged. The main reason the city got its nickname - the City of Thieves - was due to the infamous Thieves' Guild that lay somewhere beneath the city.

"I haven't been here in some time," Antaeus commented. The Elf rested his hands easily upon his sword hilt as he studied the city."Actually," he said with a slight curl in his lip,"I haven't left

Elvenméson in about thirty years."

"Just how old are you?" Karlos asked.

"Let me just say that I wandered Sarophia before Izonda had built its first city." Antaeus replied.

"But that's..." Anthron began until the Elf waved his hand.

"Time means very different things between our races," Antaeus pulled his hood up then began walking the last few miles to Kutporn.

Anthea stole a quick glance at Anthron before saying,"Come on, we want to get there before it gets too dark."

* * * * * * * * * *

The companions joined the short queue at Kutporn's southern gate, where late travellers and merchants were awaiting entry to the city. The tall stone wall was unkempt. Jelik spotted several loose bricks from his position in the line. He decided confidently that if they were for some reason refused entry, he could scale the wall fairly easily without tools. To the left of the barred gate stood a large hut that puffed a healthy amount of smoke from the chimney. As the group joined the queue behind a merchant's wagon, two unshaven guards approached from the hut, dressed in chain armour and carrying long halberds.

One guard stood back and lazily chewed on a fingernail as the other examined the group."Sorry 'bout the hold up, neighbour," he addressed Anthron."The baron wants us to inspect everyone coming and going a bit more thoroughly that usual." The guard sniffed loudly, then turned and spat out phlegm. Wiping his mouth, he continued in a bored tone, obviously having recited it often,"Please state you name, company, or business and your purpose in Kutporn."

"I am Lothor, and this is my company - Lothor's Maunders." Anthron replied just as they had rehearsed.

The guard scoffed."Since when have women become mercenaries - and such fine looking whores too."

Anthron smiled wickedly."They're with us for that exact reason."

The guard glanced at the exposed skin of one of Gen'vieve's legs through her leggings, then grunted."And you let them carry swords?" He looked to Anthea.

"If a whore can't look after herself, what good is she?" Anthron replied casually.

Nodding slowly, the guard squinted at the group of nine.

Jassnik moved forward, and asked quietly,"Is there still the after dark entry tax?" The bard subtly showed he held a gold coin in his palm.

The guard stuttered, but recovered quickly."As a matter of fact, there is an after dark entry tax." He took the coin then waved them past the merchant's wagon. The merchant glared at the party of nine overtaking him as another guard searched through his goods.

A sentry from the inside opened the gate leading into the city, and they passed through without comment.

It was an hour past sundown, and the streets were still filled with traffic. The main road that ran straight through the city to the northern gate was unpaved, so dried mud was splattered along the shops and houses on either side. The wide street was filled with wagons, carriages and riders, with pedestrians being forced to wade through the body of merchants and peddlers. Street lamps burned, radiating a flickering light upon the group as they stood in front of the gate.

"There's an inn not far from the eastern gate, next to the Merchant Quarter. I suggest we head there for the night." Jassnik suggested.

No one disagreed, and Jassnik led the group off the main road down a side street, heading east.

Anthron had never been in such a large city before, and didn't care much for it either. The streets were milling with people from various cultures, races and economic backgrounds. Most he saw were human - looking to be commoners dressed in patched hose and tunics - but he thought he caught sight of a dwarf that had ventured down from the mountains and a halfling. Anthron didn't mind the crowds nearly as much as the stench. The smell of human and animal excrement, body odour and rotten food assaulted his nostrils, particularly as they passed the multitude of alleys and side roads. Glancing at the others, he noticed only Sudenora and Gen'vieve seemed in similar discomfort.

Sudenora glanced about nervously, one hand resting upon his purse. There was something about this place, he thought. Something familiar. A hawker hooted his silk prices as they passed and suddenly jolted Sudenora's memory. The scene reminded him of his dream from Lotheric. Sudenora walked on silently as he noticed a baby was crying nearby.

"You okay?" Kielmark asked.

Sudenora nodded."Fine, just a little *déjá vu.*"

* * * * * * * * * *

The weathered sign depicted a large brown mug of ale. Under the picture was painted *The Mighty Mug,* with a crude *'er'* scratched into the wood underneath. A filthy ragged man sat on the muddy road near enough to the entrance to accost any patrons, guarding a metal bowl. The beggar looked up hopefully as the companions stopped outside the inn, and wiped a filthy hand to clear the drool from his black beard.

"Coin for old hungry?" The beggar pleaded as his grey eyes studied the group.

Jassnik waved the man out of his way as he pushed open the inn's door. Jelik stopped, and without a word tossed several silvers into the beggar's bowl.

As the beggar began to say something, Jelik pushed inside after the troubadour.

Anthea raised her eyebrow in surprise at Jelik's action, and wondered whether Jelik had once been a beggar in Smazorok. She walked past the beggar; being unwilling to make eye contact with the man as he streamed blessings after the thief.

The Mighty Mug was full. To the left ran a long bar with two bar staff struggling to keep up with the shouted orders over the din of the taproom. At the end of the bar was a door to what Anthron assumed was the kitchen. A chalkboard hung on the wall next to the kitchen which were written various order numbers. A large damp log smoked on the choking fireplace in the middle of the right wall, which had caused the immediate seats around the pit to be vacated. On the far side of the room was a set of stairs leading up to a balcony where young ladies attempted to sell themselves.

Noting that the empty table by the fireplace was the only place where they could all sit together, Jassnik weaved through the crowd and threw his Elven cloak over the back of a chair. Examining the fire, he turned to the others as he waved smoke from his face, "Anyone good with fires?"

Anthea smirked. "You could say I have a talent." She waved Jassnik aside, then subtly invoked *Pharson* to dry the wood and set it alight healthily.

Fairly soon afterwards, the smoke had cleared and the patrons of the inn began to shed their cloaks as the temperature rose. The companions ate plain soup and average bread, then relaxed over well-chilled ales that were served in enormous mugs.

Jelik rocked back on his chair legs as he drank, and closely watched the ladies on the balcony above.

"Which one do you like the look of?" Karlos nudged Jelik, disturbing his thought.

Jelik merely answered, "Who is picking up what tomorrow?" He looked in Anthron's direction for an answer.

Anthron looked to Anthea before replying, "We were thinking that Kielmark can pick out and buy the horses, with someone along to help."

The Arrolokian nodded, knowing he was the logical choice to finding sound mounts. Karlos raised his hand to indicate that he would assist the horseman.

Anthron continued. "We need travel rations, cooking equipment, tents..." he counted on his fingers.

Jelik nodded. "I have a couple of things I'd like to do as well..." The thief let his voice trail off.

"I think Jelik and I can snoop around a bit," Jassnik mused. "Gen'vieve can use her abilities to help."

Jelik nodded quickly, "Yes. Amongst other things, Carl Mort'l and Zathorn Sabriski may be somewhere in this city."

"Good idea," Anthron agreed.

"I'll get the cookware," Sudenora offered as he finished off his ale."I've only had a couple of those...must be the heat." The Elementalist began standing then stumbled before sitting heavily.

Anthron and Anthea excused themselves."We've got four rooms upstairs," Anthron motioned up the stairs.

"Just knock first," Jassnik chuckled, which caused Anthron to blush.

Soon it was just Jelik and Antaeus left in the hot taproom. The Elf seemed quite content to sit quietly, sipping at either ale or wine he had in front of him, observing the common room. Several patrons had already begun to make their beds under a table, making ready for the night.

Antaeus noticed Jelik watching him. The Elf waved his hand towards where the majority of the patrons still drank."I still don't understand the world of Men." He casually ran his long fingers through his nearly white hair."But I will always try."

"Well," Jelik pushed back his seat and stood."I'm going to relieve some tension. Night." Jelik nodded to Antaeus, then set off up the stairs to select the woman he would bed for the rest of the evening.

Antaeus watched after Jelik. The Elf emptied his wine, then his ale. Smiling to himself, he said,"...but I will always try."

* * * * * * * * * *

"Could be anywhere." Jelik whispered as he, Jassnik and Gen'vieve pushed their way into the centre of the City of Thieves amongst the early afternoon traffic. The wind whipped at the red flags of Kutporn that were erected upon the tall buildings around what was referred to as Gallows Square as they braced themselves with their Elven cloaks.

Jassnik had led them around most of the Poor Quarter that morning, searching for an entrance to the Thieves Guild. He had made several well-known thieves' hand signals as they walked the alleys to signify that he wanted the Guild to get in contact with them, but to no avail. It was only when Gen'vieve 'heard' by using her talents that the major intersection of Kutporn where all four quarters of the city meet was also the major entrance to the Thieves Guild.

It was an hour after midday and they were becoming increasingly hungry and irritable as they entered the large intersection. Gallows Square, given its name by the massive hanging stage that occupied the centre, acted something like a roundabout for horses, wagons, carriages and prison cages while pedestrians stayed safely to the crowded paths that ran alongside the muddy roads.

Jassnik looked uncomfortably at the gallows and flexed his neck subconsciously."Let's split and keep alert. The Guild might be our only way of finding information on our friends."

Jelik pulled his Elven cloak closer as a sharp gust of wind escaped through the mass of bodies and struck him. Shivering slightly, he made his way through the throng, glancing at several merchants' wares as he worked his way closer to the Industrial and Rich Quarters.

Kutporn reminded him of home. Smazorok had a similar area for public executions and government announcements - fairly similar things he sniggered. Smazorok was larger, with a population of around twenty thousand - the biggest population in a non-port city in Sarophia - and the main streets were paved. Jelik eyed the host of commoners moving through the stalls and remembered back to his first theft. He had been just a boy, and had been running from the Ruby Brotherhood after his parents' murder. He remembered running through the Merchants Quarter, taking a dagger from a smithy as he passed. The blacksmith had given chase for two blocks. Jelik subconsciously checked that he still had that very dagger concealed on his left forearm, followed by an inventory check of several key daggers, his two swords, and his money pouch...

Jelik moved with incredible speed and grasped the child's hand as he backed into an alley. The boy, no older than thirteen or fourteen, revealed a long dirk, which Jelik possessed within seconds. Jelik squatted casually and pressed the boy's dirk lightly into the would-be-thief's neck.

"Now," Jelik said calmly, his nose inches from the terrified boy's."You can show me where the Thieves' Guild is."

* * * * * * * * * *

Sudenora re-read the letter for the sixth time. Had he said everything he'd wanted to? He thought of Carlae's reaction when she opened it back in Eurgonok and smiled. Yes. She would know that he hadn't deserted her, and that he was still alive. She would know that he wanted to meet and be a father to his child. It had been just over seven months since he had disappeared - what if she had found someone else? What if she thought he had run scared from his responsibility?

Again Sudenora forced himself to calm down and think straight. He couldn't go back now - not until the Selection was stopped and Sarophia was cleansed of its agents. Squinting at the angry sky through the taproom window of *The Mighty Mug*, he considered what else he could do. I could send her money, he thought. Hire someone to look after her...He gritted his teeth in frustration, and bashed his fist on the table causing several patrons to turn their attention to him. Why had he been taken? Why had *he* been selected?

Sudenora wrote several more lines and signed the letter, and sealed it in an envelope. He melted red wax onto the back, pressed it, and then scratched an *S* into the warm seal. He hoped she would understand. As an afterthought Sudenora dipped his quill into the ink and wrote in his flowing handwriting on the back, *Please reply to Platown*. When the ink was dry he placed the letter inside his robe, returned the ink and quill to the innkeeper, and set off to post his letter and purchase the cookware for the following day's travel.

* * * * * * * * * *

"Do you see it?" Jassnik asked.

They stood in a rubbish-strewn alley after Jelik forced the boy thief to show him the alley where he could gain access. The boy had managed to escape, which Jassnik claimed he wasn't worried about since he now knew where to look for the 'signs'.

Jelik shook his head."I've never been registered with a Guild, and Furnar didn't teach me..."

Jassnik signed."Every thief needs to know the symbols. That's how they survive in new cities," The bard looked at Jelik to see if there was any recognition. When Jelik stared blankly back, Jassnik continued,"Do you see anything out of the ordinary on the wall there?" He pointed next to the reeking body of a small dead dog.

Jelik studied the wall, then said,"I can see a scratch in the brick...and lots of rubbish..."

"We're starting to get looks," Gen'vieve chimed casually from the alley entrance.

Jassnik nodded."Okay Jel, if you look really closely, that scratch looks like a lock pick. It shows thieves that there is a Guild around here. I'll take you through the symbols sometime..." Jassnik used his foot to push open a box that was covered with rotten food. He peered inside then took a deep breath and entered the box.

To Jelik's surprise the little blonde man disappeared into the filth. Crouching, Jelik peered after Jassnik to see him crawling through a dark hole in the side of a house. Motioning for Gen'vieve to follow, Jelik crawled after the dark outline of Jassnik through the dingy tunnel of filth.

* * * * * * * * * *

"This way," Jassnik motioned.

Gen'vieve followed Jassnik, with Jelik somewhere behind her in the dark. They scrambled through the small passage that led into a large round pipe. The pipe continued on a downward angle for five minutes before it opened out into what smelt like the sewers. Jassnik had sighted another sign not far from the pipe - a barely visible line with a tiny triangle at one end - another lock pick symbol.

The sewer tunnels were made of red brick that had become stained with slime and excrement. The tunnel roof was about twenty feet above water level; the dark pungent liquid of sewage flowing widely down the middle with a three-foot pathway on either side. The three followed the major tunnel north in the darkness before Jassnik noticed a smaller tunnel heading off in a general northeasterly direction.

"I think it's that way," Jassnik whispered with a smile."Towards the Rich Quarter."

Gen'vieve paused as she examined the darker passage."I can *hear* something," she whispered.

Jelik cocked his head."I can't hear anything."

"*No*," she spoke inside his mind, causing the hair on the back of Jelik's neck and arms to prickle."*I can* hear *something.*" Jelik could barely see her tapping her temple.

Suddenly a flash of light from the new tunnel temporarily blinded the three, and then they could hear movement and hushed voices within the darkness. Another flash sparked a hooded lantern into life, revealing a dozen men dressed in black with loaded crossbows leveled at them.

Jelik heard movements behind him and knew they were trapped. Sheathing his daggers, he saw Jassnik react a similar way. Gen'vieve held her dirk with white knuckles as she looked near panic.

An average looking man with black hair and beard pushed through the ring of bowmen that surrounded the three. He looked Gen'vieve up and down then glanced quickly at Jassnik and Jelik."We'll keep the woman, kill those two."

"Wait!" Jassnik cried, loud enough for his voice to echo some distance through the sewer tunnels. The crossbow men hesitated as the bearded man regarded Jassnik.

"What?" the man asked gruffly."You are obviously too stupid to live if you walk uninvited on the Thief's Highway. And besides," The man smiled, revealing rotten teeth,"There's a fair price for heads."

Jelik assessed their assailants. Including the bearded man, he could pick out fourteen other thieves. Five to one odds. With crossbows. Jelik let out a long breath as he readied for a backward somersault and began visualizing the wraith form he had taken on in the Urgar Dungeon.

"Who's put a price on our heads? Carl Mort'l? Zathorn Sabriski?" Jassnik stalled.

The man laughed coldly."It is good that you know your enemies."

211

He motioned for one thief to fetch Gen'vieve. She looked to Jassnik who nodded solemnly for her to go without a struggle. She relinquished her dirk to the thief.

"Ironic, isn't it?" Jassnik spat."We were looking for the Guild in order to purchase information about those bastards."

"It is convenient that our assassins won't have to kill you tonight at, where is it...The Mighty Mug?" The bearded man sniggered evilly."You," he pointed to the thief manhandling Gen'vieve."Take that whore to my chambers. You others report with their dead bodies." With that, the bearded man disappeared into the darkness after Gen'vieve.

Jassnik held his hand out in a sign of peace."I don't suppose we can talk our way out of this, can we?"

Jassnik was answered by the twang of a dozen crossbows firing.

CHAPTER NINETEEN

The bolt punched through his leg.

Jassnik threw himself out of the lantern light to the sewer floor and vanished. Cringing in agony he sunk his teeth into the hilt of his dagger to stop himself from screaming, and remained as still as possible. Only his ability to bend light had saved him from the thieves. He attempted to slow the blood flow - the only thing that would give away his position - and waited silently as the thieves searched.

Jelik had launched himself into a backward summersault, invoking the special rings' powers simultaneously. Within quarter of a heartbeat four crossbow bolts flew harmlessly threw his insubstantial form. Jelik willed himself into a tight cloud out of the lantern's radiance and searched for Jassnik.

He waited several minutes, floating above the dozen alarmed thieves who whispered sharply to each other. As he waited, Jelik noticed his vision slowly changing - it was becoming easier to see in the darkness through a red tint. After another minute the thieves had expanded their search, swords drawn, and Jelik could see them clearly from his vantage point near the ceiling of the sewer. Willing himself to follow, he glided silently just below the ceiling. He noticed the huddled form of Jassnik below, and for some reason ignored him. Not quite understanding why, Jelik continued to stalk the thieves.

Another minute passed, and Jelik found himself above a thief. He was surprised at the anger he felt towards the thief below, and he fought the urge to attack. Through the wraith's eyes, Jelik watched the thief with abhorrence. Jelik began to hear faint voices, distant whispers, chatter in his mind. He assumed that in the form of a wraith he had superior hearing. Jelik willed himself lower...lower...until he was inches above the thief's head. His vision was now completely red, and the unknown rage seemed to match. He could feel himself tremble in anger, the feeling of his parent's murder coming to the surface of his thoughts.

He visualised what he wanted to do to the Ruby Brotherhood, stabbing his dagger into their eyes and cutting off their fingers, toes, noses...torturous visions flooded over Jelik.

Below Jelik the unaware thief continued his stealthy search, sword stabbing into the darkest niches within the sewers' main tunnel. The thief motioned for one of his companions to investigate further down the sewer passage.

Jelik's fury was so intense he felt like his head would burst as he floated silently above. He slashed out with a gaseous limb, only to find it pass harmlessly through the thief's head. The thief shivered, suddenly aware of Jelik's presence.

"Vai!" the thief yelled."There's something here!" Jelik's wraith form parted as the thief's sword attacked.

Jelik was aware of the other thieves approaching, nearly drowned out by the chanting voices within his head. Whispers, suggestions, some in languages he had never heard, all telling Jelik one thing: destroy the thief.

His head pounded, his senses dulled. Through his red vision he watched the thief futilely attack as if he was watching through someone else's eyes. Jelik lashed out again, and the thief backed away unharmed. The enchanted rage took control of Jelik as he pursued his quarry. Lowering, Jelik entered through the terrified thief's screaming mouth.

Darkness. Jelik's wraith form entered the body of the thief through his clenched teeth. The voices he heard were now chanting loudly, almost screaming inside his head. The pain within his head was so intense, as if the blood supply to his head had ceased. Jelik felt like he was going to be sick...he had to do something...make it stop.

The body of the thief exploded as Jelik transformed back into his body. Body parts splattered in a wide radius around Jelik as he fell to his knees vomiting. Blood rained, dripping from the sewer's ceiling as he wretched again. The approaching thieves ran. As Jelik's vision cleared, the noise in his head hushed to whispers, then ceased.

Jelik then collapsed on the sewer floor, amongst the filth and body parts.

* * * * * * * * * *

Jalesia smiled. The bodyguard pulled her fur-lined hood over her head, then dug her heels into her horse's flanks to set off at a canter. She looked to the grey skies, and assessed that it would be raining again within the hour. Sighing, she focused on arriving at *The Dusty Traveler*, a little inn a days ride from Trendrik. Waving to Yarlyn over her shoulder, she left the palace courtyard through the guarded gates that led to the city, leading twelve Trendrik soldiers.

Jalesia wore her usual travelling clothes, consisting of brown leather pants and boots, and a chain mail jacket. Overtop her armour she wore the King's white tabard depicting a castle across her chest, and her favourite red cloak. Her sword belt was fastened tightly around her waist over her cloak to keep her warmer and to hinder her cloak from flapping in the wind as she rode.

Yarlyn watched until Jalesia and the dozen soldiers were out of sight before turning on his heel and marching back to his office. Trendrik spanned out for miles, consisting of a population of fifty thousand as it counted the two dozen towns within two days ride as part of itself. The massive walls that used to signify Trendrik's border around the city proper was now used to indicate where the richer estates and merchants stalls began. The wall was guarded during the day for the purpose of customs, and closed at nightfall. Outside the wall the city had grown over the years to three times the size of what the commoners referred to as 'the Walled'. Every street within the Walled was paved, with proper drains running down each side alongside a footpath for pedestrians. Commoners generally only ventured into the Walled to witness an execution, or for one of the royal family's birthday festivities. Even though those who live within the Walled considered themselves the upper class of Trendrik, Yarlyn knew all too well the seedy underside of the inner city.

A squire sidestepped Yarlyn with a nod as the King's Adviser marched down the glorious marble hall of the servants quarters. Rounding a corner Yarlyn pushed through the heavy red velvet curtains that covered the large double doors leading into the palace proper. The passages were wide enough for four soldiers to march shoulder to shoulder. Fifteen feet above the floor hung exquisite crystal chandeliers. Tapestries and portraits sparsely populated the cream marble walls. The doors were made of massive polished oak with the King Rogor Trendrik's castle symbol carved into each. Every handle and hinge was polished gold or silver.

Yarlyn had spent most of his adult life living in the palace, since becoming a squire at age thirteen. He had made senior squire by his sixteenth birthday, and had proved to be a quick student of politics and court procedures. He became the youngest minister in Trendrik aged twenty-eight and became the King's adviser two years after thirty. Three years later and Yarlyn was still Minister of Foreign Affairs, and had guided King Rogor through several major issues. Now there was the Selection.

Yarlyn passed several servants with a quick nod, then proceeded to climb the massive stairs to the third storey. Striding with purpose, Yarlyn pushed through the door leading to his office, startling his secretary Sion.

Sion, a fairly ugly short thin man with a large protruding nose jumped from behind his desk in fright. "Lord Yarlyn!"

"Bring my special drink, Sion," Yarlyn said as he walked through the door to his private office. The room's main feature was a huge polished oak table, covered with papers and maps. Two of the walls were covered with maps of various places in Palandra, and a large bookshelf ran along the left wall. Behind the leather bound chair was a large window and balcony where Yarlyn could sip at a drink during the summer afternoons.

Yarlyn closed the heavy curtains and stirred up the embers in the small fire pit opposite his desk. As he sat heavily in the leather chair behind his desk, Sion rapped on the door with bony knuckles and entered, carrying a silver tray with a crystal decanter and glass.

Yarlyn half filled his glass with clear liquid from the decanter, and tested it. Nodding in satisfaction, he looked to Sion,"You can get a glass for yourself if you want."

Sion nodded and retreated through the door, to return with his own crystal glass. Pulling a seat closer to the desk, he poured himself a drink then reclined into the soft leather.

"I think we've done it," Yarlyn raised his glass in the gesture of clinking them together, although he made no effort to move closer to Sion.

Sion raised his glass in a similar fashion, then grimaced as he sipped the strong clear alcohol."Well done. So King Rogor agreed to send someone to find the group then?"

Yarlyn nodded as he poured himself another drink."He sent Jalesia and a dozen soldiers!" Knocking his drink back he let out a small cough before refilling his glass."Yes, my friend. Thanks to the messenger pigeon sent by our agents in Kutporn, we may be able to meet this group that managed to have escape the Selection. With their inside knowledge of the Selection, I think we can stop it for good - and find out who's responsible and what this group is doing."

Sion smiled, making his nose wrinkle unattractively."Excellent."

Yarlyn Kontar leaned back in his chair and peeked between the curtains as it began to rain again. He was pleased that things were working out. If everything went to plan, he would be singularly responsible for stopping the Selection in Sarophia. He'd have to get a statue made of himself near the palace, he mused. All that needed to happen now was for Jalesia to find this group in Kutporn, and return to Trendrik with them. Yarlyn believed that his suspicions would be proven true, and he, acting as Minister of Foreign Affairs, would be sent to Panthorian to sort through the issue before talks of war began. After that, he could retire a famous politician...or perhaps take up politics in Panthorian as things would be shaken up fairly soon.

Yarlyn sipped his drink, ignoring Sion as he excused himself, visualising ultimate wealth, women and power.

* * * * * * * * * *

They ate quietly. After Jelik, Jassnik and Gen'vieve had returned from the sewers with the assistance from some paid thugs Gen'vieve had found near Gallows Square, the group made ready to leave. Karlos healed Jassnik's bolt wound, but found Jelik and Gen'vieve physically unharmed. Jelik had cleaned himself as much as possible before emerging back on the streets of Kutporn. The thief had rid himself of his blood-soaked Elven tunic and pants, and rolled his chain and boots inside his cloak. After stealing a plain tunic and hose for their return to *The Mighty Mug*, Jelik now wore his black leather tunic and pants again. He wore the Elven chain underneath the studded vest, and had spent some time trying to clean his boots and cloak. He had said very little since Gen'vieve had found him. She had used her mental abilities to cause enough pain inside her two assailants' heads that she was able to grab her dirk and stab one. The other had fled. She had used her mind to search the immediate area for help, finding several bashers for hire. Karlos had spent some time healing Jassnik, however Jelik complained of a headache that Karlos just couldn't help.

They made a cold camp several hours after dark off the Kutporn-Platown Highway, nestled amongst a group of pine trees. After eating a meal of trail rations, each person went about their own business in silence, with Kielmark taking particular care of their new horses.

Karlos sat heavily next to Jelik."You okay Jel? I haven't known you to be this quiet in all the time we've known each other."

Jelik shook his head,"I'd rather not discuss it." He half smiled at Karlos to ensure he knew it was nothing personal."Scary things going round my head," he added."I just need some time to sort them out."

Karlos nodded."Well, if you want to talk..." The Healer left the invitation hanging, then shifted under their camouflage canvas with a blanket."Better get some sleep Jel, you and I are on the last watch."

Jelik nodded in reply. It seemed like only several minutes later that Karlos was lightly shaking him awake.

"It's three hours after midnight," Karlos whispered."At least the rain is light."

Jelik forced his tired muscles into action, pushing himself to his feet for his watch duty.

* * * * * * * * * *

Anthron studied the clouds and the position of the sun. He judged it was just after noon on their fifth day out from Kutporn. The travel southeast had been uneventful, with the exception of riding off road to avoid two suspicious looking groups of mercenaries who loitered along the highway studying each traveller that passed. It had rained nearly constantly, and Gen'vieve and Karlos had caught headcolds. Jassnik had developed a sniffle, but claimed adamantly that Gen'vieve hadn't passed her bug on.

"Impressive." Sudenora gasped.

Platown was about the size of Mosorac, surrounded by a square thirty-foot high stone wall, with silvery symbols reflecting upon its surface. Blue flags with an image of a book tugged in the wind atop the turrets that emerged another thirty feet from each corner of the complex. There was only one way into the Great Library - a massive gate in the centre of the northern wall, big enough that Anthron thought the great golden dragon Rhailk could walk through it. Four soldiers rested easily on the other side of the gate, and Anthron observed there was a regular patrol of sentries on top of the wall. He could see the library itself towering at least fifteen stories high from behind the walls. His initial thoughts of the impressive castle-like library was that it appeared over guarded.

Jassnik nudged his horse forward and pointed to the silver symbols."I heard once that every civilised culture in Palandra wrote their promise on the walls, never to endanger or threaten Platown, or anyone within."

"Are you saying that every culture in the *world* agreed to leave this place alone?" Sudenora looked impressed.

Gen'vieve pointed."Is that what the silver on the walls are - writing, or signatures?"

Jassnik nodded."From what I heard."

The party set off at a lazy trot towards the library.

"A little over guarded, don't you think?" Jelik commented, breaking another of his long silences.

Jassnik adjusted his sodden blue-brimmed hat and released a puddle of rain."These guards have nothing to do with the Kingdom soldiers - Platown has its own police. They strongly enforce the library's laws, funded by the Chorsar family who have lived here for centuries."

"A soldier could grow fat out here." Kielmark observed.

Gen'vieve shivered, then sneezed suddenly. Wiping her nose, she said,"Someone with evil intent is watching us." She looked over her shoulder and searched the horizon.

"There." Antaeus pointed.

Anthea followed the Elf's gaze and spotted a lone rider far behind them."I can't quite make out..."

"Male, human, dressed as a mercenary. Mid thirties, unshaven..." Antaeus stopped as all eyes turned to face him. He shrugged,"We Elves have good eyes."

"I can't see anyone." Karlos sniffed.

"Let's get indoors." Anthron suggested, and kicked his horse into a gallop.

* * * * * * * * *

Anthron took a long pull from his cold beer. He sat in the most spectacular taproom he had ever seen. Located in the first of what was referred to as the residential blocks was the exquisite tavern named *The Polished Platter*. There were four long residential blocks that ran from north to south, two on either side of the giant building that was the library. The residential blocks were made up of houses, inns, taverns, shops, and several estates, owned by rich Elementalists or clerics who had chosen the life of study. South of the library was a massive park, with neatly trimmed grass, an enormous fountain featuring a well endowed woman, and many benches on which to sit during the warmer weather. Beyond the park lay the Chorsar Estate, which resembled a small castle - bar the moat.

Anthron surveyed *The Polished Platter*. Smaller than most taprooms, it was immaculately tidy. The floors were made of streaked grey marble, the walls made of a shiny metal that reflected like a warped giant mirror. Silver candelabras sat on each polished oaken table, and the entire ceiling was covered with paintings of Platown's construction and signed by various races. Along the western wall was the bar and kitchen. The eastern wall opened into a massive fireplace that warmed the entire room. The southern wall gave way to a stairwell circling up to the first floor and their rooms.

Finishing his beer Anthron let out a sigh. It was good to be warm and dry again. He smiled to himself as he considered the delights of again having privacy with the half-Elf. He blushed furiously as he caught Gen'vieve looking at him. She just winked and went back to talking quietly with Jassnik.

Anthron studied Gen'vieve. She wore her black leggings that exposed the side of her legs from hip to knee, laced together with a scarlet binding. She wore her Elven boots and a loose navy pirate-style jerkin. Her long hair was plaited around her neck, which Anthron thought looked like a strange kind of hairy necklace.

Sudenora let out a loud sigh. "When is this guy meeting us?" He fidgeted absently with his empty mug.

Jassnik looked up from his conversation with Gen'vieve. "Troy should be here shortly. He's a busy man."

Jassnik had organised for Troy, the younger of the Chorsar brothers, to guide them through the library 'to save them months of searching' as he had put it. The Chorsars were a family of historians who had helped establish the great library within Platown centuries before. The wealthy family had lived in Platown since, taking care of the library and grounds. They hired their own security, to act as police and peacekeepers. Over the years, the Chorsar family tended to act as something of a collective mayor of Platown, ensuring the residential blocks and roads were tidy, and that the merchants and tavern owners adhered to fair trading.

The door to *The Polished Platter* opened, revealing the dismal weather outside. The rain had increased to a heavy tattoo on the tavern roof, drumming constantly throughout the afternoon.

A soldier rushed through the open portal and closed it behind him. Anthron could tell that the soldier was a veteran by the polished plate and chain armour, the worn but cared for broad sword at his belt, and the steely look in his creased dark eyes. The soldier then shook his cloak out in the doorway and hung it on a peg. Surveying the empty taproom he then removed his silver helmet, revealing a weathered face and grey hair. Using the nosepiece as a handle, the soldier approached the group.

"I am looking for Jassnik Corline," the soldier announced.

The blonde troubadour raised his hand."Here. You must be Monalo."

The soldier bowed stiffly."If you are ready to go I shall take you to the library while it is still light, to meet Mr. Chorsar."

Jassnik stood and clasped his cloak around his neck."Lead on."

Gen'vieve, Anthron, Anthea, Sudenora, and Antaeus followed after Jassnik and Monalo.

Karlos yawned, then sneezed. Blinking his puffy red eyes, he said,"I'm off to bed. Wake me if the place is on fire." Hauling himself to his feet, Karlos slowly made his way up the stairwell to their rooms.

Glancing at Kielmark, Jelik let out a sigh."Just us again, huh?"

As Jelik was about to excuse himself, the tavern door was opened again. A beautiful woman; long red streaked brown hair, stunning blue-green eyes, stepped through the door. She removed her fur-lined red cloak revealing two swords and armour. Jelik could tell by the snugness of her chain mail vest that she had a slim curvy figure underneath.

The woman turned to speak to someone outside,"Desen, I want you to feed and water the horses yourself. Check their hooves..."

There was an acknowledging voice from outside and the woman turned back smiling. Catching sight of Jelik her smile lingered, taking the thief's breath away. She slowly moved towards the bar where the eager innkeeper rubbed his hands at the new custom.

When she had broken eye contact with Jelik, he found his heart pounding heavily. He barely noticed the eleven Kingdom soldiers enter and sit themselves near the bar.

"Perhaps we should make ourselves scarce," Kielmark said nervously, nodding at the soldiers.

"Our next stop is Trendrik," Jelik replied."Perhaps we can head back with them."

The Arrolokian shook his head, then whispered,"They may not be heading that way, besides, I don't want to go to Trendrik in shackles."

"Fair point," Jelik conceded."Shall we?" Jelik motioned for Kielmark to stand.

"We shall," Kielmark returned, and they followed after Karlos up the stairs, the woman watching them both closely.

* * * * * * * * * *

"Do you think you can read it?" Sudenora asked.

Jassnik held a thick ancient book in both hands. Placing it delicately on a table under the light of a silver candelabra, he let out a sigh."I don't think so. The cover is written in the Ancient Language..."

"I can read the Ancient Language," said Troy matter-of-factly before sniffing. Troy Chorsar was a man in his late forties, of average height and build. His skin was pale from spending most of his time indoors, and his mouse-coloured hair was cut short with a straight fringe. He wore spectacles, and was dressed in a thick crimson robe and cloak. He was a pleasant sort of a man, even though he had an annoying habit of loudly sniffing and swallowing phlegm.

With Troy's assistance, they had been searching the Great Library for the past six hours. Thankfully the library was well lit with amazing crystals on the ceiling that ebbed a yellow light, and a large candelabra on each table.

"Is it the right book?" Anthea asked. She had spent the last half hour resting at their table.

"I certainly hope so. *Tolorel* wasn't all that specific when she referred us here. Hopefully this is the book that 'has all the answers'," Jassnik replied.

Troy sat down in front of the book, rubbing the palm of his hand across the cover. Peering over his little glasses, the scholar quaffed,"The cover is human skin." He tilted the book and studied the spine."Looks like it was written during the Great War period. Interesting, I shall look up where we came upon it later. Let's see what it says about Xycermon." The historian-scholar opened the large book delicately, revealing yellowed pages.

The first page depicted a seven-pointed symbol. Sudenora leaned closer to study the picture."That's the dagger - or should I say - the seven daggers." The symbol was of the seven bat-shaped daggers, joined at the pommel. Blood dripped from each blade, the same colour as each of the ruby sets of eyes.

Troy turned the ancient page. For the next couple of hours Troy translated relevant passages, with Sudenora scribbling everything onto parchment.

"Red Eye, or Xycermon," Troy droned,"is also one of three components required for the conjuration when joined as one."

"That must mean when the seven daggers are joined." Jassnik said.

Troy continued."The second is a candle of human fat, inscribed with blood quoting from *The Book of Passage.*"

Sudenora stifled a yawn."Could that be what the Selection was for?"

Troy frowned at the comment."You are investigating the Selection? Is this what this is about?"

Jassnik nodded."Yes. And as for your suggestion Sudenora, that would make one *big* candle if all the people from the Selection are being used to...melt."

Troy thought for a moment."You can halve my fee, since this is a noble cause."

"Fee?" Gen'vieve asked.

"Never mind." Jassnik muttered, waving his hand as he peered over Troy's shoulder.

"What's the third component?" Sudenora yawned.

Troy ran his hand down the page of symbols before continuing,"The third is something called the Ring Bearer. The collective Xycermon must have blood from the Ring Bearer's heart spilled onto each blade."

Gen'vieve gasped."*Jelik*?"

Jassnik shrugged."It could be any ring, Gen." The troubadour looked dubious.

"What is the spell to conjure?" Sudenora asked the historian.

Troy read through the ancient pages for several minutes in silence. Looking up, he removed his spectacles and rubbed his eyes."It looks to be something like a resurrection spell, but not like *Bormal's* necromantic ways. It's almost like it's to raise something that's not dead..." Troy read several more passages before the colour drained from his face. He closed the book and pushed himself away from the table.

"What is it?" Jassnik asked. Turning to Gen'vieve, she too had gone pale.

Troy stood shakily and addressed the group."This is a spell to raise Molath, the Ruling Lord who disappeared during the War of the Giants. According to this," he motioned at the book;"Molath rests somewhere in Palandra, awaiting his servants to awaken him and again rule the Men..."

"And Elves," Antaeus, who had quietly observed for most of the evening, said."And dwarves, halflings, Issa, orcs, goblins, trolls..."

"Quite." Troy said quietly.

After a moments silence, Jassnik said,"Let's get back to the others."

* * * * * * * * * *

Jelik woke instantly. Before he was fully awake he was crouching next to his bed, dagger in hand. He sat silently for several moments, trying to ascertain what had woken him. He jumped as Antaeus whispered;"I heard it too. Sounded like metal scraping on the roof."

Jelik looked around their room. Karlos and Kielmark were still fast asleep, the Healer quietly snoring.

Suddenly the window next to Jelik shattered inwards. Jelik fell back as Antaeus somehow managed to notch an arrow and fire upon a black figure that had entered through the broken window. The figure fell backwards onto the cobblestones one floor below. Another black clad

225

figure swung from the roof through the window. The assassin was dressed in black cloth, with cloth wrapped around his head allowing only his eyes to be seen. From his belt the assassin withdrew a pair of sai - long metal fork like weapons from Kortusia - and launched towards Jelik as Antaeus shot an arrow through the assassin's throat.

"Quickly," Antaeus said calmly, motioning towards the door."There may be more."

Jelik avoided the broken glass as he pulled on his Elven boots and strapped on his sword belt. Karlos and Kielmark did likewise. As Kielmark went to grasp the door handle, the portal swung open from a kick. Kielmark raised his blade quickly, but lowered again as he recognised Anthron.

The blonde warrior, wearing only breeches and boots, carried his sapphire-encrusted long sword. Anthea, Sudenora, Gen'vieve and Jassnik gathered behind Anthron.

"What's going on?"

"Assassins," Kielmark replied as he passed a backpack to Anthron. Within a minute they had cleared out their room of luggage and equipment. Kielmark, Jelik, Karlos and Antaeus ventured quietly into the dark taproom with their equipment as Anthron and the others gathered their gear.

The taproom was dimly lit from the outdoor street lamps. Jelik could make out the dozen Trendrik soldiers sleeping under the tables on the tavern floor. The thief thought it strange that the soldiers slept on the floor when there were spare rooms upstairs.

Antaeus placed his hand on Jelik's shoulder, and motioned for him to crouch. Kielmark and Karlos followed suit. Antaeus silently withdrew an arrow from his quiver, and drew his longbow. Several tense moments later, the Elf let the shaft fly into the darkness.

Jelik squinted into the shadows as a black form hit the taproom floor, rousing several soldiers who slept nearby. Quicker than Jelik thought possible the Elf notched another arrow and sent it into another corner to the room, followed by a gurgling and the sound of a body falling.

One soldier called the alarm, and the rest were quickly on their feet with their broad swords drawn.

"Light!" commanded a woman's voice. Shortly after, a lantern was lit, at the same time as Antaeus shot down another assassin. Once the room was lit the assassins had no need for subterfuge. Ten dark figures moved from the shadows with weapons drawn.

"Make a circle!" the woman ordered - the attractive woman Jelik had seen earlier that night. She spun her two swords expertly as an assassin closed in on her and another soldier. The dozen Kingdom soldiers kicked the tables aside and formed a circle in the centre of the taproom.

Then the assassins attacked.

SAROPHIA BY STU DUNN

CHAPTER TWENTY

Anthron raised his sword.

The assassin hesitated as Anthron's sapphire encrusted sword buzzed in his ears and made his eyes sting. Within seconds he had cut the assassin down. Chancing a look around, Anthron noted that only seven soldiers and the woman were left fighting in the middle of the taproom, and there were only six assassins left standing.

Antaeus fired his last arrow, killing another assassin as Sudenora contained an electric pulse in both hands, waiting for an opportunity to unleash it upon the remaining enemies.

The tide had turned considerably, and the five remaining assassins began backing away. When Kielmark, Anthron, Jelik and Jassnik blocked their way, one assassin signaled the others. They simultaneously reached into their black tunics.

"Stop them!" Jelik cried. "They're going to kill..."

Before anyone could react, the assassins dropped to the floor after placing something in their mouth.

"*Damn!*" Jelik swore. Sheathing his weapons, he stooped to check the pulse of the nearest body. "Dead."

"This one's not yet," the brunette warrior kneeled and wrenched the wrapped cloth from the face of another, the one that had signaled their suicide. Roughly tearing the last of the assassin's guise away, she rocked back in shock. "*Kros!*" She hissed, her eyes narrowing dangerously as she fingered her sheathed dagger.

"Jalesia." the assassin croaked then coughed blood. The assassin was an ugly unshaven man with unnaturally large lips. He had filthy red hair that was cut at different lengths, and his green eyes locked with the woman who was called Jalesia.

"What...are you doing here?" Jalesia stuttered. "I thought you were a..."

Kros attempted to laugh, settling for a gurgling in his throat. When he spoke, Anthron could hear blood in his lungs."Agent." he coughed, spraying Jalesia in blood.

"Who do you work for?" Jalesia demanded.

Kros replied by dying with a bloodied grin.

"Looks like bresac," Jelik observed."Bresac's a fairly nasty poison that eats a hole in your lungs."

Jalesia stood, her face expressionless."Search them." she ordered two soldiers. Turning to face an older fighter with grey streaks in his black hair, she said,"Desen, can you check on the fallen?"

Desen nodded and began checking the five soldiers bleeding on the taproom floor.

"I'm a Healer," Karlos said."I may be able to help."

Densen appealed to Jalesia, who agreed. The warrior woman finally regarded the companions."I think we have some talking to do," She studied the group for a moment longer, then shook her head."Forgive me, I took you for a group I was looking for. Thank you for your assistance during the fight. I am Jalesia Enos, bodyguard to the King." She offered her hand in greeting.

Anthron stepped forward and took her hand. As Jalesia smiled Anthron could clearly see a greenish yellow aura around her, and he felt at ease that she was an ally."I am Anthron Mikolnic of Vemmlok."

"You *are* the ones..." Jalesia started just as a soldier called out.

"We've found something on the assassins," The soldier held up a little ring, with a glistening blood red ruby."They were all wearing one of these. Looks like the Ruby Brotherhood is moving east again."

Jelik calmly moved past the frantic innkeeper who had finally ventured out from the safety of his home through the kitchen. The thief scooped up one of the rings, righted an upturned table and chair, and examined the ring silently.

"What's going on!" The tall thin innkeeper wailed.

Jalesia let out a sigh."Master Innkeeper, would you be so good as to alert the local authorities, and have a wagon take these bodies away."

"There's one upstairs, and another outside," Antaeus added.

The innkeeper stuttered, then fled outside in his nightshirt.

Turning to Anthron, Jalesia said,"Now, let's get to the bottom of this."

* * * * * * * * *

Anthron's teeth chattered. It had been ten days since the attack at *The Polished Platter*. From the five soldiers that had fallen during the fight with the assassins, only one had been dead. Karlos had cared for the four wounded, refusing to allow them to travel for at least three days. So on the fourth day after the attack the company set off at a slow pace, accompanied by Jalesia and her soldiers.

The companions and Jalesia had spoken at length. Afterwards, Gen'vieve had separately assured the group that Jalesia really did work for the King and had been assigned the mission of finding them somewhere around Kutporn. Jalesia hadn't been too interested in the details they knew about the Selection, claiming that she would hear everything when they spoke to King Rogor.

Jalesia had sent word to the castle as they passed through the main entrance at the outer wall that once signified the border of Trendrik City. Anthron was impressed with the city. He could see the massive castle rising up from the centre of the city, four hundred rooms Jalesia had informed them. The streets leading into the city were fully paved with gutters, drains and footpaths. The lampposts that lined the streets were polished, and in the centre of every large intersection stood a life-sized statue of powerfully built past kings of Trendrik.

"The Kings seem quite," Anthron delicately searched for the right word,"Stronger looking than I expected..."

Jalesia smiled as she rode."Every heir to the Trendrik throne is expected to spend three years on the Euroness and Parntorn border."

"That's a mean land." Jassnik thought aloud.

"Yes it is," Jalesia replied."King Rogor lost his older brother along the borders from an orc raiding party."

Thirty minutes from the main gate they reached what Jalesia referred to as the middle wall. Two soldiers wearing the King's tabard saluted and stepped aside as Jalesia passed.

Anthron was stunned. Between the middle and outer wall was rich - but this was far greater. The houses they rode past looked more like mansions, with large lawns and gardens, each surrounded by large iron barred fences. Anthron noticed there were no shops, nor were there any merchants or street hagglers. Several richly dressed nobles walked the footpaths talking together and an expensive horse-drawn carriage rattled past the companions along the paved road as the light of day began to fade. Anthron decided that the area between the inner and middle walls was too clean, too rich if there was such a thing. His mind drifted back to Lotheric with half their town in ruins - with just a fraction of the wealth displayed here the entire town could be rebuilt...

They were admitted through the inner wall into the palace courtyard, where they were introduced to a slim man in his mid thirties, with short curly brown hair and blue eyes. He was dressed in a fine scarlet tunic and hose, tall black buckled boots, and a heavy fur lined red cloak similar to Jalesia's.

"Jalesia! You're back much earlier than I expected." the man held out his arms.

"Yarlyn, it's good to see you again." Jalesia replied.

Jelik shrugged. He'd thought a few times over the last week that a woman like Jalesia wouldn't be single - and it looked like she was with a powerful nobleman of the Trendrik court. Sighing, he was pleased that he hadn't made a fool of himself trying to get close to her.

Quick introductions were made, and the man introduced as Lord Yarlyn seemed very pleased to see them. Jalesia dismissed the eleven soldiers, then Yarlyn led the group into the palace as two boys rushed from the stables to care for their mounts.

None of the companions, with the exception of Jassnik and Antaeus, had ever been around royalty before. Sudenora found himself awkwardly nodding a greeting to each servant that made way for them as Yarlyn marched with purpose past them.

"Very nice." Jassnik commented as he walked beside Gen'vieve. She clung to his arm, looking very uncomfortable.

"Here we are." Yarlyn stopped at a side corridor, sweeping his arm to indicate the companions should venture down the new passage. "There are several suites for your use. I'll arrange to have hot water brought to you shortly, and will send for you in one hour." He then turned to Jalesia and held out his arm. "Shall I escort you?"

"Please," Jalesia answered, taking his arm. Turning back to the group, she said, "See you all in an hour - 'til then." With a smile and a wave, from Jalesia, Yarlyn led her back the way they'd come.

"Well," Anthron said nervously. "Better get cleaned up. We're meeting the King in an hour."

* * * * * * * * *

"Tell me what happened?" Crysin calmly asked as he sipped a green drink from a shot glass.

Kadash ran his hand over his smooth scalp, wiping off beads of sweat as he let out a long sigh. The assassin winced and shifted uncomfortably as he nursed his injured shoulder. "Lorol turned up with Kros where you'd told us to be," Kadash began. "He said you wanted us to follow that group, and that Kros would be heading the mission. When they got to civilization, we were to get a dagger they carried and take out as many as we could," Kadash shook his head. "We followed so far behind, we didn't know they had an Elf with them."

Smit-Myer Crysin nodded slowly. "Just be glad you rolled with the arrow and fell out the window. The entire team is dead now." He finished his drink then ordered another.

The two assassins sat in *The Open Book*, a small tavern in Platown, east of the great Library. Crysin had arrived in Platown nine days after the attack at *The Polished Platter* and had found Kadash nursing himself to health.

"Why did you follow Lorol's orders?" Crysin asked, his expression neutral.

"He knew where we were, he knew our passwords, our signs. He convinced us you had sent him." Kadash dabbed a cloth across his forehead.

"What did your instincts tell you?"

"They told me never to trust Lorol the Blade."

"Then your instincts were correct," Crysin let out a resigned sigh. After a minute, he said,"I'm getting out of the game, my old friend."

"*What*?" Kadash nearly choked on his beer."How can you get out? They will hunt you."

"They've already started. I think my team was selected to test the strengths and weaknesses of the group - in other words - to get slaughtered. Getting the dagger would have been a bonus."

There was a long silence before Kadash said,"So, what now? I'm no good for another month at least. Will you stay here...or follow the group?"

Crysin stroked his goatee in thought."I don't know. I may track Carl Mort'l and that Elementalist, since they are my biggest threat in Sarophia - besides Dernas." He reached into his tunic, retrieving a full pouch. He placed it in front of Kadash."Here, consider yourself unemployed. Our team is no more, and I haven't the want anymore to set up another. Do what you will from here."

Kadash didn't look surprised."You know, if I resurface they'll want me to go after you."

Crysin nodded."Or they'll kill you. That's your choice, I just hope we never need to cross swords my friend." Crysin pushed back his chair and rose.

Kadash struggled to his feet and held out his hand."I hope we don't either. I know you're better."

They forced a quiet chuckle.

"Goodbye Kadash."

Kadash smiled."Goodbye." They shook hands, and Smit-Myer Crysin dropped several coins for his drinks on the table, and left *The Open Book*.

Kadash watched the closed door for several moments, before saying quietly,"Goodbye my old friend. I hope we don't meet again."

* * * * * * * * * *

"King Rogor, this is the group I have been telling you about." Yarlyn said as the companions entered the King's study.

"Show them in." Rogor said in a clear commanding voice as he stood from behind his paper covered desk.

Rogor Trendrik, the King of Sarophia, was a broad middle-aged man with shoulder length curly brown hair and a neatly trimmed beard. He was dressed in a heavy red velvet robe and cloak, and from his belt hung a jewelled rapier.

Anthron could instantly tell that the King of Sarophia was a fighter of some talent. He also noted a strong green aura surrounding the man.

The King's study was a large red carpeted room; the walls lined with overflowing bookshelves and rolled maps. While the King's large desk rested near the back of the room, another part of the room was obviously used for entertaining. Several luxurious four-seater couches surrounded an open fireplace, with a small table placed in between each. A crystal chandelier hung from the centre of the ceiling with enough candles flickering to make the room seem bright. There were two other exits, besides the door they had entered.

King Rogor gestured to the group to seat themselves on the couches. then eased himself into a soft leather chair with a pleased groan, motioning for Yarlyn, who was standing at his side, to make introductions.

Yarlyn inclined his head in response - close to a bow but not quite, Jelik noted."I shall ask Lady Jalesia to assist as I have not yet committed all names to memory," Jalesia smirked as Yarlyn began speaking in what she called his 'court voice'. Yarlyn continued as he waved his arm towards Rogor,"May I introduce King Rogor Trendrik, ruler of Sarophia."

The heavily-built King smiled,"I believe you are going to unlock the mystery of The Selection for us."

"We certainly hope so," Yarlyn commented with a nervous chuckle."This is Anthron, Kielmark, Jelik, Sudenora and Karlos - all from Izonda." The King lazed on his couch and nodded. He waved for Yarlyn to continue."Lady Anthea from the Forest of Ithren, Jassnik from..." The King's adviser regarded Jalesia, who shrugged.

"Jassnik Corline from Cyermyth," the troubadour replied.

Yarlyn's eyes widened, and the King let out a loud laugh."You're part of the Panthorian Royal Family?" Yarlyn's eyes narrowed."Where's your family ring?"

Jassnik withdrew a ring from a chain around his neck and dangled it in front of Yarlyn.

Yarlyn stammered slightly, recovering quickly."If we had known..."

Jassnik smiled and replaced his neck chain inside his tunic."No worries. I've been travelling somewhat disguised over the last while, having a try at travelling merchant. Well, had a go..."

Yarlyn eyed Jassnik suspiciously before continuing."You know Antaeus of Sambethe," With that, the Elf and King nodded in silent greeting."And finally, Gen'vieve from..."

As Yarlyn looked to Jalesia for assistance, Gen'vieve interrupted."I'm from here and there." She smiled sweetly, her smile emphasising her dimples.

"Yes," If Yarlyn was irritated at Gen'vieve's reply he didn't let it show."Let's get down to business then, shall we?"

"Who leads?" King Rogor stated, his expression suddenly very serious.

Anthea elbowed Anthron before he replied,"I am our spokesperson, Your Majesty."

Anthron felt sweat trickle down his back as Rogor focused his attention on him."Then tell me who is behind The Selection?"

Anthron cleared his throat."There are two major players in Sarophia that appear to be running the Selection - the first is Carl Mort'l..."

"First knight of Queen Kilandra's personal guard," Yarlyn dubiously supplied to the King. With a wave from King Rogor, Anthron continued.

"The second is an Elementalist name Zathorn Sabriski," Anthron waited for Yarlyn to interrupt, but no explanation of Zathorn was forthcoming."We first came across them at Urgar Keep."

The King and Yarlyn asked questions of each of the companions late into the night regarding the Selection, how they were taken from their homes, transported in cages, and ended up in Ithren. Anthron and Anthea described the events leading up to The Great Library, then Jassnik explained the spell they had researched, the components required, and finally Xycermon.

"I thought the Ruling Lords were legend." the King said wearily, sipping at his brandy."This is much bigger than I had first thought. Yarlyn, what are your thoughts?"

Yarlyn let out his breath slowly while he thought."We must become active in trying to stop this spell from being cast. Even the Elves think it important enough to send Antaeus here."

"I agree," King Rogor nodded."We could send an army against the enemy, but who is the real enemy?"

Jassnik cleared his throat, and Yarlyn said,"Yes?"

"From what the King of Elves told us, Queen Kilandra's adviser, Aracon, fits their description of *Le Shoft Tear*," said Jassnik."He may be the leader of the cult behind the Selection."

Rogor looked to Yarlyn who began gnawing at a nail. When he realised he was being looked at Yarlyn shrugged."I don't know. I've met Aracon before - boring sort of a guy. What we need to do is label Carl Mort'l and this Zathorn Sabriski as outlaws of Sarophia and post a warrant for their arrest. Offer an appealing reward - perhaps one thousand gold pieces? Our inquisitor will be able to extract the information we require from the comfort of the Trendrik dungeons.

"However, it might be prudent to send an emissary to Cyermyth, to investigate what we may."

"Someone like the Minister of Foreign Affairs?" the King raised an eyebrow.

Yarlyn did his best to look surprised."Why me? Of course I would go if you asked it of me. I would require soldiers to escort me of course, and..."

King Rogor let out a long sigh."It is late. This is what I shall do. You shall go to Panthorian, and take this group with you. Captain Saralon will arrive back in five days - he shall escort you with fifty of my best soldiers. Jalesia?"

"Yes, Your Majesty?" Jalesia said.

"You shall go also, as the Minister's body guard."

"Yes, Your Majesty."

Rogor finished his brandy with a cough."Yarlyn Kontar, I want one thing very clear. We are not going to start war - even though we've heard one is brewing. You are to find out as much information as you can then return in one piece. We know something's happening in Cyermyth, now's your chance to find out what."

"So we leave in a week then." Yarlyn rubbed his hands together.

* * * * * * * * *

"I've just received word that Captain Saralon has arrived. We shall be leaving at dawn tomorrow." Jalesia said.

The group sat in their communal lounge, as they had done for most of the week. Severe rain and winds had been assailing Trendrik, and they had paced the halls of the palace like caged animals, waiting for the weather to let up. Jassnik had occasionally entertained the group by teaching them several card and dice games, singing, and telling stories from Panthorian. Only Sudenora and Karlos had spent any of their time elsewhere - at the palace's library and amongst the Royal Healers of *Termolen*. They were both present when Jalesia called by.

"We leave tomorrow?" Kielmark asked.

"Just in time to miss the Heart of Winter Festival too," Gen'vieve screwed up her nose."I was looking forward to that - a royal booze up."

"The King wants us to leave as soon as possible," Jalesia shrugged."We're leaving by road since the work on the Trendrik Port hasn't been finished yet. We're catching a ship from Sornc now. Your uniforms are ready for their final fittings, so report to the armoury within the hour." The King's bodyguard then left.

"I don't see why we have to all dress as Trendrik soldiers," Sudenora moaned."I don't suit chain."

Karlos patted his stomach,"I was beginning to need another set of armour any, as my scale was becoming too big for me."

It was the first time Anthron really noticed that the party's Healer had in fact lost quite some weight during the two months since leaving the Forest of Ithren."I agree with the disguise." he said.

"Well, you're not a washer woman are you?" shot Gen'vieve.

Anthron blushed." 'The washer women are an integral party of any army...' " he repeated Yarlyn's words with some accuracy, the rest of the group laughing.

"Don't worry Gen," Anthea smiled."At least you'll have company."

* * * * * * * * * *

Antaeus ran back into view along the Platown - Trendrik Highway. Anthron was amazed at the Elf's stamina - he never seemed to tire, and he never looked fatigued.

To Captain Saralon, Antaeus said,"There appears to be some kind of disturbance about five miles north Captain."

Captain Saralon rubbed his chin in thought. The Captain stood just less than six feet, wearing a broadsword at his belt and a coat of chain mail, over which he wore the King's white tabard with a black castle. He was in his thirties with shoulder-length brown hair, blue eyes, and a weathered face. Over the last week of travelling under Saralon's command, Anthron had come to respect him as a blunt honest man with compassion for the men under his command. Anthron, Jassnik, Kielmark, Karlos, Jelik and Sudenora made one of nine groups of six soldiers. Each group of six appeared to know each other very well, and Anthron noticed they treated each other like brothers. Anthea and Gen'vieve, wearing fairly unflattering peasant dresses, travelled inside one of the supply wagons situated amongst the middle of the troops near Yarlyn's carriage. With Anthron and the others trotting right behind the Captain, Anthron hadn't spent much time with the half-Elf at all since leaving Trendrik behind a week ago. Jalesia had taken the role of rear guard of the troops. The last two soldiers to make the fifty the

King had assigned as their escort were the Captain's sergeant and corporal. Sergeant Loucas was a bull of a man about half a foot shorter than Anthron. His greying hair was cut short to match his beard, and he bore an ugly purple scar across his forehead. The rumours amongst the men were that the sergeant had got the scar from wrestling with a young lion, which from the size of Loucas, Anthron believed. The sergeant was a gruff man who commanded the soldiers with a harsh respect, however he didn't seem obliged to treat Anthron and the others with any form of courtesy. Anthron assumed that Sergeant Loucas only paid respect to soldiers who had earned it.

Corporal Olin, as it turned out, was from Vemmlok. Olin was a tall gangly man in his mid twenties with curly brown hair. Even though Anthron didn't actually know him from his hometown, they reminisced about some of the townsfolk they both knew and the nicer weather that Izonda usually had. In Izonda it was common for the sun to shine at some stage during the Heart of Winter Festival.

Captain Saralon leaned down from his horse and whispered something to the Elf, who nodded. Antaeus gave Anthron and their group a quick nod before turning and silently running back the way he had come, securing his bow and quiver with one hand as he disappeared.

"Elven endurance," Saralon said, shaking his head."He can easily move as fast as a trotting horse - could probably run for longer too..."

Anthron smiled. On the first few days he had tried to make small talk with Saralon several times. He decided that if he were going to break the silence, it would be by the Captain's prompting."Has the King met Antaeus before?" Anthron thought back to their introductions to the King back in the palace.

Saralon pulled his uniformed red cloak closer as the afternoon wind picked up."Antaeus used to visit Trendrik about thirty years ago. That was around the time when Rogor's older brother was killed along the Euroness and Parntorn border, and he became Heir to the throne. Rogor's father, King Gathor, ordered him back from the borders, to return to Trendrik and be taught the ways of the court. I believe Antaeus had fallen in love with our King Rogor's sister, Arleia. Arleia may well have loved him too, but six months after Rogor returned, King Gathor had her marry a nobleman in Panthorian."

Saralon shrugged."It's probably for the best, as I believe she hasn't aged well in Gwilieth - the King seems to think Antaeus doesn't seem to have aged a day in thirty years."

Anthron went silent and slowed his horse so he was by himself. What about him and Anthea? She may only be half Elven, but she would still outlive him...how many times?

"Back in formation!" Sergeant Loucas cried from somewhere behind, and Anthron nudged his horse forward, again next to Kielmark. Anthron silently cursed the sergeant, then swore to himself that he would never join the army.

SAROPHIA BY STU DUNN

CHAPTER TWENTY ONE

The wind howled outside.

Yarlyn glared at the skies from his carriage as it started to spit again, and wrapped his fur lined red hooded cloak tighter around him. He wore tan coloured leather breeches and jerkin, black leather gloves and his favourite black knee high buckled boots. Sitting on the seat next to him was his crossbow that could load three bolts at once, and in his belt he wore several jewelled silver daggers. Yarlyn had to admit that he wasn't the best traveller, particularly during winter.

Jalesia laughed at Yarlyn from horseback. She had plaited her long red-streaked brown hair back for the journey, and wore a red headband. She wore a cloak identical to Yarlyn's, and was dressed in fitting brown leather pants. She wore a vest of chainmail over which she wore the King's tabard, and elbow-high brown gloves covered her hands. Her twin swords were both sheathed on her left hip.

"I don't think we've ever travelled together, Hawke," Jalesia said, still referring to the name Yarlyn went by at *The Drawn Bow*. "Why don't you stop hiding in your carriage? Come out and enjoy this beautiful weather."

"You know, you could always travel in here with me...you are meant to be protecting me." Yarlyn grinned.

"Oh Yarlyn." Jalesia laughed, not seeing Yarlyn's look of disappointment as she dropped back as rear guard once again.

Yarlyn had spent the nine days since leaving Trendrik mostly drunk, as there was no one to share his carriage with and he refused to ride when he didn't need to. He had earned his right to ride in style.

Yarlyn woke as the carriage stopped suddenly. He could hear the obnoxious sergeant barking orders, and the corporal ensuring the orders were followed. Wiping sleep from eyes, Yarlyn was fully awake when he heard a soldier scream.

Flinging open the carriage door, Yarlyn saw what the commotion was about.

Standing amongst the soldiers was what appeared to be a beautiful Elven woman dressed in a black robe. The Elf's long honey blonde hair flowed hypnotically in the wind, and Yarlyn found it difficult to concentrate on anything else. He forced his eyes away, then looked back and saw the rest of the creature. Her naked scaled body was jet black, similar to an obsidian ring Yarlyn wore.

As a soldier attacked, the creature flicked him away with ease, then with powerful arms lifted another dazed soldier and ripped his throat out with her long talons.

"It's a *Crasheiar,*" Yarlyn breathed as he reached for his hip flask.

The *Crasheiar* turned her gaze upon two soldiers who were attacking. One stopped mid-swing, and Yarlyn could tell that she had successfully charmed the soldier as he lowered his weapon and allowed the beast to tear his face off.

"Form a defense! Archers behind, take out the head!" Loucas ordered, and the King's soldiers quickly formed defensive lines to protect the archers and wagons.

Suddenly Jalesia was next to Yarlyn."Get on," she dismounted and handed him the reins."Get behind the supply wagons." Once, Yarlyn was mounted, she handed him his crossbow from the carriage then slapped the rump of her horse to start it cantering.

Anthron pointed his sapphire encrusted sword at the *Crasheiar,* noticing it stop and shake its head. The *Crasheiar* searched past the first line of soldiers, ignoring the rain of attacks via sword and arrow, until it saw Anthron. As she locked eyes with him, Anthron felt his knees go weak, and his sword lowered slowly.

"Anthron!" Kielmark slapped the blonde warrior across the face as the creature's charm began to take hold.

Coming to his senses, Anthron rubbed his jaw,"Thanks." He looked around quickly, stopping suddenly in alarm - he was unable to see colours surrounding half the soldiers in front of him.

"What is that thing?" Jelik interrupted Anthron's thought. He stood as part of the second defense line with Anthron and Kielmark, with Jassnik, Sudenora and Karlos joining the third.

The *Crasheiar* launched herself into the air while extending her sixteen-foot wings that had previously been folded at her sides. Arrows continued to rain upon the flying creature, harmlessly deflected by her black scales. As the *Crasheiar* paused to take a deep breath, Sudenora felt the hairs on the back of his neck prickle as magic was being summoned.

"Back!" Sudenora called, then pushed Jassnik and Karlos away from the creature. Anthron turned to see the Elementalist retreating. He motioned for Jelik and Kielmark to follow.

Suddenly the ground shook, and Anthron was hurled from his feet by an immense heat. He collided into a wagon wheel with such force that his shoulder smashed one of the spokes. Still lying on the ground, Anthron turned to see what had happened.

Instantly the fetor of burnt flesh filled his nostrils as he saw the destruction the creature had inflicted. Roughly a twenty-foot ring of charred smoking bodies littered the highway. Anthron estimated that maybe a third of the King's soldiers had just been killed. He could hear the injured moaning, or screaming in agony as half of their bodies had been burnt. Smoke stung his eyes as he pushed himself back to his feet. The King's tabard he wore was scorched, and he threw off his uniform red cloak as he noticed it was smouldering. He located his long sword as Captain Saralon shouted,"That thing is still up there. Archers! Spread out more, aim for the head and the wings!"

Jelik appeared through the smoke, a large cut across his forehead."Where's Kielmark?"

Panic gripped Anthron as he scanned the bodies nearby. He felt his throat tighten as he spotted Kielmark lying motionless, his chain armour and tabard melted together to expose his badly burnt flesh. Then Anthron saw his fingers clasping into a fist...he was alive!

Anthron heard the remaining soldiers firing upon the *Crasheiar* as she taunted them from the air with her magical charms and unnatural beauty. Anthron and Jelik pulled Kielmark under Yarlyn's carriage to inspect him as Sudenora, Karlos and Jassnik reappeared. Damn it, Anthron thought, I need Anthea here.

Karlos quickly examined Kielmark,"He'll live - no doubt because of that silver helm of his. He's healing nearly as quickly as if I'd asked *Termolen* myself."

"Right," Anthron said,"Let's kill that thing."

Jassnik stayed with Karlos as Anthron, Jelik and Sudenora marched into the smoke.

* * * * * * * * * *

Anthea finished drawing symbols in the air, then spread her arms wide. A tingling sensation spread throughout her body and Gen'vieve nodded that she also felt it. Now the immediate area was immune to fire.

"I have to stay still and concentrate to keep this protection up," Anthea said."Stay safe."

Gen'vieve drew her long dirk from her boot."I'm staying right here."

"Thank you."

You're welcome, Anthea heard Gen'vieve's voice in her head.

* * * * * * * * * *

Sudenora finished his incantation, then released a crackling bolt of lightning from his fingertips at the *Crasheiar*. The creature folded her wings and dropped sharply before opening them again, avoiding most of the damage. She sucked in her breath again, and breathed another fireball onto the panicked group below. To their amazement as the fireball hit the ground it dispersed into nothing. Heartened, the soldiers doubled their efforts to shoot the *Crasheiar* down.

"I was sure we were dead that time," Sudenora said, wide eyed.

"Not just yet," Jelik replied. The thief strode towards the creature, Elven blade in one hand, his short sword in the other.

The *Crasheiar* screeched as an arrow finally pierced her scaly armour, injuring her wing. Soon another arrow struck the same spot on the *Crasheiar*, followed by another, then another.

Anthron smiled. Antaeus had returned.

The blonde warrior charged as the *Crasheiar's* clawed feet touched the earth once again and the rain of arrows ceased. The beast viciously lashed out at a soldier in front of Anthron, who fell back decapitated. Anthron stepped over the body and stabbed his sword towards the *Crasheiar*, the enchanted blade biting deep into her scaled side. A cheer went up from the immediately surrounding soldiers, and within another minute the creature's head was bleeding dark red. The *Crasheiar* suddenly turned on Anthron, slashing at his face. He dropped to the ground as he lifted his sword, then awkwardly rolled over his shoulder, back to his feet. As Anthron readied himself for another attack, he found the *Crasheiar* was down to one knee, with at least ten swords raining upon her - with other soldiers waiting to fill a gap if someone was to fall or tire.

Anthron rejoined the fight, and soon after the *Crasheiar* crashed to the earth motionless, covered with a mixture of her own and the soldier's blood.

"What in all the levels of hell was that?" Captain Saralon exclaimed, as he wiped his sword blade. The left side of his face was blistered, and some of his hair had been burnt away.

"That was a *Crasheiar* I believe," answered Yarlyn, who approached with Anthea and Gen'vieve. "I obviously haven't seen one before, but..."

"It would be hard to mistake for anything else?" Gen'vieve finished.

"Quite," Yarlyn nodded as he covered his nose with his cloak.

Saralon went about ordering the wounded to be looked after, and the dead buried some distance to the west of the highway. The *Crasheiar* was burnt. The death count was twenty-three - including Sergeant Loucas. Corporal Olin took charge of the situation straight away, ensuring the twenty able soldiers were kept busy.

A tent was set up to the east of the highway where the wounded were taken. Karlos invoked *Termolen's* power to relieve the five wounded men of some of their burns. To even Karlos's amazement, Kielmark was on his feet again by the time the tent had been erected.

The heavy storm clouds began rolling away as night fell upon the encampment. A high sense of paranoia gripped them, and even though everyone was exhausted, no one slept.

"What was that thing?" Saralon leaned back in his padded wooden chair as he studied the companions, then turned to Yarlyn and Jalesia.

They were seated at a long table in a large green tent which was Saralon's private sleeping quarters. It had a cot at the far end with a wooden chest at the foot. There were two guards outside the tent flap, monitoring all that requested entry.

"Well," Yarlyn began to explain, pausing to take a sip from his hip flask."Our Intelligence Service picked up sightings of these *Crasheiar* about five years ago, up north," He nodded towards the north."I don't know much about them, just a description. Once, our agents near Sorne saw one and reported it, then they began turning up floating in The Deep Sea after that. You know how hard it is to get good agents in Sorne or Brane these days?"

Saralon smiled weakly as he ran his hands through his matted brown hair,"Where was this creature sighted?"

Yarlyn took another long drink."There were three reported to be flying north of Brane. We assumed they were heading back to their lair or something."

Captain Saralon let out a long breath."You know you should have..."

Yarlyn held up his hand."I know I should have, but things happen. I didn't want to send our army north, only to find the sightings fictious - some ploy to weaken Trendrik's defenses. Since I didn't get any more reports, I forgot about them."

"Your reports stopped due to your agents being killed," Jalesia repeated.

Saralon sipped at his wine as he studied the others in the group who had remained silent. To Antaeus, he said,"At least we know what the disturbance was." He then addressed the rest of the group,"So, what are we to do now? We may have at least two more of those things out there, and we have to march right past their doorstep..." The Captain fell deep in thought.

"What is further north than Brane?" Sudenora asked rhetorically."The Three Towers," he answered before anyone else was able.

"They're ruins at any rate," Karlos said.

It was fairly widely known that three towers stood at the northern most point of eastern Sarophia, where great Elementalists trained and taught, also known as a magic academy of sorts. As the stories were told, twenty-seven centuries ago the legendary Veckros Ipisimus contested with a rival Elementalist by the name of Sauros Loklin. There was no clear winner after their three-day magical battle, which ended with the destruction of the Three Towers and the surrounding towns and farms.

"What are you alluding to?" Captain Saralon asked Sudenora.

"The Ruins of the Three Towers are far enough away from everywhere to be a good place..." Sudenora rolled his hand as he was trying to find the right word.

"For Carl Mort'l and Zathorn Sabriski to use as a base of operations?" Gen'vieve finished, and Sudenora nodded.

"Ah," Saralon said."I see where you are going with this."

"When was the last time anyone has been up there?" Anthron asked.

Yarlyn tugged on his ear as he thought."I don't know," he said vaguely."The Kingdom pretty much ignores the Three Towers. They aren't even on the new maps..."

Jalesia said,"Are we looking at heading there on our way to Sorne?"

Saralon unrolled a map of Sarophia. Pointing to Brane he said,"Brane is nearly a day off the road." He then pointed to the northern cliffs."To get to the ruins would take another four days."

"If we cut across here," Jalesia indicated a line just north of Platown straight up to where the ruins were,"we can save quite a lot of time."

Saralon looked to Yarlyn,"Yes, but since we'd be going off the highway, someone wouldn't be able to ride in their carriage..."

"Fine," Yarlyn folded his arms,"*If* we're going."

"I think we should take a look." Jalesia said.

"I do too," Sudenora agreed.

"And I," Anthron nodded.

Yarlyn held up both hands in defeat."Okay, I get the picture."

"At first light tomorrow we'll send the carriage and supply wagons back with the wounded, and we'll carry everything we need on our horses or backs," Saralon poured another wine."It's late people. Remember your watch shifts - you are in the army."

The group exited the Captain's tent as he collapsed into his cot for what he thought would be the last night in a long while.

* * * * * * * * * *

They stayed at Platown on the second night since the fight with the *Crasheiar*. They decided to stay at a different inn - besides, Jalesia thought the innkeeper of *The Polished Platter* probably wouldn't let them back in due to the destruction during their last visit. The *Highway Rest* was similar to the previous they had stayed at, but instead of shiny metal walls; these walls were covered with beautiful mosaics.

Sudenora was distraught that still no letter had arrived from Carlae, when he returned to Platown.

Three days later along the highway, they crossed the only bridge that allowed passage across The Long River. They came across a band of fifteen mercenaries who looked like they were harassing anyone who wanted passage, for a toll - but at the sight of what appeared to be thirty Kingdom soldiers they promptly ceased their loitering.

They left the highway and headed north for another hour before setting camp along a fairly defensible rock face, then set about cooking. After a dinner of stew and bread, the companions relaxed, enjoying an evening of no rain and slightly warmer weather.

"How are you doing?" Anthron casually asked Anthea. Now that the number of soldiers had halved and there were no longer any supply wagons, Anthron had been able to ride near Anthea without appearing like a disobedient soldier.

Anthea smiled, and snuggled closer into Anthron's arms in answer.

Since hearing Saralon recounting Antaeus's story, Anthron had been thinking about himself and the half Elf he loved. He studied her golden hair, her peaceful expression as she dozed. His heart still beat faster when he looked at her. He smiled as he replayed several of their intimate moments together, until he found himself becoming aroused. Knowing there was no chance of privacy with Anthea, he chose to look around the surrounding camp. Some soldiers were sleeping and a couple were quietly playing cards. On the inside of the trench that signified the outside of their camp he could just make out in the darkness the still forms of Jelik and Kielmark on the southern watch. Jelik had kept pretty much to himself since leaving the Kutporn sewers. Whatever happened down there seemed to change the thief. Not only was he quieter, but Anthron thought Jelik looked to be struggling with something also.

Kielmark was again lucky to be alive. The Arrolokian now wore his own mismatched armour of leather, chain and plate since his Kingdom chain mail had been ruined from the *Crasheiar's* fire. He wore a new tabard, and like Anthron, Jelik, Jassnik, Karlos and Sudenora, he wore his Elven cloak instead of the soldier's uniform. Kielmark had discussed his latest near death experience with Karlos in Platown. Karlos reported that Kielmark thought he could see shadows moving out of the corner of his eye every now and again. Anthron wouldn't have thought much about it, accept the aura he saw around Kielmark had changed from a green to a more yellowish colour.

Anthron realised now that if he looked hard enough at any living thing he could see the surrounding colours. He wasn't sure what each colour meant, but he now knew that to not see any was a very bad thing. Of the soldiers fighting the *Crasheiar*, the ones that Anthron saw as having no aura had died that day.

Anthron let out a long sigh. He would ask Sudenora and Jassnik more about it when they had more time. Checking that his enchanted long sword was by his side, Anthron allowed himself to finally drift off to sleep.

* * * * * * * * * *

The next two days were uneventful as they followed the western bank of The Long River in a roughly northeastern direction through the long grass. Anthron and the others were now fairly proficient in picking defensible campsites and fortifying them thoroughly with spiked trenches, getting to practice every night. The Captain had promoted Corporal Olin to Sergeant after Loucas's death, and appointed a veteran soldier by the name of Wilon. Corporal Wilon took his new role seriously, and had Anthron's group of six performing all tasks the usual soldiers were required to do.

It was sweaty work digging the deep trenches that surrounded their site, and filling them with sharpened branches. A large hole was also dug aside as the latrine. Anthron understood very quickly that if a soldier irritated Sergeant Olin or Corporal Wilon during the day, that man and the other five in their group were assigned to stand watch next to the ditch of human waste during the night.

Anthron watched his breath as he let out a long sigh. It was about midnight, the evening being clear but very cold. *Lithloren* was full tonight, illuminating the campsite with her violet touch as *Tolorel* had already sunk a half-hour before. Squinting up at the massive range to the east known as the Snowcaps, the fighter let his mind wander.

"Peaceful, isn't it?" Jelik disturbed Anthron from his thoughts. Anthron hadn't even heard the thief approaching. Jelik stood over the warrior while he surveyed the violet landscape.

Anthron nodded,"Yes. I was just thinking about home. I remember going out into the cornfields when *Lithloren* was full one time..."

"Say no more," Jelik smiled."Sounds like the sort of story that ends with a woman on her back."

Anthron began to protest, then let out a quiet chuckle. Anthron stopped suddenly as a deep moan sounded from somewhere in the mountains, followed by a distant roar.

Karlos and Sudenora appeared within moments from their post."What was that?" Sudenora whispered.

Anthron and Jelik shrugged. Anthron said to Sudenora,"Let the Sergeant know there's something up there. It didn't sound close, but he'd have our ears if we didn't tell him."

Sudenora nodded and headed for the middle of the camp.

Another roar sounded.

"That sounded a bit like an angry barbarian." Karlos said.

"Look," Jelik pointed. Anthron stared for a few moments before spying two humanoid shapes half way up one of the many peaks of the Snowcaps.

"What are they?" Anthron asked no one in particular.

"Most likely hill giants," Anthron jumped as Sergeant Olin appeared with Sudenora."There's a large colony of those giants up there. We've had to get physical a couple of times when they've gotten too interested in Brane and Platown," Olin pointed at the two silhouettes."I'm just pleased they're up there. Sounds like they're fighting over territory. Wake me if they get much closer. Night gentlemen."

Anthron looked back to the giants. He couldn't make much of them out, being too far away, but he could tell they were huge - possibly twelve to fifteen feet tall. The giants were obviously strong too - hurling boulders at each other that would have been twice his size. The duel lasted for some minutes as the giants bellowed at each other, until finally a rock caught one giant by surprise on its head. Another bellow echoed through the mountains as the winning hill giant watched its foe fall to its death.

"We need one of those if we come across another of those devil Elves," Karlos said after the successful giant had wandered out of their earshot.

"That *Crasheiar* took out about twenty-five of the Kingdom's best soldiers." Jelik pointed out.

"True," Anthron breathed.

Karlos indicated over his shoulder with his thumb."We'd better get back. There's only an hour of watch left."

"Night Karlos," Jelik waved. After Karlos and Sudenora had left, the thief fell silent after a deep breath and fidgeted with a dagger.

Anthron struggled for several minutes as to what to say to Jelik before he blurted,"How are you doing?"

Jelik stopped spinning his dagger."Fine," he said casually.

"I mean, about that ring. I don't know what happened in Kutporn..."

"It scared the hell out of me Anthron, and every now and again I can hear voices. Occasionally I feel like a rage is coming over me, and I have the urge to cut my own finger off...Come on Anthron, how am I doing?" Jelik began twirling his dagger with some urgency, then stopped. Removing his right glove, Jelik displayed the marks around his middle finger."If I don't find a way to get this off my finger soon, it looks like I have two options. First, I can cut it off. Second, I can get myself sacrificed in some cults' attempt to revive a Ruling Lord."

"I don't know what to say..." Anthron said quietly.

"It's okay Anthron. I appreciate your concern; I'm just having some difficulties. It's nice to just sit here under *Lithloren's* gaze and not think about anything."

Anthron was pleased that Jelik had said what was on his mind. Anthea had attempted to talk with him to no avail during their stay in Trendrik.

* * * * * * * * * *

They got to the Kutporn-Sorne highway after dark the next day and negotiated accommodation for themselves and their mounts on a large beef farm. After the tents were set up, Captain Saralon purchased the troops a worthy meal of cooked beef, potatoes and vegetables.

"I don't think I've ever eaten meat this good," Jelik commented as he sat cross-legged with a plate on his lap.

"That's because you don't often get unsalted meats in a city like Smazorok." Anthron said.

"I heard the Captain picked which cow we were going to eat." Karlos said as he washed his food down with a mug of water.

Antaeus approached, with Anthea on one arm and Gen'vieve on the other. Anthron felt pangs in his chest as he saw the two Elves together...then he noticed Gen'vieve watching him with a sad expression.

"Anthron," Antaeus said as Anthea sat on the blonde warrior's knee."When you and the others are available," the Elf motioned to Jelik and Jassnik."I wish to bring something to your attention."

Anthron started to push the half-Elf from his knee when Antaeus raised his hand and smiled."There is no hurry."

After an hour, Antaeus led Anthron, Jelik and Jassnik to the east of the farm. After ten minutes of walking it began to rain, and the Elf began jogging. After another five minutes Antaeus stopped and crouched, using his cloak to cover something on the ground.

"I found this earlier," Antaeus said."It may be too dark for your eyes to see in this light - I didn't think of that sorry."

"I have a candle on me," Jassnik offered, then proceeded to light it as Anthron and Jelik provided shelter with their cloaks.

"What do you have to show us?" Anthron asked.

"This." The Elf drew back his cloak, and in the candlelight they could make out a footprint in some dried mud.

"A footprint?" Jelik asked.

"An orcs' boot," Antaeus replied, then pointed to the northeast."There are a few more about a mile that way."

"Have you told the Captain?" Anthron asked.

Antaeus nodded."He recommended that I show you three also, as we have been selected to scout ahead of the main party. Saralon now believes that Ruins of the Three Towers aren't as deserted as he first considered."

"So just us four are going on ahead?" Jassnik asked as he examined the imprint in the mud.

"That's correct," Antaeus said."We go on alone one day ahead of the others from Brane."

"Sudenora, Karlos and Kielmark won't be happy." Anthron said as he let the candle go out. Jassnik took it and placed it back in his belt pouch.

Antaeus indicated they should head back."I believe the Captain has something else lined up for them."

* * * * * * * * * *

The orc crouched low as the Elf glanced his way. Gruin had fought

Elves before, and was painfully aware that their eyes were better than his at detecting heat around a body. Gruin waited until the Elf and three humans were far enough away so he could steal away into the night undetected. Setting off at a fast pace, the orc scout began his four and a half-day run northward. There was much planning to be done in order for the trap to be laid, and Gruin had every intention of making the Master very happy.

CHAPTER TWENTY TWO

They disappeared into the fog.

Anthron, Jelik, Antaeus and Jassnik led their horses away from Brane just after dawn through the long grass. It had taken most of the previous day to reach Brane from the small farm, and they had at last stayed in beds at the small town's only tavern.

Captain Saralon assured the companions that he had specific plans for Kielmark, Sudenora, Karlos, Anthea and Gen'vieve, which was why they were not part of the scouting party - however he would not tell them what. When there had been protest, Saralon merely reminded them that the King had put them under his charge.

They discarded the royal tabards for their regular clothes. Saralon had provisioned them with light packs and enough food for a week.

They led their horses for another ten minutes before mounting, and rode for the next hour in silence as the fog dispersed. Anthron brooded at having had to leave Anthea behind. He had tried one last time last night to argue with Saralon, claiming that if they were a scouting party, who better to have along than a half-Elf? The Captain had just waved him out of his room, and ensured that no one else could get in to see him. Anthron had spent most of the night making love to Anthea, which for some reason felt desperate. It was as if both of them knew they'd never see each other again. Anthron had lain awake in the hours before dawn, willing the sun not to rise.

The sun rose anyway.

"What do you think the Captain has in mind for the others?" Anthron broke the long silence.

Jelik shrugged, and Jassnik said,"I really don't know. It's a shame...I think I will miss Gen."

Antaeus let out a sigh."I haven't been privy to Saralon's plans, but I spied a map he had been studying. It detailed the northern coast where the ruins are, and the lands south of Brane. From what I could tell, there is a long valley leading up to the tower ruins. He had drawn an arrow pointing up the valley - possibly us - with more pointing towards the valley from the flanks. If I didn't know Saralon..." the Elf's voice trailed off.

Anthron frowned."What is it?"

Antaeus paused before replying."The valley would be a very good place for an ambush. If we get through to the ruins unnoticed, there's a chance we could get cut off from the others if there is enough of the enemy."

"Do you know what's up there?" Jelik nodded north.

"No. The Elves have not had any interest in the Three Towers since before they were destroyed."

"So you just *think* it's a good place for an ambush?" Anthron asked, to which Antaeus nodded.

Anthron squinted north across the grasslands, as if attempting to see the ruined towers that they should arrive at in four days time.

* * * * * * * * *

"What do you mean we're heading to Sorne?" Anthea yelled.

Anthea, Kielmark, Gen'vieve, Karlos and Sudenora sat at a table in the taproom of the only tavern in Brane, named *Flagon 'o*. Also sitting was Captain Saralon, Yarlyn and Jalesia and Sergeant Olin.

Captain Saralon's eyes narrowed as he regarded the half-Elf."Yarlyn, I think it's time to tell them." he said without taking his eyes from Anthea.

"Well," Yarlyn began."One of my contacts in Sorne sent a message, which we intercepted a week ago - two days after we left the library." Yarlyn paused, gauging each persons' expression - a habit he'd picked up throughout his political career."It detailed three confirmed sightings of Carl Mort'l, and one possible sighting of Sabriski."

Saralon continued."We have the full co-operation of Sorne's garrison and police. Your job is to find them before they slink onto a ship and disappear off to Panthorian."

As Anthea was about to say something, Yarlyn finished,"I sent a message back to Sorne organising the port to be closed for about a week - I bet Lord Ras was foaming at the mouth when that arrived." Yarlyn allowed himself a slight smile. Yarlyn didn't hide the fact that his job as Minister of Foreign Affairs often had him clashing with Lord Ras, ruler of Sorne - the busiest international port in Sarophia.

"How long have we got before the port is open again?" Anthea asked.

Yarlyn examined his nails as he thought."About five, six days from now. If the messenger killed several horses getting there, then you'll have about a week."

"What's stopped Mort'l from jumping onto a ship before your runner got back?" Karlos asked of Yarlyn.

"Ah," Yarlyn hesitated."The, ah...Thieves' Guild, actually. My contact ensured that Carl Mort'l would not leave the city via ship, by arrangement."

"You work with the Thieves Guild? Willingly?" Karlos blurted.

Yarlyn shrugged."Sometimes. We have a similar arrangement in most cities..."

"Except for the Mosorac Underground." Gen'vieve supplied, her dimples showing as she smiled at Yarlyn.

"Ah, yes." he stuttered, unsure how she was aware of that information.

"Anyway," Saralon's voice grated, his tone demanded attention,"Grooms have your horses ready, and five soldiers shall accompany you - including Corporal Wilon. You're to leave immediately. That will be all."

Anthea began to protest again but Karlos lightly pulled her away. They entered their rooms at the end of a short hall."You can see the wisdom in travelling to Sorne?" The Healer asked as they climbed the stairs to their rooms.

"Of course," Anthea breathed as she strapped her pack closed and hoisted it over one shoulder. Slipping a dagger into her sword belt, she said,"I know that we're better equipped for dealing with Carl Mort'l and Sabriski than the Sorne garrison and secret police are, but I don't have to like it."

"I have an interest in meeting Mort'l again," Kielmark stated,"However this time I'll be wearing armour." He motioned to the soldier's uniform he wore.

Karlos nodded."And I'm wanting to even a score with Zathorn."

Sudenora shrugged."I have no vendettas," he smiled,"Must be drinking different water."

Gen'vieve, recently dressed back in her tunic and leggings that had most of the soldiers' eyes followed her, said quietly,"I hope Jass is okay."

They were silent as they finished packing.

* * * * * * * * * *

The wind howled down the valley through the trees as Anthron and the others crouched amongst the greenery. They were three days north of Brane. The winds had picked up again, and it had been showering intermittently over the last two days.

"This has to be the valley," Anthron looked at the Elf for confirmation, who nodded.

Below them a massive valley spanned as far as Anthron could see, speckled with tufts of five-foot beach trees - blacker and more gnarled branches than Anthron had seen from his off shore home of Vemmlok. Thick brown grass covered the sandy dirt. The valley was steep where they crouched, levelling off to a slight descent about a hundred feet below, about half a mile across at its widest point.

"Not much cover," Jelik muttered.

Antaeus indicated a footprint near where they hid."And there are definitely signs of orcs having been in the area." The Elf slowly scanned the valley below."Although there is no movement other than animals for miles."

"You think we should get our horses," Jassnik indicated over his shoulder where they had tied their mounts ten minutes behind them,"We could ride down..." he finished dubiously.

Anthron looked to Antaeus, who said,"We'd stand out severely on this landscape with horses," The Elf gestured to their cloaks."These ought to be enough for us to blend in on foot."

"Let's get our gear from the horses then." Anthron made his way in a half crouch back the way they had come.

They removed the saddles from their mounts and set them free, knowing Captain Saralon and the soldiers would be arriving at the valley about this time tomorrow and there was not an adequate area nearby to graze them. They donned their packs, then set off to the north once again, into the valley that led to the Ruins of the Three Towers.

* * * * * * * * * *

Tolorel sat high in the cloudy night sky, the full moon illuminating the four figures attempting to remain hidden amongst the short trees.

"There," Antaeus pointed back the way they had come as he strung his bow. They had travelled cautiously since the morning before, slinking down the valley and weaving through the trees. Until nightfall they hadn't come across anything out of the ordinary - until the Elf noticed an orc several miles behind them. No one else could match the Elf's sight, so they periodically paused for Antaeus to scan the entire area.

"Is it any closer?" Jelik whispered, crouching next to the Elf.

Antaeus shook his head,"No, but it is definitely following our path."

"You think it best to take it out?" Anthron indicated to the bow.

"I don't know about you," Jassnik said,"But the only orcs I want behind me are dead ones."

Antaeus half smiled,"Yes, *fron amos*. I shall double back and kill the orc, then hide the body."

As the Elf began to rise, Anthron said,"Do you need any assistance?"

Antaeus again half smiled."No thank you, I will move quicker by myself." Then he was gone.

Thirty minutes later Jelik jumped as Antaeus returned silently. The Elf looked grim.

"The orc is dead?" Anthron frowned.

Antaeus nodded."And another eight. We are being tracked. They now know we are aware of them - it was unavoidable. Now that this has happened we may be in for some trouble."

"Oh," said Jassnik, looking back up the valley. Everyone turned to look.

About two miles up the valley they could see the flicker of a campfire. Within a minute, there were ten campfires burning across the valley.

"They've cut us off," Anthron breathed.

"How many do you think there are?" Jelik asked the Elf.

Antaeus calculated as another half a dozen fires sprang to life further up the valley."Orcs usually share one camp per ten, so at this stage there are about sixty up there."

The colour seemed to drain from Jassnik's face."Do you think we can slip past them?"

Antaeus shrugged."I may be able to get through, but I don't think..."

"Fair enough," Jassnik interrupted."Do we hide until Saralon catches up?"

Anthron shook his head,"If they rode down the valley where we left our mounts behind - they'll still be half a day behind at best."

"And there are only two dozen of them at best." Jelik added.

"Well," Anthron let out a long breath."We'd better get moving and see how much distance we can put between us and them. Let's just hope that whatever the Captain had in mind for the others has something to do with helping us here."

Anthron's heart sank as the first campfire was lit a mile to their left.

* * * * * * * * * *

"Look out!" Gen'vieve cried an instant before an arrow shot from the darkness took the soldier next to Karlos in the throat, throwing him from his saddle.

"Cover!" shouted Corporal Wilon as they raised their shields in the direction from where the arrow came. Another arrow struck from the opposite direction, this time killing a horse.

Just two days ride from Sorne, they had travelled through the most dangerous ambush areas through the Snowcaps Pass - known to locals as Prayers Pass for those that chose to travel by themselves along the dangerous road. Very rarely did bandits attack larger bands, and even more rare for any of the King's men to be attacked.

Several more arrows rained upon shields with no further injury as Wilon picked up the fallen soldier whose horse had died and pointed to a barn off the road,"Regroup there!"

Sudenora galloped after the others, surrounding himself with a magical shield to protect him from the deadly missiles. He noted Anthea did likewise. Spinning his horse, he scanned the rocky feet of the Snowcaps for any movement in the evening.

Anthea pointed to where a ledge overhung the western side of the highway,"There."

Sudenora caught movement from the other side of the road from a similar vantage point, then flinched as an arrow bounced off his shield.

"You never get used to that," Anthea commented, then she turned at the sound of fighting behind them. Whirling about she said,"Sounds like the barn was the real trap, which is why they left the ambush to the end of the Snowcap Pass."

Sudenora dug his heels in and raced after Anthea. As they neared they could see the fighting was fully underway. The main fighting was going on in front of the rotten barn. To the left of the barn a soldier was down, a crossbow bolt protruding from his shoulder and his broadsword just out of reach as a mercenary charged him. Without thinking Sudenora dropped his shield to begin another incantation.

Anthea saw Wilon and the remaining two soldiers fighting from horseback against eight mercenaries, alongside Kielmark and Karlos in front of the barn. Gen'vieve clutched her dirk as she watched in terror. The half-Elf was surprised how Kielmark fought - not caring about being hit. The Arrolokian had dismounted in order to fight more directly - something she thought strange for the horseman. Kielmark winced as a sword glanced off his armoured shoulder, then ran the mercenary through. Without a second thought the Arrolokian flicked his Elven blade to rid it of excess blood then assisted Karlos.

Anthea felt a shove from behind and turned to see one of the archers from earlier put another arrow to bowstring from twenty feet away. Anthea drew her blade and charged at the bowman as another arrow bounced from her barrier. She knew that as soon as she began conjuring a fireball or any other kind of offensive magic that her shield would disappear. With at least one other archer lurking she didn't want to take the chance. It was up to her to ensure her companions didn't get arrows in their backs.

The mercenary threw his bow aside and drew a scimitar as Anthea rode down on him. At the last possible moment the mercenary rolled aside and slashed out, leaving a vicious cut across the horses' rear left leg. The horse whinnied in pain and flung Anthea from the saddle. Both Anthea and the mercenary moved quickly. The half-Elf picked up her dropped sword, bringing it up before her as the curved blade struck.

Kielmark kicked the mercenary's body aside, then extended his arm, the point of his sword piercing the neck of the man fighting Corporal Wilon. As Kielmark pulled his sword free, Wilon was pulled from his saddle and took a heavy blow to his helmet from his left. Wilon slumped as blood trickled from under his dented helm. Kielmark didn't hesitate. He leapt forward to defend the fallen Corporal as Karlos dragged the injured man to relative safety away from both mercenary and horse hooves.

Kielmark breathed heavily as the remaining four mercenaries backed away, then fled behind the barn to where they must have hidden their mounts. Kielmark's armour was missing several chain links from numerous hits he had taken during the short battle, however he stood uninjured. He was just about to suggest to Karlos that he check the wounded when he saw Karlos was already doing so.

"Why did they run?" Anthea called as she approached from the highway. She bore a cut to her left forearm but was otherwise uninjured.

Kielmark shrugged. "We killed some of them..."

"At the expense of four of us..." Karlos said quietly. "And the Corporal doesn't look good - he's unconscious and has blood coming from his ears." The Healer closed his eyes as he crouched next to Wilon and prayed to *Termolen*. Slowly the soldier's eyes flickered as he regained consciousness."I didn't see that one coming." he said weakly. Karlos assisted in removing his helmet as Sudenora and Gen'vieve arrived."Where did they go?" the veteran soldier, now Corporal, asked as he propped himself up on one elbow and looked up at the sky. It was late - near midnight, and *Tolorel* was struggling to illuminate the area through the dark clouds.

"They ran away." Gen'vieve supplied softly.

Karlos noticed that Gen'vieve looked pale, her eyes darting."Are you alright?"

Gen'vieve smiled weakly,"Can't a girl get scared anymore?"

"Sorry," Karlos replied.

"Half an hour along the highway is the tavern we were making for," Wilon winced as he sat up."We'd best bury the dead quickly and be gone."

Within twenty minutes the dead soldiers and mercenaries had been buried behind the barn. None of the mercenaries had any items of interest, besides a note on one that read, '*Just slow them*,'

"What do you think of that note?" Sudenora asked as they continued along the dark highway. A light sweat covered his brow as he maintained the shield around the six horses and riders.

Wilon scoffed,"The Kings' men have never been attacked so blatantly before - those men must have been paid to stop us."

"Or bleed us a little, thus slowing us down," Kielmark offered.

"Gen," Anthea turned to Gen'vieve."Did you 'hear' anything from them?" The half-Elf tapped her own temple to emphasis her meaning.

Gen'vieve nodded."I could pick up muddled thoughts - the main one was that these men were more afraid of not attacking us. It seemed like they didn't want to fight, but they had to. As soon as they had done enough damage, they were pleased to flee."

"Interesting," Anthea mused as she stared into the distance. Squinting slightly, Karlos noticed Anthea's eyes reflecting red as she switched to her Elven infravision to detect heat in the dark."We have more company ahead," she said solemnly.

* * * * * * * * * *

"How many do you think there are now?" Jelik panted as sweat dripped from his face.

They had been running north all night, only allowing short breaks to rest. *Tolorel* had sunk some hours before, and they had been relying on Antaeus's Elven sight to guide them until the eastern horizon began to lighten. Soon after Anthron, Jelik, Antaeus and Jassnik had begun their flight, they could hear the distant sounds of their orc pursuers communicating as they followed.

Even after the grueling run, Antaeus barely looked winded."The valley behind us is swarming with orcs. I don't think I could hazard a guess."

"This is hopeless," Jassnik stood straight with his hands behind his head, trying to catch his breath.

"Unless we can make it to the ruins soon," Anthron said in between gulps of water."We may be able to hold out until..."

"Until Saralon and the twenty-five or so soldiers come to our rescue?" Jelik asked."We're in trouble. Given a day's rest, an excellent position to defend ourselves from, and another hundred soldiers we might be able to take out half of them." The thief motioned back the way they had come.

"What can we do then? Any suggestions?" Anthron asked as he pushed his wet blonde hair back.

"Okay," Jassnik returned his water skin to his pack."I could possibly bend enough light to make us unnoticeable."

Anthron nodded, remembering how the bard had rescued him from Urgar Keep."That's good. All we need now is a place to hide. I don't fancy dodging orcs out in the open with a *chance* that we'll be noticed."

The Elf pointed north."There used to be a small network of caves that ran from the towers to a rise that overlooked the clearing where the towers stood. The Elementalists used it as a passage to board the overflow of students and as a peaceful place to meditate."

"You think it might still be there?" Anthron asked as he hefted his pack onto his tired shoulders.

Antaeus shrugged."I haven't ever been there, but if they are there, they may be filled with orcs..."

Suddenly an arrow thudded into the ground, twenty feet short of where they stood, followed by the sound of orcs rustling through the trees nearby.

Then Anthron saw one draw its bow back."If I can see an orc then they're too close. Let's go!"

They set off again, this time at a more urgent pace. Anthron concentrated on where each foot went, ensuring he didn't trip, fighting off his fatigue by counting a beat to run by. He glanced at Jassnik, struggling to keep up with the taller men. It'll be a miracle if any of us survive this, he thought, then began counting in rhythm with his breathing again.

* * * * * * * * * *

Gruin grinned; his large tusk-like yellow teeth protruding from under his snout as he blinked painfully under the mid-morning sun. He clapped his hands together, drew his scimitar, then pointed to the north. Bellowing in orcish, Gruin signaled the orcs he had been given charge of since the successful return of his scouting mission, to come out of hiding and begin the second step of his Master's plan. Gruin closed his red eyes in ecstasy as the hundred orcs behind him roared in response to his command. All he needed now was the woman Elf he'd been promised to rape and he would be complete. He wiped drool from his chin with a gloved hand, then led the charge from the western lip of the valley. Within several hours Gruin would have slain the humans and Elf...then he would collect his delicious reward...

* * * * * * * * * *

"What was that?" Jelik exclaimed, staring to the left of the valley.

"Don't waste your energy, *fron amos*," Antaeus said as he ran."The orcs are trying to cut us off before we reach the ruins."

"I don't know how much longer..." Jassnik wheezed."We've been running for hours..."

Antaeus reached into his tunic, revealing a folded green leaf. As he ran, he unfolded the leaf and handed something to Jassnik."Hold it in under your tongue. It is a mixture of crushed *arbré Auréle* leaves, water from the *rivi're aué refraíce*, in a biscuit base. Elves use it when we have to travel for many days and have no time to hunt or eat." Antaeus then handed a portion to Anthron and Jelik before placing one in his own mouth. He carefully re-wrapped the green leaf and placed it back inside his tunic.

Jassnik thought the Elven biscuit tasted plain, if not a little bitter, but as soon as he put it under his tongue he felt energy flood through his veins. His arms and legs felt lighter, his muscles no longer ached. He nodded his approval to the Elf.

They could all clearly hear the orcs in pursuit as they ran on.

* * * * * * * * * *

Smit-Myer Crysin slit the sentry's throat. The man died silently, and Crysin eased the body out of sight. This was the tenth man he'd killed this morning.

Crysin had been watching the group of mercenaries since sunrise, where they were waiting in ambush just before the small village of Yun amongst the feet of the Snowcaps. He knew Carl Mort'l and Zathorn Sabriski were in Sorne, unable to leave until some dispute with the port had been settled and it was once again open. To hedge against the chance that Mort'l found a ship before the assassin returned, Crysin had bought the services of the Thieves' Guild - a high price - but with his own team dead he needed extra eyes and swords. The thieves had informed him about the hiring of mercenaries, mostly has-been fighters who frequented the brothels and pubs in the poor quarter of Sorne. When Crysin had detained one of these mercenaries, he was unsuccessful in attaining who was employing them. He did find out two things however.

Firstly, the mercenaries were setting up ambushes to slow the progress of a particular group, who he assumed were what he now referred to as 'his Selection group'. The second thing the assassin discovered was that no matter how much pain he caused to the captured mercenary, he was more afraid of his employer than he was of the assassin. That irritated Crysin.

It also scared him, because after some reflecting he decided who the employer was.

Gwyerson Dernas, his ex-employer.

This is why Smit-Myer was crouching low amongst the brown rocks, waiting as the midday sun shone down on him. In order for him to retire in relative safely, Carl Mort'l and Zathorn Sabriski must die. The assassin was confident about fighting Mort'l, even with the fighter's healing abilities gifted by Dernas. No, it was Sabriski that bugged Crysin. He had no protection against magic. Had he brought his Selection group in for Dernas, the reward was a magical shirt that had energies that absorbed or reflected magical attacks, and was enchanted to keep the wearer as protected as a soldier in full plate. That one item had nearly bought his loyalty.

If he could help his Selection group to reach Sorne, he could point them in the direction of Sabriski and have them take care of him. Crysin closed his eyes for a moment, resting them. Once out of the wind, he thought, it was a fairly warm day. He decided that the mercenaries above hadn't heard the assassination, so he began his silent climb to do what he did best.

* * * * * * * * * *

"The ambushes seem to have stopped." Kielmark observed from the front of their small column. They had managed to ride through two more attacks with the help of Sudenora and Anthea's magical shields that morning, however it was taxing on them. They had feared that an arrow had struck Sudenora from his horse, only to find him unconscious from fatigue. Karlos secured the Elementalist to his saddle as Anthea replaced Sudenora's shield with her own once again.

They had now travelled quietly for two hours.

"Don't push our luck," said Sudenora, who looked pale and tired. His head flopped lazily on his shoulders as he barely remained conscious in his saddle. Karlos had convinced him to leave the ties around his arms and legs in case he did, in fact, fall asleep.

Anthea studied the position of the sun, judging the time to be about two after noon.

"If we keep at this pace we should reach Yun just after sundown." the Corporal said.

Karlos said,"Good. Sudenora needs rest, as does Anthea..." the Healer stopped talking as he looked back at Gen'vieve, whose face was white, tears brimming in her eyes."What is it?" he asked.

The group stopped, noting Karlos's sudden change of tone.

The way Gen'vieve looked into Karlos's eyes made his heart sink as feelings of despair and hopelessness washed over him."It's the others," Gen'vieve said quietly."They are in real trouble, and I know that I am never going to see any of them again."

* * * * * * * * *

Another arrow buzzed past Jelik's head as he ran."They're getting closer!" The thief sidestepped a small tree as they fled.

"That way!" Antaeus pointed toward a long steep rise, and he changed directions to the north and east. The others followed.

Anthron chanced a look over his shoulder and nearly lost his footing.

The massive valley was swarming with orcs. The orcs were about fifty feet behind them, the occasional one pausing to fire an arrow as the host carried on. Thousands upon thousands of orcs tirelessly ran after them, all baring their teeth and shaking their crude weapons in excitement of killing the humans and Elf.

CHAPTER TWENTY THREE

The great golden dragon stirred.

Rhailk raised his mighty head from his horde of treasure, unsure what had woken him. He angrily snorted a ring of smoke, then sent out a magical search. There was nothing nearby that had woken him.

Help!

Rhailk let out a roar that shook dust from the ceiling of his massive cavern. Something was speaking directly into his mind without his consent, something familiar. Rhailk sniffed the air; a habit the great dragon had since well before his magic had developed. There was no one there.

Help Rhailk!

Snorting in rage, the enormous wyrm sent out another enchantment, this time tracking the intruder. The dragon's mind's eye sped north east, across the Forest of Sambethe, over grasslands, the highway, the Snowcap Mountains, before honing in on the little village of Yun.

* * * * * * * * *

"Come on!" Anthron hauled Jassnik forward as the little blonde bard stumbled in fatigue. They scrambled up a tall bank of sandy dirt, the base of the small trees and roots being the only sturdy ground they had. Since reaching the bank they had put a little distance between them and the orcs, although some had sheathed their weapons and had again begun closing the gap.

Antaeus stopped running, turned while reaching into his quiver, and killed three orcs with three movements. The Elf shot dead another two orcs that had been closing in, before spinning on his heel and easily catching up with the other three.

"I'm down to my last quiver of arrows." Antaeus said.

Suddenly the landscape before them opened out. They had reached the top of the bank. A steady downhill led to the ruined towers set in a clearing on the edge of the coast about half a mile away. One tower was mostly intact, looking like a crooked black finger pointing accusingly at the late afternoon sky. The two other towers were crumbled empty shells with blackened bricks scattered around the clearing. In between the triangle of the three towers was a massive crack in the ground, like the earth had opened. Anthron thought that if a magical earthquake had caused the chasm, it was surprising that even one of the three towers was still standing.

"That way." Antaeus pointed, then in one fluid motion put an arrow into another orc that was getting too close.

"Down!" Jelik shouted, then dived down the other side of the bank in a flurry of arrows. Just as Anthron shifted, arrows began dotting the ground where he had been.

"Any more of those biscuits?" Jassnik asked, clutching his side as he breathed through his teeth.

Antaeus said,"No, I am afraid not." The Elf bounded down the slope, aiming slightly away from the ruins towards what looked like a small cave in the distance.

As Jelik ran he considered the burnt symbols around the middle finger of his right hand. Seven symbols, he recalled. The wraith, the cat's eye, the feather, the closed eye, the spider, the skull and the fist. He had warily studied the scars since the Kutporn sewers, not wanting to accidentally activate the ring. However, during the exhausting flight from the orcs he had reconsidered his options. He knew what happened with the wraith, and that while he was under control of himself he was quite safe from physical attacks. The cat's eye, feather and spider he wasn't sure about. The closed eye Jelik thought could be useful...perhaps it could blind the orcs or make him invisible. The skull and fist the thief had no idea about.

Jelik leapt over a short tree. As he landed he felt the ground begin to give way. Throwing himself forwards, Jelik rolled heavily, then crashed through a small tree. Gnarled branches scratched at his face as his momentum saw him to his feet, and the thief kept running.

Suddenly to his left Jelik heard a trumpet, followed by a thunderous roar. Looking in that direction Jelik nearly gave up. He felt his pace slow as about a hundred more orcs raced towards them from the new direction, making it look impossible for them to reach their destination. Anthron gave Jelik a shove from behind to hurry him along. The thief's jaw tightened - if Anthron can make it, so can I, he thought.

"Where's Jassnik?" Antaeus called from the lead, turning to assess the need of his bow once more.

Panic gripped Anthron, and he stopped running to examine the landscape behind. He placed his hands on his knees, gulping deep breaths as he searched. There was no sign of Jassnik. The host of orcs raced on, now about forty feet behind them. It was his fault Jassnik had faltered, the blonde warrior thought as he sank to his knees. His hands were shaking so badly he could barely unsheathe his sapphire-encrusted sword. Gritting his teeth, Anthron raised himself to his feet and gripped his sword in both hands, readying himself for the impossible number of orcs approaching.

The arrows stopped as the front orcs saw one of the humans had stopped running. The first orc that reached Anthron was cut completely in two, the second orc sliced from groin to chin. Anthron ducked under an attack as he severed an orcs' arm, then kicked out at another. The blonde warrior's black blade lashed out killing another orc, to be replaced by two more. He received a deep slash to his leg as he elbowed an orc in the snout, then Anthron was covered with orcs.

* * * * * * * * * *

The man screamed as Sudenora's lightning bolt passed through him, leaving behind a smoking corpse with convulsing muscles.

Sudenora covered his nose from the stench of burnt flesh, then motioned for Karlos to watch behind him. The Healer turned and threw up his shield, defending himself until Kielmark had unlocked himself from the three opponents he was currently battling.

Even though Yun was a small town, they had still found trouble.

They had been in Yun for an hour before mercenaries and four assassins ambushed the tavern they stopped at. Corporal Wilon had been killed in the first flurry, and Anthea had been knocked unconscious as the assassins bent their attention towards the half-Elf. It was only because of Kielmark's regenerating helm once worn by Sir Rodol the Invincible that they were still alive. Several farmers who had been drinking in the tavern hefted pitchforks and beer mugs at the attackers until they too had been knocked out of the fight. Gen'vieve had gone to lie down as soon as they had arrived, and was hopefully safe.

Sudenora was horrified at how efficient the assassins were at dispatching life. Now two of them and a mercenary were fighting Kielmark, which left two assassins unaccounted for. Out of the corner of his eye, Sudenora spied a flash of silver to his right. Without even thinking, he raised a shield that deflected the throwing star that would have killed him. He began the necessary incantation to *Servas* as he strained to keep the shield in place, then released his shield as a white arrow materialised in front of him. He detected what looked like a shadow shifting directly underneath a burning torch on the wall and released his missile. The arrow looked like a white streak as it sped into the darkness, letting out a short scream as it flew. Sudenora heard a cry and wood splinter, then the missile dissolved into nothing.

As Sudenora turned back to Kielmark and Karlos, he heard Gen'vieve's voice inside his head, *That assassin isn't dead!* Sudenora ducked quickly behind an upturned table and drew his Elven blade as a shuriken spun through the space he had just occupied. Glancing upstairs to where Gen'vieve had been sleeping, he spied the brunette on the top platform clutching her dirk. He gave her a nod of thanks.

Karlos parried the mercenary's mace with his sword, then bashed his shield into the man's face. The man faltered, then stepped back, temporarily stunned. Karlos swung a heavy blow that put a hole in the mercenary's neck, then again smashed his shield into his head. The man collapsed as Kielmark disposed of the last mercenary.

The two assassins withdrew a step, aware that the battle had turned somewhat against them. One nodded to the other, then the assassin to

Kielmark's left attacked in a swift and precise routine with his katana. Kielmark's blade rang as he deflected most of the attacks, drawing his attention from the second killer.

The other assassin is putting poison on his blade! Gen'vieve's voice sounded in Karlos and Sudenora's minds.

Karlos immediately began praying to *Termolen* for the ability to neutralise poison as Sudenora ducked away from another shuriken thrown from the darkness.

Gen'vieve peered into the dark corner of the tavern, sending out a probing thought. As soon as she found the mind of the assassin, she visualised her hands squeezing his brain. From the shadows came an anguish cry, then a shout in Kortusian. Then silence.

The assassin engaged with Kielmark kept the Arrolokian too busy to notice the other black clad man look up the stairs and spot Gen'vieve. Somersaulting backwards, the assassin let several shuriken fly up the stairs, striking Gen'vieve down. As the man in black landed lightly on his feet, Sudenora stood and thrust his sword towards the assassin's stomach. The agile killer sensed the Elementalist's approach and easily stepped inside of Sudenora's guard, knocking him unconscious with a solid palm strike to his chin.

Kielmark took another hit to his side, but was able to grasp the assassin's sword arm with his left, then severed the assassin's arm from the elbow. Kielmark finished the man off quickly, as Karlos finished his prayer.

Only one assassin was left, ready to fight. Karlos's right hand glowed green colour and he held it delicately in front of him as if he was nursing something precious. Glancing upstairs, Karlos picked his way carefully behind Kielmark across the slippery bloodstained floor towards the staircase.

Kielmark flicked the blood from his sword as he stalled long enough to allow most of his wounds to heal. The assassin that had taken Gen'vieve down backed away as the big black man regenerated, until the Arrolokian was completely healed. The assassin fled with Kielmark hot on his heels.

Gen'vieve lay sobbing at the top of the stairs, two throwing stars embedded in her stomach. The colour drained from the Healer's face as he saw the wounds. He knelt next to the injured brunette and placed his glowing green hand lightly over her wounds as he carefully removed the throwing stars. Examining them, he could instantly tell they had both been poisoned.

"It hurts!" Gen'vieve cried."I wanted to warn...Jass is..." She coughed weakly, blood trickling from the corner of her mouth.

"Shhh." Karlos said gently as he released his God's magic into her body. Gen'vieve began convulsing, sweat pouring from her. Karlos mopped her forehead as he finished his attempt at neutralising the poison. His heart sank as her lips started going blue and her breathing became shallower and more rapid.

"Karlos," she whispered.

Tears rolled freely down Karlos's cheeks as waves of panic and pain hit him from Gen'vieve's thoughts."I am here."

"I can't see." Gen'vieve stared blankly where Karlos knelt.

Karlos grasped her hand as he began praying again. Releasing healing energies into Gen'vieve's body caused her to convulse again - fighting against the assassin's poison. As soon as he had finished the prayer he began another, hoping that he had enough strength to combat the lethal poison.

* * * * * * * * *

Antaeus released his arrow, then knelt and spun as he withdrew his slender Elven blade. The Elf turned back and fired another arrow, his sword already sheathed as an orc gurgled next to him on it's knees, it not quite realising that it was dead.

Jelik took a punishing hit to his back, mostly protected by the Elven chain, wielding his two swords in unison as he got closer to where Anthron had fallen. Jelik ducked and kicked the legs from under one orc, parried an attack with his left sword while running another through with his right. Almost overwhelmed, the thief used an orc's head as leverage to somersault, then roll away. He was hit from behind again, shoving him forwards into another attack. He managed to avoid being skewered by awkwardly parrying the oncoming sword with his left before losing his grip. Jelik kicked out, twisted and ducked under a high swing then sunk his Elven blade through another orc.

"Anthron! Jass!" Jelik cried, rolling backwards and throwing a dagger into an oncoming orc. As he gained his feet he tripped on a body and fell. Scrambling backwards, he was relieved when several arrows killed the orcs charging the fallen thief. Climbing back to his feet, Jelik withdrew another dagger, his eyes narrow and his jaw set. He was not going to die today.

Suddenly Antaeus was next to him, moving impossibly fast, wielding his long sword. The Elf ducked, killed, spun, killed. Antaeus never stopped moving as he pushed towards Anthron, orc bodies dropping with every movement of his blade.

Jelik threw his dagger, then threw another while his right hand kept several orcs at bay. The thief chanced a moment to survey the area, noting that the next wave of orcs were going to hit them very soon. Jelik leaned back to avoid his head being severed, then lashed out with his sword, only wounding the orc. The orc reeled back, then slashed at Jelik's arm. Pain erupted up the thief's arm and he lost grip of his last sword, once again thanking *Sorel*, the Goddess of Luck, for the Elven chain. Jelik threw his last boot dagger, then was shoved from his right. Crashing through a tree, Jelik hit the ground hard. Slightly stunned, the thief rolled painfully over his left shoulder, into a crouch. Without thinking, Jelik reached for his last weapon inside his tunic - the bat shaped dagger.

The orcs beside Jelik began backing away, and as the thief rose, the fighting ceased. The orcs surrounding Anthron slowly backed away as they saw Xycermon, and Antaeus pulled the blonde man from the mountain of orc bodies. Anthron leaned heavily on the Elf as he retrieved his black sword.

Jelik picked up his Elven blade then moved next to Anthron and Antaeus while holding Xycermon high above his head, the orcs giving them about a twenty-foot radius of space."What do you make of this?" Jelik panted.

Antaeus said,"Let us ask that question when we are safe. They're talking amongst themselves, repeating 'Get Gruin, dagger here.' I think we want to be elsewhere when this Gruin shows up," He pointed, at what looked like a cave entrance forty feet away."That's where we're trying to go."

Jelik, still holding the bat shaped dagger high above his head, set a cautious pace toward the cave. He was drenched in sweat, blinking painfully as it stung his eyes. His muscles shook, and it took all of his concentration to keep walking. The thief stumbled on a tree root, but Antaeus's strong grip caught him and they continued on slowly as the ring of orcs moved with them.

Twenty feet now.

Behind them Jelik could hear more orcs joining the circle, and what must have been an argument.

Fifteen feet. Jelik could see that the cave was more like a doorway leading into the side of the valley than a cave. Just above the entrance was a large flat piece of land, absent of trees - probably what would have been the Elementalist's meditation spot. There were periodic small holes in the bank further along, which could have acted as windows along the passage.

Snarls erupted from close by, followed by the sound of steel on steel.

Ten feet. There was now a clear path to the cave entrance.

A commanding growl issued from behind them, followed by a deafening roar of reply from the thousands of orcs that now surrounded them.

"Run!" Antaeus shouted, and virtually carried both Anthron and Jelik. Within seconds they were through the door. Antaeus drew his sword, and defended the entrance as the orcs came on again.

* * * * * * * * * *

"She is resting." Karlos sighed, slumping onto his bed. The Healer had dark rings around his eyes, his face drained of colour.

"Will she live?" Kielmark asked after it appeared Karlos was drifting off to sleep rather than elaborate.

"I think so," Karlos said."Whatever that poison was...if I had taken any longer to get to her...she...can't..."

Kielmark and Sudenora left Karlos's room and closed the door as he fell asleep.

"I don't think I've ever seen Karlos so drained," Sudenora said as they climbed down the stairs of the tavern. Soon after the fight had ended, Kielmark had rounded up a dozen townsfolk to assist with removing the dead, cleaning the tavern and reinforcing all the windows and doors. A man named Pono had enthusiastically picked up the bartending duties, and had been serving chilled beer to the workers.

Kielmark declined a drink from Pono as they neared the bar, however Sudenora eagerly took a foaming mug."I'm sure Karlos will be fine," Kielmark said as they sat away from the townspeople who drank at another table."I am worried about Gen'vieve."

"Yes," nodded Sudenora, taking a long pull from his drink. Wincing slightly as he moved his bruised chin, he said,"Anthea seems fine though."

Kielmark said,"Anthea and I will have to round up some new mounts by tomorrow, since ours seem to have disappeared," The Arrolokian scratched at his chin."It seems that the closer we get to Sorne, the more trouble we get."

"Well," Sudenora shrugged."Looking on the bright side, we only have one more day's ride 'til Sorne."

The dark Arrolokian shook his head,"No. Madly riding northeast could be dangerous, and we may damage the horses. Even when we arrived in Yun earlier, our horses were nearly lame. We need to find a way to travel to Sorne as soon as possible, in some kind of disguise..."

Sudenora leaned closer,"What did you have in mind, my friend?"

"You ever been a farmer?" Kielmark replied with a smile displaying his white teeth.

* * * * * * * * * *

Antaeus had received numerous wounds, but was still fighting strong. Countless orc bodies littered the doorway, with thousands more trying to find a way past the Elf, Anthron or through one of the windows.

Jelik peered through a window. Orcs covered every visible part of the valley, with more appearing over the horizon every second. Where had they all come from, he thought. Scanning the clearing skies, he judged it was between three and four hours after midday. Suddenly an impossibly huge shadow covered the land. Panic gripped Jelik, and his knees went weak. Stumbling backwards to the passage floor, a slightly familiar voice spoke inside his head, suggesting he escape while he still could. Without thinking, Jelik visualised the skull on his finger. A tingling sensation flowed through him, and he instantly felt rejuvenated. Next he pictured the cat's eye, and he found he could now see every crack in the darkest parts of the passage. Lastly Jelik saw the closed eye, and the thief vanished.

"Dragon," Antaeus breathed as he fought the waves of dragonfear that was assaulting the battlefield. He could see the orcs outside turning on each other in chaos as the massive gold dragon swooped over the valley.

As Anthron recovered, he looked out the door past Antaeus. "Rhailk, thank the Nine Greater Gods!"

"I'm pleased he's an ally, I don't fancy our chances against this army *and* a dragon." Antaeus said with a straight face. "We'd best retreat while we have a chance as these orcs are starting to overcome their fear of the dragon."

"Where's Jelik?" Anthron frantically looked about.

"He won't be far ahead of us." Antaeus replied, giving Anthron a light push indicating he should move on.

Anthron rushed down the passage, passing the intermittent windows on his left. The passage seemed to be following the contours of the valley.

"Look." Antaeus said as he stopped running, and pointed through one of the holes in the bank.

Panicked orcs scrambled over each other as Rhailk swooped low over them. Hundreds of arrows bounced harmlessly off his golden scales that gleamed in the sunlight. The great dragon flicked his tail in irritation, then buffeted a hundred or so orcs to the ground with one powerful sweep of his wings, instantly climbing hundreds of feet in altitude. Rhailk looked to be thinking for a moment before inhaling deeply as he lazily hovered.

"I'd cover your eyes..." Antaeus ducked back as Rhailk let out a long powerful breath. Fire so hot that Anthron could feel it through the earth struck the middle of the orc host. High pitched screams filled the air for a brief second, before an enormous explosion silenced them. The ground shook as Rhailk's fire breath discharged into the valley.

Then there was silence.

* * * * * * * * * *

Jelik silently descended the stairs on his right, his enhanced vision enabling him to see clearly in the darkness. Pausing at the last step of the narrow staircase, he examined a raised tile that attracted his attention. He ignored the explosion from outside as he studied what he was now sure was a trap. He finally decided to avoid the trap rather than disarm it, since his hands or tools were invisible.

Stepping over the suspect tile, Jelik arrived at a T-junction. After listening intently it was obvious that no orc lingered in this place. He crouched and examined the floor. Unlike the first part of the passage, the floor here was smooth stone. No dust covered the surface, making the corridor either well used or well kept.

Looking to his right, Jelik's enhanced vision could see several doors leading off to the left. The passage came to a halt with what looked like a collapsed ceiling. Following his rule of thumb, the thief crept the other way.

The passage curved at an easy angle to the left, with a door on the right hand side every fifteen feet or so. Jelik examined the first few rooms - plain ten foot by ten-foot rooms, which contained the remains of a bed and a hardwood locker. Having found nothing of interest in the first three rooms he decided to ignore them.

Come, this way. A shiver ran down Jelik's spine. He gripped his sword as the familiar man's voice continued in his mind. *Take the next right. There you shall have the choice.*

Jelik resisted the calling. He crouched and closed his eyes, trying to remain in control. His mind began swimming with images, voices, and he could taste blood in his mouth.

"How can I fight against this magic?" Jelik cried, suddenly aware of his voice echoing throughout the empty passages and rooms.

Sheathing his sword, Jelik withdrew Xycermon and crept on slowly.

* * * * * * * * *

Anthron ran his hand over his face in exhaustion. He sat next to Antaeus, who stood in the meditation clearing above the passage. The great gold dragon sat on the valley floor below. Not one orc remained - the smell of burnt flesh, leather, and melted metal permeated into an odour that made the fighter sick to his stomach. Black smoke rose from the scorched sea of bodies. Rhailk appeared unaffected by the smell.

Antaeus wrinkled his nose as the late afternoon breeze changed in their direction. "Thank you for your timely arrival." He bowed low with his right hand over his heart, an Elven sign of respect.

Rhailk snorted before fixing his giant amber eyes on them both. "Your mind witch called. She was worried about the singer and pleaded with me to come." The massive dragon stretched his forty foot wings with a yawn, revealing rows of sword-like teeth.

Anthron's shoulders slumped. "The little singer didn't make it." He rested his head into his palms, feeling tears coming on.

The dragon remained impassive as something approached.

"That was not much fun," Jassnik huffed into view. His Elven cloak was blackened, his face scorched, but he bore no wounds from the orcs.

"Jass!" Anthron leapt to his feet and bounded down to where the troubadour limped."How?" Anthron gave Jassnik a hug, then assisted him up to the clearing.

Jassnik sat heavily, then drank from the water skin Antaeus offered. He then looked around,"Where's Jel?"

Anthron shrugged, and Antaeus said,"I think when Rhailk appeared, Jelik retreated further in there," The Elf indicated the cave entrance below them."He'll come out again soon enough."

"So?" Anthron urged."What happened?"

"Well," Jassnik began."I was following right behind Jel. He jumped over a tree that I chose to run around, but he landed on unstable ground. Jelik dive rolled then kept going, but I fell into the hole," Jassnik pointed back, along the curve of the valley."I think I found part of the caves we had been looking for - there were small rooms on one side. Looked like they were used as bedrooms. Anyway, when I fell in I bent light straight away and hid in a corner catching my breath. Quite a few orcs fell in as they ran, but I left them to fight amongst themselves. It appeared that they knew they weren't allowed there and were panicking to leave before being discovered. They dragged a few old beds out and made a ladder just as our giant friend here arrived. The orcs above roasted, and I have to admit to being a little toasted myself. Anyway, to cut a long story short, after finding the passage was blocked, I made another ladder and climbed out. It wasn't hard to see Rhailk from over there..."

"I'm so glad you're okay," Anthron breathed.

"So am I, my friend!" Jassnik chirped back.

"Now, I guess, we wait for Jelik to return..." Anthron let his voice trail off.

SAROPHIA BY STU DUNN

CHAPTER TWENTY FOUR

The farmers cheered.

The sun had just sunk beyond the horizon in Yun, and the wind had picked up, promising to make the night a cool one. Kielmark and Sudenora sat on their new mounts, surveying their handiwork.

Twenty families of farmers stood in a semi-circle around them, whistling and yelling encouragement while shaking their picks and hoes into the air as Sudenora finished his speech.

"That didn't go too badly," Sudenora smiled as he steadied his frisky mare.

Kielmark nodded. The Arrolokian had come up with the idea of rallying the villagers of Yun together, then enrage them regarding various 'injustices' done by Lord Ras, who counted the village under his protection. Kielmark's plan was to get the farmers angry enough to pack their bags the next morning and set off to Sorne, demanding a garrison be posted to Yun. Sudenora had taken things a step further, invoking a rage in the crowd due to high taxes, low trade, no constables in Yun, and the disappearances of their people - Sudenora avoided using the word 'Selection'. Now the crowd of farmers had gathered their families together, packed several wagons, and were ready to leave for Sorne tonight.

Anthea approached, leading her chestnut horse."Karlos doesn't want Gen moved."

Sudenora sighed,"I know she shouldn't be moved, but I'd rather she was with us than left behind in a deserted farming village."

Kielmark nodded."I agree. Perhaps we can put her on one of the wagons?"

Anthea curled her lip as she thought."She's very sick - I'm inclined to agree with Karlos. I think Karlos will choose to stay here with her if we leave tonight."

"We must leave tonight!" Sudenora exclaimed, waving his arm at the gathered villagers.

Anthea said,"I can't help think that the more we divide, the more we bleed."

"What do you propose then?" the Elementalist asked.

Anthea shrugged."I don't know. Maybe you and Kiel go on to Sorne. At least then Karlos and I can look after Gen here. When she's stabilised we can follow on..."

"What about 'the more we divide'?" Sudenora grated."I don't know if Kiel and I can take Mort'l and Sabriski by ourselves." He glanced at Kielmark who gave no sign as to whether he agreed or not."Let's go talk to Karlos," Sudenora dismounted."We have to sort something out soon, or this group will disperse and we'll have lost our cover to Sorne."

They found Karlos sitting next to Gen'vieve's bed. Karlos had regained some of his complexion, but the dark rings around his eyes remained. Gen'vieve slept peacefully. She was pale, with her temple veins slightly raised. Around her eyes were red, otherwise Sudenora thought she looked good.

Karlos looked up as they approached."She woke half an hour ago, wanting to know how the others were. She said something about sending help, then fell asleep again." The Healer rubbed his eyes."She is not going to be moved," he said firmly.

Sudenora let out a long sigh before replying."Fine. Kiel and I will head off." He looked to Anthea."Please secure this place, and stay alive."

Anthea smiled warmly, then leaned forward and kissed Sudenora on his bristled cheek."I promise. You two go," Anthea hugged Kielmark.

Karlos stood and shook both their hands."Thanks for understanding," He wearily smiled."You two also keep yourselves alive."

Sudenora clapped the Healer on his back."We promise."

* * * * * * * * * *

Jelik lost count of how many hours he had studied the passage leading off to the right. Looking through one of the little windows he could see the sky lightening as night drew to a end. Judging at last that the narrow corridor was safe, he plucked up enough courage to venture down. The passage opened into a large round cavern. It looked like it had been cut from rock, although the land around the ruins was sandy soil. Jelik assessed that the cavern was about thirty feet in diameter with three doors above which burnt torches - he spied one door in the south, one to the east, and the third on the western 'side'. The room was empty except for a large cloaked figure that stood in the middle.

"Jelik Qualis," the man said, his voice cold. As he brushed his cloak aside, Jelik instantly recognised him. The large man was dressed in a baggy brown robe. His pale skin contrasted to his red lips, which were parted in a smile revealing his serrated teeth. Jelik noted that the man's right hand was missing, and that he wore no weapons.

"Gwyerson Dernas," Jelik said coolly,"I would shake your hand, but..."

Anger flash across Dernas's face before he waved his remaining hand and Jelik found himself visible again."Enjoying the ring I see. Come closer Jelik," Dernas motioned for the thief to approach."It is time for The Choice."

Jelik's heart pounded as he approached cautiously, Xycermon gripped tightly."What Choice?"

"You give me the dagger, and I give you power, status...protection from magic." Dernas smiled at Jelik's reaction to his last comment.

Jelik's eyes narrowed."I know your plans for me - we found out at the library."

"What a naíve view, thief," Dernas chuckled as he began to pace slowly around the room. He walked with his right arm posed behind his back, while his left gestured in front of him as he walked."I assume you think that the bearer of the ring must die in order for the summoning to be successful."

Jelik faltered,"That's what the text..."

"Wrong!" Dernas bellowed, his voice echoing throughout the tunnels."It says 'the collective Xycermon must have blood from the Ring Bearers' heart spilled onto each blade'. Does that say you *must* die?"

Jelik remained silent; his muscles taunt as his eyes followed Gwyerson Dernas around the room.

"No it doesn't. If you give me the dagger, you will not die. You will be much more than you ever dreamed - the abilities of the ring at your disposal all the time. You could have full control of its powers..."

"And how am I to live through my heart being cut open?" Jelik said calmly.

Dernas's smile grew."Why, become one of us. Just as Carl Mort'l has made his Choice, so you can now."

"I don't know what you are."

"Something that never has to fear anything ever again," Dernas replied."Give me the dagger of your free will and you can start your new life right now. I've tasted your blood already...you just need to taste mine and you'll be halfway there." Dernas stopped pacing and held up his stumped arm. Using his long thumbnail from his left hand he pierced his wrist. First nothing happened, then slowly blood began to trickle to the smooth cavern floor.

Jelik remembered when he had first met Gwyerson Dernas, and had sunk two daggers into the man's chest. The thief recalled Dernas pulling the daggers free with not one drop of blood being spilt."I am not going to drink anyone's blood." he said defiantly.

Dernas growled, his features shifting for a moment, reminding Jelik of a wild animal. The man's eyes glowed redder as his rage intensified.

"However," Jelik continued."I am willing to negotiate."

Gwyerson's anger began to subside,"Just what do you propose?"

Jelik let out a deep breath."You know that I can't give you Xycermon and return to my companions, however I have no interest in leaving them at this stage either."

Dernas nodded and began pacing again; his wounded wrist already healed.

Jelik went on."You must already be aware of my aversion to magic. My gaining a measure of defense against magic would be... how can I put it... would be well received."

"Go on," Dernas urged.

"How can we meet in the middle, where I get this gift *and* keep the dagger?"

"Simple," Dernas replied."I kill you, take Xycermon, then cut your hand off and find a new ring bearer." As Gwyerson finished his sentence, Jelik could see a rippling in the air directly in front of him. The hair on the back of his neck prickled as magic was being summoned.

Jelik acted instantly. He visualized the closed eye marking on his finger, and disappeared. As he somersaulted to his left, he activated the spider symbol. As he landed, Jelik sprang to the wall. The thief found his feet somehow gripped the wall, and he began to run straight up it. Jelik heard Dernas release a blast of magic below him. Then he pushed himself from the wall. Jelik spun backwards twice before landing silently in his Elven boots directly behind Dernas.

Jelik activated the fist image, and then grasped Dernas around his neck with one arm from behind, the other holding Xycermon to his throat. As he did so, Jelik became visible once again."Shall we start the negotiations once more?" Jelik whispered.

Gwyerson roared in rage as he tried to tear Jelik from him, but the thief now had strength to match his own. He finally relaxed,"What do you want?"

"You know what I want," Jelik pushed Xycermon harder against his throat."I want protection from magic." Jelik began feeling his control slipping as his head began to pound.

"It is in my robe, a black shirt. It reflects offensive magic and will protect you as would plate," Dernas said calmly."You have certainly proven to be a resourceful..."

Dernas never finished his sentence as Xycermon plunged through his windpipe.

"Damn!" Jelik cursed as Gwyerson Dernas disappeared into a gaseous form, similar to Jelik's wraith form. The bat-shaped dagger passed harmlessly through the form as the thief wildly attacked."You're not going anyway 'til I get my shirt."

The gaseous form slowly floated towards the left door, then seeped through the cracks under the great hardwood portal. Jelik tried the door but found it locked. Fumbling for his lock picks, the thief decided to force the door instead, as his mind grew cloudier. Dropping his shoulder he barged the door. Even with his enhanced strength the door barely budged. Picturing the ghost image, he was past the door and solid again within seconds.

The room was small, with what looked like a coffin on a dais placed in the centre. Jelik caught a glimpse of the gaseous form of Gwyerson Dernas disappear into the coffin. Rushing to the coffin he opened it with Xycermon held in front of him.

Gwyerson Dernas lay still inside the coffin, displaying a large hole in his throat. Jelik quickly searched through his robe, producing a black silk shirt.

"I believe this is mine." Jelik muttered as his vision began reddening. He steadied himself, and then with his last hint of energy he plunged Xycermon into Dernas's chest.

* * * * * * * * * *

The salty breeze blew as the sun rose. Anthron sniffed the air as the northern breeze gave the fighter his first scent of the ocean.

Jassnik closed his eyes and breathed deeply."When you've lived your childhood next to the sea, it's no wonder I appreciate the beautiful fragrance of the crystal wonder that is The Deep Sea."

"Very poetic," Anthron murmured. They had spent an uneasy night waiting for Jelik to return, resting inside the passage door as Rhailk hunted."Well, it's dawn, and there's no signs of any other *Crasheiar*. We'd better start looking for Jelik."

Presently a chilling cry echoed from deep within the passage that set Anthron's teeth on edge."What was that?" he exclaimed.

"Something evil," Antaeus muttered as he drew his slender sword.

"When is Rhailk due back? I thought he was going to be back by now." Jassnik asked as he followed the Elf into the passage.

"He's a dragon Jass. I don't think he answers to any kind of curfew." Anthron grated.

Antaeus led them through the passage, then down a set of stairs."He spent some time here...maybe a trap," The Elf tapped the ground at the base of the last step with the tip of his sword, then heard a deep rumbling."Back up the stairs!"

As they reached the top of the staircase they heard a crash and they were thrown to the ground. Picking themselves up, they could see a slab of rock had fallen from the ceiling, and lay smashed at the base of the stairs.

"I would say yes, it was a trap," Jassnik said.

"Yes," Antaeus said, his cheeks reddening slightly. The Elf descended the stairs to the T-junction. Pointing left, he said,"Jelik went that way."

They passed the rooms Jelik had explored, then found the passage leading off to the right, to the cavern.

"Jelik's lock picks," Antaeus noted, approaching the door to the west. Trying the door, he found it locked.

"Jelik?" Anthron called, then peered through the keyhole."I can see him lying on the floor next to what looks like a coffin." Anthron shook the door, but it didn't move.

"If I may," Jassnik said, taking the set of lock picks from the Elf. Crouching in front of the door, he probed the lock."Nasty," Jassnik breathed as he leaned to the side of the door."Out of the way. Looks like a poison needle trap." As Anthron and Antaeus shifted, Jassnik prodded the lock and a small missile the size of a needle shot out with enough power to strike the far door."Right, let's get this open." Jassnik settled back in front of the lock.

After several long minutes Jassnik pushed the heavy door open on well oiled hinges. They raced over to Jelik lying next to an empty coffin. Blood trickled from his nose. In one hand he clutched the bat-shaped dagger, in the other, a black shirt.

"Let's get him out of here." Anthron said.

As they emerged outside into the morning, Rhailk was waiting for them. The great dragon sniffed in their direction."That is a truly evil scent thou dost carry."

"It wasn't a nice place." Jassnik commented as he and Antaeus placed

Jelik down.

"The soldiers thou hast been waiting for are camped," Rhailk sighed, flicking his giant tail towards the south."There."

"Good," Anthron's eyes narrowed.

* * * * * * * * * *

Saralon's head spun back, and then he hit the ground heavily. Sergeant Olin began drawing his sword until Antaeus placed his hand over the hilt and shook his head.

Anthron stood over Saralon, fists balled, breathing hard."You have no idea! Look at the number of bodies out there!"

Saralon propped himself up on an elbow as he rubbed his chin. He was about to yell but stopped himself."Fair enough Anthron." He held out his hand, which Anthron took and helped the Captain to his feet."Fair enough. Let's sit and talk this through."

Quickly, with drilled efficiency, Saralon's tent was erected, furnished with folding chairs and a makeshift table. Wine was brought out, and the soldiers began brewing a stew.

Saralon rubbed his bruised chin."The original plan was for you four to scout ahead up here. We were to arrive a day later to provide back up if required. However the real mission was to get Carl Mort'l and Zathorn Sabriski cornered and captured. We had confirmed sightings of them in Sorne, so I sent the others with an escort there. They should be arriving today." He sipped at his red wine."Yarlyn insisted that we needed to cover both bases by splitting the group. He was hoping that we'd find the missing people from the Selection hidden up here..." He looked to Anthron, Jassnik and Antaeus with raised eyebrows.

"Jelik's the best one to ask about that," Anthron answered the unasked question."But until he recovers..."

"I recommend that you send several units to inspect the ruins themselves." Antaeus said."I've seen orc footprints around the chasm."

Saralon nodded, then gestured for Olin to comply.

"It's in our interests to get to Sorne as soon as possible," Jassnik changed the subject.

"Understandably," the Captain nodded."After we have searched the ruins and cave we will pick up Lord Yarlyn and Jalesia. If we ride hard we should reach Sorne in two weeks..."

Antaeus shook his head,"If we may leave sooner, when Jelik awakes, we have arranged a quicker form of transportation."

"What, magic?" Saralon scoffed.

"Not quite," Anthron answered."A dragon."

* * * * * * * * * *

The city of Sorne was in chaos. The port had finally been opened the same day as Sudenora and Kielmark arrived with the small group of farmers. As time had worn on more and more Yun villagers had turned back, finding various excuses to avoid confrontation. Now it was about an hour before sundown and Sudenora and Kielmark sat in one of the hundreds of taverns Sorne had to offer.

Sorne was divided in two by the main road, also called The Tavern Strip, as taverns, inns and brothels lined both sides of the whole street - from the highway right through to the docks. The left half of the city was mostly the markets and merchant quarter, with some of the richer establishments nestled near the permanent stalls. Lord Ras lived in this area, performing his court duties from the lower portion of his castle-like home. On the other side of The Tavern Strip lay the fishing quarter, the tanners and other repugnant smelling establishments, and the poor quarter. Part of the poor quarter was known as Seedytown - filled with rough taverns, whores, drugs and seemingly random murders - also rumoured to be run by the Thieves' Guild.

The Tavern Strip ended at a large iron gate that signified the beginning of the docks. Due to Sorne being the largest port in Sarophia, efforts had been made to establish a vigilant customs department. Within the docks were hundreds of warehouses where stock was unloaded awaiting the tax bill or was ready for shipment, and it was highly patrolled. There were enough moorings for over one hundred ships in the built-in harbour. The man-made stone banks that arched out in a semi-circle created a calm bay around the harbour, the thick chain that could be hung across the harbour mouth closing the port having been removed the day before Sudenora and Kielmark had arrived.

The results of the busy port being closed were phenomenal - hundreds of ships had been forced to anchor outside the harbour, merchants had rioted, the Thieves' Guild had stolen a vast amount of goods from the warehouses, and the markets had closed for the first time in over eighty years. Lord Ras had dealt with the unrest without sympathy, outlawing the docks while the port was closed and very nearly announced martial law. The spokesperson for the Merchant's Guild had met with Lord Ras, resulting in the co-operation of the Guild during the remainder of the restriction.

Now merchants hurried to get an edge on their competitors by setting up their stalls before their neighbours while the city was overrun with an additional five thousand or so sailors who had spent the last week sitting in the harbour.

"This is madness," Kielmark whispered as he watched every person that passed the tavern window with suspicion."The city is too busy."

"I wonder if Yarlyn thought of that particular consequence when he came up with his plan to close the port," Sudenora absently chewed on a nail. Shrugging, he said,"Probably. He's a shrewd man."

Kielmark finished his mug of water."So, how do we find Mort'l and Sabriski in this?" The Arrolokian waved out to the teaming street."They may have already left Sorne".

"True," Sudenora nodded; nursing his very average ale."We have to..." Sudenora stopped talking as he noticed something going on outside."What's happening out there?" He stood.

Kielmark followed the Elementalist outside into the crowds of people, who were all milling down The Tavern Strip, away from the docks.

Sudenora stopped a young woman carrying a child, his mind instantly thinking of Carlae back in Eugernok."Excuse me, what's going on?"

"There's a dragon out the front!" the woman replied before rejoining the sea of bodies moving towards the city entrance.

"Dragon?" Sudenora and Kielmark said simultaneously, and they joined the throng of people massing to get their first glimpse of a dragon.

* * * * * * * * * *

"That wasn't very subtle." Anthron grated as they finished their last circle of Sorne.

Rhailk flicked his long tail in irritation before landing in the fields south of the city. The great gold dragon had grudgingly transported Anthron, Jassnik and Antaeus to Sorne, taking minutes rather than days. Jelik had remained behind with Captain Saralon at the ruins as he still hadn't regained consciousness by mid afternoon, and Rhailk had refused to carry the unconscious Jelik. Anthron hated having to leave the injured thief behind, particularly as he considered Karlos would be in Sorne to help - whatever it was that was wrong with Jelik. Saralon would complete his patrol, pick Yarlyn and Jalesia up from Brane, arriving in Sorne in about two weeks. He hoped within that time they had sorted out Carl Mort'l, Zathorn Sabriski, and had enough time for a rest while Jelik recovered...

He hoped.

"We'd best move on, as we're attracting quite a bit of attention," Jassnik suggested, pointing to the growing crowd of Sorne residents.

Rhailk released his spell that kept the three riders on his back, then lowered his head. Antaeus leapt the remaining fifteen feet, followed by Jassnik and Anthron.

"Thank you again, Rhailk." Anthron said.

The dragon rose up to his full height."Thou art welcome. I shall hunt." When the three were far enough away, Rhailk unfolded his massive wings and sped off into the southern skies.

"Let's find the others then," Jassnik said, starting off towards Sorne.

"It may be easier for them to find us here," Antaeus commented.

"Anthron!" A voice came from the crowd. Emerging from the throng was Sudenora, dressed in chain and carrying a sword, followed by Kielmark similarly dressed."Jass, Antaeus! That was quite an entrance!" Sudenora cried as they approached.

"Sudenora! Great to see you," Anthron clapped the Elementalist on the back."Where are the others? Anthea?"

Sudenora glanced at Jassnik before replying."We had some trouble getting here. Gen was hurt pretty bad - she's okay," he added as Jassnik looked about to panic. "Anthea and Karlos stayed in Yun with her, until she's better."

Kielmark looked behind them."Where's Jelik? The Captain?"

Anthron pointed over his shoulder with his thumb."They are back at the ruins. Jelik isn't too good, but we don't know what's wrong with him."

"You should have brought him here..." Sudenora started, but stopped as Anthron's expression clearly showed he had thought of that."Let's get inside," the Elementalist motioned towards the city."Kiel and I have a room, and we can catch up."

"Then we can go about finding our men." Anthron said coldly.

* * * * * * * * * *

Smit-Myer Crysin shook his head in disbelief. The group had obviously befriended the great gold dragon whose lair he had found near Urgar Keep. They had gained protection from King Rogor, and had survived everything Carl Mort'l and Zathorn Sabriski had thrown at them.

Yes, he thought, his Selection group would succeed. With his help.

Crysin merged back into the crowd, making his way to the poor quarter. Stepping into an alley, he spied a dirty beggar boy with a missing leg. The assassin made the hand signal of the Sorne Thieves' Guild, and the boy promptly unfolded his hidden leg and approached.

Crysin revealed a gold coin."I need you to do a small job for me."

The boy nodded eagerly.

* * * * * * * * * *

"So, how do we find Carl Mort'l in this chaos?" Anthron asked the group.

Sudenora shrugged."We were thinking the same thing." They had spent most of the evening in the taproom of the tavern Sudenora and Kielmark had been at earlier, catching up, telling stories, relaxing and eating.

Jassnik scratched at his blonde stubble."I could try getting in contact with the Thieves' Guild, although that didn't go so well last time."

Suddenly a filthy little boy appeared at Anthron's elbow."Excuse me," he said in a quiet voice as he held out a rolled up note, sealed with a red ribbon."For you."

Anthron frowned, then took the parchment. Untying the ribbon he unrolled the message and studied it. Letting out a sigh, he passed the message to Sudenora,"I'm not that good at reading." he muttered quietly.

Sudenora took the parchment and read through it, his jaw dropping."This tells us where Mort'l and Sabriski are held up currently - until dawn. Looks like they are catching a ship to Panthorian on the morning tide."

Anthron grabbed the boy's arm before he could retreat."Where did this come from?"

The boy squirmed."I was given a gold to bring it to you."

Anthron relaxed his grip."And who paid you to bring us the message?"

The boy smiled,"I was given another gold not to tell." With that, he wrenched out of Anthron's grip and sped through the taproom and out the door.

"Well then," Anthron said."It's nearly midnight - if we trust this information, we have a long night ahead of us."

They all nodded.

SAROPHIA BY STU DUNN

CHAPTER TWENTY FIVE

Jassnik examined the lock.

"It's got to be a trap," he said as he returned from the gate leading to the docks to the alley where Anthron, Kielmark, and Antaeus were hidden. There were no clouds in the night's sky and there was a thin fog forming. Jassnik rubbed his hands together to warm them as best as he could."The lock was already open..."

"You do think we're being set up then?" Anthron asked the bard.

He screwed his face up;"Things are *too* easy. We weren't challenged getting here, by guard *or* cutpurse, and the gate was unlocked..."

"You and Antaeus go on ahead," Anthron whispered, his breath visible in the cool air."Make sure the way is clear, then one of you come get us."

The Elf and troubadour nodded, then slipped off into the fog through the heavy iron gate signifying the entrance to the docks and warehouse district.

Ten minutes later Antaeus returned through the gate, shaking his head."The way is clear - Jassnik thinks too clear."

Anthron assessed the situation. They had received an anonymous note clearly stating that Carl Mort'l and Zathorn Sabriski were staying in a warehouse in the northern part of the docks - and they were leaving that morning. He knew it was a long shot that their enemies were actually there, but he couldn't think of another solution. Anthron had to admit to feeling nervous about confronting the two men, but what choice did they have? The city proper was still in so much chaos that the authorities weren't interested. Jassnik had tried to see Lord Ras to explain, however he was unavailable at such a late hour. But those two men had been major players behind the Selection in Sarophia, aided by dark sorcery, and harming the innocent - they could not get away with it. Anthron clenched his teeth as he stood straight, something he did that made him feel more confident."We have to try."

Antaeus nodded, then pointed to the north."Jass picked a path behind the first row of warehouses. Follow me."

Anthron, Sudenora and Kielmark followed the silent Elf through the gate. They turned left and crept through the shadows for a block before turning right. Anthron was nearly overwhelmed by the reek of human waste and rotten food as they passed between two buildings. He noted that no one else complained so he chose to cover his nose and mouth with his Elven cloak.

Antaeus led them another three blocks north before Jassnik appeared from the shadows in front of them."Let me see the parchment again," the bard requested, and Anthron offered the note. Jassnik re-read the note then studied the surroundings. Pointing to the two-story warehouse to their left, Jassnik whispered;"I think it's this one."

Anthron let out a slow breath, releasing a frosty cloud into the air. He checked his sword was loose in its scabbard and that his dagger was in place on his belt. He quickly tightened the ties on his boots while the others readied themselves in their own way.

"Okay," Anthron said quietly."What's the plan?"

"We have to discover the layout of the warehouse, and just how many are in there," Jassnik started."There may be some Knights of Protection in there too."

"I don't think an all out brawl will work," Anthron said after a moment."No matter what happens in there, we have to be aware of each other. If someone's in trouble..."

"Then that's where I'll be," Antaeus finished matter-of-factly.

"That's where we will all be," Jassnik corrected."Are we ready?"

The group nodded.

* * * * * * * * * *

Smit-Myer Crysin crouched on the rooftop in silence. He breathed through his cloak to reduce the visibility of his breath in the cold morning as he watched the five figures below. Satisfied that he had done what he had set out to do, he climbed down from the roof and headed back towards the city.

By dawn, he knew, the matter would be sorted one way or the other. Crysin paused for a moment as he considered lending his skills towards eliminating the two men who would cause him the most grief in his retirement, then continued. No, it was up to the remains of his Selection group to set things right.

As Smit-Myer Crysin left the docks and entered the merchant quarter, he pulled his hair from its ponytail and ran a gloved hand over his freshly shaven chin. He would miss his moustache and goatee, but it was time for another identity - Teshar the Merchant - at least for a couple of years. He let his mind wander back to Sasha Quevnon - or Quabeth White - at the Mosorac Underground. He visualised his arms around her curved supple body as she lay on him, her sweet smelling hair, those full lips...

Yes, he thought. Teshar will set up in Mosorac until he can convince Sasha to leave the Underground, maybe live in Bayton. He may need to eliminate Lorol the Blade though...

Crysin smiled as he entered a tavern next to the already stirring markets as he considered the benefits of retiring from the role of hired assassin, for a normal life.

* * * * * * * * * *

Jassnik opened the lock and checked for immediate traps. "I wish Jel were here," he muttered to himself. "This is his forte."

Anthron motioned the troubadour to be silent. Jassnik nodded, then continued to examine the area inside the doorway. They had examined the outside of the warehouse, finding only two doors - front and back. The only windows were on the second level, and all were closed. They decided to enter the warehouse through the back door.

Jassnik swept his hand forward, indicating that the way was clear. Antaeus entered first, bow at the ready.

Antaeus stepped through the portal into a small dark room. Along the left wall hung half a dozen cloaks on hooks, and along the floor of

SAROPHIA BY STU DUNN

the right wall sat several pairs of muddy boots. A dirty mat rested on the floor in front of the door opposite, light seeping from underneath. Antaeus approached the door cautiously, and listened for several minutes before returning to the others."It sounds like one large room, multi-leveled. Somewhere near the middle of the warehouse floor there must be a table, at which at least half a dozen men are seated. I heard one set of footsteps upstairs."

"Well done," Anthron whispered."Let's look at taking out the people at the table first." He pointed up,"Stay under cover as much as we can from who ever is up there. Antaeus, if you get the opportunity, take out Sabriski first."

The Elf nodded.

There was no lock on the door leading into the main part of the building, so Jassnik examined for traps. After finding none, he decided to oil the door's rusty hinges before testing the handle. Slowly he pushed the door open.

The room was much as Antaeus had described. Seated at a large round table in the middle of the room were eight mercenaries - most likely the Knights of Protection in disguise he thought - playing cards. On the left of the warehouse sat three massive wooden crates, with one placed to the right. Along the left and right walls, two rickety-looking staircases led to the second level, which appeared to be a ten-foot wide floor running around the inside parameter of the building. From his vantage point, Jassnik could also see two doors along the wall to his left. The door blocked his view to the right.

Jassnik held up eight fingers indicating the number of enemies he could see, then slunk silently through the door. He could now see three closed doors to his right.

Antaeus came through next, an arrow already notched. The rest followed.

Anthron froze as he heard voices from upstairs, then heavy footsteps walking directly above where they hid. Anthron motioned for them to spread out quickly, each ducking into one of the doors on the southern wall.

Sudenora entered a room that could only have been the latrine and gagged instantly. Covering his nose, his eyes adjusted to the dim light as flies buzzed around him. He glanced around the small room; there was a filthy hole in the ground on the far corner - what Sudenora guessed was the smell from the alley earlier - and a male and female body. The man looked like he had been executed by strangulation, the woman however...it appeared she had struggled terribly from her fate. He tore his gaze away from the bodies, assuming they were the unfortunate ex-owners of the warehouse, and peered through the partly opened door back into the main room. As he looked out, two figures walked down the left-most set of stairs.

The first figure was a huge man with wide shoulders and a bull-like neck. Sudenora didn't recognize him initially, but it was definitely Carl Mort'l. His long black hair had been shaved, leaving a scarred scalp. His pale features were fixed in a sneer as he talked, and his grey eyes looked tired. The tall leader of the Cyermyth Knights of Protection was dressed as a simple mercenary in brown leather leggings and tunic over which he wore a chain mail vest. At his hip he wore a broad sword.

Mort'l said to the other man in his deep voice,"I want them found."

Sudenora instantly recognised the man who walked beside Mort'l as Zathorn Sabriski, his tormentor at the prison in Urgar Keep. The mage's brown hair was tied back, and he wore grey leather breeches and jerkin, with several daggers tucked into his jewelled belt. His tanned face wore a twisted smile, while his striking blue eyes studied the now silent knights at the table."They've had help - probably that renegade assassin Lorol had issues with."

"Maybe," Mort'l reached the table of knights and poured himself an ale. He sipped at it while he thought."I haven't heard from Dernas either," he mused."We can't blame this assassin for every bit of bad luck we've had."

"Gods," said one of the soldiers."We're outlaws in Sarophia now! What happened to becoming Dukes and Earls of this little nation?"

Mort'l's eyes narrowed."Silence, Hernos!" The soldier flinched, and tried to look busy shuffling the deck of cards."I admit that things haven't gone as planned," Carl spoke to all the soldiers."However, when we get back to Cyermyth those fools will come trailing after us. They'll bring the last of the daggers with them, and Dernas will ensure that the ring will follow. We have succeeded!" Mort'l's voice echoed throughout the warehouse as Zathorn watched on, appearing bored. The leader of the knights continued,"When this is all over, and we have fulfilled our roles, Sarophia will be ours to rule - as will Panthorian! Hernos, how would you like Kortusia for yourself - I don't want it, it's filled with Kortusians!" The soldiers laughed, and the tension was released.

"And what would you leave for me?" Zathorn asked, his blue eyes locking with the taller man."Might I have what's left of Syphora? Maybe you'll save me the Wastelands of Bone to play with?" The mage's tone was mocking, baiting the huge knight.

As Carl Mort'l spun on Zathorn to retort, an arrow struck the mage's chest, then dropped to the warehouse floor with a clatter. Zathorn looked in the direction of where the arrow had come as Mort'l and the soldiers drew their weapons. The leader of the knights waved the eight soldiers forward.

"Looks like the rats have come to find us," Zathorn smiled wickedly, licking his lips.

"Now!" Anthron shouted as he burst from the door he had hidden behind. The blonde fighter charged, Mort'l's old sapphire-encrusted sword ready.

Antaeus changed his tact immediately, deciding that raining arrows upon the protected magic user was futile. Instead, he began firing arrows at the charging soldiers, ensuring that he didn't endanger his companions.

Due to Carl Mort'l and Zathorn Sabriski holding back, Kielmark was the first to enter combat. He ducked under a high attack and swung his blade mid-height. He was satisfied as his sword bit deep into the soldier's stomach, then used his weight to slide his sword free. The knight-mercenary fell screaming, vainly attempting to hold his entrails inside his stomach as Kielmark took a punishing hit to his back. Falling to one knee he narrowly missed decapitation, then stabbed into the groin of another of the mercenaries. Wincing, he rolled backwards over his shoulder to his feet as Anthron joined next to him.

Jassnik looked on helplessly. He knew he wasn't skilled enough to get right into what now looked like a full-scale brawl. His skills lay with surprise, or at the very best one on one. Glancing at Sudenora, he decided the Elementalist was safe enough for him to disappear. He quickly sent out a thought to *Lithloren*, and to anyone who was watching, Jassnik Corline appeared to fold out of sight.

Sudenora finished his request to *Servas* and felt a tingling as his protection from magic took effect. The Elementalist scanned the scene - Antaeus had downed two knights using his bow before the fighting had become too chaotic for him to shoot without endangering Anthron or Kielmark. The Elf waited calmly, his sword ready for where he could best be used. Sudenora noted Kielmark and Anthron were being pushed back by the remaining four knights. The Elementalist spoke to *Servas* once again, then held out his hand. Blue sparks erupted from his palm, jumping and spinning, intertwining within themselves as Sudenora looked for an opening.

Sparks flew as Anthron parried an attack and sidestepped. He chanced a dangerous move by spinning, turning his back on his opponents, with his sword extended at head height. As he completed his spin, only one of the two knights he fought pulled back, and Anthron's black blade sliced through the slower man's throat.

"Nice," Kielmark panted."Get to Mort'l if you can."

Anthron nodded. As he began disengaging himself from the remaining soldier Antaeus was there to cover him."Thanks," Anthron said as he sought the leader of the knights.

Carl Mort'l stood next to Zathorn, his sword held in front of him."You have my sword," the huge man said matter-of-factly to Anthron."I shall have it back."

In response, Anthron leveled his blade at him. Mort'l and Sabriski smiled in return. Anthron thought quickly as he slowly approached. He couldn't detect any aura surrounding either of the men - he hoped it meant they would meet their deaths this night and it wasn't just some magical protection from the sword's ability. As Anthron closed in, Mort'l sneered and attacked viciously. The huge knight attacked so aggressively that Anthron fell back, having to concentrate solely on defending himself. Sparks flew from their blades, and Anthron instantly began sweating from the exertion. Perspiration stung his eyes, as he backed further and further from Zathorn who began casting.

Sudenora lined himself up with the evil mage, pitched his arm back and let loose his handful of sparks towards Sabriski. The sparks looked like waving blue fuses, striking an invisible barrier that surrounded the mage. The sparks spread out over Zathorn, searching for a way to get to him before dispersing into nothing. With a laugh, the mage finished his spell and pointed at Sudenora. Five black darts sped towards the Elementalist, striking his shield and knocking him backward off his feet. Smoke wafted from Sudenora's invisible barrier as he picked himself up.

Zathorn's eyes narrowed in obvious surprise that Sudenora wasn't a smoking corpse. Snarling, Sabriski began another incantation just as Jassnik reappeared directly behind the mage, sword raised. The little bard's sword ricocheted off Zathorn's protection, but it was enough to disrupt the lethal mage. Sudenora began speaking quickly to *Servas* once again as he gathered energy.

Kielmark cried out from a slash to his neck. Falling back, he clutched his wound and he lost grip of his sword. Another heavy blow landed across his back, and he felt the chain mail links snapping as his flesh parted. Gurgling as his sight blurred, he braced himself for the next strike. Dully he heard the fighting continue, seeing silhouettes of people that became clearer as his silver helm began healing him.

Antaeus parried a blow aimed at Kielmark and kicked the knight-mercenary behind the knee, then crushed the man's throat with an openhanded strike as his enemy stumbled. Antaeus placed himself between the remaining two knight-mercenaries and Kielmark, his stained slender blade waiting for their cautious advance as the Arrolokian climbed to his feet.

Never had Anthron faced such a powerful opponent - Carl Mort'l seemed quicker and stronger since their duel in the courtyard in Urgar Keep. He grunted as he lifted his heavy arms for another two-handed parry. Mort'l appeared tireless, keeping his furious attacks constant, giving Anthron no time to retaliate. The blonde warrior quickly wiped perspiration from his brow, then dived into a roll to his right. He heard Mort'l's sword passing over him, and when he gained his feet he found his Elven cloak had been ruined. Tossing his tattered cloak aside, Anthron took a deep breath and tried to relax his grip on his weapon. He aimed the black blade at Mort'l's eyes, and as the huge knight's broad sword came at him, Anthron shifted his sword into a two-handed block, then returned it to his centre.

There! Anthron thought, excitedly. He remembered what his teacher from Ithren, Lepus, had always done to best him - even though Anthron was stronger. Lepus used the centre line to his advantage, defending with minimal movements from the centre and often having a clear shot at Anthron's chest and head.

Carl Mort'l swung a fast overhead attack at Anthron. The blonde fighter shifted the tip of his blade to intercept the strike. Before Mort'l had the opportunity to withdraw, Anthron stepped forward with a quick flicking movement.

Mort'l screamed in rage and anger as Anthron's black blade struck the crown of his head. The knight dropped his sword as he fell back while Anthron's sapphire crusted weapon smoked where Mort'l's blood touched it. The sword continued to smoke until all of Carl Mort'l's blood had dissolved, leaving the black blade clean.

Mort'l half crawled, half staggered away, holding his bleeding head as he made for the remaining knights fighting Antaeus. He suddenly spied Kielmark, weaponless and dazed, slowly gaining his feet. He wasn't sure how Sabriski was faring, and he had to shift the scales of the battle quickly.

Anthron launched a kick at Mort'l, trying to stop the knight's progress. Mort'l suddenly withdrew a dagger as Anthron's foot connected. Letting out a loud breath, Mort'l cut a vicious wound along Anthron's calf, which dropped the blonde man. Winded, Mort'l threw himself at Kielmark, tripping him.

Jassnik's arms ached from the shock of striking Zathorn's shield. His hands were throbbing as he fumbled to pick up his sword.

Zathorn Sabriski raised both hands together, much like someone praying, and shouted a word Jassnik didn't understand. A crimson light appeared between Zathorn's hands, then shot forth at Jassnik. The energy struck Jassnik as he attempted to dodge with enough force to fling the little man into one of the crates. Jassnik hit the crate side on before falling motionless to the warehouse floor.

Sudenora, oblivious to the rest of the fighting, finished his casting as Zathorn turned towards him. The Elementalist smiled to himself as a shimmering globe resembling a crystal ball materialised before him. With a swift motion, Sudenora sent the globe towards Sabriski. As the crystal-looking globe hit Zathorn's magical shield it shattered, releasing a glowing glue-like substance. The thick clear substance spread over Zathorn's shield, then both the substance and the mage's magical defence winked out of existence.

Sudenora felt slightly more fatigued as the spell dissolved. Seeing Zathorn's eyes open wide with panic, Sudenora drew his sword and charged before the mage could cast again. The Elementalist swung his sword as Sabriski madly worked an enchantment. Sudenora's blade cut through Zathorn's grey leather jerkin, opening a fatal gash across the mage's chest. Sabriski's hands continued to move, trying desperately to finish his spell as his lifeblood poured to the warehouse floor. Sabriski coughed blood, then looked wide eyed at his own chest, as if finally noticing the wound, then back to Sudenora. The dying mage glanced disappointedly at Sudenora's sword."By a sword...after all this." he coughed and sank to his knees, then Zathorn Sabriski fell forward dead.

Antaeus finished off his final opponent with a quick thrust as Anthron limped towards him. His face was grim, and he nodded behind the Elf. Turning, Antaeus saw Kielmark on his knees, his silver helm having been tossed aside, with Carl Mort'l standing behind the Arrolokian with a dagger to his throat.

Sweat dripped from the huge knight who was trembling, but he had a strong hold of Kielmark's chin. The wound Anthron had given him hadn't healed properly, leaving a half-closed swollen purple wound on the top of his shaven head.

Anthron could see the whites of the Arrolokian's eyes darting anxiously, as the dagger pressed harder against his throat. The blonde warrior raised his eyes to meet those of Carl Mort'l.

"We are in a situation," Mort'l croaked in his deep voice."I found out how your black friend healed and have remedied it, so he will die if I choose."

"And then we would kill you," Anthron replied flatly.

Mort'l said,"You are a powerful group, why not join the winning side. Killing me won't stop the Summoning." Mort'l stopped as Sudenora approached.

"Sabriski's dead," Sudenora said."Jass is alive, but I can't tell how serious his injuries are." He then looked to Mort'l.

"You even think about casting and your friend will die," Mort'l sneered.

Anthron replied,"We will not join you, no matter what you offer."

Mort'l laughed,"How can you even begin to know what the Master can offer? He could give you a forest full of Elven woman to bed, or if you so wished, immortality..."

"Immortality like you have?" Antaeus interrupted.

Anger flared across Mort'l's features, causing blood to trickle down his face from the purple wound.

Anthron motioned for Sudenora to retrieve Kielmark's helm."You're not regenerating as quickly as you were at Urgar Keep." Anthron started, his sapphire-encrusted long sword anticipating any opportunity to leap forward and skewer his enemy of the last two months. As Sudenora passed him the helm, Anthron asked,"Why didn't you use it yourself?" He placed it on his own head. Mort'l remained silent, watching with interest as Anthron waited.

After half a minute, Mort'l nodded towards Anthron's injured leg."Didn't heal me either."

"Must be personalised for Kiel only." Sudenora murmured as Anthron handed the Elementalist back the helm.

Letting out a long breath, Anthron said,"It's over Mort'l. Your Knights of Protection are all dead. The necromancer is dead..."

"You have no idea," Mort'l grated."After the Master found me years ago in the Wastelands of Bone he gave me The Choice. The Master had enough influence for me to return to Cyermyth as leader of the Queen's Personal Guard, made me stronger, faster, and granted me regeneration..."

"Who is this Master?" Anthron asked.

"Is it Aracon from the Cyermyth court?" Sudenora added.

Mort'l shook his head, blood dribbling with each turn."It is NOT over!" He shouted, pressing the dagger against Kielmark's neck until a red line appeared."I was given The Choice, the same as you could have, Mikolnic. You could have been a General in the new army." Carl Mort'l looked distant, almost sad for a moment.

Anthron seized the opportunity and aimed the sapphire-encrusted sword at the knight. This time, perhaps because Zathorn was dead, whatever had protected Carl Mort'l earlier was absent. The huge knight flinched as the sword buzzed in his ears, and Mort'l's eyes began to water. Kielmark quickly forced the dagger away from his throat and lunged aside as Anthron stabbed his sword through Mort'l's chest.

"Have your sword back," Anthron said. The leader of the Knights of Protection let out a silent scream and the sword smoked. Anthron lost grip of the handle and stood back as Mort'l sank to one knee, then the other, as the wound issued a hissing sound. Mort'l finally slumped to one side, the smoke clearing as the huge knight finally died.

"I told you that sword was designed to destroy chaos and evil," Jassnik said as he approached from behind them, nursing his head.

"Yes you did," Anthron replied."Let's check the bodies and get out of here."

EPILOGUE

The trumpets sounded across the port city.

Nearly two dozen King's soldiers escorted the royal carriage down The Tavern Strip of Sorne as citizens watched from the side of the street in the heat. Standing to attention were forty of Lord Ras's garrison, trumpets in hand. Again they simultaneously blew a single note, and the procession stopped.

Jalesia rode up to the carriage as a soldier opened the door."Are you that vain, or are you trying to irritate Ras?" she smiled.

Yarlyn Kontar stepped from the carriage with a wave. As soon as it was apparent to the gathered crowd that Lord Yarlyn was the only person riding in the black royal carriage they began dispersing."Both." Yarlyn breathed deeply, soaking in the atmosphere.

Jalesia rolled her eyes, then dismounted as a soldier took the reins of her horse. She turned to see Jelik still mounted, waiting next to Sergeant Olin dressed in his black leathers and silk shirt."Come on Jel," she waved. Jalesia considered that she had gotten to know the thief from Smazorok fairly well on their trip back from Brane, and had enjoyed his company. She had played his advances down - much to her amusement - and just when Jelik appeared close to giving up she would flirt to gain his interest once again.

Jelik frowned, then looked to Yarlyn who nodded. He winced as he dismounted, then gave his reins to another solider. He had been in a coma for a week before waking stiff, every muscle aching. His head had hurt and he had vomited blood for several days before he began feeling human again. Over the two weeks since waking he had rested and stretched, and now he could walk unassisted. The thief limped towards Jalesia - her arm held out for Jelik to take.

"For support," Jalesia said with a straight face.

Captain Saralon led Yarlyn, Jalesia and Jelik to a guarded gate, and followed the wide paved path lined both sides with Lord Ras's guards that led to his castle-like home.

"Nice," Jelik approved. Ras lived in a three-story, twenty roomed house surrounded by a shallow moat. Jelik assumed the little moat was there for show, as he considered it looked more like a large puddle than a defense for the house. The roof of the house had been sculpted to resemble that of a fort - having arrow slots and a walkway that could be patrolled around if required. The grounds were lush. The lawns were well kept, roses neatly trimmed, with several bright gardens filled with orderly lilies and tulips. A row of hedges sculpted into sitting lions stood guard along the path behind Ras's guards.

One of Lord Ras's servants met them at the door, and they were led to a large study where despite the slightly warmer weather, the fireplace was lit.

"Jelik!" Karlos cried, springing from a comfortable looking leather armchair. The large Healer and thief embraced."I heard you were..." Karlos searched for the correct word, but settled for,"...sick."

Jelik clapped Karlos on the back."I was out for a week, apparently." Jelik nodded his greetings to Anthron, Jassnik, Kielmark, and Antaeus as Saralon, Yarlyn and Jalesia were also welcomed.

Jelik pausing to embrace Anthea.

"I'm so glad you're okay," Anthea whispered into his ear."I was so worried when Anthron told us."

Jelik held her tightly until he was conscious of everyone watching. Pushing her back slightly, he said quietly,"Well, I'm okay now." Jelik then noted Gen'vieve, lounging across a leather chair with a navy cloth wrapped around her eyes."What happened to Gen'vieve?"

Gen'vieve answered,"Poison actually." Jassnik moved to stand beside the mind reader and gently held her hand."Assassin's poison. I survived thanks to Karlos," She smiled in the Healer's direction,"But have lost my sight."

Jelik frowned, instantly analysing the pros and cons of having a blind mindreader travelling with them. He quickly assessed that it would be more of a hassle to have her along.

Before Jelik could formulate a polite reply, Gen'vieve's dimples deepened as she smiled."It's okay Jelik. I can't see through my eyes, but I can through here," she tapped her temple."Through here I can see through other people's eyes."

Jelik blushed at having such a thought picked from his mind.

Quickly changing the subject, he said;"Where's Sudenora?"

"He's due back in about a week," Karlos interjected."He went to Platown, following up a personal matter."

Jelik nodded. He took a goblet of wine offered by Karlos and lowered himself slowly into a chair."What happened in that cave, Jel?" Karlos asked as everyone seated themselves.

Jelik had wondered on his trip to Sorne whether he would tell the truth about his confrontation with Gwyerson Dernas. The thief looked at his companions and noted their concerned expressions."A lot I can't explain," Jelik was suddenly uncomfortably aware of having everyone's full attention."I fought Dernas, and as I am here I believe I must have won."

"*What*?" Karlos exclaimed."Not too long ago he took all of us out! How..."

Jelik held up his gloved hand, then tugged it off revealing the burnt symbols on his finger."I think it was also this that put me in a coma." He looked to Anthea uncomfortably."Dernas was somehow communicating to me, making me go to him. He wanted me to hand over Xycermon," Jelik then flicked his wrist revealing the bat-shaped dagger before anyone could speak."No, I didn't give it to him."

"That ring is too dangerous," Jassnik said."It'll kill you if you keep on using it."

"Unless you learn to control it." Antaeus added.

"So, I hear Mort'l and Sabriski are dead as well." Jelik sipped at his wine, deciding to change the subject.

"Yes," Saralon shook Anthron's hand."Well done. Everyone has done very well. King Rogor is very pleased."

Yarlyn grinned to himself, having already received word from the King.

Anthron smiled."It would seem that we have beaten *all* our enemies."

SAROPHIA BY STU DUNN

"Not all." Jassnik warned, holding his forefinger in the air.

"Cyermyth." Kielmark answered.

Jelik nodded."When do we all leave?"

"When Sudenora is back," Anthron answered.

Antaeus cleared his throat."Not quite all of us are travelling to Panthorian."

Anthea nodded to herself, as if something she had guessed had come true.

"You're heading back to Sambethe?" Anthron asked."I thought you'd come with us..."

Antaeus smiled warmly,"No *fron amos. Elvenméson* is now safe thanks to everything you have done. I must return home and see how I may next serve my King."

Anthron was speechless, having assumed that the Elf would be going with them. After a moment, he said,"I'm sorry you're not coming. You have been a great companion, and an even better friend."

Antaeus nodded his thanks. The Elf pointed to Jelik's shirt."You are wearing the shirt you found in the cave I see."

"Yes." Jelik nodded, placed his wine down then leaned forward to unbuckle his pack. He withdrew his Elven chain armour, then motioned for Antaeus to take it."I want you to have this."

Antaeus's eyes widened."I - I can not."

"Please," Jelik urged."You saved our skins at the towers. I will be offended if you *don't* take it."

Antaeus blinked his moist eyes as he took Jelik's armour."Thank you," He stood silently for several moments before turning to face the rest of the group."I have walked amongst Men many times in my life, and I have often been disappointed by their self-destructive ways and seemingly selfish nature." The Elf smiled warmly."You all have shown me that there is much more to Men than I had assessed. The conclusions I had come to so many years ago have been challenged irregularly, but since travelling with you all - I must thank you." Antaeus paused to register everyone's expressions."You have demonstrated loyalty, trust, integrity...and friendship. You have shown through your actions the traits that Elves hold so dear, that makes *Elvenméson* magical. I would like to call you family."

Anthron's mind reeled. Both with Jelik's apparent generosity and Antaeus's words. Emotions washed over the blonde warrior. He managed to croak,"We are honoured."

Anthea embraced the Elf as the others nodded quietly.

Antaeus pointed to Anthron."You should visit the Elves north of Gwilieth. Ask them of *Orlon*, as you surely have His gifts."

"*Orlon*," Jassnik mused."Oh, the colours!" He snapped his fingers."Have you been keeping track of what colours you have been seeing?"

Anthron shifted uncomfortably under the sudden attention."Not really, but I will," He turned back to Antaeus."And we will endeavor to visit the Elves."

"Well," Jelik broke the silence."I'm fairly hungry." He looked to Jalesia, who nodded in response.

"Where is Lord Ras's kitchen?" Jalesia asked Yarlyn.

The slender man grinned boyishly."It's where he keeps the liquor. Follow me."

* * * * * * * * *

Sudenora returned from Platown five days later.

"Was there a letter from Carlae?" Karlos asked quietly after the Elementalist had caught up with everyone after dinner.

Sudenora, who now wore his azure robes and the jewelled belt he had taken from Zathorn Sabriski, nodded.

"Well?" Karlos asked impatiently."What did she say? Do you have a son or a daughter?"

Sudenora broke into huge smile."A daughter!" he cried."Shelli."

"Congratulations!" Karlos beamed, patting Sudenora on the back."And how is Carlae? Did she understand about the Selection? What you're doing?"

"She still wants me," Sudenora laughed."Carlae understands that I didn't run scared from her and our baby, and will wait in Eugernok for my return - as she put it - 'after you and your friends have made this world a safer place.' She..." He felt a lump in his throat."She said..." Sudenora stopped speaking. He screwed up his face and wept, releasing months of tension and uncertainty.

Karlos smiled warmly as he patted the Elementalist on his back."It's okay. How about we tell the others, and celebrate?"

* * * * * * * * * *

Jassnik's mind raced as he escorted Gen'vieve around Lord Ras's gardens that night. He walked in silence, trying to sort out in his mind what he wanted to say. Normally the bard would have no troubles talking, adlibbing whatever topic he chose, but this was different. His stomach twisted with a combination of fear and anticipation as he began opening his mouth.

"Come on Jass," Gen'vieve stopped walking and turned to face him. Even though she wore a cloth over her eyes, she looked down to Jassnik and smiled what Jassnik thought was the most beautiful smile he had ever seen."You've been edgy since we arrived last week, but have refused to talk about it." She tapped Jassnik on the forehead."Don't make me go in there and drag it out." Her smile deepened.

Jassnik let out a long breath."Okay, I'm going to get straight to the point," Jassnik began as he summoned up his courage."I'm too nervous to...I want to say..." The bard shook his head."You have the ability to read minds. I want to ask you a question...."

Gen'vieve held her hand up to Jassnik's lips to silence him, then concentrated. She frowned as a wave of images and emotions flowed through her, and she felt her heart begin to race. As she began to sort through the chaos running through Jassnik's mind, she suddenly felt sensations of caution and fear, with more powerful feelings of warmth, appreciation, togetherness, respect, love and...

Jassnik fidgetted nervously with his family ring he kept on a chain around his neck. He relaxed when he noted Gen'vieve's features soften and a tear trickle down her cheek from under her cloth.

"You mean it Jass?" Gen'vieve asked timidly.

Jassnik nodded,"Yes I do. Sometimes, I can't find the right words to say just how I feel. You..."

"I read your *heart* Jass," Gen'vieve let out a noise which was a cross between a laugh and a sob."I have never read anyone's heart before. Oh Jass." She leapt into the bard's arms and hugged him tightly, Gen'vieve standing three inches taller than Jassnik.

"What is your answer?" Jassnik whispered into her ear.

Jassnik felt her hot breath on his ear as Gen'vieve whispered,"Yes, I *will* marry you Jass."

They held onto each other in silence.

* * * * * * * * * *

That evening and most of the next day was spent in double celebration, for the birth of Sudenora's daughter Shelli and Jassnik and Gen'vieve's engagement. Anthron hadn't enjoyed himself so much for as long as he could remember. He raised his flagon of beer in acknowledgement as Anthea looked at him and winked. Yes, he thought, very happy. Not only was he with the most beautiful woman he had met, but he had come to realise just how special his companions had become. They had become friends, perhaps as Antaeus had put it - they had become family. Even Yarlyn and Jalesia had spent a fair amount of time socialising with them. They had hardly seen Captain Saralon as he been heavily involved in reinforcing order back to Sorne after the docks had been closed. Yarlyn had often boasted about the havoc shutting the port had caused Ras.

Anthron looked around the room, studying everyone. He paused on Antaeus. The blonde fighter was really going to miss the Elf, who was leaving on the morrow. Anthron and the others had promised to visit Sambethe again.

Antaeus turned to catch Anthron staring, and nodded, as if the Elf

317

had read his mind. This was their last day of rest before boarding a ship bound for Panthorian. Anthron drank his beer, wiping the foam from his top lip.

Off to Panthorian tomorrow. It was the first time any of them will have stepped on anything bigger than a raft, and Anthron couldn't deny he was a little nervous. Yes, he mused. Off to Gwilieth, then east onto Cyermyth to confront Queen Kilandra and her suspect adviser Aracon, and possibly stop the Second Great War from occurring...

"You look so serious," Anthea said as she approached. She knelt down in front of Anthron and kissed him. "Why don't you let yourself have one more night off."

"You're right," Anthron agreed. He took her hand and easily pulled the half Elf onto his lap and kissed her again. "One more night off,"

THE HISTORY OF THE WORLD – RECORDED BY THE FAMILY OF CHORSAR

Unknown	War of the Giants. Powerful giants ruled the Men of Palandra, named The Ruling Lords, but mysteriously disappeared. Rumours began stating the Nine Greater Gods – OBPSULTTN – came to Palandra and offered The Choice. This was to join them in the Heavens as Lesser Gods, or be destroyed.
000	The Earthquake of Change. The continents reshape, new mountain ranges appear, and volcanoes erupt. All previous records are destroyed. The land between Sarophia and Panthorian sinks. All buildings were destroyed. The Elves are separated by the sunken land, and hide away.
380	The Great Lake Floods. A year of rain in Sarophia. Izonda and Thinstor are flooded, which creates a river through Thinstor.
382	Platown Treaty. Signing of the wall. This begins intercontinental trading.
389	Marshes of Cone created by *Nermion*.
490	The Three Towers destroyed by dueling Elementalists - Veckros Ipisimus and Sauros Loklin. Surrounding towns are destroyed. As a result magic is outlawed in the Trendrik Kingdom Territories.
600	Trading between continents prospers
628-630	The Great War. People throughout Panthorian disappearing. Parntorn over runs Eurnoness and Cyermyth, ships dispatched to Gwilieth, Sarophia and Kortusia to destroy their ports to avoid the chance for

319

help. Gwilieth and Scyermor joined with Sarophia and won against Parntorn. Creation of Scyermor South – The Free Land. Sarophia lost most of its army. In the final battle Veckros Ipisimus aided them. Magic no longer outlawed. Trading decreases.

802-803	Thinstor vs. Arrolok I.
804	Isle of Syphora – Town built – gold miners.
806	Trading re-established.
810-900	Kortusian Wars – Emperor Chan Lo'un I ascends the throne.
906	Isle of Syphora invaded by Parntorn.
1021-1031	Plague of Gwileith.
1280	Piracy becomes a problem – Trading becomes more difficult. This creates the Meeting of State, held in Cyermyth.
1314-1321	Kortusia invades Cyermyth – Panthorian and Sarophia fight and win.
1322	Peace established.
1418	King of Cyermyth, Trendrik and Scyermor assassinated.
	Parntorn suspected – The Poison Capital.
	Euroness and Gwileith plot – an assassination attempt on the King of Parntorn is failed.
1420-1520	A plot is revealed that the Emperor of Kortusia hired the Ruby Brotherhood from Sarophia to kill the Kings so he could invade again.
	Sarophia's under threat of invasion for one hundred years until a threat that Veckron Ipisimus is still alive is sent to each state. Threats cease.
1520	Daughter of King Trendrik marries the new Emperor of Kortusia. This guarantees the peace.
1548	The body of a 40-foot Ruling Lord is found in Panthorian. A cult starts, worshipping the Lesser Gods, and rumours begin that there are still several Ruling

Lords alive on Palandra.

1600	Piracy confined to The Deep Sea around Gwileith.
1718	Ithren Forest Fire – Carson built in its place.
1727	First dungeons discovered across Palandra. Many adventurers die. Creatures begin to surface.
1741	A red dragon destroys Northern Kortusia over the space of three weeks, due to the Kortusians' killing the dragons' mate. Maj-Aktor built on the desolation.
1767	Euroness sights the first Cat-People.
1812	Ogre marries human woman in western Kortusia.
1813	Ogre kills woman – ogres hunted and killed. Orcs and goblins attack Carson.
1820	Urgar Keep built over dungeon to stop creatures roaming. Dungeons sealed.
1918	Urgar Keep becomes a prison.
	Creatures appearing – no organised attacks. They keep to themselves.
	Merchant Stop built.
2110	The Smazorok Butcher caught and publicly executed. He had killed 8 men, 47 women, and 29 children.
2208	Hill giants come from the SnowCaps and cause trouble. Trendrik army called to push them back.
2219	First Elementalist translator appears in Panthorian. Learns orcish and goblin. His son learns hill giant, but is killed by one. Languages are now taught.
2228	First Elementalist transformation. Turned into hawk but didn't successfully change back.
2328	First successfully returned transformation.
2420	Sighting of Veckron Ipisimus. If true, he would be over two thousand years old.
2500	Cyermyth royalty changes family. First woman to rule the Panthorian Kingdom - Queen Kilandra I.
2601	Queen Celena II of Cyermyth poisoned after Parntorn offered "Fountain of Youth." Her son becomes King.

2810	An outside adviser is brought into Cyermyth to assist the Queen on her return. From 2810 onwards - all advisors in Cyermyth are named Aracon.
3181	Thinstor vs. Arrolok II.
3192	People start disappearing throughout Sarophia – "The Selection" begins.
3193	Today.

PANTHORIAN:

Cyermyth	Queen Kilandra V
Parntorn	King Bornine
Gwileith	Duke Mathorn
Euroness	Prince Galvin
Scyermor	Queen Moria

KORTUSIA:

All Lands	Emperor Chi Amorg

SAROPHIA:

Trendrik	King Rogor Trendrik

ELEMENTALISTS – WRITTEN BY THE CHORSAR FAMILY

Magic is gifted; you must be born with it. Like any ability, magic must be studied and practiced for it to strengthen within an individual. There are some gifted who never know of their potential.

The only exceptions known to the Chorsar Historians are those that study the dark-hearted sorcery -practitioners of what has become known as Item Magic.

We've collected some notes to explain the Greater Gods, the Nine Gods; or OBPSULTTN (pronounced Ob-sult-in).

THE SYMBOL OF OBPSULTTN

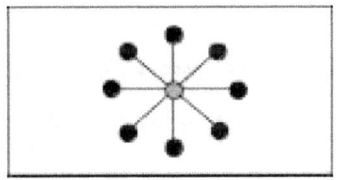

GODS	NATURE	MAGIC USEAGE
Orlon	Aura	The Ruling God. Innate
Bormal	Darkness Item	Magic & Symbolic
Pharson	Fire	Symbolic
Servas	Air	Verbal – Spell Words
Utor	Earth	Request Channeling
Lithloren	(Violet Moon)	Deception. Item Magic,

		Request Channeling
Tolorel	(White Moon)	Truths. Item Magic, Request Channeling
Termolen	Earth	Request Channeling
Nermion	Water	Concentration and visualization

The main points to note are that
1) *Utor's* main followers are Rangers, whereas followers of *Termolen* are often named Healers.
2) *Nermion* no longer has a large following.
3) To worship *Bormal* is illegal in any of the Kingdom Territories.
4) Finally, *Orlon* was supposably killed during the War of the Giants. Although there is no proof, *Orlon* has had no recorded followers since the Earthquake of Change. There are too many Lesser Gods to list.

The last thing we feel we need to have you watch out for are mind readers. Mind reading is not magic. They do not answer to OBPSULTTN. They are dangerous, so be warned.

HELIOS AND TROY CHORSAR

RECORDED AND WRITTEN IN PLATOWN, IN THE YEAR 3193

THE ELEMENTALISTS' LEVEL OF ADVANCEMENT

The Elementalist' Greater Gods:

Bormal, male God of Darkness	Item focusing
Pharson, male God of Fire	Symbolic
Servas, female God of Air	Verbal
Utor, male God of Earth	Requesting permission verbally
Nermion, male God of Water	Intense concentration

Calling Power:

1) Basic calling (create a small flame, cause sparks, create dust, create water)
2) Secondary calling (fireball, lightning, ground shudders, dehydration)
3) Third calling (two fireballs, chain lightning, earthquakes, part waters)
4) Fourth calling (becoming one with the element, can not harm Elementalist)

Level 1 - The Elementalist is at the beginning of their progress, being able to manipulate their element (e.g. flaring fire, making a breeze, moving dust, rippling water).

Level 2 - The Elementalist is now able to exert Calling Power 1.

Level 3 - The Elementalist can now control their Calling Powers (throw flame, aim sparks).

Level 4 - The Elementalist increases to Calling Power 2.

Level 5 - The Elementalist understands their element better, and reduces any damage by their element by 1/3.

Level 6 - The Elementalist gains more control over their element, their Calling Power doubles in speed. Can create a shield against normal missiles.

Level 7 - The Elementalist can conjure a minor protection against magic.

Level 8 - The Elementalist can summon their own elemental creature, although find it difficult to control.

Level 9 - The Elementalist increases to Calling Power 3.

Level 10 - The Elementalist understands their element better, and reduces any damage by their element by 2/3.

Level 11 - The Elementalist gains more control over their element, their Calling Power doubling in speed again (now x4 of beginner).

Level 12 - The Elementalist gains the ability to conduct their element to channel their power. Can shield themselves from physical attacks.

Level 13 - The Elementalist can now control their Calling Power totally.

Level 14 - The Elementalist increases to Calling Power 4.

Level 15 - The Elementalist is now a Master Elementalist of their God. They are granted immunity to their element, and are considered about their race. They have special allowances by their God – being able to ignore the usual restrictions (like using symbols, vocal, items etc). The Elementalist begins to age much slower than normal for their race.

THE THIEVES' LEVEL OF ADVANCEMENT

Level 1   - Test sleight of hand

Level 2   - Test lock picking

Level 3   - Test trap setting / disarming

Level 4   - Test stealth

Level 5   - Test the combination of levels 1 – 4 together, by collecting an item specified by the Guild's Number 1

Level 6   - Test unarmed fighting

Level 7   - Test dedication and skill, by completing a job specified by the Guild's Number 1

Level 8   - Test the combination of levels 1 – 7 under time pressure in a scenario specified by the Guild's Number 1

Level 9   - Test endurance capabilities

Level 10   - Test advanced sleight of hand techniques, including razors

Level 11   - Test sensory skills

Level 12   - Test the combination of levels 1 – 11 in The Maze

Level 13   - Test of advanced stealth

Level 14   - Test of puzzle solving and reading (including magical scrolls)

Level 15   - Test the skill of the combination of levels 1 – 14, by completing a Quest specified by the Guild's Number One. Upon completion of this Quest, the thief is recognised as a Master Thief, and may challenge a Guild's Number One, or set up their own Guild. Because of this, not many thieves become Master Thieves…

*Stu currently lives on the
Kapiti Coast, teaches Wing Chun Kung Fu,
and is New Zealand's leading expert
on micro expressions, body language and
detecting deception.*

www.MicroExpressions.co.nz.

SAROPHIA BY STU DUNN

www.ingramcontent.com/pod-product-compliance
Lightning Source LLC
Chambersburg PA
CBHW062025170626
46813CB00001B/291